PRAISE FOR *FAKE ID*

"A taut, suspenseful thriller filled with unexpected twists. I loved *Fake ID*!" —Michelle Gagnon, author of *Don't Turn Around* and *Don't Look Now*

"From the first sentence to the last, this mystery delivers code-red, heart-thumping action." —Crystal Allen, author of *How Lamar's Bad Prank Won a Bubba-Sized Trophy*

"Fast action, judicious plot twists, and sufficiently evil teens and adults should keep thrill-seeking readers awake long into the night." —*Kirkus Reviews*

"[An] engrossing thriller." —*Publishers Weekly*

"Conspiracy theorists and thriller fans alike will be guessing right up to the end of this exciting debut." —*Booklist*

"Smart, punchy teen dialogue; a strong African American protagonist; and non-stop twists and turns make this mystery pop." —*The Horn Book*

PRAISE FOR *ENDANGERED*

"Fans of Giles's *Fake ID* will be overjoyed to find his debut
success was no fluke. This title delivers another skillfully devised
plot, supported by a fully fleshed cast." —*The Bulletin of the Center
for Children's Books* (**starred review**)

"A dynamic, dangerously suspenseful, contemporary adventure that
also leaves room for introspective soul-searching." —*SLJ*

"Suspenseful and often wise." —*Kirkus Reviews*

"[The] exploration of good and evil, justice and culpability,
and anger and guilt gives this psychological thriller the thematic
and emotional depth to match its full-throttle plot. A strong
choice for lovers of suspense." —*The Horn Book*

"Giles (*Fake ID*) crafts an unpredictable psychological thriller. . . .
A timely and unsettling story . . . The novel's strength rests in its
underlying moral complexity." —*Publishers Weekly*

"Giles writes a fast-paced, gripping suspense novel with an
engaging whodunit mystery. . . . A good choice for reluctant readers
and fans of strong female heroines." —*VOYA*

LAMAR GILES

NOT SO PURE AND SIMPLE

HARPER TEEN

An Imprint of HarperCollinsPublishers

HarperTeen is an imprint of HarperCollins Publishers.

Not So Pure and Simple
Copyright © 2020 by Lamar Giles

Library of Congress Cataloging-in-Publication Data

Names: Giles, L.R. (Lamar R.), author.
Title: Not so pure and simple / Lamar Giles.
Description: First edition. | New York : HarperTeen, [2020] | Audience:
  Ages 13 up | Audience: Grades 10–12 | Summary: High school junior Del
  Rainey unwillingly joins a Purity Pledge class at church, hoping to get
  closesr to his long-term crush, Kiera.
Identifiers: LCCN 2019025683 | ISBN 9780062349194 (hardcover)
Subjects: CYAC: Dating (Social customs)—Fiction. | Christian life—
  Fiction. | High schools—Fiction. | Schools—Fiction. | Family life—
  Virginia—Fiction. | African Americans—Fiction. | Virginia—Fiction.
Classification: LCC PZ7.G39235 Not 2020 | DDC [Fic]—dc23
LC record available at https://lccn.loc.gov/2019025683

Typography by Molly Fehr
20 21 22 23   PC/LSCH   10 9 8 7 6
❖
First Edition

FOR ADRIENNE, WHO WAS THERE ON
THE NIGHT OF
&
FOR THE CURIOUS

CHAPTER 1

PASTOR NEWSOME'S RULES FOR FIRST Missionary House of the Lord were simple. Every head bowed (mine wasn't) and every eye closed (nope) while he went on and on with his crazy freestyle prayers.

"Lord!" He gripped his lectern as if fighting a holy tractor beam trying to drag him to heaven right before our eyes. "We know they need to feel that touch from your never-changin' hand, and we know someone is out there hurtin' this morning..."

Hurtin'? For sure. Between my near-empty wallet forcing me to sit lopsided on that pew-of-steel and yet another infinity sermon, my pain was not in short supply. Newsome was on a roll. He ranted, threw in weird stuff no one seemed to notice, the way he totally did *all the time.*

"... and we see the evil on our TV and in our news reports, Lord. Bless those endangered spider monkeys of the Amazon rain forests!"

Like that.

"Yes, Lord, yes," Mom mumbled. She squeezed my hand, nearly crushing my fingers with pulsing robot strength on each word. It sounded like she was cosigning on the old man's insanity, but over the last few weeks I'd noticed her lips moving even when he wasn't saying stuff. Not repeating Newsome's lines. Having her own conversation with God, I guessed. The protocols of Mom's Sunday worship were still fairly new to me.

We Raineys weren't hard-core Church People. At least we didn't used to be. Christmas, sure. Easter. Mother's Day (which always felt weird because if Mom didn't normally go, why was it so important to be in service *on Mother's Day*? We could've been getting those early seats at the Golden Corral buffet). We mumbled grace before we ate meals. When terrible things happened in the world, my parents posted stuff about thoughts and prayers on their Facebook pages. We were *that* kind of religious.

Dad still was that kind of religious. He's remained dedicated to not dressing beyond b-ball shorts and slippers on Sunday mornings. As he said, that was his "Adult Privilege." I probably could've exercised my "Teen Privilege" and done the same thing . . . if I was stupid. But, Mom was one-half of the votes on my "Driving Privilege," and my Spider-Sense warned me that refusing church would have had consequences.

So, each of the last four weeks inevitably gave way to a moment of temptation where I wanted to gnaw my arm off, dive through a stained-glass window, then Usain Bolt my way home, yet I endured. Partially to not endanger possession of my car keys. Though, if I was being honest, there was another incentive for my continued attendance.

Kiera Westing.

While Pastor Newsome ranted, I watched her. She sat across the center aisle, on the same row as me and Mom, so Prayer Peeking was the only time I could really look at her. Otherwise she'd see me, too.

Head bowed. Eyes closed. Kiera leaned far forward, her bare fingers interlaced as she whispered her own prayer. No promise ring in sight.

She'd switched up her hair—a move I recognized thanks to my sister Cressie cycling through hairdos with pop-star frequency, "testing looks" before she left for college. Girl stuff.

At school on Friday, Kiera had been happy, smiling, and rocking springy twist outs that bounced when she passed me in the hall. Since then, she'd flat-ironed her hair into black waterfalls that crested her dark shoulders and the thin straps of her wine-colored dress.

She hadn't smiled once since service started, though she still looked *hot* hot. Volcano *hot*. Dragon *hot*. Summer barbecue in southern hell *hot*. Happy or sad, there was no changing that.

With effort, I tore myself away. There's Prayer Peeking and there's Prayer Staring. I wasn't a creepy dude.

Plus, if all went well after service, I wouldn't have to sneak glimpses anymore. In the meantime, there were other entertaining sights in the church.

Along the side of the sanctuary, six prismatic windows stretched high. On sunny days, the eastern glass turned outside light rainbow and doused chunks of the congregation in paintball colors. All our varying shades of brown got psychedelic.

3

Missus Baines, the old lady in the pew ahead of me, who shambled in with a cane every week, and smelled like the inventor of cigarettes *and* peppermints, turned Oompa-Loompa orange. Almost had to squint to look at her. I liked her because she was unpredictable. For the moment, she was quiet, but at any given time she might catch the Holy Ghost, pop up from her pew, and sprint the aisle, swinging her stick. Get too close, she'd knock you out.

Three rows back was another of my Prayer Peeking All-Stars. Coach Scott, tinted leprechaun green, with his eyes squeezed shut hard. He was one of the few First Missionary House of the Lord members I ever saw outside of church. Usually barking at my school's JV basketball team from the sidelines.

My boy, Qwan, perpetual benchwarmer, claimed Coach Scott wielded curse words like the Force. When the guys were goofing off in practice, he'd hit them with f-bombs that slammed them into stuff. Here, in the house of the Lord, he was still loud, but high-pitched, a weird cartoon-mouse voice. Hands raised and spread wide to catch all those blessings from heaven. He shouted, "Thank you, *Jay*-SUS!"

A lot of little shows played out among the eighty or ninety people in the congregation every week. There were nose pickers, and throat scratchers, and nail biters, and ear diggers—and all of them wanted you to shake their nasty hands after service. Mom thought I was OCD the way I hit up that little bottle of Purell in her purse some Sundays. Mostly, it was funny to me. Seeing what I wasn't supposed to see, and knowing what I wasn't supposed to know.

"We praise you, Lord! We love you, Lord! We need you, Lord!" Newsome, barely taking breaths, kept at it. No sign of slowing down.

I couldn't resist another peek, and was right back to eyeballing Kiera and her family. The way I was with her, you'd have thought she was a new girl. A transplant from some big city, here to shake up the status quo. Someone from another world. Like the movies. Naw, though. We were born in the same hospital, right here in Green Creek, Virginia.

I'd known her since kindergarten. Had a thing for her *since kindergarten*, when I was her leading man in the class production of *The Wizard of Oz*.

(I mean, she was Dorothy, and I was the Cowardly Lion, so there were three leading men if you weren't counting the kid who played Toto—and I wasn't; dude didn't have any lines. Regardless, me and Kiera had obvious chemistry.)

So, what happened? A smooth brother like myself must've made a move sometime in the last decade, right. Right?

No. Because Kiera Westing had never been single. Nev. Er.

Actually, there *was* a brief window from kindergarten to almost the end of elementary school, but—I can admit this—I was more cowardly than lion during those years, and didn't know we were working a deadline.

On Valentine's Day during fourth grade, Devin Thompson hit her with some sick game. A homemade, *purple* "Do you like me? Yes/No/Maybe So" card. She circled yes, and they were like engaged all the way to sixth grade, where they realized they were different people with different dreams. By the time I heard about the breakup, later that afternoon, she was with Corey Thurgood, who wooed her with some lackluster trumpet play.

If she'd watched him drain his spit valves—think water-slide—something I witnessed during my brief stint as a band xylophonist, she probably wouldn't have found it all that sexy. Neither here nor there. Corey was her boyfriend all the way to the summer before freshman year, when Corey's mom got a job with some company in Chicago and his family moved, leaving Kiera heartbroken.

My family was doing the vacation thing down at Disney World in Florida, so the heartbroken part I got from a Qwan text. Girls, gossip, and b-ball, in that order, were life for him.

Qwan: Dude! K. Westing is a free agent.
Get your game right.

Me: I'll be back in 3 days.

Qwan: I suggest you start running now.

Three days later, in the airport waiting to board our flight to Virginia, an alternating soundtrack of J. Cole and Kendrick thumping in my headphones, I got the last text on the matter.

Qwan: Maybe next time. Colossus, yo.

I snatched my headphones off, cussed loudly. It drew the attention of my sister, my parents, a TSA agent coming off her lunch break, and some lady's toddler, who immediately started machine-gunning the four-letter word I'd released into the ether. If Mom wore pearls, she would've clutched them.

That kid's mother did *not* accept my apology. Worse, they sat right behind us on the plane, and Dad wouldn't allow me the use of my headphones, so I had to listen to the mini Samuel L. Jackson I created all the way home.

As unpleasant as that was, it had nothing on what awaited me back in Virginia. Kiera's new boyfriend. Colossus Turner.

Who named their kid Colossus? Maybe psychics who knew their son would grow into a thick-necked state champ wrestler incapable of un-shrugging his shoulders.

Colossus and Kiera's relationship . . . two years strong. He gave her a promise ring that she wears on her left middle finger. Wore.

I'd given up hope. Even though I saw her every day at school, and now here on Sundays, I came to terms with never having a shot.

Until last night.

Me and Qwan were on a double date. Sort of.

Really, *he* was on the date with some girl named Erin or Erica, engaging in backseat debauchery while I drove and my uninterested date, whose name I don't even remember, rode shotgun. Over sloppy sounds of making out and my not-quite-loud-enough music, Erin or Erica's friend said, "Oh my God!"

Then, she had the nerve to mute my music.

"Never touch my radio," I said, ready to crank my barely alive tweeters back to max.

She ignored me, contorted into the space between our seats with her phone held out like the Olympic torch, passing it to Erin or Erica. "Look! That hot wrestler boy from Green Creek broke up with his girlfriend."

All the wet smacking stopped. The girls went Gossip Level Orange talking about Colossus cheating, and how it was only a matter of time, and "some heifer named Angie." I caught Qwan's gaze in my rearview, but we didn't say a word. We didn't have to.

It was my time.

Kiera's deacon and deaconess parents were bodyguards on either side of her. Her mom was closest to me but sat stiff and straight and didn't obstruct my view despite a cream-colored hat that was as wide as a UFO. Her dad's consistently conservative blue suit looked presidential on her far side.

My plan: after service, I'd catch the Westings in the foyer, where they hovered every Sunday, shaking hands and exchanging niceties—"have a blessed week, brother" and "have a blessed week, sister." I'd approach Kiera's dad first, like, "Deacon Westing, I hear you're in charge of the Ushers' Board."

Just curious enough so all the Westings thought *What a fine young man this is* but not so gung ho that I committed myself to any real work.

We'd chat like that a minute, then Pastor Newsome would come, right on schedule, talking church business with the Westings. Instead of Kiera huddling up in the parking lot with the other church girls, it'd be me and her. At the very least, I'm walking her to her dad's Cadillac. *Talking* her to her dad's Cadillac. I contemplated hitting her with some Langston Hughes poems, or some Drake, but this was short notice. No time to rehearse.

Anyway, I'd be letting her know, in no uncertain terms, that I'm into her, and I want that next-boyfriend slot. Just needed Newsome to let church end. Then I could execute the pl—

Hold up.

Kiera stood. Excused her way past her mom, continued to the front of the church while her dad slow-clapped. He wasn't the only one.

The applause went viral throughout the congregation, creating a pattering echo under the high ceiling, while Newsome uttered, "Hallelujah, hallelujah."

Six more kids, some I recognized from school, rose and approached the altar, forming a line when they faced the rest of the congregation. Shanice Monroe and Helena Rickard were sophomores at Green Creek High. Ralph and Bobby Burton, who were eighth graders at the middle school, I believed. Mya Hanson, a fellow junior and my super-serious coworker. Then Jameer Sesay, class Golden Boy. With the exception of Mya, I only knew this group well enough to speak to, nothing more.

"Hallelujah, hallelujah," said Newsome.

Over the last couple of months, I'd gotten my black belt in daydreaming during sermons. Usually a good thing, but this time I'd missed something important.

A lady approached the pulpit. She was a grown-up, old, like

twenty-five. I'd seen her around, but never met her. Flowery sundress. Plump cheeks, light brown skin, a forever smile.

When she stepped to the pulpit, she reached for the mic, an act that seemed to make Newsome uncomfortable enough to abruptly cease his hallelujahs. He gave her the "wait a minute" finger.

One final, emphatic *"Hallelujah."* Then he handed over the mic.

She said, "Are there any other young people who'd like to join us on this wonderful journey?"

Oh! An opportunity!

In the early moments of service, before I zoned out, they'd talk about volunteering. Go read to old folks at the nursing home. Help scrub graffiti off the community center. Whatever it was, Kiera would be there. If I got in now, I could still execute the plan, with the added bonus of an obvious shared interest. We'd be volunteering *together*.

"Excuse me," I said.

Mom's head tilted, all confused when I brushed by her.

I hit the aisle; the varnished wooden planks creaked loudly under my weight. Every eye in the place seared me, making my belly feel twisty and moist, giving me second thoughts. I only kept going because it would be more embarrassing to turn back, and I could not be embarrassed in front of Kiera.

While the other kids lined up to Kiera's right, I took a spot to her left so we were side by side. It sort of wedged me between her and this potted fern Pastor Newsome kept near the pulpit, but I wasn't going to risk anyone getting between us.

Because I took that spot, when the lady stepped to us with the wireless mic, she came to me first.

"Tell us," she said, beaming, the happy-face emoji come to life, "why do you want to remain sexually pure until you're joined in holy matrimony?"

I said, "Huh?"

CHAPTER 2

"WHAT'S YOUR REASON FOR WANTING to remain sexually pure?" the friendly lady repeated, shoving the mic in my face. My stomach churned so loud I was afraid it'd come through the surround sound. Everybody in the place was waiting. Kiera included.

I leaned in and said, "Because I love God."

Casual Churchgoer pro tip: know the appropriate answers. When you did something good, and someone asked why you did it: "Because I love God." If you did something bad, and someone asked why you shouldn't do it again: "Because God loves me." If you threw a Bible verse on top of it, even better. I wasn't so great at that, so I kept it simple.

My heart rammed my sternum in the silence that followed. A lone moth fluttered across the sanctuary.

Then, the church went stadium crazy. Claps, shouts, cheers. I wondered if I was going to get a Super Bowl ring.

"That's awesome," said the woman. "Bless you, young man." She moved on to Kiera. "And you?"

Kiera said, "I also love God. And I want to be sure I'm with someone who loves me the way He does before I give away any part of myself, because I value my body. My temple. First Corinthians 6:18 says: 'Flee from sexual immorality. All other sins a person commits—'"

Her answer was comprehensive. Debate team worthy. She got those good chastity belt cheers, same as me, and the mic went down the line. Everyone's answer was some version of what me and Kiera already said. Jameer Sesay was last to go.

He was a dude I only knew by reputation, his name and face mounted in the cafeteria under our class banner every grading period for Honor Roll and Perfect Attendance. Type of guy who said hi to teachers he wasn't even taking classes with. I expected a State of the Virginity Address from him, but when asked the magic question, he gave the shortest answer. "God."

By then, you could feel the end-of-service fatigue in the room; he still got the victory cheers, though.

The lady wrapped it up with, "Purity Pledge will be a ground-breaking, heart-changing, soul-enriching journey. At the end of this eight-week period—"

Eight? *Weeks?*

"—these young people will be ambassadors of God serving as positive influences for their peers and the community at large. The course culminates with our Purity Ball, where the parents, and any of you in the congregation who wish to attend, can bear witness as they pledge, before the Lord, abstinence until the day they're married. I'm so excited, by—"

"Amen, Sister Vanessa," Pastor Newsome said, reaching for his microphone.

She—Vanessa—lost her smile; she passed the mic. Newsome swept a hand from us to the congregation, giving us permission to return to our seats. Kiera broke formation first. Of course, I was right behind her, enjoying the view, because *that dress*, oh my *Gawd*. Kiera was what you'd call slim thick. There are whole Instagram accounts dedicated to booties like hers. How could I not follow her? And the rest followed me.

The benediction was as long as ever, padded with additional prayers for I don't know what. I couldn't even pretend I was paying attention at that point. I was Prayer Peeking again, zeroed in on Kiera, still thinking my plan could work. Further down her pew, two arms raised. Wide at first, before crossing into an X, then wide again. Jameer Sesay, Prayer Peeking like me. *At* me. Trying to get my attention.

He shook his head. Mouthed something. It looked like *Don't do it*.

"Amen!" Pastor Newsome said, the band giving us a free-to-leave musical cue. Everyone stood, and white-gloved ushers got to work extinguishing candles with brass snuffers. Mom shook hands with folks around us. Some patted me on the back for joining Purity Pledge. A thin sea of people parted as Jameer wedged his way toward me.

I told Mom, "Be right back."

Skirting around folks, I met him halfway, all while flicking glances at the Westings. Didn't want this interruption messing up my operation.

Jameer was a little shorter than me. Way skinnier, with a Gloworm's complexion. He wore black-framed glasses, and pristine suits with his neckties done in intricate knots.

We'd only exchanged "what up" nods in passing. So, when he slapped my palm, and pulled me into a bro-hug, I thought this was more Purity Pledge nonsense. But, he whispered in my ear, "I know what you're thinking. Don't. Bad timing."

I backed out of the hug, stomach churning again.

"Yeah," he said, "I'm talking about her."

The Westings were in the foyer shaking hands. The group gathered around Kiera was thicker than usual, giving her arm extra pumps of encouragement. I was missing my in.

Jameer laughed. *Laughed.* "You look so thirsty. Let me guess. You're thinking she broke up with Colossus. You need to rush in, right now, profess your undying love."

"How did you—?"

"Please. You and half the school. Three guys already asked her to prom."

Three? Prom was nine months away. And I was going to take her. Bet that!

"Relax," Jameer said, "they all got noes. You're going to get a no if you don't listen to me."

My head was all over the place. The other times I'd waited and lost. Three prom invitations? In less than twenty-four hours? "How you know any of this? Why tell me?"

"Walk with me." He took the aisle to the pulpit, where a couple of deaconesses tipped collection plates into buckets, the loose change clattering. The crowd in the foyer thinned. Pastor

Newsome worked through a few straggler parishioners, his dark robe swishing, patting backs en route for the Westings. If I was going to execute my plan, it had to be now.

Jameer's warning, though.

He swung a sharp right and took a side door outside. I rushed after him, emerged in a grassy, fenced-in side yard. A swing set, slide, and monkey bars occupied a rectangular patch with a plank-board border, filled end to end with crunchy broken seashells that definitely have skinned and definitely will skin knees. Giggling young kids with sleepy-looking young parents played. They all waved at Jameer and he waved back as I caught up, in time to see a couple of parents turn their children away from my new friend.

Forgetting that oddity almost as soon as I saw it, I said, "Does Kiera know what's up? I mean, that I wanna get with her?"

"Not really. It's shocking how oblivious she is about how many of you are unhealthily obsessed with her." He leaned on the fence and stroked all three of his chin hairs, enjoying this. "*I* know because you're just not very original."

"What?" Were we about to fight? It felt like we should fight.

"You're doing what everyone else is. The day after someone she thought she loved betrayed her. You want to get in on the ground floor when the building's not open."

"You a poet or something?"

"I dabble."

Awesome analogies aside, I still had suspicions. "Why are you even talking to me right now?"

"Because I've seen you looking all enamored every Sunday. I know we don't know each other like that, but you seem like a *good enough* dude. Someone should tell you you're doing the most right now, and it's not cute."

"Maybe you're saying all this so you can snake me. Knock out a contender."

He laughed. Again. "Hardly. Living within one hundred feet of her for as long as I can remember inoculated me. Thank God. I'd hate being like the rest of you puppies nipping at her ankles. Plus, I don't know how much of a contender you are, rocking a clip-on."

My hand floated to my tie involuntarily. I forced it back down.

"Not to be all demanding," Jameer said, "but I like my favors returned."

"Favor? I didn't ask for your help."

"Be glad you didn't have to. As I said, I'll be collecting. Not sure what, yet. When I know, you'll know."

This guy. "I'm not promising you anything."

"Reevaluate." He approached a latched gate that opened on the church parking lot. "You're in this Purity Pledge with us now. Maybe you can get to know her better, with some assistance. Though, considering the class, what you probably have in mind might be a bit counterproductive." He shook his head and was gone.

I took the side entrance back into the church. The foyer was clear. The Westings had left. I felt deflated, my clothes suddenly baggy on me. Mom sat in our pew, patiently flipping through a packet of paper she didn't have before.

"Here." She thrust a folder the color of communion wine into my hands. "From Sister Vanessa. You'd run off, so she gave it to me."

A white mail label affixed to it read: *Purity Pledge Materials and Activities.* Spreading the folder wide, I noticed the first page was a schedule. Assignments and due dates. "There's homework?"

"Apparently. Y'all meet on Tuesdays and Thursdays after school. I'm really proud of you. I had no clue this was a commitment you wanted to make."

Yeah, Mom. Sometimes I even surprise myself.

CHAPTER 3

"YOU SORRY PIECE OF SH—" Dad clipped his profanity as we emerged from the garage into the kitchen, Mom leading me, shaking her head. A thick simmering beef-and-spice aroma clouded the air. Dad hunched over the slow cooker with the lid off, steam billowing up around his shaved face and head, making him look like a genie escaping a Crock-Pot. An angry genie, with a view of the football game playing on our living room TV.

"The Dolphins losing?" I asked.

Dad gave me the "of course they are" shrug, then asked Mom, "How was church?"

"You'd know if you'd go," she said in her standard tone. Upbeat. Hopeful.

Dad adhered to the script, as neutral and noncommittal as ever. "Maybe next time."

They kissed, a quick peck, no hard feelings since Dad's hand slipped below the counter to do-a-thing-I-didn't-want-to-think-about, causing Mom to jump and slap his fingers from her backside playfully. Sultry looks were exchanged, and I'd for sure need to charge my headphones later tonight if I was to avoid traumatic bed squeaking.

"Cressie called," said Dad, sounding cranky. Crankier than he was about the Dolphins losing.

Mom whirled, and snatched the cordless handset from the wall mount, dialing my sister's number. "Is everything okay?"

"You tell me, Tina. Because right now I'm worried the massive tuition payment we made is not okay."

Mom ceased dialing. "Really."

"It's been a month since we moved her on campus. She's popped up back home twice already, and she's on the phone with you nearly every day. Is she going to class? Have you seen any grades yet? I know you miss her, but damn."

Mom's new look—definitely not sultry. She turned the corner, the squawking tones of dialed numbers drowned by her stomping footsteps ascending the stairs.

Dad shook his head and went back to stirring his meat. Mysteries of the nightly meal intrigued me way more than Cressie's drama, so I said, "Smells good. What is it?"

"Slow-braised beef. Going to hook up some street tacos."

"Nice." This was the unforeseen benefit of our relatively new weekly church tradition. Since Dad refused to go, he'd cook us a banging meal every Sunday as a peace offering. I don't know what Mom prayed about up in First Missionary, but I'd been asking God to keep these meals coming. Guess that spiritual stuff really works. Still, I could use a break. "Dad, how about we switch it up next week? You hit church with Mom, and I stay behind to cook."

"Wow. It's not just the Dolphins making bad plays today." He dumped a small mound of chopped onions into his cauldron, then held up a torn envelope from Nationwide Car Insurance as a reminder that I had more pressing concerns than weekly worship. "Don't you have somewhere to be? Freedom ain't free, young man."

On the TV a pass grazed a receiver's fingers before sailing out of bounds, and Dad resumed his cursing (quietly), our conversation over. Unclipping my tie, I made my way upstairs to get ready for work.

Mom's voice echoed in the hall, cheery and skeptical in a way only moms could pull off. ". . . I don't know what a YouTuber is, but it doesn't sound like a real career to me, Cressie."

She saw me pass, and shouted, "Del, come talk to your sister."

I leaned into the room. "Mom, I got work."

"Talk. To. Your sister." Mom shoved the phone into my hand. I said, "Hey, C."

"Hey, D."

"So, have you flunked out yet?"

"No," she huffed. "Asshole."

"Mom, Cressie said a bad word. On Sunday."

But Mom was in the walk-in closet, changing. I sat on the edge of my parents' bed, then flopped backward, stared at the slow-whirling ceiling fan. "For real, school going okay for you?"

"School is school."

"That's real disappointing. I always thought college supposed to be fun. Are you doing college correctly?"

"How's school for you, big-time junior?"

"You already know. Ain't nothing changed at Green Creek."

Not exactly true. But I wasn't about to get into the latest GCHS drama with Mom a dozen feet away. Plus, I'd give my sister some credit; what interest would a college student *really* have in the petty nonsense happening in my high school's hallways?

"No girlfriend?"

I almost said "soon," but, again, Mom was right there. "On that note, I gotta get to the gig."

"You know you can always ask me for advice when you need it, little brother."

"Cold day in hell, big sister."

"Del!" Mom barked from the closet.

"Now you care about bad words?"

Cressie said, "Love you, punk!"

"I know." I passed Mom the phone and made my way to my room.

Inside, door closed and locked, I peeled off my church clothes and excavated my closet floor for faded jeans, my wrinkled official company shirt, and my catfish-stenciled hat. After suiting up, I grabbed my phone, earbuds, and car keys to pull a paper chase at the least appetizing restaurant in all of Green Creek.

"Welcome to Monte FISHto's! What are you casting your hook for?" I was on autopilot, immune to the clotted smell of Old Bay batter.

My register's touchscreen glowed, and I tapped in an order of two Cra-Burgers with extra Sea Sauce, Filet Fries (they're regular fries, but the FISHto brand insisted on everything sounding extra), and drinks. "That's twelve ninety-eight."

I'd been there an hour; my first customer of the day, reeking of musty weed smoke and problems, handed me a crumpled, expired 50-percent-off coupon.

"Sir, I can't take this."

"What you mean you can't take it?" He expected his red-eyed gaze to be the tiebreaker in our little dispute.

I said, "It expired last year."

"No it ain't."

"Sir, this coupon is no longer valid and I, literally, can't do anything about it. It's got a bar code, and the system won't even let me scan it." I showed him the error message on my register—like it'd matter.

"Hell, naw." Now he was loud. "I ain't come here to be cheated out of my dough, lil' man. Where the manager?"

"Tyrell!"

My manager, Tyrell, waddled around the corner, his belly stress-testing his button-up boss shirt that had a fancy version of the Monte FISHto mascot "The Count"—a red cartoon catfish dressed all British with a sword—stenciled over the heart, fronting like the Ralph Lauren polo horse. Tyrell had fat fingers, fat knuckles, and the kind of hair like the seats on public toilets. U-shaped, rimming the side of his head, while the rest of his scalp was completely bare. His eyebrows were raised so they were the closest things to a hairline he'd had in a while. "What's going on, Del?"

"This customer wants to use this coupon." I handed the flimsy, faded paper over.

"I'm sorry about the inconvenience, sir." Tyrell punched his manager's code into my register, taking half off the meal. "Go grab his order, Del."

"Yeah, go grab my order, lil' man." He paid his $6.50 with a fifty he peeled from a thick wad of bills. I turned away to meet Stu the Cook at the counter between the kitchen and the front line.

When the food was claimed, and Weed-Douche bopped out with World Champ swagger, I waited for Tyrell to give his usual spiel. "Customer's always right, Del."

"Except when they're wrong. Dude cheated us."

"True. He seemed like a troublemaker though. What do we not want in our restaurant?"

He wanted me to say trouble. I said, "Roaches. Might be too late, though."

Stu cackled, but my other coworker gave a slow headshake from her post in the drive-thru hutch, then went about polishing up the Coke machine with a damp cloth.

Mya Hanson had made the transition from First Missionary Holy Youth to Fish Flinger same as me. A FISHto's uniform was not flattering, and Mya didn't put any effort into enhancing the look. Her shirt was a size too large, her pants too baggy and dusty with batter. I mean it was the same deal with my uniform, but she's a girl. Don't get me started on that sloppy ponytail sticking through the back of her signature Monte cap. In church you could tell she tried a little. Here? I don't know. To each his, or her, own. I guessed.

Our shifts often aligned because we had the same school (and now church) schedule. We never talked much, despite all that overlap. She was a nose-to-the-grindstone, on-to-the-next-task kind of person. Killing herself like she didn't recognize FISHto's for the joke that it was.

Tyrell disappeared to the back, doing whatever the manager of an unappetizing Long John Silver's knockoff did, leaving Stu, Mya, and me to our respective stations.

Except Mya crossed the imaginary border between drive-thru and front line, wiping crumbs off a counter that was technically my responsibility. I never felt possessive of FISHto squalor until that moment. Well, maybe possessive was the wrong word. Judged?

Quickly, I snatched a clean cloth from a bin on the wall, soaked it in the nearby sink, then began scrubbing the opposite end of the counter while eyeing her. "I was going to get that, you know."

"It's slow right now. So we help each other."

It's always slow at FISHto's, and I'd never helped on her station. Something was off here.

Mya Hanson was—how to say this? Like the out-of-focus ghost in the background of a quiet horror movie. There, but not. I mostly only ever saw her out the corner of my eye.

With a second dry rag she produced from her apron pocket, she went back over the streaks she'd left on the counter, buffing the tiles to a glossy shine, really exercising attention to detail while working closer to me. I was focused on her, barely paying attention where and how I dragged my sloppy wet cloth. "There's something you want to say, Mya. I can tell."

The gap between us closed to whisper-distance. She did this exaggerated glance toward the back like we were coconspirators. Stu was the only possible witness, and he had his chin propped in his hand, dozing. A dangerous thing to do over the hot grill, but he'd beaten the odds so far.

Mya, hushed, but excited, said, "Purity Pledge!"

"What about it?"

"We're doing it!" Her brown cheeks turned rosy. "I don't mean doing *IT*. Obviously. We're on the same journey."

That's what she wanted to talk about?

With the Mya mystery solved, I abandoned counter cleaning completely, shooting my rag toward the sink like a Steph Curry three-pointer. The wet cloth smacked the floor about a foot short of the basin. Mya flinched at my horrible miss.

"I didn't warm up." I rotated my shoulder, wincing like I might be injured. "Go on. Purity Pledge."

"I don't know if you know this, but me and my mother are part of the First Missionary Welcome Committee."

I did. Mrs. Hanson had been cozying up to Mom about us transitioning from frequent visitors to official church members. My mother was one of those use-the-entire-trial-period kind of people, so she was taking her time on the decision. "That keep you busy?" I said.

"Not exactly. There aren't a ton of new people coming to our church."

I nodded, well aware.

"As someone with a mandate of making all who step through the church doors feel a part of something bigger than themselves, I was very happy to see you so eager to be a part of PP . . ." Her voice trailed off, a weird hesitation. ". . . though, I do have a question."

"Okay."

"I was . . . under the impression . . . that you weren't exactly," she did another glance toward the back, embarrassed to look me in the eye, "*pure?*"

"What?"

Her voice sped up. "Not that I'm criticizing. But, I mean, don't you have a sort of reputation?"

I had no response. I was still processing the Purity Pledge thing myself, and Mya Hanson was vetting my virginity?

The door chimed before I could formulate a solid answer. When I saw who it was, I felt saved.

"I'm going on break," I said to no one in particular.

But saying "break" was like saying "Voldemort"—Tyrell appeared from the back in a cloud of Trout Breading. "Company policy says employees have to work a minimum of three hours before taking a maximum of fifteen minutes' rest, and by my count—"

"Or," said Qwan, my best friend, and former Monte FISHto's coworker, "you could pass him the mop and let him improve these dirty-ass floors."

Tyrell waggled a finger Qwan's way. "You're not even supposed to be in here. Thief!"

Before those two could really get going, I gripped the nearest mop with two hands and steered a bucket of stagnant gray water onto the main floor. "Call me if you need me."

Given the nonexistent flow of customers lately, that was unlikely.

Mya looked put out, like she'd wholly expected our conversation to continue . . . or at least officially end. Nope.

At the back of the restaurant, out of Tyrell's sights, Qwan splayed in a booth like it was his living room couch. Ball cap cocked, blue hoodie jacket, matching LeBrons with laces loose in a way that would make me lose a shoe.

He dripped swag, as usual. Made lounging in a fast-food joint look like a mixtape cover. Made me want to be free of my trash uniform so I could do the same. But, money. I squeezed extra water from my mop and did the thing.

Qwan lifted a foot away from my swishing mop head. "Tyrell really still tripping about those nasty Cra-Burgers?"

"You stole food. You were wrong, dude."

He flopped back, hands behind his head to support the wide grin on his face. "It was so worth it, though. I bet you wish you'd done it."

The "it" he was referring to . . . he'd given that food away to a couple of *bad* Carolina girls who'd crossed the southern Virginia border into our part of the world for . . . reasons. I'd been working the drive-thru the night it happened. Tyrell caught him immediately. Fired him immediately. From my window perch, I watched Qwan stroll into the parking lot, FISHto shirt untucked and flapping in the wind like an action movie hero walking away from an explosion. He enthusiastically accepted a ride from the grateful ladies. What he said happened after that, I want to believe it's a lie, because if it's not a lie, it makes him a legend.

"What are you doing here?" I asked. "I know it's not to eat."

"Hell naw. I should whistle-blow on this place. Tell the Environmental Protection Agency or something. I walked all the way up here to find out what happened with Kiera. You make a move?"

A particularly sticky milkshake stain snatched my attention. "D," Qwan said. "No."

My mopping trajectory shifted and I left him in the booth. "I didn't punk out. Timing wasn't right."

On his feet, he paced me. "Timing? If you didn't do it now, it might already be too late. Kiera Westing is Green Creek's Most Wanted."

"You don't think I know that? It's different this time."

"Damn right. Because if you're not going to step to her, I might. That girl is *fire*."

I whacked him across the chest with my mop handle. He raised his hands in surrender. "Joke, joke. I know Bro Code's in effect here. Alls I'm saying is—"

"I'm working on it. See, we're both in the Purity Pledge at church now. That's going to give me some time with her." Working backward, tracing big wet arcs along the perpetually filthy tile, I left a cock-eyed Qwan stone-still on the other side of a widening soap-and-water moat. He shook off the momentary freeze and stamped alternating sets of Nike swooshes across my floor to rejoin me.

"*Purity* Pledge?"

"Yeah, it's when you agree not to—"

He sliced a hand through the air, cutting me off. "I know what it is. I saw a Netflix documentary on that creepy shit. Dads were taking their daughters to the prom."

"I don't know about all that."

"It's No-Bone Zone, though. Right? Voluntary celibacy."

"If you're going to be crass about it, I guess."

He knocked the mop from my grasp, and the handle clattered loudly. "Worst. Plan. Ever. We already don't agree about this one-true-love stuff you been on with Kiera since birth. But, fine. You haven't necessarily let it hold you back. When's the last time you got some, though?"

I glanced over my shoulder, concerned Mya, my new purity monitor, might hear. My voice low, I said, "What's it to you?"

"Tanisha Thompson's basement party. It almost doesn't count because everybody smashed. And it was two years ago. It's like you took a Purity Pledge right after."

A name I hadn't thought about lately bobbed to the surface

of my thoughts, like those Magic 8 Ball answers floating up from black water. Shianne Griffiths. Me and her in Tanisha's dark, private guest bathroom, a single candle burning on the marble sink.

"Get out the way!" I hit him with an NFL-caliber stiff arm and snatched my mop up. "One of us cares about not being fired."

"And one of us cares about you using your little wee-wee before you die."

"Stop thinking about my wee—my *dick*, Qwan."

"Somebody got to."

"Bro. I gets mine. All right? Just because I'm not telling you all my business . . ."

"That's just sad, D. You told me when your mom found those limited-edition sparkle Pop-Tarts you like. You hit me at midnight about them shits. You'd definitely tell me if you were getting some booty."

"Dude, I'm good." I wasn't.

We were back in front, and Mya was too busy with a drive-thru order to pick up on the context clues about that "reputation" she'd heard about not being all that.

Tyrell leaned over a clipboard, jotting down managerial stuff.

I said, "Hey, Tyrell, Qwan's trying to convince me to steal a case of Flounder Patties. You should kick him out."

Tyrell didn't look up. "Get out, Qwan."

"Fine. I got ladies to check on anyway. Hopefully the stench of this place hasn't stuck to me, messing up my game so that it's like yours, Del."

My mop became a bat, the mold-smelling drenched end cocked over my shoulder and ready to fling gross water. "You should go."

He flipped both middle fingers and backed into bright afternoon sunshine. "Later, Mister Clean."

Though he was gone, Qwan's evaluation remained. Purity Pledge. Worst. Plan. Ever.

That stung. But it also held weight because, statistically speaking, Qwan was mad successful with girls. Since he lost his virginity three years prior, he'd been obsessed with getting more, more, more. He treated Instagram like it was Amazon, always shopping, always sliding into some new girl's DMs looking for nothing longer than two-day delivery. He swore he smashed as much as he did because he didn't do emotion. Told me *I* shouldn't do emotion, that girls liked it when you weren't all soft and fuzzy.

His thinking wasn't much different than most of the dudes at school.

Qwan thought I was too picky. According to him, if Kiera Westing didn't exist, I'd be saving myself for some hot actress on TV because that's the next level of unattainable after Kiera. I let him think it. It was easier than the truth.

Doing it the way he did, the way most dudes talked about . . . I envied it, really. I wished I was built like that. It seemed fun. Somehow easier. Until it went wrong, anyway. Something everyone at Green Creek High had witnessed.

I'm not built that way though, not the smash-on-the-couch-after-school-before-some-adult-got-home type. I liked the way Dad sat on one corner of the sofa with Mom wedged in his armpit, her feet tucked under her, while we all watched *Jeopardy!* or *Black-ish*. I liked watching them hold hands in the Costco before I was old enough to skip the trip. That's the kind of thing I wanted. With Kiera. And it wasn't unattainable. I wouldn't let it be.

I mopped until my arm ached. After, I stowed my bucket. There were three hours left in my shift. Then Tyrell let me know to adjust my math.

"Business is slow. Gotta send you home early, Del."

Not the news I wanted. Two hours' work for the whole week wasn't even a full tank of gas, let alone car insurance money. Mya remained in the drive-thru nook, filling a couple of Whale-Sized cups with ice and Sprite, no signs of slowing down.

"Just me?" I asked.

Tyrell gave me a half grin. "We've got the rest of the evening covered."

My driving privileges were on the line here. "Can I get on the schedule some evenings this week?"

Tyrell held his clipboard to his chest like a shield. "I'll call if I got something."

Not down for answering any "why you home so soon?" questions, I caught a movie at the two-dollar theater in Old Town

Green Creek, then made my way home around the time my shift should've ended.

Mom's car was MIA when I pulled into the driveway. She was back at church, for the special Sunday-evening worship First Missionary did every other week. Like, seriously, how much praying did you need to do in one day? Dad was zonked out on the couch, snoring, an NFL game watching him. I slipped to the kitchen quietly, huffed down three—maybe four—tacos, then made my way upstairs to the Sanctum Sanctorum, aka my room.

Mom had left my Purity Pledge folder on my keyboard. But, it wasn't the only item.

There was also a signed permission slip I'd brought home weeks ago and forgotten about, with the Green Creek High crest printed at the top. It said:

Healthy Living Elective Opt-In Form/Grade 11

If you wish to opt your student into some or all of the grade eleven Healthy Living Elective (HLE) lessons, please complete this form and return it to your student's Health/PE teacher by the Week 1 date on your welcome letter.

PLEASE NOTE: You MUST return this form if you wish for your student to participate in the Grade 11 HLE activities.

CHILD'S NAME: Delbert Rainey, Jr.

Directions: Please check ONLY those lessons in which you want your child to take part.

"Healthy Living" . . . was sex ed. Last year it was "Family Living" . . . but still really sex ed. Why they didn't call it that had always puzzled me. And the lessons . . .

Below the instructions was a list of lessons, divided up over eight weeks. I skimmed phrases like "strengths of my inter-personal goals," and "maturity and decision making," and "A thorough review of STD prevention and contraception." For some reason, that one was in bold type.

Rocking back in my chair, eyes rolled back, I groaned. Eight weeks of Purity Pledge *and* this?

Sitting up, I said, "Eight weeks."

I set the permission slip aside and opened my Purity Pledge folder. The first page had a weekly breakdown of our purity lessons. Immediate phrases that jumped out: "strengths of bib-lical principles," and "God's will vs. my will" and "A thorough review of why Jesus wants me to abstain."

In bold type.

Snatching up my Healthy Living permission slip, I held the breakdowns of the two classes side by side. Each week, each lesson, was like Bizarro World opposites. Whatever was on the books for Healthy Living, Purity Pledge went the other way. And vice versa.

What the hell?

Or what the heaven? I mean, this definitely wasn't a coinci-dence. The parallels were too exact, right down to the fonts. The image that popped in my head . . . tug-of-war.

But, why?

This felt important. I would've pondered it more, but I got a text from Qwan.

> **Qwan:** Got a new IG follow for you.
> MzIndependentNCS. She's Nigerian,
> Colombian, and Swedish bro. Bikini shots
> are bananas!

And then I moved on to Instagram. To explore the nations of the world.

CHAPTER 4

MORNING

PERSON

THOSE WERE THE TOP and bottom captions in Kiera's IG story, paired with a Boomerang of her flipping her hair back and forth like a shampoo ad. Back and forth, back and forth. *Flip-flap, flip-flap.*

It was the latest in a series that posted overnight. Some stills. Some video. A few with the goofy filters that made her eyes cartoonishly big and/or distorted her head. All positive, upbeat. Overly.

She was broadcasting to all of GCHS that everything was fine. Nothing to see here.

The views were in the hundreds and climbing.

I tapped my phone, intending to check Colossus's story while barreling down the stairs loud enough to trigger a "Walk!" from Mom. At the front door, car keys jingling in my other hand, I felt the rush of unsupervised transportation that still hadn't gotten old. Before I could escape, Dad's office door slid open.

"Junior, let me holler at you a sec."

"Dad, I gotta pick up Qwan."

"Just a few minutes. You'll be fine."

My backpack tugged tight on my shoulders, I flopped onto the center cushion of the couch inside his "home office." Dad had a sweet job writing technical documentation for a company that made productivity apps. He never had to go into a "real office," like he used to. Now he was "work from home" and a "telecommuter," terms that he tossed around at family functions when folks asked how things were going.

It was good he could say those things now. Better than when he was out of work and could only mention "prospects" and "you know how the economy is." He was happier than those days, though he worried about money a lot more.

He parted the drapes, exposing the open blinds beneath, and the laser lines of sunshine beaming through the cracks seemed to slice up the room and everything in it. "Son, what's up with this Purity Pledge thing at your mother's church?"

My stomach fell into the crawl space under the house. The same feeling I got on the rare occasion I'd watch a movie with my parents and there's suddenly a sex scene no one knew was coming. "It's like, a class. We learn about ways to not, you know."

Dad took his high-backed desk chair, swiveling to face me. In the tiny space, our knees almost touched. His legs were bare because he was in a bathrobe, T-shirt, and shorts with tube socks pulled just below his knees. His go-to work uniform these days.

The only time we'd ever come close to discussing anything remotely related to Purity Pledge was three years ago. I'd been in my room playing *Gears of War* and he'd gotten home from work, back when he still wore pants.

"It's time we had a conversation," he'd said then, closing my bedroom door. I wondered what I'd done wrong.

Instead of him listing my crimes and passing my sentence, he pulled a shiny wrapper from his shirt pocket. Held it to me, gently, like precious treasure. The impression of a ring was clearly visible through the foil packaging. "You know what this is?"

A condom. Mike Brooks stole some from his brother's closet and showed us at lunch one day, but I only said, "Yeah."

"You know how to use one?"

"Yeah." A lie.

Grinning with every tooth in his head, he said, "My boy."

He laid the loose condom on my Avengers comforter, popped the latches on his briefcase, and removed the open twelve-pack that the loosie must've come from. The box said they were "ribbed," and all I could think about was summer barbecues. I liked ribs a lot.

He placed the box—one I still had tucked in the back of my underwear drawer—on my bed, too. "Then you know to always keep one with you. Gotta be safe, son. Got any questions for me?"

"Naw."

He clapped a hand on my shoulder, winked. "Good talk."

In his office, his face was flat. Waiting. Were we remembering different things?

"What I'm trying to understand, son, is if this Purity Pledge's some sort of reset for you? Because I assumed you'd been, you know." He made a fist, did this weird slow extension punch that was some signal for sex, maybe.

Focusing on the rainbow spines of the various technical manuals lining his bookshelves, I conjured the most plausible response I could manage. "Purity Pledge, it's a, a volunteer thing. It'll look good for, like, college applications."

That hung between us awhile. His next words: "Seems kind of extreme. You could go fold clothes at the Goodwill, right?"

He didn't mean extreme. That was his "son, this is weird" voice. That tone I'd heard too many times in my life. When I joined the band as a freshman instead of the JV basketball team (like that was my choice; not even Qwan would choose me in a pickup game). Or when he caught me trying to move the TV remote with the Force. Or when he thought I was too slow getting into girls.

Dad didn't ever say what really bothered him, but I'd learned to complete his half judgments on my own.

He pushed. "Aren't there other volunteer opportunities at the church, or around town?"

"Like what, Dad?"

"You tell me. I'm not the one trying to get into college." That was his version of "I don't know." Like when I used to ask him what a word meant, he'd say, "Look it up, I can't do everything for you," meaning he didn't know either, but he wanted to seem wise.

Leaning closer, he checked our perimeter. Grinned. "Are you really trying to tell me a Rainey Man doesn't want to get some?"

God. I blurted, "Kiera Westing's doing it."

A slow blink then. He'd caught me eyeing her at a parent/teacher night a bunch of years ago, knew about my thing for her. He pressed back in his chair, his posture was proud, his bathrobe draped his seat like a hero's cape, and that warmed something inside me. "Oh," he said. "Ohhhhhhh. I see now."

With a fist pump, I said, "Rainey Man."

"Damn straight." Though he still seemed troubled. It came off him in waves.

"Is there something else, Dad?"

"One thing, and don't tell your mother I asked this."

Uh-oh.

He said, "How much does this Purity Pledge cost?"

"Ummmm. Nothing. I think."

His widest grin yet. "Exactly what I wanted to hear."

"I gotta go, Dad. Qwan."

"Of course." He stood before I did, like he needed to show me the door. "You two. I remember those days. Best time of your life, son. Enjoy it."

Enjoy what exactly? Dad was hard to read, never ever said precisely what he meant, and the whole conversation was mad weird. On my way out, I almost asked for clarification. But, when I faced him, he winked.

And I didn't want to ruin that.

● ● ●

"Ninja," Qwan said, reclined to near horizontal in my passenger seat, his phone held so close to his face I wondered if he needed glasses, "shit's getting crazy on Snapchat."

Despite Kiera's cheerful social media show, the rest of Green Creek High was treating her breakup like the small scandal it was. Qwan viewed and reported while I made the slow drive to school. He had to be my eyes and ears because my driving privileges were also dependent on me never doing any of the following things:

Texting while driving.

Web surfing while driving.

Talking on the phone without a hands-free setup (currently unavailable in my used economy Nissan—I was lucky to have air-conditioning) while driving.

This was one of the many topics on which my parents were a united front. "It only takes a second to make a fatal mistake, and if you don't concentrate fully on the road, you don't deserve your own transportation," they often said. In unison. As if possessed by twin safety demons.

Never mind that there was barely a street in Green Creek with a posted speed limit over 45 MPH. Whatever. Since gas money was always an iffy proposition with him, it gave Qwan a chance to earn his keep.

He said, "People acting like they died."

That wasn't surprising. Not that breakups weren't a thing at Green Creek High. We had couples get together before lunch and be exes by final bell. Kiera's breakup strayed from the standard because of her relationship's length, intensity, and effect on school morale. So, the grieving was real.

Her and Colossus had been class couple every year since they got together. There were dumb rumors of them getting married at our graduation ceremony. Like the principal's gonna be all, "Here's your diploma, you may kiss the bride."

The point was people rode hard for "Kee-Lossus."

Yeah, that was a thing, too.

I said, "Kiera post anything new?"

"Naw. Still that same Molly Sunshine mess. I been on Colossus's account." Qwan giggled. "He singing love songs."

"Stop playing."

Qwan turned his phone speaker to max, and I got a sample of some off-key screeching.

"Turn it off." Surely that horrendous sound violated one of my parents' Driving Don'ts.

Colossus had always been on some true romance stuff with Kiera. Flowers on Valentine's Day. Stuffed animals on her birthday. Most dudes got clowned for such PDA. Most dudes couldn't put you in a chokehold that'd have you sleeping through college.

When either Kiera or Colossus posted pics of them bowling, or strapping on helmets at the Go-Kart Village (always coordinated to hit both of their accounts simultaneously, maximizing exposure), mad girls would repost those joints like they were celebrities. #relationshipgoals or #BAEenvy. For them, "Kee-Lossus" was a Green Creek fairy tale.

Guys—myself included, with the couple of not-so-serious girlfriends I'd had—saw a hard standard to live up to. As Qwan once put it, "Colossus take Kiera to Outback Steakhouse, then every girl I'm trying to holla at need a Bloomin' Onion. He must be stopped." I agreed.

We finally got our wish.

We parked in the student lot and made our way into the building with fifteen minutes to spare before homeroom. Enough time for Qwan to cop one of the brick-hard sausage biscuits from the cafeteria (I stuck to chocolate milk, thank you very much), and for us to absorb the latest drama in real time.

I'd hoped to catch a glimpse of Kiera at her locker, but she was nowhere in sight, though a few of the more gossipy girls hovered in the general vicinity like paparazzi waiting on Rihanna.

At my locker, Qwan stayed at my side, giving me a running report of all new info.

"Angie Bell is catching it," Qwan said, swiping and scrolling. "There are like eight different versions of what she did this weekend. 'Angie knew Colossus's people were out of town and showed up at his house in nothing but a trench coat.' 'Angie saw Colossus at the Sonic Drive-In, climbed in his backseat.' 'Angie has *always* been into Colossus, and wore him down after he had a fight with Kiera.'"

He kept going, kept indicting Angie. Everybody liked Kiera. So, what happened to the girl who did her dirty? *All* the girl hate got aimed at her.

Qwan said, "The comments, bro."

I could imagine, but didn't have to. Neck-deep in my locker, excavating for my books, I heard a shady, cough-shout, "THOT!"

That Ho Over There.

I turned around as Angie passed us. Head down, face mean. A bunch of people laughed so I couldn't tell which asshole said it. People took it too far going at her like that. Way I saw it, I owed Angie Bell a fro-yo.

Qwan's head swiveled with her, leering, tracking her movements until she turned the corner. He said, "It's amazing how you be around someone for months and never notice their inner beauty."

"Oh my God." I knew where this was going. I slammed my locker, and we joined the foot traffic to class. Approaching from the opposite direction was Antoinette Petrie, who was low-key hot in her tight sweaters and bright green glasses. She was a current Qwan work-in-progress.

"Nettie, you get my DM?" Qwan said.

She giggled. "You wild, Qwan."

"All I'm saying is we should hang."

"I'll think about it."

Then she was gone, and with the attention span of a hummingbird, he flitted back to the previous subject. "Anyway, Angie. I hear she's got a sensual soul. Real *deep*."

"Never use the word 'deep' like that around me again."

"I'm trying to appeal to your delicate nature, D. If you want the real . . ."

Qwan began a rapid-fire, triple-X version of what supposedly transpired over the weekend. Information that couldn't possibly be accurate, though when has that stopped anybody at Green Creek. He was still telling me about what Angie did, what Angie could do, and what Angie invented (like something called a "Yorktown Pancake Bend" that involved syrup and tremendous dexterity) in excited whispers as we took our seats in social studies. While our teacher wrote on the whiteboard, he continued his recap on sheets of loose-leaf with crude stick figure drawings.

I was happy for a break during English—my favorite class, with my favorite teacher, Mister Jay, aka "MJ"—because Qwan's schedule differed from mine until lunch. By then, his perv battery had run low, and he moved on to the day's other significant topic. Healthy Living. We both had our signed permission slips.

"Why you think they're all parental approval with it this time?" I asked.

Qwan said, "I don't know, but I should be the one teaching it. Bet I know more than Coach."

He was probably right. Coach Scott never struck me as much of a ladies' man, particularly with those Mickey Mouse prayers at First Missionary, but the point was moot. For the second time that day I was face-to-face with my favorite teacher, MJ, waiting in the door of Health Sciences Room 1.

Beyond him, at Health Sciences Room 2, was one of the guidance counselors, Mrs. Gaither. Without being told, boys with permission slips handed them over to MJ, while the girls with permission slips continued on to the second room. Anyone without slips kept on to the gym, where they'd probably run laps for the next forty-five minutes.

"What up, MJ?" I handed over my slip, then engaged in a fist bump. His calloused knuckles always hurt a little, but I made sure not to flinch.

"So we meet again," he said.

MJ's English class wasn't exactly fun. He made you work, and you better not be behind on the reading and trying to focus on your desk so he didn't call on you, because then he'd call on you first. I don't know, though, it was still better than most everything else in school. From day one he told us his class wasn't one where "old dead white dudes" (MJ's *actual* words) rule. We still had people like Dickens and Steinbeck—*Of Mice and Men* was dope—on our summer reading list from before the school year started, but there was also Gloria Naylor, and Walter Dean Myers, and Meg Medina, and graphic novels by people like Gene Luen Yang to pick from now that school was in. Writers I didn't know about before I knew MJ; writers I couldn't wait to read.

None of that had a thing to do with Healthy Living, I didn't think. So why was he here?

Inside the Health Sciences room, another oddity. The rumpled gray suit that was our never-happy vice principal. Mister Terrier. He hovered in the corner, scowling at nothing in particular, his cheeks and crinkled forehead an irritated red with beige splotches peeking through. He usually lurked in the halls, giving people detention for the most minor infractions or yelling at them to go to class. I'd never seen him *in a class* before.

Qwan and me took seats among classmates who were all going for different levels of aloofness as we filled the twenty-plus available desks, the same dudes in the same general sectors we'd occupied for most of our school careers. Slouched weed-heads gravitated to the center of the desk grid, stretching legs into the aisle, playfully tripping those walking by. Burnouts settled on the back row. The JROTC crew, led by future supersoldier Mason Miles, came in all buttoned up in their olive-green uniforms, and took seats at the front. Me and Qwan were in the row closest to the door, him ahead of me. Slack, annoyed facial expressions were set. Any visible interest—even though I was hyped about MJ being in the mix—was unacceptable.

"Settle down, guys," MJ said. That command from any other teacher might've needed to be issued a couple of times, but MJ, with his shoulder-length dreads, and his sweater sleeves rolled up revealing the various tattoos running up his ripped forearms, never had to issue any orders more than once. "I know you're probably wondering why I'm the one teaching this course instead of Coach Scott. The simplest answer is I volunteered."

He let it hang, his gaze sailing to Mister Terrier, whose chin cocked like some kind of silent dare in the back of the room. MJ rolled his eyes, kept going. "The more complicated version has to do with there being some changes to the approved sexual education—"

"*Healthy Living*, Mister Jay," Terrier interrupted.

MJ heavy-sighed. "—*Healthy Living* curriculum. When my colleagues and I were informed, and some of the physical education faculty expressed discomfort with the changes, I felt compelled to step in. This happens to fall during my free period, so it worked out."

Qwan's hand popped up.

MJ said, "Yeah, Qwan?"

"What changed? Healthy Living seem the same as when it was called Family Living last—"

"That's enough with the interruptions," said Terrier.

"I didn't interrupt anything. I raised my hand and MJ called on me."

"You know that tone doesn't fly with me, young man." Terrier unstuck himself from the wall, trudged toward us, reaching into his jacket pocket. Damn Qwan.

"What tone? All I'm doing is asking a question."

Terrier's pad of detention slips appeared like a gunslinger's six-shooter.

"That's not necessary." MJ's words dripped disgust.

If Terrier cared about MJ's assessment, we couldn't tell. He scribbled Qwan's name and particulars on the slip, and handed over a carbon copy. "For disrupting class, Mr. Reid. See you this afternoon." Then, to MJ, "Continue."

When Terrier turned away, Qwan mouthed *What the fuck?*

MJ's scowl was ice. "Regarding the change, there's been a push to augment the abstinence-only aspect of the program formerly known as Family Living. So, while topics will be similar to the old format, there will be some additional direction on contraception, STD prevention, and resisting peer pressure up to, and including, any sort of ill-advised pacts."

I straightened in my chair, understanding. Others did too, evident by the chuckles around the room.

Pacts. It all made sense now.

MJ was talking about The Baby-Getters Club.

To be clear, there was no pact. Or outbreak—another word the TV stations ran with before they settled on the most popular term for what happened. All of that conspiracy BS was fiction. The simultaneous pregnancies were real, obviously. All nine of them.

Nine girls of different grades—freshman to senior—different races, family income level. Nothing in common except aspirations to have a diploma from Green Creek High School someday. How'd it happen? That was the part the adults couldn't wrap their heads around. To be honest, I don't think they tried very hard. When bellies swelled, and the state of things was impossible to ignore, the town mostly discussed the pregnancies in whispers. As if speaking on them too loudly would spontaneously create another baby.

The mystery/crisis/apocalypse reached critical mass one morning last spring. My bus turned onto the road leading to the school, and there was a city cop directing traffic with one of those Slow/Stop signs you flip when part of the road's blocked and cars coming from both directions gotta use the same lane. Usually it's because of road work, or a breakdown, or a storm knocking down a tree. That day it was news crews from Richmond.

All of the major networks sent blimp-like vans parked half on the road, half on the shoulder, with satellite arms stretched high. Reporters in suits held their big lollipop mics before bulky cameras wielded by bulkier cameramen.

We nearly tipped the bus when everyone rushed the side closest to the cameras to see what was up. Of course, we got no direct info. During homeroom, Terrier announced that we should not let the media disrupt our school day, and though he couldn't make us avoid the reporters once we were off school grounds, we should consult our parents before *wah-wanh-wah-wah*...

It took all of five seconds for people to get the scoop on their phones. When we did, it was a letdown, because it wasn't news to us.

The word was a bunch of girls made a strange, strange pact to get pregnant because of their music, or something they saw on TV, or video games. *The word* was some epic unknown threat had come to Green Creek and corrupted the minds of the youth in one of Virginia's most peaceful towns. What else might the kids be plotting? The horror! *Dun-Dun-Dunnnnh!*

That *word* was trash. I'd never heard a song, or seen a movie, that made me make a baby. And, what senior's conspiring on anything with a freshman?

If they wanted the truth, they should've asked Freya. That was the name of the out-of-nowhere freak blizzard that blanketed our part of the state in snow last October. School got shut down for a week. But parents still had to go to work. A lot of boredom set in. It was that simple.

When Cressie was still at home, we tripped out about how wild the stories got. How it became about everything but time and opportunity.

My sister said, "Sometimes I think simple hurts worse. So people make stuff complicated because there's more ways to toss around blame."

The news, and on some level, I think, our town, liked the pact angle most, though. Enough to run with it for the better part of a week, throwing "alleged" in front of it, until they managed to get class clown Kent Oster on camera.

Reporter: "Young man, do you know anything about the alleged pregnancy pact that took place at your school?"

Kent: "Pact? Oh, you mean The Baby-Getters Club?"

That's how Green Creek became the home of The Baby-Getters Club.

We weren't great in sports. Our academic ratings were middling. Graduation rate was only slightly above average. But, where Green Creek reigned was highest per capita teen pregnancy rate in the state of Virginia. So, we were the best at something. Go team!

MJ brought up a video player on the smartboard. "We're going to watch a short introductory film, guys."

Someone on the other side of the room yelled, "Is Lindy Blue in it?"

Cheers and claps. Lindy Blue was a porn star. I knew because, you know, I'd heard it around.

When the applause ceased, Terrier issued more detention slips.

MJ dimmed the lights, and a dull movie-guy voice began talking over stats about diseases, and pregnancies, and lifetime income of teen parents versus people who don't have babies until after college. At some point Terrier slipped from the room—probably as bored as we were—and by the time the lights went up and class was dismissed, I debated whether running laps with the kids who didn't have permission slips would've been a better use of my time.

In the hall, Qwan revved up, crumpling the detention slip in his fist. "Terrier, bro. I'm gonna be late for conditioning over this. Coach is gonna make me run hella laps. Yo, you listening?"

Kinda. But Jameer from church leaned on the bleachers by the half-court line, grilling me with his stare. Kiera, coming from the general direction of the girls' locker room, smoothed wrinkles in her blouse, a moment that felt worthy of slow-motion and love songs in my opinion, and joined him. She didn't see me, or even look in me and Qwan's general direction. Too busy being chased.

Colossus skulked behind her. The Green Creek *G* on his letter jacket stretched across his broad back, ready to tear if he flexed any harder. I couldn't hear what he was saying this far away, but I didn't need to. He was expressive, emphasizing each word with his open, stubby paws. "Please, baby, please" in bootleg sign language.

Kiera shook her head, not having any of it. He reached for one of her hands, which she snatched away. Jameer pushed off his bleacher perch like he might intervene, and I took a stupid step forward thinking, *What if I . . .*

Someone on the basketball court yelled, "Qwan, no look!"

There was time to register Qwan swiveling at the hip, dodging, right before a spinning orb eclipsed my vision and smashed my nose. A bright white starburst exploded my world, and the pain followed quickly.

Bystanders emitted a collective "oohhhhh." I went from upright to sprawled on the floor like a kindergartener at naptime.

"D?" Qwan said. "D, you good?"

I was, definitely, not good.

The blinding white from the collision faded to gray then to a fuzzy, pulsing view of beams and ventilation shafts overhead. I touched my fingers to my nose; they came away wet and red. With each thumping heartbeat, an invisible hatchet chopped me between the eyes.

Don't. Cry.

The weapon, a basketball that might actually be made of iron, lazy-rolled away from me.

Qwan said, "D, my bad, man. I should've caught it."

The dumbass who threw it said, "Yeah, you should've!"

I rolled to my side, then to my knees, red drops leaking between my fingers to the floor. I sniffled, bit back a whimper. Do not cry.

Every agonizing move I made getting to my feet was confirmation that I wasn't crippled or dead. Lack of permanent injury gave my classmates permission to crack up. Murmurs became snickers became deep-throated, knee-slapping laughs. I was their ridicule highlight of the day.

Hunched, I pressed my shirt to my nose, ruining my outfit but, literally, saving face. I smeared blood into my leaking tears so my cackling peers wouldn't know the difference.

Qwan gripped my arm. "I'll help you to the nurse's office."

A solid plan, but I had other concerns. Were Kiera and Jameer laughing, too?

I peeked over the bunched, stained fabric of my shirt to where they'd been before my mauling. Though Colossus had come closer, smirking with the rest of my audience, my church mates were nowhere in sight.

The school nurse screwed cotton into my nose, and I drove home breathing through my mouth with a pinkish swab protruding from each nostril. I arrived to an empty house, my voice echoing. "Mom! Dad!"

My phone shook as I made my way upstairs. Qwan.

Qwan: Yo, did the nurse amputate your nose?

Me: No. Dick. What you want?

Qwan: Angie was in detention with me. Got her number. Gonna see what's up.

Me: You don't care people treating her like typhoid mary right now?

Qwan: Ty-who?

Me: Damn dude! Read. Something. I'm saying you don't care that she's like shunned?

Qwan: Maybe by the girls . . .

I mined cotton from my nose, and tossed the swabs in my trash can.

My phone kept buzzing, more of Qwan's schemes, no doubt. I had the house to myself, though, and I needed to feel something other than the pain behind my eyes, and the lingering embarrassment from getting my face smashed.

I threw my phone on the bed, and locked my door to be safe. At my computer, my Purity Pledge folder rested on top of my keyboard. Tossed that aside, too. I opened a private browser window, turned the volume low, and searched for Lindy Blue.

CHAPTER 5

GRAVEL CRUNCHED UNDER MY TIRES the following after-noon when I pulled into the church lot for the first day of Purity Pledge. With the exception of a couple of cars in re-served spots near the main door, the place looked deserted. Haunted-house creepy. There had to be another way to get time in with Kiera. I considered bailing on the whole thing and driving home.

Before I could jerk my gearshift into reverse, a car turned into the lot, rocks crackling beneath it. It was a newish Buick, dark green, three passengers. Jameer opened his door and ejected from the backseat before it came to a full stop, rolling his ankle slightly but not considering, even for a minute, wait-ing until the car was actually not in motion before exiting.

The day was cool, so I had my window down. I heard every-thing.

From the car's passenger window, Mr. Sesay yelled, "This conversation isn't over."

"Oh yes it is," Jameer said, on a beeline for the door, limping slightly.

His mom turned the car in a wide arc as if angling back toward the road, but stopped short of a complete turn to lower her window and yell, "You better remember what Proverbs 6:20 tells us. 'My son, observe the—'"

Jameer spun on his heels and stood at attention like a military man. "'—commandment of your father and do not forsake the teaching of your mother.'" He snapped off a salute paired with an exaggerated smile. "Ma'am, yes, ma'am! Sir, yes, sir!"

"God don't like ugly, Jameer," his mother said. "Go in there, let Vanessa knock some of that sin off you, then get your disrespectful butt straight home. You hear?"

He didn't respond, simply hobbled up the church steps while his parents' car spit rocks on its way to the road.

I intended to wait until he went inside, embarrassed to have even witnessed whatever the hell that was. But he lingered on the porch landing, rolling his shoulders, as if bracing himself to go in. Was I not the only one having a change of heart?

Suddenly, like he heard my thoughts on the breeze, he turned, eyes pointed my way. I fought the urge to duck.

He quickstepped down the stairs, still limping, and made his way over to the passenger side of my car with the intense purpose of a Terminator; I pawed at the power lock button out of reflex. I actually hit the power *window* button, and while the glass sailed up, Jameer yanked my door open and flopped into my passenger seat. "Are you a spy now?"

"Man, I was just sitting here."

"You heard that." He leaned across the console between our seats, too far in my personal space.

"Maybe. I guess. Yo, you need to relax with that energy right now." For the second time in as many conversations with Jameer, I wondered if we'd have to fight.

His chest heaved slowly, then he sat back, stared straight ahead. "We should go in."

Exiting my car, Jameer limped back toward the church. I snatched my bag from the backseat and scrambled after him. "Hey, we're not going to discuss what happened?"

"Nothing to talk about."

"Dude, you did like a John Wick roll out of your people's car and they weren't even concerned. Your ankle might be broken."

"It's not broken." He climbed the steps gingerly. "Slight sprain at most."

"Okay. I feel like we're not addressing the core issue here."

"How's your nose, Del?"

"My—?" Crap. He did see me catch that basketball to the grill. Did that mean Kiera saw, too?

"As I thought." Jameer twisted the knob and let us into the warm church sanctuary. "Let's discuss something other than our injuries then."

"Fine." I chased him down the aisle between all the empty pews. "What's up with Kiera and Colossus?"

"A lot of him begging. A lot of her not having any of it."

I felt a rush, and a grin lifted my cheeks. The incident with Jameer and his parents flitted to the back of my mind, when I grabbed his arm and spun him toward me. "You and her are tight, then? Can you put in a word for me?"

He scoffed. "Like a college reference letter? 'Dear Kiera,

Delbert Rainey is a fine student and an innovative thinker.'"

No. I mean, yes. It sounded dumb when he put it that way. "You don't have to be a dick about it."

At that, he flinched. I didn't know if it was what I said, how I said it, or that I'd said it in church, but he squeezed his eyes shut a second, pinched the bridge of his nose, and said, "Look. Let's get through this class first, then we can talk about it. Can you give me a ride home?"

"Cool."

In my head, I heard his mom yelling, "Get your disrespectful butt straight home."

So, I'd probably have to drive fast.

"Welcome to Purity Pledge!" Sister Vanessa bounced on her toes in front of a wall-to-wall whiteboard, a blue dry-erase marker in her hand, uncapped and ready.

We were in a wood-paneled Sunday school classroom at the back of First Missionary. Mostly empty corkboards lined the walls with the exception of a giddy cartoon Jesus poster that had Our Lord and Savior sitting on a rock, surrounded by cartoon kids of at least three ethnicities. There was a white kid, a brown kid, a Simpsons-yellow Asian kid and, for some reason, a happy goat. There was an aggressively bright sun with sunshine spokes shooting over Jesus's head, and a rainbow. The bubble print overlaying the blue sky read: *Jesus Loves Me, Yes I Know!* It seemed encouraging, blasphemous, and racist all at the same time.

Rows of worktables aligned in a way that mirrored the pew setup in the main sanctuary, creating an aisle in the middle of the room, separating all the Purity Pledgers by gender. Boys on the left, girls on the right. Sister Vanessa said, "Who wants to lead us in prayer?"

No one raised a hand.

I didn't know any prayers other than the "God is great, God is good" one I learned as a kid, and wasn't confident I could go off the top of my head like a bunch of people in the church seemed to do. It's like being at a party and someone asked you to rap when you're not a rapper.

The tense "no volunteers" moment stretched another half second before Kiera rose from her neatly organized workstation that occupied most of an entire table on the girls' side of the room. She had a fresh white binder with *P. Pledge* written on the side in black Sharpie, three different highlighters, and multiple pens—all making my single dull pencil feel inadequate. She joined Sister Vanessa at the front of the room, clutching her worn Bible with colorful tabs protruding from the pages like the flags of tiny pastel countries. "Dear Lord, thank you for this opportunity to gather and discuss the temples you constructed, our bodies, and . . ."

Everyone's heads dipped, their eyes sealed. I slipped my phone from my pocket and checked Instagram.

I scrolled through several of my favorite model accounts, and saw a couple of funny memes while Kiera got winded by such fervent prayer. ". . . oh Lord, please guard over all the innocents in the room, so that they won't be corrupted by the predatory influences around them . . ."

Something about her tone, something pointed, drew my attention. When I glanced up, my stomach clenched. Kiera did not have her head bowed, or her eyes closed. She stared directly at me.

My phone slipped from my hand, clattered to the floor. My neck craned, searching for any other witnesses. A few chins tilted in my direction, but all other eyes remained squeezed shut. Just me and Kiera, in an uncomfortable staring contest.

"Let us all be faithful to the vow we made before you on Sunday," she said, sneering, "as Ephesians 5:6 states, 'Let no one deceive you with empty words, for because of such things *God's wrath* comes on those who are disobedient!' In your name we pray. Amen!"

Sister Vanessa's eyes popped open, her smile crooked and confused. "My, that was certainly passionate. Amen."

Kiera continued staring me down, and something stubborn in me refused to look away. Did others in the room see this? How could they not? Sister Vanessa definitely did a double take, though I was unsure what she read in the moment. I was unsure what *I* read in the moment. Whatever she saw, she felt compelled to beckon me over. "Del, would you come up for this next part, please?"

Helena, one of the younger girls, giggled when I stood. The sound became a contagion infecting everyone on the girls' side of the classroom except Mya, who looked as confused as I felt.

Kiera crossed her arms tight over her chest, and she had the stern teacher's look I'd expected from Sister Vanessa. Our Purity Pledge leader remained sunny while I dragged my ass to the whiteboard.

"Where's your Bible?" asked Sister Vanessa.

"Uh, I left it in the car." So that was a lie, in church. I didn't have my own Bible. I always read from the old, cracked-spine copies in those cubbies on the back of the pews.

Something hard and angular pressed into my palm. Jameer stretched over our table to pass me his Bible. I took it, grateful.

Sister Vanessa said, "Can one of you find Psalm 51:10 while the other turns to Matthew 5:8?"

Kiera flipped her Bible open, leafed through a few pages. "Got it."

I was still on the table of contents. "Which one did you do?"

"Psalms."

"Sweet. Love those Psalms." I struggled to find the book of Matthew—was that in the Old Testament, or the New? Sister Vanessa prompted Kiera to read.

"'Create in me a pure heart, O God, and renew a steadfast spirit within me.'"

"Del?" said Sister Vanessa.

"Right. Matthew 5:8." I was in the book, but overshot the chapter and verse. I flipped pages and tried not to look up, though all eyes were on me. "Got it. 'Blessed are the pure in heart: for they shall see God.'"

"Excellent," Sister Vanessa said. "Why do you think I asked

you to read those verses? What do they have in common?"

The question was tossed out casually; anyone could've answered. Kiera said, "I'm sure Del knows."

The hell?

It wasn't what she said, as much as *how* she said it. Her voice as cold as summertime A/C.

Sister Vanessa waited on my response. I'd already forgotten the verses, so how was I going to BS my way through this?

Jameer came with the save. "They're about pure hearts, and that's what we're all here for."

If Sister Vanessa minded the interruption, she didn't let on. "Excellent, Jameer! Pure hearts lead to pure souls lead to pure bodies. Please, you two, sit down."

Kiera re-joined the still-giggling girls, scowling at me. I returned to my seat.

"We've got much to cover in our sessions," Sister Vanessa said. "We're going to have so much fun." She lifted a cardboard box that had been resting against the wall. Starting on the girls' side, she circled the room, passing out glue sticks and colorful plastic kid scissors.

Hush-voiced and a little frightened, I said, "What is this?"

"Wait for it," said Jameer.

Sister Vanessa put the box away, approached a table stacked with the kinds of magazines you see in doctors' offices, about gardening and world events. Several pieces of blank poster board sat beside them. "Everyone, I want you to grab a poster board and a magazine. We're all going to find pictures of things we think represent purity and make Covenant Collages!"

Across the room Mya squinted, and turned an ear toward Sister Vanessa like she'd misheard the direction. Her nose crinkled like she detected a bad smell. Jameer smirked and shook his head, the smug look of someone who'd predicted the worst possible outcome and been proven right. Similar cool, confused reactions played on everyone's faces, with the exception of Kiera. She obediently led the charge, rallying the girls. "Come on. Like Sister Vanessa said."

They complied, and it occurred to me that me, Kiera, Jameer, and Mya were the elders of this purity class. All of the other girls were underclassmen at Green Creek High. Ralph and Bobby were still eighth graders at Baldwin Middle School.

Kiera's intense gaze swept my way. Not as angry as before, probably because she wasn't looking at me. Her attention was on Jameer. She made a jerky nod toward the magazines.

Jameer heavy-sighed, and pushed up from his seat slow, like a weightlifter squatting his max. "Come on, little duckies. Follow the leader."

He lined up behind the girls, the twins followed, then me. We collected our arts-and-crafts materials for an activity that felt suited for seven-year-olds. With Thanksgiving coming up, maybe we'd get to do handprint turkeys, too.

DEL

Written in graffiti-styled block letters at the top of my board, headlining snipped photos of a man jogging on the beach at sunrise, and a sweet red Mustang, and a business meeting. After flipping through the magazine three times for those pictures, I started cutting anything that didn't have a hot girl in it.

The door creaked. Pastor Newsome stepped into the room. I'd seen him up close before, but always in the burgundy Emperor Palpatine robes he wore in the pulpit, towering over the congregation. In his high-waisted khakis with the tucked-in golf shirt, he looked like a professor. A tiny one.

"Well, isn't this a blessed sight," he said. "There's nothing sweeter to my eyes than young people showing their obedience to the Lord." He folded his arms behind his back, and walked the center aisle, greeting the others and reviewing their work. Most everyone met him with a "Hey, Pastor" or "Good afternoon, Pastor," to which he nodded his approval. When he reached Kiera, he placed a hand on her shoulder, squeezing gently. "Your collage is lovely, dear. Deacon and Deaconess Westing have done well with you."

"Thank you, Pastor."

He turned his attention to the boys' side of the room, tipping his head toward the twins. "Nice job, young men."

"Thank you," they said in unison, then gave each other dirty looks—also in unison—for the unintentionally harmonized response. Pastor Newsome kept it moving to me and Jameer's table.

Jameer didn't make any special effort to acknowledge Pastor Newsome. He focused on his poster board, rolled his glue stick along the back of his final picture. He flipped it over and it wasn't a picture, but a block of text from some article, too small for me to make out. His whole poster board was that way. No actual photos. Only text, under his name, which was spelled in individually clipped letters like ransom notes in movies.

Pastor Newsome's previously jovial warmth chilled considerably. "Mr. Sesay."

"Pastor."

Newsome stared at the mass of letters that was supposed to be Jameer's collage. It looked more like something a serial killer would put together, something full of secret messages only he could decode. I glanced around the room, and everyone seemed to be holding their breath.

Pastor Newsome said, "Perhaps there was some confusion about your project."

"I like words better than pictures."

"It's not a writing project, Jameer." Pastor Newsome looked to Sister Vanessa. "Perhaps you weren't clear."

"It's the first day," she began, but the temperature in the room dropped another few degrees, and she said, "I'll be particularly clear from now on."

Jameer chewed his bottom lip but remained silent. In the little time I'd known him, I'd come to think that was a difficult task for him.

Pastor Newsome shifted focus to my project. Grinned. "Now that's a fine collage, Mr. Rainey."

It was odd to hear my name, so formal, cross his lips. He said it with reverence, the way he pronounced religious names like David and Moses from the pulpit. I didn't think he knew who I was.

"We need more fine young men like you in the congregation. You're a shining light for your generation, and you'll help guide up the young boys in the right way." He motioned to Ralph and Bobby, who grinned, but I had a hard time sharing their enthusiasm because I knew enough to recognize that by praising me he was also, somehow, dissing Jameer.

Pastor Newsome's eyebrows arched. He was waiting for something, and I knew what. Even though it made me feel slightly nauseous, there was too much I didn't understand here and I wanted—needed—him to move on. So, I said it. "Thank you, Pastor."

Sister Vanessa said, "Hey everybody, take a moment to hang your collages. We'll keep them up for the rest of our sessions as reminders of how we recognize the pure."

Kiera retrieved a tape dispenser from Sister Vanessa's other supplies and began rolling short strips into sticky loops for her girls. That's how I thought of them now, *her* girls.

Jameer saw me watching, as if daring me to critique his art.

Patiently, I waited for my turn with the tape.

When all the collages were hung, Sister Vanessa ended the session with a prayer of her own, dismissed us, then stepped into the hall to speak with Pastor Newsome. The girls hustled out of the room in a tight, Kiera-led huddle while me and the other guys gathered our things with sloth-like cool. Ralph and Bobby chatted about chores they needed to do after dinner as they exited the room. Jameer stared at me.

"You know that's super annoying," I said.

I figured he was tense over the way Pastor Newsome played him in front of everyone (and used me to do it). I figured whatever came next would be about that.

He said, "You're taking Healthy Living at school, right?"

Now that was unexpected. "Yeah. Sure."

He checked over his shoulder, a schemer's glint in his eye. "You know nobody else in here is allowed to take it."

"Why?"

"You still cool giving me a ride home?"

Dude apparently could not answer a question straight. "Fine. Whatever."

We stepped into the corridor together, and Jameer said, "Bye, Sister Vanessa."

She was so deep into her conversation with Pastor Newsome, her hands moving around, explaining . . . something, I don't think she heard him at all.

On the church steps, the Purity Pledgers waited on their rides. It was one of those springtime-warm nights that was very Virginia because it was actually fall and it had been ten degrees cooler two hours ago. If not for the sky darkening to purple when it was barely five p.m., we could've been in mid-May. Kiera noticed Jameer walking with me. Her classroom scowl returned.

"Jameer, my dad'll be here in ten minutes," she said.

"Tell him I'm okay tonight. I'm riding with Del."

"You're sure?"

It wasn't an upbeat "You're sure?" Oh no. It was someone

about to stick their hand in a porta potty to fish out some loose change. Like, *You're sure you want to do that, because I wouldn't.*

That "you're sure" had me doing something I never thought possible in all my Kiera fantasies. I scowled back. "Chill. I got him covered. Thanks for your concern."

Maybe I did more than scowl, and maybe I was louder than I thought. Because everyone turned my way, meerkat-style. Mya mouthed the word *Dude.*

Then, I was locked in a staring contest with Kiera.

She broke from her troop, came straight at me. Angry, aggressive. "Can I talk to you?" She clamped her teeth together after she spoke.

"Yeah. Whatever." I bristled.

"Around the corner." She stomped over to the church's shadowy side yard, assuming I'd follow.

I almost walked to my car. She was bossing me around all crazy, everybody watching. Sure, our conversation might be private, but her owning me in front of the Purity Pledgers was public domain now.

Facing Jameer, I gave the "what's up?" shrug. He only shook his head.

Fine. I rounded the church, ended up under a bulging globe fixture that anchored an orbital spiderweb and drew a squad of moths in its wash of yellow light. Kiera poked a finger in my chest hard enough to hurt. "Delbert Rainey, I know what you're doing, and I want you out of this class. Gone. Tonight!"

DEL-bert RAIN-ey! Spoken like our first-grade teacher, Mrs.

Martin, used to say it. The way I hate.

I felt the strangeness of how little we'd been around each other, even to say hi, the last few years. Struggled with how little sense this conversation made.

"People call me Del now." It was all I could manage.

If she called me out about trying to get with her, I'd deny it. Double down. As Qwan said way too often, die with the lie.

She said, "I know about how you and your boy Qwan are out with different girls every weekend. People still talk about that little orgy you two were in at Tanisha Thompson's freshman year. And I know you're only in this class so you can 'get your stats up' or however you nasty boys talk about your escapades."

"Get my stats—*what?*"

"Right. Play dumb."

I wasn't playing, though. She said so much in that one breath it actually made me dizzy. "You've got it all wrong, Kiera."

"I don't think so. You and Qwan have reputations."

Qwan. Qwan had a reputation. Him. I was his transportation. I couldn't say that, though. Bro Code. You didn't throw your friend under the bus to save your own ass.

"If you two want to be man-whores in this state and the next, it's not my business. But I won't let you be a predator with them." She pointed back the way we came, to her girls. "All they see is a cute boy who's rough around the edges and obviously hasn't been properly churched. You want to keep up your little charade, I can't stop you, but you won't get near them. I'm betting once you see there are no easy targets here, you'll get bored and move on. So save yourself some time and get to stepping now. Before your nose gets busted by something worse than a basketball!"

She smacked me in the chest and stomped away. I stood there a moment longer, stunned. Maybe for the wrong reason.

All they see is a cute boy who's rough around the edges . . .

Was that their assessment, or hers?

"Del." Jameer lingered at the building's corner. "You ready?"

Kiera wouldn't bother looking at me, though all the girls she wanted me to stay away from were. I went for my car and settled behind the wheel. Jameer drifted into my passenger seat all feathery, with a big ole grin.

"You really pissed her off," he said. "There may be hope for you yet."

CHAPTER 6

JAMEER SHUFFLED HIS LOAFERS, kicking aside empty water bottles, gas receipts Mom always insisted I get (". . . even if you have to walk inside for them because they can't ever say you stole it if you got your receipt!"), and burger wrappers spotted with dried grease. "I'm going to need new shoes after you drop me off."

"You know what else would make you need new shoes? Walking."

"Your anger is misdirected."

"Tell me how to get you home, Jameer."

"You know Stafford Woods?"

"Sure." It was a subdivision on the east side of Green Creek. I'd taken Qwan to see some girls out there before. Five-minute drive at the most. I flicked on my turn signal to make the next right, a straight shot.

Jameer said, "I'm not in a hurry if you aren't."

Braking at the stop sign with no traffic behind me, I did not turn. "Will you stop with all your Riddler BS and answer some questions for me?"

"Not about my parents."

"Why would I care about your parents?" They were religious and weird and not my problem. I said, "Kiera."

"I can probably shed some light on her current situation."

I flicked my turn signal off and kept going straight, toward Old Town Green Creek. "Yo, what happened back there? Why'd she get in my face all aggro?"

"She told you. You and Qwan Reid have a certain *reputation* at school."

"No. No. No."

"So it's not true? You and Qwan Reid don't go out with different girls almost every weekend?"

"It's complicated."

We sailed through the uncrowded, tree-lined streets of Green Creek. The one car ahead of us was nothing but glowing red taillights. The scene in my rearview was ink black. I said, "Am I sunk?"

Jameer answered quickly. "Honestly, I don't know. She's in a strange space right now."

"What really happened with Colossus? Some people saying him and Angie Bell made a sex tape."

His shrug about shook the car. "That I don't know. She won't talk about any of it in detail. It's like she's traumatized. I guess he cheated, but between you and me, that wouldn't be new information. They never broke up over it before."

I'd heard Colossus got it in with girls at different schools, too. It pissed me off because, as Jameer said, it didn't ever put a dent in "Kee-Lossus" before. "What should I do here, Jameer?

You know I want to holler at her, but it's like I'm moving in the exact opposite direction of where I want to be. And this Purity Pledge feels like the ultimate mistake. She wants me out of it, and, real talk, I want me out of it, too. I mean, I joined accidentally."

"You can't quit, though."

"Why?"

"God."

Then he laughed. And I laughed.

When he was done laughing, he said, "Seriously, if you quit, you prove her right. But if you're hanging in, maybe I can help."

We cruised into downtown, a few cross streets bordered by a dozen or so storefronts that were already closed because most of Green Creek shut down when the streetlights came on. Jameer's offer of assistance sounded generous. It also bugged me. I didn't express my concerns, just said, "How?"

"We need a strategy. A way to flip Purity Pledge to your advantage. Pastor Newsome won't like us treating it like a dating app. But it's the one thing you and Kiera have in common, right? So, we work it."

Me and Kiera had more than Purity Pledge in common. *The Wizard of Oz* came to my mind. Also, hot wrinkle-free outfits. And well-moisturized skin. For the sake of this conversation, I nodded, kept trying to feel him out. "*You're* cool with using Purity Pledge that way?"

"Totally fine."

Okay. The alarms in my head were blaring loud. Couldn't hold it in anymore. "Like, me and you ain't close. We barely

talked before Sunday, but now you want to be my personal matchmaker? I'm not trying to insult you—but it's suspect, bro. Why you want to help so bad? What's in it for you?"

"I already told you."

I tapped the steering wheel. Waiting.

He said, "Pastor Newsome won't like it."

Seriously? "Look, I'm new at First Missionary. I don't really get all the dynamics or whatever happening in that church. I know I'm not comfortable with you weaponizing me because you're pissed at your pastor."

"He's your pastor, too. If you're not pissed yet, give it time."

I swung a right at the next corner, put us on course for Stafford Woods. "Thanks, but no thanks. I'll figure the Kiera thing out myself."

His voice rose, slightly panicked. "Del, wait. I'm not using you to mess with Pastor."

"You said—"

"I mean, not exclusively. It's a bonus for me, I won't lie. But, I was hoping we could sort of trade favors. I help you with Kiera, and you do something for me."

"Something like what?"

"Healthy Living."

My foot slipped off the gas and we coasted, our speed decreasing incrementally, the scenery around us going from blur to crawl. "Sex ed? What about it?"

"Is it," he seemed to struggle for the right word, "informative?"

"We watched a stupid video about STDs. So, not particularly."

"There's going to be more to it? A lot of different topics?"

My thinning patience made me get real direct. "Tell me what you want."

"Are we trusting each other? I keep Kiera stuff in confidence, you keep my stuff in confidence."

"Bro, I'm about to kick you from this moving vehicle."

A resigned sigh. "Fine. Next time you're in Healthy Living, can you ask a question for me?"

"Depends on the question."

He rubbed his hands along the fabric of his pants like he was trying to burn his palms off. "I want to know if certain . . . *dreams* are . . . normal?"

I considered what he was saying a moment. Questioned if I heard him right. "You're talking about wet dreams."

He grabbed the "oh crap" handle above his door like I'd suddenly swerved toward a ditch. "I . . . I suppose." He kept glancing through his window like he was waiting on some other ride to come get him.

"Dawg, we can look that up on your phone right now."

"No, we can't." He fished something like a clamshell from his pocket. Took me a second to realize it was an old-fashioned flip phone. I remembered Dad having a phone like this when I was a little kid, a decade ago.

I said, "That works?"

"At the most basic level. I can call my parents. They can call me."

That they still made phones like that was amazing. I didn't

get on him about it. It could be a money thing. Maybe all his people could afford. Only, his clothes told a different story. Always pressed. Always smelling like soap and cologne. Not everyone at Green Creek High was as fortunate. Those shoes he'd been worried about ruining might've cost more than my Xbox.

Then "wet dreams" popped back in my head, and derailed my flip-phone deductions. "Look it up on my phone."

I grabbed my cell from the cup holder, handed it over. Though, from experience I didn't want to tell him about, I was sure wet dreams were pretty normal.

He shook his head. "I don't want to look it up. I want a *professional opinion*."

MJ? A professional? If we were talking the Harlem Renaissance . . . sure. "I'm not asking that question in class. Not in front of everybody."

"Do it after class. Or before. I don't care."

"No! Why don't you ask yourself?"

"I'm not allowed."

"Says who?"

"Pastor Newsome! No one in Purity Pledge is allowed anywhere near that Healthy Living class. Except you."

My thoughts began circling the opposing curriculums of Purity Pledge and Healthy Living I'd discovered the other night, the tug-of-war. It was the pastor's doing, then. Not a total shock that a church didn't want kids learning about sexual stuff—but saying the kids in the congregation weren't *allowed* to take the class? I said, "Okay, but Wikipedia. Or Google that shit, bro."

When I glanced right, and I saw him staring at the scrolling scenery and clutching the fabric of his pants with nervous little pinches, I backed off. "Your people really that strict?"

The window fogged when he spoke. "I do my homework on a computer in a nook next to our kitchen. My dad installed three different Safe Browse programs on it. Anything those don't block, he reviews by checking my browser history and cache when I'm done for the night." Jameer faced me, shrugging the way you do when you've told an old, boring story. "My parents are *that* strict."

Lindy Blue, and Instagram models, and *Call of Duty* Kill-streak videos, and everything else I ever surfed on my Mac . . . I never worried about how much Mom and Dad knew about private time in my room. But, I never *really* expected them to go all Homeland Security, searching my personal stuff for unsanctioned activity. "Is it like that for everyone in Purity Pledge?"

"Maybe. Or I might be special. You gonna ask my question for me or not?"

While I pondered, he directed me to his street, and to his carnival-bright house, light beaming from every window. You couldn't look at it without squinting. I braked at his driveway, and he waited for his answer.

"Fine," I said, "I got you. Then I want some results on this Kiera thing. For real."

Cue slick comeback, right? I expected something to put him back in charge. That's how I thought of Jameer until that moment. In charge. He only said, "Thanks for understanding."

Didn't have the heart to tell him, no, I didn't.

When he disappeared into the blinding lights of his smothering home, I glanced toward the dark windows of the house next door. Kiera's.

Soon.

CHAPTER 7

MY HOUSE HAD TWO BATHROOMS. The one in my parents' room: shut, steamy from Dad's hot shower, and unapproachable due to his loud, bad singing. The other one was in the hall between my room and Cressie's. I'd forgotten the hectic mornings pounding on the door because Cressie was barricaded in there, doing whatever sorcery was necessary to become publicly presentable, leaving me a solid ten minutes to perform my own hygiene duties before rushing off to school. So, imagine the trauma on a random Wednesday when groggy, barely functioning me went to nudge my never-locked bathroom door open, only to nearly dislocate my shoulder when I walked full speed into unyielding wood.

I bounced backward, first checking for a bone bruise, then I beat on the door with the meaty part of my fist, thinking my sister had made another surprise visit home. "Cressie?"

"It's me, sweetie," said Mom. "Hang on."

Okay. Made sense. Dad was in the other bathroom. Mom had to go.

Except, I heard whispering. "Mom? You talking to me?"

I leaned toward the door, nearly pressing my ear against it, when it swung open so quickly I almost tipped over. Mom thrust her iPhone at me. "Your sister's on the line. You want to talk to her?"

"It's six thirty in the morning." I motioned into the bathroom. "Can I?"

Mom sidestepped and allowed me in. I was so sleepy, and so irritated, it never once occurred to me that Mom talking to Cressie in a locked bathroom when the sun wasn't up yet was . . . unusual. Before I closed the door, I heard Mom padding downstairs, saying, "I don't think it's a great idea. People your age want to put everything online. Seems reckless to me . . ."

Uncapping the Listerine, I swigged the burning blue liquid, swished, and spit. Didn't give my mother or sister a second thought.

The ride to school with Qwan was quiet. Healthy Living was after lunch, and Jameer's question was on my mind. It felt dumb as hell to go through all this when I could grab him between classes and look up "wet dreams" on the library computer.

Wait. No.

I abandoned the idea as fast as it had come. Maybe his super-strict parents couldn't monitor his web activity there, but the last thing I needed was some asshole like Kent Oster looking over our shoulders at the exact wrong time and blasting to the school that me and Jameer were wet dream research buddies.

He'd made it clear that my own internet research wouldn't do, no Wikipedia printout. So we were back to me asking a "professional" if I wanted his assistance on my Kiera goals.

At a red light, I said, "What are you doing?"

I knew why *I* was quiet, but Qwan was uncharacteristically silent. "Texting," he said.

"Who?"

He tapped his screen, but was slow answering. Almost like he was stalling.

"*Who?*"

"Angie." He put his phone to sleep, slipped it in his pocket.

"Don't stop on my account."

"She about to get on the road and shouldn't be texting anyway."

"Huh?" He sounded like her dad. Or my dad. Or anybody's dad. Weird. The light changed and I welcomed this distraction from Jameer's uncomfortable mission. Easing us closer to school, I said, "She tell you anything about what went down with Colossus?"

"It's bullshit. Said she ain't do nothing with him."

"You believe her?"

"Don't know. That's what she was in detention for, though. Arguing about it with Tiff Burrell in Spanish class. You know Señora Ortiz don't play."

"Lucky you, right?" Ever since he got her number, I hadn't heard much from him. It had only been a couple of days, but the way Qwan ran game, that was like they'd been dating a month.

He grinned. "Remains to be seen. Working on it, though."

We got to school, made our cafeteria breakfast run, then went for our lockers. We passed Kiera's locker, where she was flanked by Helena and Shanice from church. Each of them greeted me with a "Hey Del." Kiera's expression hadn't changed from the night before, still icy.

Qwan, as elegant as always, said, "Man, she looks like you farted in her elevator."

"That's not an expression."

"Whatever. I guess that Purity Pledge plan is going awesome for you."

"Leave it alone. I'm working on it."

We rounded the corner, on course for my locker. My neck was craned, evaluating Kiera's reaction to me. Qwan snapped his forearm across my chest, stopping me dead. "What—?"

"Del."

I followed his line of sight, no explanation needed. Walking toward us, escorted by Vice Principal Terrier, and her parents, was Shianne Griffiths.

Her head was down, like she was trying to ignore the obvious stares or barely concealed whispers of the classmates surrounding her. What they were talking about was anybody's guess.

Could've been the legendary orgy she participated in our freshman year.

Or the fact that I was her partner at said orgy.

Or that she was a charter member of our school's infamous Baby-Getters Club, having given birth maybe two months ago.

You know, the basics.

As she got closer, her name slipped from my mouth like a gasp. "Shi."

She looked up, smiled with half her mouth, showing one dimple. A finger wave before she focused on the floor again. Her parents had more to say.

"Hello, Del." From her father.

Her mother said, "We hope your family's well, Del."

Me and the Griffiths family always got along.

Then they were past us, on the way to Terrier's office, I supposed. When they were far enough away that the gossip could resume at a comfortable volume, the chatter ramped up. Shianne wasn't the first Baby-Getter to return to Green Creek, but the "glad it's not me" relief we felt all around didn't seem to decay.

Me and Qwan kept it moving. He said, "You talk to her since she had the baby?"

"A text here or there." An overstatement. I sent her a "congrats" when I heard through the Green Creek grapevine that her kid made it into the world. She hit me back a week later with "thx." That was the most communication we'd had since school ended last year.

"If you ask me—"

Sensing ignorance, I said, "I didn't."

"—that's who you need to be focusing on. I mean, y'all already got a kid together."

I lunged like I might punch him. "That ain't funny."

He threw up his hands in mock shame. "My bad. Too far. I'm saying though, y'all used to smash. I never got why you backed off her at all. Shianne cute as hell."

"It's complicated."

"Because you probably made it that way."

If only he knew. Me and Shianne had a secret, one that made Mya's interrogation at FISHto's, and Kiera's warning at church about my "reputation," so much more ridiculous than anybody knew.

Shianne was the only other person in Green Creek who knew that, really, my participation in Purity Pledge was completely aboveboard. Even if involuntarily.

While she went and got a baby, my sexual status remained unchanged. The same as it had always been. Despite the legend.

I, Del Rainey, was, and still am, a virgin.

CHAPTER 8

I MEAN, I'VE DONE STUFF. Not a lot of stuff. Some stuff.

You can't go on as many double dates with Qwan as I do and not get physical occasionally. I've had a girlfriend or two. I've touched a boob. Once.

I just, you know, haven't had need of my trusty condom. Yet.

Though everyone at Green Creek who had knowledge of the infamous basement party would tell you otherwise. Me and Shianne included.

The rest of the morning became a stomach-twisting blur of guilt, math, paranoia, science, and a bunch of other things I wasn't excited or prepared for.

Shianne coming back . . . I wasn't necessarily worried about her, I didn't think. She'd kept our vow about what really happened (or didn't happen) in that bathroom two summers ago at Tanisha Thompson's for this long. But seeing her again mixed with Jameer's plan, Purity Pledge, and Kiera's reaction to my so-called reputation hit like an anxiety bomb.

Tanisha's party had been billed as a barbecue/cake/ice-cream thing; not even my mom had an issue with it. Us kids would play music and watch movies. Mister and Missus Thompson would be there the whole time! No big deal.

Except, the Thompsons' house was huge, one of the biggest in Green Creek (next to Shianne's), making supervision this fluid thing. Either the parents stayed in the exact same room as us at all times, or they didn't exist. Mister Thompson vanished to the golf course early. Missus Thompson lost track of time with her friends over a bunch of margaritas waaaayyy upstairs. And, wouldn't you know it, the basement door locked from the inside.

Tanisha set it off with the Spin the Bottle app on her phone. That escalated to Truth or Dare. Nobody even fronted like truth was an option, so when Shianne was up, her challenge came directly from the hostess herself.

"Shianne, I dare you to lock yourself in the bathroom with . . . Del! And don't come out until you're a woman!"

Shianne hit Tanisha with a wide-eyed, horrified look I'd think of later when it got around school their relationship had morphed from sorta friends, to frenemies, to outright enemies (something that took all of a day). But, in that instant, I was horrified, too.

Was Shianne hesitant (Angry? Disgusted?) because it was my name in the dare? Would she have jumped and cheered if it was Qwan, or Mason Miles, or Rashad Jackson?

Though I was braced for a refusal, that horror went away when Shianne hopped to her feet without a word, grabbed my hand, and led me to our assigned location. She closed and locked the bathroom door behind us.

New hope and fear collided: was this happening? I patted my back pocket, confirming the lone condom Dad insisted I carry at all times was there.

Shianne looped her arms around my neck, tilted her chin up, and brought her face close to mine. Not a kiss; she shifted left, and put her mouth to my ear. "Don't even think about it, Del. Here's what's going down . . ."

For five minutes we rustled the shower curtain, and I thumped the door with my sneaker at odd intervals while Shianne issued the occasional Moan of Ecstasy. When the nosy a-holes on the other side of the door applauded, we giggled into cupped hands. Soon, the crowd outside dispersed to what we'd later learn were their own "encounters." But we hung out in the space we claimed for a whole hour, talking in whispers, enjoying each other's company in the stress-free wake of fake sex.

When someone knocked—they really needed to use the bathroom—we made *our* pact. Die with the lie.

After that party, me and Shianne bonded over the ultimate in-joke. We found it hilarious how people spoke about us like folk heroes. The couple that set off the Tanisha Thompson orgy. There was even this short-lived shipping situation—"Shi-Del," which had *no* ring to it—that died a quick death once upper-classmen took notice of her.

I'd only ever discussed the bare-minimum false details about our time in the bathroom with Qwan, yet the stories I heard about my own deflowering were way more . . . *limber* than I could've ever concocted. Some of it was flattering, but most of it was about her. How good she was supposed to be at things that never happened. Shianne went from mostly unnoticed to coveted sex goddess.

We got good laughs from that, too. Sometimes. Other times, I could tell that being supposed sex pros was losing its charm. When dudes said wild gross things in the hall. When girls who weren't in attendance cracked on "the party hoes."

Last summer, I started seeing less of Shianne. I'd text, but her responses were anywhere from slow to never.

I remembered when her clothes got tighter, her walking around the halls with her stomach poking out extra far while she massaged her lower back. Her belly button protruding a little farther than everything else, like the baby was trying to show everyone at Green Creek its thumbprint. One day, Shianne was gone. Now she was back. With a whole new human to care for.

Sometimes, for like a hot second, I wondered if we hadn't lied and kept lying, would things have turned out different for her? Or, if I'd just told the truth, snapped on dudes calling her a "party ho" instead of riding the lie, could I have made things different for her.

Would've. Could've. Should've.

The truth wasn't gonna help anyone now.

At the class-change beep, my anxious thoughts shifted from "lying on my dick"—Green Creek's preferred phrase for the act of falsifying one's sexual conquests—to "wet dreams," and I couldn't decide which one was worse. I was heading into MJ's English class, where I'd decided I'd ask Jameer's question at the end instead of waiting until Healthy Living. That way anyone who saw me hang back would assume it was book related, not, er, penis related.

We were currently reading *Invisible Man* by Ralph Ellison to discuss next week. But, today, we had presentations on a novel of our choosing. We were supposed to talk about the plot, themes, symbolism, and the work's relevance to modern society. This was a pretty cool unit because MJ let us pick anything. Novel, short story collection, graphic novel, whatever. I went on Monday, talked about *Invincible: Vol. 1*, a comic book trade collection where the son of the world's greatest hero finally gets his own superpowers only to find out his dad really has plans to take over the world. MJ gave me a B plus because he said I slacked on symbolism and relating the story to our real, modern world. I disagreed, but wasn't salty about it, or anything.

Today, three more people were presenting. Among them, Mason Miles. I steeled myself for what was coming.

MJ said, "Mason, you're up. What do you have for us today?"

Like he didn't know. We all knew.

Mason unfolded from his desk, tall and slim, with protruding veins running up his military-pushup-molded arms like drawings. I didn't think the JROTC guys had to wear army stuff every day, but Mason did anyway. Today it was camouflage pants, tucked into tightly laced tan boots, and an olive-green T-shirt with dog tags hanging over the collar. He smiled at Lacey Bishop on his way to the front, and she showed him every last tooth in her head. A lot of girls got super goofy when Mason looked their way. As if his head wasn't big enough.

Clutching some papers in front of him, he cleared his throat and said, "So, the book I picked is *Factions of Fire*, part nine in bestselling author Ron Shapiro's Jack Jake series. A little backstory: Jack Jake is an ex–Green Beret, Navy SEAL, CIA operative on the run from homegrown terrorists that have taken over . . ."

Lacey Bishop's grin slipped away. She was new to Green Creek, barely here a year. She didn't know about Mason's obsession with the Jack Jake books. She was going to learn today.

Zoning through Mason's lengthy recap, and the next two presentations, I thought about the least awkward way to approach MJ at class change. My palms were sweating, and I considered abandoning the whole plan until the bell dinged through the PA and I was still zoning, so none of my books were packed and ready. Everyone beat me out of the room, leaving MJ *right there at the front*, alone.

"MJ?"

He swiped the eraser along the whiteboard, cutting wide arcs through all the topics we'd halfway discussed today. "Del, you're still here."

"Yes. I kinda gotta ask you something."

"About the Ellison reading?" He finished cleaning the board, sat on the desk's edge.

"Naw, it's not about English. It's about the other class."

"The other—oh. Right." He scanned the room, maybe making sure we were alone, and that brief hesitation made me want to sprint away. I held my ground.

This better be worth it, Jameer.

"I need to know about dreams. Sexy ones," I blurted.

"What about them?"

Shit. What about them? Jameer hadn't specified anything, and I didn't think to clarify. I tugged a pen and notepad from my bag to make sure I got everything I could, because I was never asking about this again. "I guess, whatever, you know. Like, are they normal?"

"Sexy dreams? I assume you're referring to the kind that trigger a *physical* response."

"Yeah." My stomach got fluttery, and I focused on a specific brick on a nearby wall.

"The technical term for what you're referring to is nocturnal emissions. Though I'm sure you're aware of the more common term."

I nodded so he didn't have to say it.

"If you're experiencing them—"

"This ain't for me."

Quick nods. "Sure. Of course."

"I mean, for real. It's not for me."

"Of course."

My shirt was sticky. Sticky. We were talking about wet dreams and I was thinking of being sticky. Ugh! Had to hurry this up. "Can you tell me anything else about them?"

I was deep in it now, and Jameer would not accuse me of half-assing.

"They're the result of the hormone levels in your—I mean

anyone's—body changing around the start of puberty. You're producing testosterone, and semen, and when you're sleeping the body's doing some test runs to make sure the plumbing's working, so to speak. Ejaculation is the result."

Oh God, he said "ejaculation." Scribbling fast and furious, I asked, "Girls don't have them?"

"They can. It's not as common and doesn't have the exact same result. Obviously."

"Doesn't mean anything's wrong with you, though? If you're having them?"

MJ shook his head. "Quite the opposite, really. It's the mind and body doing what ensures there will always be new humans."

"Got it. Thanks." I about dived for the door.

"Del."

Facing him, I expected an interrogation. Why was I asking him? Was there anyone at home I could talk to about this stuff?

Instead, he said, "Hey, keep this chat between us. I'm not totally sure this is a topic the school board would be happy about me discussing in this context, particularly outside the Healthy Living classroom. Okay?"

This context? What context? Asking would've meant more conversation about . . . this, though. I wanted to be gone. "Uh, okay."

"See you later this afternoon."

I thought I'd feel better once I was out of the room, job done. Too much had happened today, and I had questions that lingered through lunch, my afternoon classes, another Healthy Living class focusing on the dangers of diseases of sex.

It wasn't better once I got home. I wanted the night to be dinner, and Xbox, and maybe . . . Lindy Blue?

Aside from dinner, I never got around to the rest of it. Homework—math, history, and English—was a beast. Whenever I switched gears between subjects, MJ's weird comment came back to me. He was the guy responsible for teaching Healthy Living. I asked a Healthy Living–type question. Why would the school board be mad at him for doing his job?

Thought about it all night. Even in my dreams.

I got to First Missionary a few minutes early the following afternoon, found Jameer waiting alone on the church steps. He met me at my car, read my "nocturnal emissions" notes like he was going to give me a grade. Nearby, somebody was burning leaves. He held the paper in two hands; the torn spiral edges fluttered on the oaky brimstone breeze.

I said, "You happy now?"

Because he didn't look happy. He'd been staring at the page for a while. I didn't write that much. "Jameer?"

"Your handwriting is terrible. But, yes. Thank you for this."

"You're welcome. We had a deal. Kiera. Now what should I do?"

Creasing the sheet, he slipped it into his back pocket, said, "You need to win Purity Pledge."

"Win it? Like the Hunger Games?"

"Kiera's betting you're an opportunistic lowlife who'll quit if you get too uncomfortable. We have to make her think different. We need to turn you into a wholesome boy. The kind her parents want to invite to dinner, and who will never ever cheat on her. You have to become the best Purity Pledger."

Gravel crunched under the tires of a polished, scab-colored minivan turning into the church lot. The Burton Brothers hopped from the sliding side doors, gave us an enthusiastic wave, and jogged inside. Right behind them, Shanice and Helena in Helena's mom's car. They snuck glances toward me and Jameer, giggled their way to the church steps, where they sat and chatted.

Win Purity Pledge, huh. Weird thinking of it that way. I said, "How?"

Jameer lifted the flap on his satchel, produced a brand-spanking-new Bible. "That's yours. No more borrowing. I'll help you read up on appropriate scriptures ahead of time. You'll use them to be proactive. After tonight, you're the first to answer at least two of Sister Vanessa's questions each session. Got it? Should be enough to get you started. Don't look at me like that."

Were my teeth showing? Was I snarling? "Like I don't have enough homework already. I'm taking a lot on faith here."

He swept a hand toward the church doors. "Great place for it. Have I led you wrong yet?"

"You haven't led me anywhere."

"Yet!"

Mya pulled up in her beat-down Subaru, a car as old as us, that had, on more than one occasion, required me, or Tyrell, or Stu the Cook to break out some jumper cables and resurrect her finicky battery in the FISHto's lot after a shift. It was pine-forest green in the places where the paint wasn't splotchy and worn down to the gray chassis. A neat row of GCHS Honor Roll Student bumper magnets decorated the back end, and the odor from the exhaust pipe was of environmentally unfriendly scorched oil. She parked beside me, shouldered open her dented door, and emerged looking distraught. Her phone—a modern Android, not a throwback like Jameer's—was in her hand. She looked at it, to the church doors, back to her phone, frowned. Like she was double-checking the GPS coordinates of somewhere she did not want to be.

She spotted me and Jameer, came over. My immediate thought: What'd I do now?

But this wasn't about me. Not even close.

"Hey guys," she began, still flicking glances at the church doors. "Is Kiera here yet?"

"She's inside," Jameer said. "You know her. Early is on time, on time is late."

Another odd glance. "Is she okay?"

Jameer stiffened. I leaned toward Mya like I was having trouble hearing her. "Why wouldn't she be?"

"I don't like spreading gossip."

Video was playing on her phone, obvious flickering movements. I pried it from her hand. "I will relieve you of the burden, Mya."

She didn't resist. This was something we'd end up seeing with or without her help. Which kind of made it worse.

It was an IG story from one of our classmates. Blond, freckle-faced Taylor Burkin, who dressed up like Scarlett Johansson's Major character from *Ghost in the Shell* last Halloween and immediately got sent home because Vice Principal Terrier wasn't having any sexy skin-tight suits in his hallways, thank you very much. That outfit didn't fit her very long because she was also one of the Baby-Getters. Like the rest of them, she'd had her kid over the summer. Taylor had yet to return to school, but she had a pointed message for her GCHS classmates.

"You know what," she said, staring down at the camera, the puppy filter on so she had a dog's nose and ears for some reason, "I see all of y'all talking a bunch of mess about me and the other Green Creek ladies who have kids now. 'The Baby-Getters this' and 'The Baby-Getters that'—everybody got an opinion, huh? Well, I got opinions, too."

The clip jumped to the next video in her story. She was in a different part of her house, that K-Pop band BTS was visible on a poster in the background. She'd switched to an IG filter that gave her a French beret and pouty red lips. "What about the guys? It takes two, folks. Or, I guess, eighteen, since there are nine babies. You know what I mean. I don't see y'all saying a thing about the daddies. Let me be the one to start *that* conversation, because I got plenty to say about *my* baby's daddy!"

Another jump, another location. Jameer pressed against my shoulder so he could see. Mya remained where she was, obviously familiar with what would surely be the talk of the school tomorrow. Whenever someone snapped and went off on social media—it happened a few times a year—it made the week so much better. This should be a really good one, too. Because I didn't know who Taylor's kid's dad was.

No filter this time, but with a runny-nosed, light brown infant on her hip, Taylor showed us a cluttered kitchen with a row of baby bottles drying on a mat next to the sink. "My baby's daddy doesn't want to take any responsibility for what *we did together*. He wants this all to be a secret, like he's Drake or something. But I'm tired of all y'all acting like I'm some whore, or I made my son in a lab. So let's see what kind of judgment you got for your little wrestling golden boy Colossus Turner? Hey Colossus, you watching? I'm going to go feed your son now. Toodles."

Taylor finger-waved at the camera, and the screen flipped to someone else's IG story.

Oh. Shit.

Colossus had a kid?! He was a Baby-Getter?

I returned Mya's phone. Stunned. Silent.

On the steps, the previously giggling Shanice and Helena leaned into one another, attention on a single phone. They looked up, slack-faced, turned toward the church entrance as if afraid. The IG story was spreading.

Jameer said, "We should probably go inside now."

But I didn't think anyone wanted to.

The church doors cracked, and a smiling Kiera beckoned Helena and Shanice inside. She spotted us, and said, "We're starting soon."

Nobody moved. She didn't know.

Slow, like a death march, Helena and Shanice peeled themselves off the stairs and trudged inside. Me, Jameer, and Mya followed. When I passed Kiera, she said, "You're back."

"Yeah."

She took a deep breath, as if preparing to light into me again. I probably would've let her, all things considered; she had something much worse than my harsh words coming.

What she actually said: "I'm sorry for the way I spoke to you the other night."

My knee-jerk response: *You should be.* This wasn't the time. "Um, I appreciate that."

Jameer, visible over her left shoulder, lingered.

Kiera said, "Jameer told me I was too hard on you. I prayed about it, and really felt God told me it wasn't my place to judge anything you've done prior to joining the Pledge. That I wasn't modeling the kind of love that Jesus has for saint and sinner alike. So, if you're serious, and here for the right reasons, I support you."

She clasped my shoulder, and her touch was like electricity. It was the first time we'd had actual physical contact since— when? Elementary school during some stupid playground games? Damn, she smelled good now. Like sugar.

Jameer told her she was being too hard. He really was holding up his end of our agreement. But was it going to matter when Taylor Burkin's bomb hit?

Kiera withdrew her hand, sensed . . . something from everyone around us. "What, guys? You act like you've never seen me apologize before. I know it's rare, but . . ." She let her thought trail off, forced a chuckle in the midst of the strange vibe.

So, nobody was going to tell her?

Jameer gave a slow head shake. His intuitive ass must've sensed me already deviating from his simple Win-the-Pledge strategy. I couldn't play dumb, though. I wouldn't want people knowing stuff about me that I didn't know about myself.

"It's not about your apology," I said. "Can we talk over there?"

I motioned to a nearby pew, tried to make my voice even, or sympathetic, or something other than the confrontational tone we'd both had during our last private chat so she knew this wasn't a fight. She moved with me. When she sat, I opened IG and pulled up Taylor's story. I passed it to her, then sat, waiting. My phone volume was low, but everyone else had already heard. They flitted toward the Purity Pledge room, Jameer the last to go, his eyes wide and apprehensive.

I don't know what comes next either, bro.

Taylor's story reached its thrilling conclusion. Kiera immediately tapped back to the beginning and watched it all again. I stared at the lectern Newsome preached from each Sunday because I didn't want to look at her face.

She pressed my phone back into my hand, and I dared a glance in her direction. I prepped for whatever. Tears. Rage. Her face gave nothing away.

Kiera stood, brushed phantom lint from her jeans. "We should join the class."

As she scooted past me into the aisle, I wondered if I'd created a kill-the-messenger situation, completely trashing all her apologetic goodwill. She said, "Thank you for showing me, Del. I wouldn't have liked finding out everyone but me knew later."

Those were words I was happy to hear. I hoped she meant them.

In the Purity Pledge classroom, Sister Vanessa asked someone to start with a prayer. Helena volunteered, and we got right into more prompts on why we should remain pure. There was reading, and crafts, and conversation, and though Sister Vanessa often looked to Kiera to jump in, she didn't utter a word the whole afternoon.

Over the next couple of weeks, though, Green Creek High had a lot to say.

CHAPTER 9

#BABYGETTERSTOO.

It was a thing, coined by another new Green Creek mom who took Taylor's lead and called out her baby's daddy on Snapchat: a freshman at Commonwealth University, where my sister attended. A third Baby-Getter did the same, her kid's father being a local burnout who'd been a senior at Green Creek last year, but never actually graduated. We all sat back watching the debacle with equal measures of glee and horror, speculating on how bad (exciting) it could get. What if one of the dads was a perv-teacher like at the school where that nosy photographer chick was taking sneak pictures of everyone's business for her secret blog? Or what if one of the dads was Vice Principal Terrier? (That theory was immediately met with mad vomit emojis and no one wanted to bring it up again.) So far, Colossus was the only guy currently in school with us who'd gotten called out, and he loudly denied even knowing Taylor. Bullshit, basically. Green Creek wasn't that big.

We waited on more social media blowups. For the two weeks

following Taylor's bombshell, the #BabyGettersToo movement went from three to five to seven baby daddies getting exposed. And there were ripples . . .

First, a decree from Terrier that anyone caught spreading "maternity-related gossip" would face "stiff penalties" (trigger more vomit emojis). Like, was the faculty spying on our social media? It didn't slow down the ogling, but everyone felt some kind of way about the implication. School was supposed to be school, we got to be free when we were on our own. Right?

Second, Kiera. She'd stopped posting. Stopped talking, really. Mad people came at her like, "Did you know? When did you know? What do you know?" She handled it all like a champ with side-eye and no comments. Even in Purity Pledge she seemed less there, but I think Sister Vanessa knew what was up, and didn't make a big deal about it. Jameer tried to keep me in the loop on how Kiera was doing with his spotty insight.

"She won't talk about it," he said. "Not even to me."

I was thinking, isn't it part of our agreement that you get her to talk about it so I can be better prepared for what's next? Instead, he kept molding me to be the Purity Pledge champ with choice scriptures and observations that I parroted through the next few sessions at church.

Matthew 6:22 was about turning your eyes from worthless things—like hot cars, and IG models in bikinis. It was supposed to make you stronger to focus on worthwhile, pure things. I talked about that.

Exodus 20:14 flat-out said don't commit adultery—which

was pretty much any sex where you're not married. I became the Exodus 20:14 spokesman.

There were other verses too that Jameer passed me on Post-it Notes that were stuck to my desk at home. From Genesis, and Romans, and 1 Thessalonians (which you said like "*First* Thessalonians" not "*One* Thessalonians" even though there was clearly a "1" there—weird, right?).

Sister Vanessa seemed "impressed by my spiritual growth"—her words—but I didn't think anyone else was. As much as I wanted to, I got it was probably better that we didn't press Kiera during these trying Baby-Getter times.

Even Qwan agreed. Sorta. One day on the way to school he asked, "None of those other church girls throwing you any vibes, man? I know you been All-Kiera-Everything forever, but there are no unattractive ladies in that Pledge. Got me ready to get some religion."

"Would Angie be cool with that?"

Annnnd, he shut up. We'd yet to get into how much time he'd been spending with her. It was very un-Qwan-like. Two weekends passed without a single request to chauffeur him to some new girl's house. I almost wanted to press my hand to his forehead and check his temperature the way Mom did when she thought I wasn't feeling well.

Speaking of Mom . . .

Third ripple, even my parents and Cressie knew about #Baby-GettersToo. Each asking me about it on separate occasions.

Dad's was a casual, "What's up at the school with those

pregnant girls?" I explained they technically weren't pregnant anymore. And lied about not paying attention to any of it so he'd leave me alone. He accepted my explanation, went back to work at his computer.

Cressie hit me with a text that was a little strange.

Cressie: Lil' Bro. #BabyGettersToo. You got details or what?

Me: Or what. Don't you have college stuff to do?

Cressie: Do you think any of the girls would talk to me about it? Maybe Shianne?

Me: Talk to you? For what?

To which she never responded. Cressie was good for a nonconclusive text, and I wasn't pressed to keep talking #BabyGettersToo. As far as I knew, we'd both moved on.

Ten days after Taylor Burkin set it all off, on a sleepy Sunday after I'd worked a closing shift at FISHto's, Mom finally got around to asking. Newsome preached on accountability that day, how God's natural order meant men and women had different roles and responsibilities during our time on earth. Though sleepy and yawny from work, I paid more attention

than usual because the sermon seemed to align with our next Purity Pledge session.

At one point, Newsome said, "In Proverbs 5 we're told that the lips of a seductive woman are oh so sweet, her soft words are oh so smooth. But it won't be long before she's gravel in your mouth, a pain in your gut, a wound in your heart."

A few folks, Coach Scott among them, shouted loud amens, but all I could think was, wow, that sounded dark. And wrong. Somehow.

Mom squirmed next to me, the lines around her mouth made more pronounced by her new frown. Newsome had more to say on the subject, but she'd closed her eyes, mumbled her secret prayers for the rest of service. I twisted in the pew, checking reactions from my fellow Pledgers, the girls in particular. Mya was stone-faced, unreadable. Helena and Shanice seemed to be in another world. I couldn't see Kiera's face because she was a couple of rows up, but her dad nodded vigorously. Her mom, not so much.

Pastor Newsome kept it moving.

During the car ride home, Mom brought up the hashtag. "Is it true some of the girls from the pregnancy pact are publicly exposing the boys who were involved?"

"There wasn't a pact, Mom."

"Fine. What about the rest?"

My turn to squirm. I hated talking about this stuff with her. "Yeah. A couple have been talking on IG and Snap."

"Those are internet apps?"

Close enough. "Yeah."

"Are they being well received?"

"Internet apps" I was able to translate, roughly. I didn't know what she meant about "well received."

I said, "A lot of people are paying attention."

"What are they saying? Are they supportive of the girls?"

"It's all anyone's talking about."

"That's not the same thing as being supportive, Del. Tell me the ways people are responding."

Aggravation crept into her voice, and I wasn't trying to bring on what me and Cressie called a Mom-Storm, so I opened my "internet apps" and scrolled through some of the replies on IG. "It's mostly laughs and people instigating. Anything to keep it going. Some name-calling. Why you want to know?"

"You're not saying mean things to those girls, are you?"

"Naw. I mean, no."

"You better not be."

"Dang, Mom! Why are you coming at me like that? What I do?"

Her jaw clenched, and she patted my knee. "You didn't do anything. How's Purity Pledge going?"

Though her voice softened, the subject change didn't inspire more comfort. "It's, you know, pure."

"Sister Vanessa says you've been studying hard. You've been a good example for the other kids. Particularly the Burton twins."

"Have I?" I fought to keep my annoyance in check. I had a theory about that great evaluation from Ralph and Bobby Burton.

We turned onto our street. Mom pressed the button in the ceiling that opened our garage door. We pulled into the driveway while the door clanked up. When it was fully open, she didn't drive in. Instead, she started talking fast, like we were on a timer. "I want to apologize to you, son. Admittedly, I was shocked when you joined Purity Pledge. I questioned your motives. That was wrong. I'm proud of you for the decision you made, and I'm glad that you're taking such steps to being a good man."

Then she drove us inside. The door ratcheted down behind us, and she was quickstepping into the house before I could undo my seat belt, or say thanks, or clarify what she meant by "good man."

All righty then.

I was waist-deep in the cabinet beneath the FISHto's drive-thru Coke machine, swapping empty syrup and carbonation tanks for new ones. The sickly-sweet scent of congealed sugar water accumulated in the corners from old spills was gag-worthy, but I didn't dare complain for fear of Tyrell sending me home again. The checks I was pulling from my shortened shifts could barely buy air fresheners for my car, let alone keep covering gas, or my part of the auto insurance bill.

My phone buzzed in my pocket. Already knew who it was and ignored it. This had been the pattern for the last two weeks since Jameer started "helping" me.

My new Purity Pledge coach hadn't kept all of our secrets. Somehow the other Pledgers got it in their heads that my Healthy

Living connection meant all of their weird-ass questions could get answered with no real paper trail for their parents to flip over. Jameer played middleman. With a strong implication that I'd provide the requested information if I wanted his help to continue. Asshole.

"Del," Mya said from somewhere above me in her fresh-air perch at the drive-thru window. "How much longer? It's slowing down my fulfillment time when I gotta run to front line for drinks."

"Do you want to do this?" I unsnapped the Barq's root beer hose and tossed the empty syrup box at her legs.

"Watch it, mister." She kicked me in the thigh, passed me a replacement.

Spending time together in Purity Pledge led to more casual conversations here at FISHto's. I knew the restaurant was her way of saving for college; specifically, for her own apartment, because her grades were good enough for scholarships. I knew she wanted to be a software engineer after college. I knew she wasn't one of the Purity Pledgers feeding me anonymous sex questions through Jameer because she told me so, and Mya Hanson did not lie.

My phone kept vibrating.

Barq's was done. I swapped the Orange Fanta, and the Caffeine-Free Diet Coke, then closed up shop, crawling out of the cupboard. "Done."

Not that there were any customers to appreciate it.

Mya, gracious, said, "Since we're slow, I'll take care of the front-line condiments for you. First Missionary Crew!"

She raised her hand for a high five, and I slapped her palm even though I thought the greeting was corny. One of Jameer's tips was "embrace the corniness." First Missionary Crew!

While Mya refilled my tartar sauce and ketchup packets, I checked my phone for this week's haul.

Jameer: New Qs from the PPers

1—What should I smell like? Down there.

2—How long should erections last?

3—Should I get tingly when I watch
the morning news with my parents?
Specifically when it's channel 12 and mete-
orologist Ashley Eubanks is on?

4—What about feet?

"Feet?" The questions had gotten so much stranger lately. I had a gut feeling the weirdest ones were coming from Ralph and Bobby, thus them gushing about how great I was to whoever would listen. Nobody else was entertaining their fetish-y urges.

I wondered how Jameer even managed to do this with his parents clocking everything he did. He proudly explained that their insistence on such a low-tech phone is what gave him the freedom to harass me. They couldn't put any parental spy apps on a phone that old. All he had to do was delete his messages after he sent them. Sneaky. And annoying.

"You started this," Mya said, popping open a fresh box of cocktail sauce packets, referring to my Healthy Living double-agent duties.

Pocketing my phone, I knelt with her, transferred packets from the box to the bins beneath my register. "Just because you said you hadn't sent questions to Jameer before doesn't mean you didn't change your mind. For all I know, it's *you* asking about feet."

"Nope. Not even close. I don't have to tiptoe—pun intended— around my curiosity like the rest of them. I have working Wi-Fi. Also, I guess I'm not that curious about sex stuff. Not the way everyone else seems to be."

"Why not?"

She shrugged. "After everything with the pregnancies, I don't know, sex seems like more trouble than it's worth."

"Is that the Purity Pledge talking?"

"No. It's not. But if it was, would it be a bad thing? I mean, you've really been crushing all of the scriptures and activities lately. So sex must not be a huge deal for you either if you stopped doing it and are focusing on a different path."

"Yeah," I said, uncomfortable skirting around the topic of my "reputation" pre–Purity Pledge. "You have a point. Is that why you don't take Healthy Living at school?"

Mya shook her head. "That was Pastor's call. My mom was

going to sign the permission slip until he preached against it. I wasn't that excited about it, anyway. I like playing basketball during gym."

Of all the new conversations and connections between me and Mya, we hadn't really discussed this. "Why did Newsome tell the church not to let anyone take it?"

"He said he didn't think it was the sort of thing we should be learning about at school." She moved on to refilling the salt and pepper packets bin.

I said, "Did you know the Healthy Living lessons and the Purity Pledge lessons are kind of, like, opposites?"

"That makes sense. He talked about it in the same sermon where he told the church not to let us take it. He's part of the board that helps set the curriculum at the school."

"Wait. What?" A civics class lesson came back to me in the moment. How our country was supposed to be big on keeping religion out of its many functions. Like education. It was a thing. My parents sometimes brought it up when they watched the news after dinner, and I said it the way they would. "What about separation of church and state?"

"This is Green Creek," Mya said, as if we existed outside of the normal rules of America. "Pastor told us that impropriety had set in over the meetings and was influencing what the educators allowed into our classrooms, and no matter how much he fought, the school embraced an unholy spirit, or something."

"Unholy spirit? That's extreme. He really said that?"

Mya stopped filling her bin, a scowl twisting her face. "Del, you were there. It was the first Sunday you and your mom showed up at church. Do you really daydream that much? You don't remember any of it?"

Welllll . . .

Mya said, "Yes. He really said that."

"So, did he come up with Purity Pledge like counterprogramming? Something to fight Healthy Living?"

"I don't know about that. He's never mentioned the Pledge from the pulpit. At least not that I recall. It always seemed more Sister Vanessa's thing."

"What's up with them? Their relationship seems weird."

"She's his niece. Pastor and First Lady Newsome raised Sister Vanessa."

"First Lady Newsome." I'd never heard about her before. "Where's she?"

Mya got bashful, focused extra hard on the condiments in her hand. "She passed away last year."

"Oh. I'm—I'm sorry. That sucks."

"It did. Pastor didn't preach for like a month after. The deacons just rotated, giving short sermons and letting us go home early. Then he came back, the church moved on." The drive-thru buzzer sounded. Mya popped up, a fish-themed superhero ready to save some hungry stomachs. "Duty calls."

I stored the condiment boxes, leaned on the counter almost hoping (praying?) for a customer so I had something to do. My phone buzzed again. I slipped it out and found another Jameer text.

Jameer: 5—What is the best way to watch porn without anyone knowing?

I said, "Are you serious?"

Tyrell, emerging from stealth mode, said, "Del."

Scrambling, I went to slip my phone in my back pocket. I missed completely, and it clattered on the floor. Crap. "Tyrell, my bad, I—"

"You're not supposed to have your phone out while on the floor. We've been over this."

"Yeah, but there's nobody—"

"It's fine. As you mentioned, we're not that busy. I'm sending you home. It's all good."

I couldn't go home. I couldn't explain to Mom or Dad why my shifts were getting cut short. I'd need to crack the code on this money situation soon. Just not that afternoon.

I shot Qwan a couple of texts before leaving FISHto's.

Me: Ninja, you up?

Me: I'm coming through

Fool was probably up all night watching Netflix. I'd have to be his wake-up call. Dropping my phone in my cup holder, I set off for his crib.

Qwan lived in a beige, weather-stained townhouse wedged

between other beige, weather-stained townhouses in a community called Delany Groves. There weren't driveways, only designated parking spaces along the curb. Because of the designations, guests like me could only park in spots where "VISITORS" was stenciled on the asphalt. Normally, it wasn't a problem. The neighborhood wasn't crowded, and there was typically a prime VISITORS spot right by Qwan's door. Not so today. An old tan conversion van—the kind that looked like a fat diving bell and had a couch in the back—occupied the space.

The next available spot was a ways down, so I parked and walked. When I knocked, Qwan's mom let me in. She had curlers in her hair, and a terrycloth housecoat tugged tight. "Hey, baby. You here to study, too?"

"Yeah," I said, cosigning the lie automatically. There had never been a study session at Qwan's house. Davonne, Qwan's little sister, scrolled through Hulu options in the living room, while Ms. Reid returned to something sizzling in the kitchen. I climbed the stairs, anticipating discovery.

Shouldering open his door, I cast hallway light into Qwan's dim room. Two wrestlers broke apart like they'd heard a referee's whistle. As I flipped on the ceiling light, my gaze snagged on the one who wasn't my best friend.

Well, hello, Angie Bell.

They weren't doing it, THANK GOD. Still fully dressed, but ruffled. They'd been doing *something*. Angie was more self-conscious of it than Qwan. He'd long given up any shame around me.

She shifted around in his desk chair, crossing and uncrossing her legs in an audition for the part of Nothing-to-See-Here Girl. Even if she'd found the perfect posture, the giveaway would've been her body lotion. It had glitter in it, so her skin glistened when the light caught it right. It was most noticeable above the barely-a-collar of her low-cut tee, right where sternum became cleavage. The same glittery lotion was all over Qwan's face, sparkling, turning his grin into something as magical as a unicorn's horn.

"D," Qwan said.

"Yoooo!" I couldn't hide my smirk.

Angie said, "What up, Del Rainey?"

"Hey, Angie."

We'd never had a conversation before, me and Angie, but when you went to Green Creek introductions weren't often necessary.

Qwan eyed my uniform. "Tyrell let you out the shark tank."

"Kinda. Thought I'd swing through. But, you're busy."

Angie stood, catching the strap of her unopened school bag. "I'm leaving. I think we've studied enough for one day."

"I don't know," Qwan said, his hand grazing her thigh above the knee, "we could hit the books a little harder."

"So corny. Bye, Qwan. Bye, Del Rainey." Halfway out the door, she spun and said the strangest thing to me. "And tell your sister I'm a fan."

She'd descended the stairs too quick for me to respond. Qwan hustled to my side, looped an arm over my shoulder to watch her go. "I hope your weekend's been as good as mine."

"She knows Cressie?"

"Not personally. She talking about YouTube."

"YouTube? What?"

His mouth stretched into an O. "Shit, D. You don't know?"

Qwan tapped his phone screen rapidly, then flipped it around so I could see. Yes, that was my sister in a frozen You-Tube thumbnail, face frowned, one hand raised in what might be the universal gesture for attitude.

I snatched the phone from him. Above the thumbnail, the video title: "*FemFam* with Cressida Rainey."

There were two "episodes" posted for her first season. One called "Allow Me to Re-Introduce Myself," the second, "The Trouble with College Bruhs." Each video had netted a couple thousand views, and her channel had a respectable 657 subscribers.

I returned Qwan's phone.

"You ain't trying to watch?" he asked.

Truth: I felt weird watching . . . whatever Cressie was doing for the first time with a witness present. Maybe this is what her and Mom had been talking about? Why hadn't I paid more attention? I played it off. "Not really. I watched her live show for sixteen years. When did Angie tell you about this?"

"I told her. Cressie's, like, my first bae, so I saw when she posted about her new channel on the Gram. Why you acting salty about it?"

"I'm not salty." My best friend's unhealthy obsession with my sister aside, I didn't expect today to be a Cressie day.

"Well, keep not being salty while I smash you on 2K?" He powered up his Xbox, and rap music from the basketball game start screen bumped through his speakers.

I reached for my preferred controller, stopping short when I noticed a sprinkling of glitter on it. "Dude, what were y'all doing in here?"

He grinned. "Maybe when you're older, D."

Qwan took the first game playing as the Milwaukee Bucks, but I was handling him after switching from the Raptors to the Rockets. And we talked. Not about his weekend with Angie. My preferred topic.

Qwan bricked a three-pointer, said, "It was probably smart to back off Kiera with Colossus getting blown up in the Baby-GettersToo thing, but, I'm going to keep it one hundred with you, I think you're a little too casual. Ain't nobody else trying to run a long con like you. I saw Ricky slip his arm around her waist the other day between classes and start whispering in her ear, in front of everybody."

"Ricky Nestor?"

"Yep."

"And?"

"She slipped loose and bounced. Ricky's game is nonexistent. I'm just telling you nobody else has an elaborate twelfth-dimensional chess game going to get at her. They're shooting their shot. You should shoot your shot."

On the screen, I threw a garbage pass straight into his defenders' hands. Qwan lazy-jogged it to the basket for an easy lay-up.

I said, "It's different this time. The church and the Pledge are important to her. I'm putting myself in a position, so she can't slip away."

"Yeah, but—" He didn't finish his sentence, focused on a baseline drive to the basket that I blocked with my center.

"You obviously have something to say."

"Kiera is fire, like easily one of the five hottest girls at Green Creek. That part make sense. Only dudes that aren't attracted to her, they kinda know . . ."

I paused the game. "Dude, say it."

"They're not going to get any. In my experience, in this town, that whole church-girls-are-freaky stereotype is big wrong. I've hollered at a couple, and it was all watching Hallmark movies with their parents in the room. Wednesday-night Bible study. It makes me have to ask you flat out—do you not like sex?"

I unpaused the game. "Of course I like sex." I think. It looked fun when Lindy Blue did it.

"That's what I thought. That's why you might need to consider some different goals, D." He drove the Greek Freak into the paint for a monster, uncontested windmill dunk.

My phone buzzed in my lap. And I paused the game again, freezing my player on the baseline, looking for open guys to pass to. The text wiped all digital basketball concerns from my mind.

Jameer: Code RED! Get to my house ASAP. Park on Kensey street, and come through my backyard.

My stomach fell through the floor.

Qwan said, "Dude, we doing this or what?"

His voice barely registered.

Me: What's wrong?

But I knew. Deep down, I did.

Jameer: Someone is at Kiera's

"I gotta go." I pushed up out of Qwan's chair. "It's . . . my dad. Errands."

If Qwan suspected the lie, I couldn't tell. "That's a forfeit, right?"

"Yeah. You win."

"It's the natural order of things."

Him winning, or me losing?

I made it to my car, and gripped the steering wheel extra tight to keep my hands from shaking. If I was right, the next thing I'd be gripping extra tight might be Jameer's neck.

The neighbor whose lawn I had to cut through to get to Jameer's was on his knees, in his flower bed, pruning something. I was so mad that I stomped across his grass, gave a semi-polite wave, and kept on through his backyard like me trespassing on his property was our old routine. Nearby, loud and annoying, a lawn mower motor snarled.

Jameer waited for me where the property lines met, leaning on the short chain-link fence that enclosed his family's yard. I planted two hands on the top rail—extra tight—and hopped over. When me and him were eye to eye, I said, "Who is it?"

For the first time, he looked rattled. Couldn't tell if it was from the rage radiating off me, or something else. I hoped it was me. His little fake mastermind ass should be terrified.

He said, "Come inside and keep your voice down."

"Tell me who it is, Jameer. Who's the new boyfriend that didn't wait around for you to deliver like my dumbass did?"

"There is no boyfriend." He looked at my shoes instead of my face. "Not yet. Come on."

Inside a linoleum-floored mudroom, he stomped his feet on a woolen mat, shaking loose a few blades of grass. Then we were in a kitchen where every wall was covered by stainless steel appliances, or darkly rich cabinetry. Every horizontal surface was some kind of exotic rock with the edges left rough on purpose, a chosen imperfection in the flawless room. Even their cereal was in foggy, perfectly aligned glass canisters so the corn-flakes and raisins seemed frozen in a glacier.

"Your people here?" I asked. There was a slight echo.

"No."

He took me through a museum-quality dining room with unused place settings and fancy paintings of gangly, exagger-ated black folks playing piano and trombones on the wall. A front foyer. Up wooden stairs with a thick carpet runner on the risers so it felt like climbing mattresses. We ended up in a bedroom. At a glance, I wasn't sure it was his. It was so plain. Something was off here, and I was too mad to see it right away.

The walls were bare, except for textured wallpaper lining the room in vertical pastel patterns that looked like bars. There was a desk, and a bed with a comforter that matched the wall. A dresser with a porcelain dove perched near the edge. That was about it. No computer. No TV. No games. Maybe a guest room?

A Bible I recognized sat in the windowsill. The one he lent me that first night of Purity Pledge. On the floor under that window, the satchel that bounced on his hip when he walked the halls at school. The closet door was cracked, and I spotted some familiar plaid shirts on hangers. This *was* his weird-ass room.

He walked me to his window, shoved binoculars into my chest before I had time to ponder. "Look! But don't stand too close."

Like a sniper. I was thinking in *Call of Duty* terms. My mind prepped for war games. Or, maybe just war.

Standing where Jameer directed, I raised the lenses, then adjusted the focus until I had line of sight on cars parked in front of Kiera's house. Two crammed the driveway. A Cadillac and a Chevy SUV that often served as Sunday vehicles for the Westings. Along the curb was a Ford truck that did not belong to the Westings. Stenciled on its door: *Handy Lawn Care Company*. Hitched to it, a long trailer with the ramp lowered, presumably for the riding lawn mower doing the last few passes. Its driver was an older man in a straw hat, and at first I fooled myself into thinking this was the threat that had Jameer call me over. Then I panned the binoculars right.

"Oh my God!"

Near the porch steps, where the manicured shrubs began, was Kiera sipping a can of lemonade, chatting with the second man on the Handy Lawn Care Company crew. This landscaper was in an army-green shirt, soaked dark with sweat. An oversized pair of shears was tucked under his arm as he enjoyed a lemonade as well. It had to be the best damned lemonade on earth the way the two of them were cheesing between chugs.

I mumbled the words. "No. Not Jack Jake."

Jameer said, "Who?"

"Mason. Miles."

Their conversation stretched, she fanned the collar of her blouse like it was hot—it wasn't—then casually tugged the rubber band off her ponytail, shaking her hair out in a way that made my knees weak from equal parts desire and jealousy.

She was flirting. *Flirting!* With Mason f'ing Miles.

"You said it was all about timing." I lowered the binoculars. "That's what you told me."

This was supposed to be my time. He didn't bother to say what we both knew.

My time had run out.

Raising the binoculars again, I strongly wished that I could read lips. Since that wasn't one of my actual skills, I superimposed my own dialogue over Kiera's and Mason's magnified image. My words matching their lips as closely as the English in those badly dubbed kung fu movies Dad watched sometimes.

Him: So, hey, look at my abs.

Her: I can't see them with your shirt on, silly.

Him: We'll have to do something about that.

Her: Oh yes we will.

"Argggh!" I tossed Jameer's binoculars on his bed, my fury nearing the point of eruption.

"Del, listen." He raised his hands to chest level, palms out, like he was going to hold me in place, but stopped an inch shy of actually touching me. A wise decision. "This isn't necessarily an endgame for us. You need to relax."

"Relax?" I saw myself storming out, slamming the door so hard it shook the foundation.

Except there was no door.

Like, at all.

There was the rectangular frame that we walked through. There were three evenly spaced impressions along the door frame where hinges had once been. No. Actual. Door.

Who didn't have doors?

This detail, oddly, was the thing that got my mind off the nuclear assault on my dating life taking place on the Westings' lawn.

Slowly, I spun in place, taking in my surroundings undistracted. Plain walls. No door. Not even a mirror—how the hell did he tie his ties? "What's up with your room, Jameer?"

His gaze bounced about the odd space. His shoulders slumped; I wondered if he preferred me yelling at him about

Kiera. Shamefaced, he said, "I told you my parents can be strict."

My emotions shifted. I was in danger of feeling sympathy for the dude who'd failed me, so I looked out the window again. I didn't need binoculars to reignite my rage. "I can't with you right now. I'm gone."

"Del, wait." Jameer chased me down the stairs, my feet sinking into the thick carpet runner.

We hit the first floor, and he hissed, "Crap!"

The front door swung inward. His mom and dad were silhouettes backlit by the setting sun.

Mr. Sesay crossed the threshold, blinking rapidly, his eyes adjusting to the house's oppressive gloom. He stopped cold when he saw me. Mrs. Sesay walked right into him, knocking him forward like a softly tapped billiard ball.

They probably didn't recognize me. My FISHto uniform and all. "Hi, Mr. and Mrs. Sesay, it's—"

"Del," Mrs. Sesay said, with zero enthusiasm. She peeked around her husband's shoulder. "Jameer, what's going on here?"

The way she talked through me made me feel like *I* wasn't all the way present.

Jameer said, "Del's in Purity Pledge with me. He came by—"

Mrs. Sesay squeezed Mr. Sesay's arm. He said, "You're not allowed to have company if no one's here. You know that."

"It's about the Pledge, Dad."

Mr. Sesay said, "Uh-huh."

The glances his parents exchanged were the kind I'd seen Mom and Dad give each other when a more miserable discussion was being scheduled for later. Succumbing to politeness,

Mrs. Sesay held up a plastic grocery sack, fragrant with the garlic twang of rotisserie chicken. "You can stay for dinner if you like, Del."

It was supposed to sound like an invite. I felt no more welcome to sit at their table than if I'd actually been the Count of Monte FISHto himself, flopping wet and stinking of the deep sea.

"No, thank you. My dad's cooking."

"Well, then." Mr. Sesay stepped aside, and his wife did the same, allowing me full access to the exit.

Okay. "Later, Jameer."

He didn't respond. The Sesays closed the door, but before it slammed shut, I caught a "What the hell do you think you're—?"

Followed by a deadbolt clacking into place.

I was mad at Jameer for . . . everything. I was also worried about him. His room . . . no doors, no mirror, as bare as frontier cabins we sometimes read about when MJ couldn't get around state-mandated book lists. It creeped me out.

So, I didn't leave. I lingered on the shadowy porch, listening intently for danger sounds—yelling, crashes. After a few minutes of nothing, I decided he probably wasn't in physical danger, and I was totally overreacting. It was okay to go back to being mad at Jameer.

Cautiously, I glanced next door to the Westing home. The man on the riding mower finished his last swath of cutting while Mason trimmed bushes, in the landscaper zone, the white cable from his earbuds snaking from his head to his phone.

Qwan said it; I was playing this too casual. That had to

change. It would change. I wasn't about to let another dude come along and take what I'd been waiting so patiently for.

I traversed stepping-stones that led to the street. When I touched asphalt, I circled the block to my car. Moving fast, with purpose, but no plan. What now?

I still had an hour before my original FISHto's shift was supposed to end, so I drove slowly around Green Creek. Sulking, really.

How was this going so wrong again?

Toward the end of my drive, my phone began vibrating steadily. When I parked in the driveway, I found a series of texts from Jameer.

Jameer: Del, I know you're mad. But I have a plan

Jameer: And the other Purity Pledgers are going to help

Jameer: I've got two words for you

Jameer: Harvest Fest

Was I supposed to know what that meant?

Me: Explain

And for the next half hour I sat in my car, watching the details of this new plan arrive in short, slow text bursts—his flip phone wasn't built for speed. But, the wait was worth it. Me and Jameer were on the same page, throwing the "too casual" approach aside.

Now, all I needed was a disguise.

CHAPTER 10

WE HAD A FEW DAYS until Jameer's big play, and things were not uneventful in the meantime. On Monday, Taylor Burkin, the founder of #BabyGettersToo, returned to school. The hall was electric with her presence. From the time her mother let her out at the drop-off lane, to her stepping foot into the main foyer, to trekking the halls to her locker, all manner of social media buzzed.

Taylor's back!

Taylor's here!

Another Baby-Getter returns!

The biggest attention-grabber was Taylor's locker position. A mere three doors down from Kiera's.

That hall became unusually thick with spectators—more students than had ever hung around that particular set of lockers and classrooms. MJ once told us about this story by a science fiction writer named Ray Bradbury. In it, this crowd would show up around car accidents and other tragedies. Not a general crowd. The *same* crowd. Every time. Like the way crowds appeared around fights, or other hallway drama at Green Creek.

But I was no different from that ever-present crowd. I, too, was curious as to how Kiera would react to Taylor, or how Taylor would react to Kiera, or if one of them might postpone their locker stop until a less stressful time.

No. Both girls were present. Kiera lingering at her locker with Helena and Shanice, as usual. Taylor approached from the south hallway, with new additions to "The Crowd" in tow.

Murmurs became silence, and the air crackled as Taylor spun her locker combination while flicking glances Kiera's way.

Obviously, Kiera was aware of the drama leeches waiting to feed on something, despite her best efforts to maintain a casual presence. Some instigator squealed, "She smashed your man!" Attempting to spark a fire.

Kiera's lips pinched, and she stared directly at Taylor, who stared back.

"Ohhhh!" said another instigator.

Kiera shook her head, looked skyward, mumbling. I recognized this now. It was a church move, a quick prayer. She closed her locker door gently, approached Taylor with Helena and Shanice at her flank.

Taylor closed her locker door, too. Faced Kiera, radiating wariness.

Everyone in attendance leaned in, determined not to miss whatever jab—verbal or otherwise—came next.

Kiera reached striking distance, eyes focused on her target, and said, "Welcome back."

She reeled Taylor into a bear hug that took her, and the entire hall, by surprise. Kiera was taller than Taylor, seemed to yank her onto her tiptoes for the embrace, but there was no malice. Taylor hugged her back, and disappointed parties at the edge of the crowd dispersed, irritated as if they'd purchased expensive boxing tickets only to see the champ go down in the first round.

Kiera said, "I'll walk you to homeroom."

"They're staring," Taylor said.

"Let them."

Kiera passed me and gave me a slight nod. In a less tense situation, this acknowledgment might have been the First Missionary Crew! high five, as had become the custom among us Purity Pledgers. Instead, she kept it moving . . . until she passed Mason at the hallway intersection. He got a fist bump.

Qwan said, "Yo, since when does Kiera fist-bump Mason?"

"Don't know."

"Should we be concerned?"

"Don't know."

My truncated answers did the trick; Qwan didn't push. Instead, he utilized the best of his best friend instincts to swerve around the topic slightly. "I heard Mason be lying on his dick."

Lying on your dick was a cardinal sin in Green Creek. The falsifying of sexual conquests. The fictionalizing of lovemaking statistics. It was a crime I was, technically, guilty of too, but my Shianne lie was mutual and consensual. Not like the story that got around eighth-grade year when Mason said he'd smashed April Benoit, and she said she didn't even know him. I hadn't heard of such infractions from Mason since, but I appreciated Qwan reminding me of dude's darkest moment.

In English class I found myself eyeing the back of Mason's head. Sizing him up. He was taller than me, slim, and clean-cut. He wore street clothes today, but in his JROTC uniform he looked like he could teach a class. I imagined Deacon and Deaconess Westing enjoying the company of someone who looked like him. He seemed like the kind of guy they'd be happy to see their daughter bring home. That twisted my stomach until I imagined Qwan beside me, specter-like, Obi-*Qwan* Kenobi to my Luke Skywalker, yelling, "Lies on his dick!"

After English, I fell into the established routine of asking MJ off-the-record sexual questions from the Purity Pledgers (except that one about feet, I vetoed that). He answered, with his usual reminder to keep it between us. Then got on with the rest of my day. By the time we got to Healthy Living, I felt more relaxed. Even though this was yet another class with Mason. Maybe it was because of the subtle adjustments MJ made to the topics.

Like in English, he let us know there were things we had to do. Even if it seemed dumb and unrelatable, like the session when he broke down "Social Gathering Safety Zones"—places you could go and not be tempted to have sex. The mall, or the movies, or an ice-cream shop.

You know what . . . the movies, sure. Me and Qwan did that plenty. The mall, though? Every one I've been to got age limits, and curfew restrictions, and scared security guards who're ready to Tase you for walking in groups of three or more without a chaperone. At least that's how it was for the black kids. I'd seen white boys looking like a whole soccer team get a smile and nod from the mall cops.

Also, where the heck was an ice-cream shop?

To keep us manageable during those lessons, MJ made us a promise. Last five minutes of every class, if we were good, he'd answer whatever random questions we had. It wasn't lost on me that he started this practice shortly after I'd broached the topic of wet dreams for Jameer.

Checking his watch, MJ said, "It's time, guys. What you got?"

A hand went up in the back row. "MJ, you know about the BabyGettersToo hashtag?"

"I'm aware. It's hard not to be."

Back Row followed up with, "What you think about Taylor coming back to school after blowing up Colossus like she did?"

MJ shifted uncomfortably. "Nice try, but you know I'm not about to discuss another student with you. Somebody else give it a shot."

Mason's hand went up. "How'd you meet your kid's mom?"

"Wow, nice pivot." MJ stroked his chin. "It was college. I was a junior. She was a freshman."

He stopped like we were going to let that ride.

Qwan said, "What else? Was it at a party or something? How'd you run your game? Tell us how the OGs did it."

"I'm not *that* OG, Qwan. I'm only twenty-eight."

The class got raucous, egging him on.

"Okay, okay. Settle down. It happened like this. This gorgeous girl's parents knew my roommate's parents. Her people told her when she got on campus, go visit him and say what's up, so she'd know somebody. The girl came to our apartment with three of her friends. She's wearing this denim outfit that looks really good, and I immediately make a fool of myself. I say something like, 'You are really rocking that skirt, ma. If only I could be denim for a day.'"

MJ posed with his back stiff, arms crossed, a b-boy stance. We cracked up partially from his boldness, partially for the corny line.

Returning to a more relaxed posture, he said, "That didn't go over well with any of the girls, and my roommate looked like he wanted to apply for a reassignment that second."

Mason said, "Why were they mad, though? You were telling her she looked good in the skirt. It was a compliment."

"Was it?"

Mason opened his mouth, then closed it.

MJ said, "Show of hands, who thinks what I said was all good?"

Most hands went up. Including Mason's. Including Qwan's. Including mine.

With a wave, MJ signaled all hands down. "There's a room full of girls next door. I'm willing to bet if we asked their opinions, the majority would think differently from y'all."

"That's because they're stuck up!"

I don't know who said it, but it got a few cheers, claps, and chuckles.

MJ face-palmed, shook his head. "Guys, it took me a long time to get it, too. You wanted to ask real questions, so I'm trying to give you real answers. Almost everything you think you know about girls and women is wrong. That incorrect information can be dangerous."

Mason said, "Ain't no girl going to hurt me, MJ."

As serious as I've ever seen him, MJ said, "I don't mean dangerous for you. A lot of women have been hurt and will be hurt because we—men—are mostly still operating on a caveman's script."

The room was quiet. I didn't know what to make of his words. I'm not sure anyone else knew either. The bell rang.

I said, "Real quick, MJ. How'd you fix it with your lady?"

"Next time, guys. Remind me. This topic bears much further discussion."

The frustration in the room was thick. A mix of no resolution and misunderstanding. The promise of a continuation eased us a bit, though it wouldn't come.

That was the last Healthy Living session we'd have with MJ.

The school lot was well on its way to empty when I stepped outside and got blasted in the face with a cold gust of wind, surprising me enough so I lost my grip on my keys. They fell in a jingling pile, and when I stooped to retrieve them, I caught sight of a girl in a bright red jacket to the left of the school's exit. She mopped that hand across her face, smearing tears.

"Shianne?"

Her chin ticked up, and she swiped more furiously at her wet eyes. "Hey, Del."

"You okay?" I asked, getting closer and making her attempts to disguise her obvious crying more futile.

She threw up her hands, defeated. "Do I look okay?"

I said, "Yeah. Fantastic."

Shianne huffed a dry laugh. "Oh my God, your face. How did we keep that lie of ours going so long?"

My eyes cut to the school doors, checking for any classmates close enough to hear. I changed the subject. "How's your daughter?"

"Fussy. Gassy." She held up her cell. "Mom's sent me plenty of texts to let me know."

"Is that why you're crying? Because you had to leave her?" I'd seen something like that on TV.

"No. I cry when I get mad."

Once, when we still hung out like that, I'd crushed her in Scrabble and she'd gotten teary-eyed before flipping the board. I wasn't convinced anger was all there was to it this time.

"Do you know how much work I need to make up to stay on course for graduation?"

We were about eight weeks into the school year, so probably a lot. "They didn't let you do any while you were, er, home?"

She shrugged. "It's not the same as being here." She coughed up another sob. "I can't mess this up, Del. My parents . . . I can't mess up anymore."

This felt like a hugging situation. I would've had her in my arms automatically a year ago. But then some cheerleaders burst through the school doors, laughing until they saw us. When their chirpy glee turned to conspiracy whispers, I took a step backward that I hoped Shianne wouldn't notice.

She fixed on the girls strolling across the lot. They piled into a minivan, carefree. The way she used to be.

A canyon of awkwardness yawned between us, so I worked on words that might end this. Before I could produce them, she said, "Your grades are good, right?"

I nodded. I was rocking a solid 3.5 GPA.

"Wanna be my tutor?"

A 3.5 wasn't exactly Neil deGrasse Tyson. "I don't know about that, Shianne."

I thought, Be strong. You're busy. You don't have time to do favors right now.

She said, "Because my dad would be willing to pay you."

"How much?"

"Whatever is reasonable. He told me to find a tutor, and I looked at the list the school keeps. Only a few people do it locally, and they're all some judgmental bitches."

"Whoa!"

"Sorry, but many people have loud, horrible, and public opinions about all of us who had kids recently. I'm sure you've seen Taylor's hashtag, so you know."

"Okay."

"Going out of town to one of those learning centers isn't

feasible. Not with my kid at home, and Mom reminding me my kid is at home every fifth minute."

Her tutoring problem was the same as any modern convenience problem when it came to our town. Lack of Green Creek resources strikes again.

If her dad was paying—Shianne's people had dough, for sure—this could work, considering I'd been getting zero hours at FISHto's. "Let's talk about my rates."

CHAPTER 11

JAMEER BRIEFED ME ON WHAT to expect at Harvest Fest the following evening. Our typical Tuesday Purity Pledge class was being preempted so all the PPers could "volunteer" at First Missionary House of the Lord's answer to Halloween.

Since the typical ghost/goblin/monster vibe of traditional Halloween was deemed unholy by Newsome and the congregation, the church did their own thing every year during the last week of October.

After school, I ran home, ate an early dinner with Dad, showered, changed into what was going to have to pass for a costume, then ran out the door to get over to the church. Before I left my driveway, Tyrell sent me a text asking if I could come in for an evening shift because someone called out sick. I was still pissed from the way he sent me home Sunday, so I didn't bother responding. The Shianne tutoring gig was about to be a thing, so who needed all that FISHto's stress anyway?

On a normal evening First Missionary House of the Lord would've been obscured by dusk. Barely visible against the evergreens huddled behind the building, or the starless night rising over the trees. Tonight it was domed by fluorescence; the light gushing from every open door and window overwhelmed.

Renaming Halloween to Harvest Fest was an effort to snatch some darkness from an accepted tradition, I got that. The pure wattage beaming from the church felt like an effort to destroy darkness period. The bright parking lot forced me squinty and I pawed for my sunglasses.

The front lot had been transformed into a playland with a blue-pink, alluringly unstable bouncy house as its centerpiece. Wind injected the sugar scent of cotton candy and the salt-butter from popcorn directly into my car vents. I rolled my window down because why not, and sniffed the scorched oak from someone's far-off chimney. The medley smell imprinted somewhere behind my eyes so that for the rest of my life, whenever I came across any one of those smells, I'd think about all of them and what this night meant.

Rimming the fun attractions were familiar cars parked in a line, trunks open, festive with colorful construction paper, and streamers, and balloons, and, most importantly, economy bags of candy that each child would help empty. This part was Trunk or Treat. Because, as Jameer mentioned, "the 'trick' in 'Trick or Treat' doesn't seem very godly."

Since the only thing anyone might get out of my trunk was tetanus, an orange-vested volunteer directed me to the side lot with the other nonparticipating cars. Killing my engine, I spotted my fellow Purity Pledgers lounging by the wheelchair ramp.

Everyone except Kiera.

Jameer, dressed as—I didn't know what he was, he was in a robe—met me by my ride.

"Where is she?" I said.

"Inside, with her parents."

Okay, I was staying. Next question. "What are you?"

"Job."

I blinked rapidly.

"He's a guy from the Bible. Don't worry about it. What about you?"

I popped the lapels on my ebony suit, pushed my shades higher on my nose, and did my best Will Smith impression. "I make this look good."

And he didn't have a clue.

I said, "*Men in Black*? Agent J?"

Really, I didn't have a costume. Hadn't had one since I was nine. I had a black suit, and sunglasses, so . . .

Jameer said, "It's science fiction, right?"

"Yeah, real funny and— What's wrong?"

His frown, though. "They won't like it if you're dressed like something from a science fiction movie."

"Why not?" As strange as all this Halloween-as-Harvest-Fest stuff was to me, I understood. Church grounds, don't dress the kids like monsters or devils or ghouls. But what was wrong with a freaking Will Smith character? Me and Dad watched all his movies when I was a kid because for a long time he was the only Black Guy Hero, and Dad wanted me watching men who looked like us doing positive things. Will Smith *fought* monsters in *I Am Legend* and aliens in that super-old one, *Independence Day*. How could that possibly be a bad thing?

Jameer gave our immediate vicinity the I'mma-tell-you-a-secret inspection, twisting all the way around until he was sure nobody but me would hear him. "Pastor got on this thing a couple of years ago about how Hollywood is run by heathens and Satan and all the movies are coded with ways to make families turn their back on God. Like with everything he says, the congregation falls in line. Folks still go to the movies and keep their Netflix accounts, but they don't bring any of it up around here."

"What happens if you don't fall in line?"

"Some adult might pull you aside and lecture you." He shuffled his feet. "If it gets back to Pastor, it might be worse."

"Worse how?"

He chewed his lip, and his hands slid up and down his robe, like to wipe off something dirty. "If anyone asks, say you're a preacher. It'll be easier for you."

Jameer's advice on how to make things easier at First Missionary House of the Lord was creepier than any tiny monster, ghost, or demon wandering door-to-door in other parts of town. Creepier still, I'm not sure if Jameer really recognized that.

Kiera emerged from the church in her Harvest Fest costume, a denim jacket with silver zippers in odd places. Her skirt was plaid, her barely there leggings showed off a little bit of thigh and the sexy curve of her calves, slim thick, still. Red high-top sneakers finished off the outfit. I didn't know what she was supposed to be, but she was what she always was. Hot as hell.

Mya wore black-framed glasses, a red-and-white knit cap, with a matching striped sweater. I recognized her immediately. Wenda, from the Where's Waldo? books. Nice. Helena was some kind of mouse. Not Minnie Mouse, though. Her mouse was definitely more of an Every-Mouse. Shanice, Little Red Riding Hood, maybe.

Kiera flicked eyes my way, then quickly focused on her girls. To Jameer, I said, "Now what? She ain't even looking at me."

"First, we're going to get assigned stations. Then— Oh here we go, follow my lead."

Kiera's mom joined us, and Sister Vanessa trailed her. Deaconess Westing wasn't in costume—I didn't think. She wore jeans, a Howard University sweatshirt, and focused on a clipboard in her hand. Sister Vanessa had fully embraced the occasion of the Purity Pledge/Harvest Fest overlap. She came as a nun.

"Good evening, y'all," Sister Vanessa said. "You look so nice in your costumes tonight, and you're going to help bring a lot of joy to all the younger children who, believe it or not, look up to you as role models. I bet you've all been wondering what this has to do with Purity Pledge, am I right?"

Plucky carnival music from a far-off speaker was the only sound in the awkward pause after that question. Even Kiera, who kept answers loaded like ammo, was slow in responding.

"Well," Sister Vanessa went on, "we're going to show everyone the kinds of boy-girl interactions that are appropriate for people your age. You'll be paired up, and assigned a station. Then you work together in a wholesome, holy, family environment."

"As it was meant to be," added Pastor Newsome, from behind me. I almost squawked.

Did he come from the woods?

Naw. He wasn't some witch emerging from the Dark Dimension. His Audi (license plate: PRZ HIM) was parked behind my car, the automatic interior lights only now winking off.

Silence stretched, everyone waiting for more, as they'd been conditioned to do. Newsome let the moment last a beat, then, "Please go on."

Sister Vanessa said, "Right, assignments."

Deaconess Westing recited names. "Bobby and Shanice. Ralph and Kiera. Delbert and Mya."

Mya-as-Wenda shuffled over, and I shot Jameer a look. What part of that plan was this? I was told maximum quality time with Kiera all night. I assumed he'd somehow gamed the list that Deaconess Westing was reading from, but no. I was going to be working with the same girl I worked with *all the time*.

Jameer got paired with Helena Rickard on cotton candy, while me and Mya would play doormen at the bouncy house. Ralph and Kiera oversaw a prize table near the base of the church steps, topped with the cheap shit kids rarely thought about until they had reams of carnival currency in hand. Slinkys and Wall-Crawlers and Ping-Pong paddles with Spider-Man's face on them. Deaconess Westing explained there were games set up inside the church—Bible Trivia, Bethlehem Skee-ball, Whack-A-Devil—that kids could play for tickets they'd later trade for the merch. Bobby and Shanice would perform their duties there.

Places, everybody.

A steady stream of vehicles bused in kids dressed like things I didn't recognize. A lot of flowy gowns and angel wings. A lot of sports jerseys; the pro-athlete dream was always acceptable in every part of our community. The church parents let their children skitter away in all directions like tossed marbles while they angled for apple cider, pizza, and cake from the snack table.

Me and Mya had the most popular attraction. Our bouncy house rocked for a solid *two hours of the scheduled three-hour event W-T-F Jameer!* So many giddy squeals escaped the flapping nylon entrance, I expected car windows to shatter.

"Socks only," I chanted at each new bouncy house guest, holding the entry flap wide while little ones shimmied inside. A boy ripped up the Velcro straps securing his Superman sneakers, kicked them off. In the folds of what I thought was a Pick-a-Disciple robe, I spotted a toy light saber dangling off his belt. That had to be a no-no, right?

"Are you a Padawan?" I asked, because what self-respecting *Star Wars* fan doesn't want to know another fan's Force proficiency?

Shoe-free and already jumping in place, he showed me the various gaps in his grin. "Nope. I'm a Jedi Master. May the Force beeee with you."

Jameer's warning flashed in my head like the caution lights

by train tracks. I checked for nearby adults with the power to shut down the kid's fantasy, the power to shame him.

The boy followed my gaze. "Are you looking for my mom?" He pointed. "She's over there and she said I could go in the jumpy house if I want."

"Naw, not your mom. I was looking for Sith Lords. You know they're the ancient enemies of the Jedi, right?"

"Yep."

"I don't see any, though. I think they're scared of you."

That got him giggling. He made *VWOOM—VWOOM* noises like his light saber was on and sizzling air, then joined the other jumpers inside.

"You're really sweet with them," Mya said. "*Star Wars*, though?"

The disdain in her voice threw me. "Yeah, so?"

"There are like no black people in that franchise."

I was disgusted. "You're crazy. Lando Calrissian. Saw Gerrera. Finn."

"Ummm"—she ticked them off on her fingers—"traitor, dead, goofy footnote."

"Lando's getting his own movie."

"Too little, too late. Plus, that galaxy far, far away is missing some sistahs! Where the black women, bruh?"

"I—what?"

"While you're thinking, I'll remind you that Lieutenant Uhura has been an integral part of the starship *Enterprise* from day one."

"Oh my God. You're a Trekkie!"

She rushed close to me, shushing. "Keep it low. You know what it's like around here."

So me and Jameer weren't the only Rebel Scum (yeah, I'm running with that) at First Missionary.

Mya, hushed, said, "And I'm not a Trekkie exactly. I like Uhura from the original series, and Burnham from *Discovery*, and Maeve from *Westworld*, and Riri Williams from the *Ironheart* comics. Like Issa Rae said, 'I'm rooting for everybody black.'"

Mya Hanson reads *Ironheart*? This was so unexpected.

I was about to ask about some other comics, when Mya added, "That includes you, Del. I'm rooting for you, too. Get ready."

"For what?"

There was commotion inside the church. Shanice, her red hood falling back on her shoulders, burst outside. "I think Bobby's having an allergic reaction."

A pin-striped Yankee uniform–wearing Ralph abandoned his post next to Kiera. Yelled, "Oh man, does he have his EpiPen?"

Kiera asked the children thrusting prize tickets at her to hang on. "What's wrong with Bobby?"

Ralph climbed the church steps to check on his brother. Though . . .

He seemed a little lazy with it. Not the speed and urgency I'd expect from someone whose family member was having a potentially life-threatening allergic reaction. Before disappearing inside the church, Ralph twisted and we locked eyes.

He winked.

Concerned adults angled their bodies toward the building. While they did, I looked to the cotton candy machine.

Jameer wasn't there.

A quick search, and I saw his Job robe flapping by a spotlight as he tore snaking ropes of prize tickets off a roll for kids who were less-than-scrupulous about how they earned their Harvest Fest currency. He aimed each ticket-rich child toward the table Kiera now manned solo, quickly overwhelming her. When he spotted me watching, he mouthed *Go*.

Mya nodded. "I'm fine. You should get over there."

Hustling over to an outnumbered Kiera, I said, "Tell me what to do."

Her chin cocked like she might object. Then a tiny prize-ticket millionaire demanded she sell him a mini Etch A Sketch. "All the items to your left are either five, ten, or fifteen tickets, depending. The bigger the item, the more it costs. I'll cover the right side. Try to keep up."

I did.

Bobby survived.

Shanice gave us periodic updates. Apparently someone came into the sanctuary with a Reese's Cup, and Bobby thought he'd breathed in peanut butter fumes or something. It got panicky enough where Pastor Newsome thought an ambulance might be needed. People prayed. Miraculously, Bobby's breathing returned to normal before anyone dialed 911.

"Folks still praying around him." Shanice aimed a pointed

look my way. "Probably will be for the rest of the night until his mom can get back to pick him up."

"I am very, very thankful that he's doing okay," I said.

"Uh-huh." She shifted her attention to Kiera. "We don't want to mess up the night for the littles, so carry on."

Kiera rededicated herself to her prize matron role, sorting swag and sweeping popcorn crumbs from her side of the table.

"Should I count the tickets?" I wanted to sound helpful. I crouched near the cardboard box housing the tangled ticket strips.

"That's not necessary. We don't really keep track. It's just a way for the littles to learn something about value."

"Oh." I stood again. We were inches apart. We hadn't been this close since the day I delivered the news about Taylor's IG rant.

Say something, Del! "What are you? I mean your costume. I been trying to figure it out all night."

"Dorothy. From *The Wiz*. The new version. Mama showed me the old one a long time ago, but we DVR'd the new one, and I liked it better."

The answer stunned me. Kindergarten was my first time seeing her as Dorothy; it was the moment I felt our bond cement. This had to be a sign, right? God was trying to tell me something!

"You look great," I said, meaning it and regretting it at the same time. Was it corny?

"Thank you."

There was a lull, and I felt weird about pushing it, so I got back to sorting prizes.

Then she said, "What are you?"

"Oh. Um, a preacher."

She sucked her teeth. "What are you really?"

I lowered my voice. "Agent J from *Men in Black*."

Her smile lit with recognition. "I looove that movie. Me and my brother used to watch it all the time when we were little. He thought the aliens would scare me, but they didn't. I thought the one that looked like a pug was cute."

"How is your brother?"

"Stationed in Guam and loving it."

Bring it back, Del. Keep the conversation here and now. "Do you like science fiction movies? Other than *Men in Black*, I mean?"

A shrug. "They're fine. I mostly watched them with Wes."

Now, Del. Say it! *Maybe we can watch one sometime. Or talk about Purity Pledge over a pizza.*

I cleared my throat. "Kiera, maybe—"

"Excuse me, young man," Pastor Newsome interrupted.

No!

He stood at the top of the church steps, the same approximate height of the pulpit. Looking down on us. "Might I have a word?"

It sounded like a request, something optional. Then, he descended the stairs, grasped my shoulder, and adjusted my clip-on tie. "We can talk in my office."

He climbed the steps, made it to the third one when he stopped and stared at me.

A child dressed in a blue-gold Stephen Curry warm-up padded to the table and tossed a disorderly ticket bundle in Kiera's general direction. "What can I buy?"

Her gaze shifted between him and me.

"You okay?" I hoped she'd give me a reason to stay.

"I'm fine. See you later."

Trailing Newsome, I entered the sanctuary, where most pews had been pushed along the walls, clearing space for the gaming floor. One had been dragged back out, evident by its canted angle. The Burton boys were on it, their baseball uniforms visible between a circle of parishioners still praying for Bobby's health. The way Ralph looked, he might've fired a flare gun to signal a rescue, if he could. Sorry, guys.

Newsome paid the prayer circle no mind. We took the corridor past the Purity Pledge classroom, toward his office. The air got thick with a spicy incense that made my head swimmy. He entered the open door at the very end of the hall, breaking through a thin streamer of white smoke.

"Sit." Newsome took the brown leather chair on the working side of his L-shaped desk. He had a huge monitor positioned on the short side of the L, which butted the wall. His screen saver was a single 3-D word floating to the monitor's border then bouncing off in another direction like an unbreakable soap bubble. The word was "Blessed."

A single incense stick burned next to a fancy gold pen set. A heat ring had eaten it to its slim midpoint. A broken ash snake settled beneath it, and I found it hard to look at anything else when I sat.

"Mr. Rainey!" he said, forcing my attention to him.

I didn't like when grown-ups called me "mister." It felt like they were telling toddlers that they're "big boys." Still, I said, "Yes, sir."

"You're probably wondering what this is about."

My costume? Maybe someone overheard what I was really supposed to be. Was this the "let me tell you how we do things here, son" lecture Jameer warned me about?

Silently, I awaited my reaming.

Newsome said, "I hear you're taking that sex class over at the high school. I'm going to need to know more about that."

CHAPTER 12

SILENCE STRETCHED BETWEEN US WHILE I processed what I'd heard. "Healthy Living? You want to talk about that?"

"Yes, I believe that's how they're referring to it." He reached beneath his desk and brought out a legal pad and a pencil. "Tell me a bit about what they're exposing you to."

Why did he want to talk about Healthy Living?

He said, "I don't mean to make you uncomfortable, son."

"I'm not uncomfortable." Lie.

"You and your mother only been coming to service for a couple of months now? It's so nice that you've joined us. We don't get a lot of new blood, and we're always happy to see wholesome families grace our pews. Is your father in the home?"

What? "Yes. My dad lives with us."

"Awesome. I know good stock when I see it."

I had a hard time figuring how any of this stuff fit together. My dad living with me making me good stock. Healthy Living. New blood in the church. I didn't really want to talk to Pastor Newsome, in his office, alone, but we were chatting it up just the same.

"Do you like it here at First Missionary, Mr. Rainey?"

"It's okay."

"You never had the good fortune to meet our First Lady, Odessa." He motioned to a framed photo on his desk, turned outward. It was a portrait of a thin, wrinkled brown lady in a bright silver wig. "My wife loved the young people. The Lord never saw fit to bless us with children of our own, so she became exceptionally protective of the youth in our charge—and I don't just mean my niece Vanessa. In a way, every child at First Missionary became our child."

Another ashy stub fell off his incense; the glowing red heat ring crawled toward the stem.

"Odessa got sick a long time ago, and fought hard. Saw a lot of good come to fruition from her direct efforts. Our Thanksgiving program where we provide entire meal kits to needy households. Our Christmas Toy Store where the poorer children from here and surrounding communities come in and pick gifts they couldn't otherwise afford. She made sure to leave her mark."

I couldn't zone out like I did in his sermons. This was one-on-one, couldn't fake my way through this. His stare never wavered.

"I'm sad to say she saw some ugly things in her final days. Shadows descending on our community. All those young ladies at the high school throwing their lives away over momentary temptation. Just about tore Odessa's heart in half." He broke eye contact, staring down at hands he was wringing hard enough to cause a potential friction burn. "I'm sure you know two of the young ladies who made that devil's pact were members here."

I did not. Why would I? Also, the pact wasn't a real thing.

This didn't feel like the right time to bring that up.

Newsome's voice became edged. "On her deathbed, Odessa told me, 'Eldridge, you have to intervene for the Green Creek youth. That's what God's called you to do. And I won't be with you, so you'll have to look for like-minded saints to help.' She said those exact words to me, and that's why I'm talking to you, Mr. Rainey. Do you understand?"

A slow head shake was my only answer.

"I want you to help me save the youth in this town. That starts with you telling me what's been going on in that sex class." He got into a comfortable note-taking position. Wrote the number one in the top left margin of his pad. Waited.

"I'm not sure what to tell you. It's boring stuff mostly. Statistics. Telling us how to avoid places where we might get tempted."

He didn't write anything down. "You said 'mostly.' You don't find it boring all the time."

"That's because of MJ." Then I caught myself, feeling I'd made a misstep. Said too much.

"The English teacher. I know the man." He scribbled something quick and hard on his pad. "He was quite eager to take on this particular task. A man possessed, you might say. How's he handling the mandated curriculum?"

"MJ's good."

"Is he now? He lets you call him that? Just his initials?"

"I—yes. I mean, he's cool." Every answer felt like the wrong answer. Twisting in my chair, I motioned toward the corridor. "Kiera's probably going to need some help."

Newsome scrutinized me while twirling his pen between his index and middle finger like a drumstick. "I met my Odessa at church when I was about your age. It's a special bond that forms when two young people connect over holy pursuits. I can tell you that. I can also tell you that two people pursuing a relationship should be equally yoked. Do you know what that means?"

"No, sir."

"Kiera Westing is a shining star here at First Missionary. Whatever boy is going to live up to her Holy Father's standard, her earthly father's standard"—he patted his chest by his heart—"her pastor's standard, will need to be a shining star, too."

Slow anger bled into my discomfort.

"Mr. Rainey, I've been very clear with my congregation about the evils of that class. It's been the exact wrong reaction to the pregnancy pact."

"There wasn't a pact."

"Excuse me?" His smile slipped. Neither one of us was doing very good by our Harvest Fest masks at that point.

"Nothing."

"As I was saying, I'm not completely comfortable with you participating in both the Purity Pledge and that sex class. I've overlooked it because my niece says you've been doing well, but I'm on the fence about how far I should let you go. There's no telling what sort of corruption they're infecting you with. I simply need more information to evaluate. Understand?"

"It sounds like you're saying if I don't tell you about Healthy Living, you're going to kick me out of Purity Pledge."

He pressed his pen to his pad. "Shall we continue our talk?"

It wasn't our talk. It was my talk. About all we'd covered in Healthy Living. Babies. Diseases. Contraception.

Newsome interrupted me. "Mister Jay is encouraging you to seek contraceptives?"

"MJ's not saying go out and buy a bunch of condoms. Just that you should have them if you're going to do something where you'd need condoms."

He wrote down way more than what I'd said.

"Does Mister Jay stick strictly to the approved curriculum?"

"Yes."

"You said it isn't boring all the time."

"That's not exactly what I—"

"How does Mister Jay liven up the curriculum? Consider your response carefully, because I'll have much to think about once we're done."

Get up. Walk out. What could he do to stop you, Del?

All the work I'd done to win Purity Pledge, though. A word from him, and I was done. My best connection to Kiera severed.

And, it wasn't like there was any real dirt on MJ. "He lets us ask questions. Like, if something was confusing, or wasn't covered, he'll talk to us about it."

"Wasn't covered? Like what?"

"I don't know."

"Yes, you do. Don't lie to me in my house, Mr. Rainey."

I thought it was the Lord's House. I should've said it. I didn't.
"I mean, like, he's got a kid, and we asked him about how that
was. If it was hard like the lessons say it would be."

"He discusses his personal life with you children?"

"He answers our questions."

Newsome rocked back in his chair, fingers steepled under his
chin. Then, he rotated his chair toward his monitor, awaking
his computer, and typing into a blank document. "I look forward to speaking with you again soon. Close the door on the
way out, and have a blessed night."

That was it?

A good forty-five minutes had passed. Bobby and Ralph were
no longer in the sanctuary. Remaining were adult volunteers
who tipped tables onto their sides, folding the legs flat beneath,
stacked gray aluminum chairs on a rolling cart, or swept the
limp remains of ruptured balloons into dustpans. Upbeat gospel music cranked through the sound system.

I crossed the floor fast, needing to be outside, away from
there.

"Del." Sister Vanessa angled toward me.

"Yes, ma'am?"

"Is everything all right?"

"Fine."

She glanced toward her uncle's office. "Are you sure?"

"I—" What was she even asking me? "Yeah. I'm sure."

Nudging past Sister Vanessa, I escaped into the night air. The
Harvest Fest now had a deserted feel. Half-deflated, the angular

peak of the bouncy house flopped sideways like the tip of a wizard's hat. Most of the Trunk or Treat cars were gone, leaving wide gaps in the previously full lines. All the Purity Pledgers performed cleanup tasks at their assigned stations.

Jameer shoveled cotton candy clouds into a large plastic bag Helena held wide for him. His attention was on me, not the task. They'd all seen Newsome walk me off.

I shook my head in his direction. Later, bro. I wanted to pick up where I left off at the prize table. I stopped cold when I saw the new customer handing an absolutely jubilant Kiera a short string of carnival game tickets.

Welcome to the Annual First Missionary House of the Lord Harvest Fest, Mason Miles.

CHAPTER 13

HOW? HOW WAS HE HERE?

I reclaimed my previous position behind the table, coming into the middle of Kiera and Mason's conversation. They didn't even notice.

Mason, motioning at his outfit, a black trench coat with a dark turtleneck underneath, said, "—he wore in book five of the series, when he was off the grid in New York City and acting as an urban mercenary."

Kiera's grin was wide. "Wow! That sounds cool."

"Hey." I cleared my throat. "What are we doing here?" I kind of waved at the table, like that's what I meant.

Mason, oblivious to the deep-sea pressure from tension squeezing us on all sides, said, "What up, Del!"

I nodded.

Kiera said, "Mason was telling me about his costume."

"Jack Jake," I said. Monotone.

Mason's goofy, idiot face lit up. "You like the JJ series, too?"

"No, Mason. I don't. It's just, whenever you do book reports—"

Kiera said to him, "I didn't think you were going to come by."

He said, "When you told me about it Sunday, I didn't know if I'd have to help my sisters with their homework. Our mom works night shifts, so if the twins are having a hard time with math or science, that's on me. But we wrapped up early, so I figured I'd at least get them out the house and see if you were still here."

"We are," I said.

We all bobbed aimlessly. Kiera crossed her arms, bounced on her toes. I stood my ground. Mason made awkward glances over his shoulder at the two tall, gangly girls tossing bean bags at a cornhole board.

He broke first, and said, "I oughta get my sisters so that cornhole guy can go home."

"You should've come earlier," Kiera said.

No. He shouldn't have.

Mason stepped backward, moving toward his sisters while never breaking eye contact with Kiera. He tapped his temple. "Noted. I will always listen to Kiera Westing's advice on events and timeliness going forward."

She said, "You better."

"See you in school tomorrow." Then he spun on his heels, jogged to his sisters. No bye for me, huh, Mason?

The twin girls, maybe nine or ten years old, in costumes that seemed like Disney princesses, though I couldn't tell from which movies, squealed their disappointment when he told them it was time to go. He was stern, not mean, and Kiera watched the interaction the way an animal lover watched sloth videos on YouTube.

Enough.

I said, "Pastor wants us to get together."

Her chin whipped my way with ample speed to cause a neck injury. "What?"

"To discuss ideas for our final Purity Pledge presentation. The week-eight assignment." I didn't know where it was coming from. It was like my tongue belonged to someone else, some-*thing* else.

Was this divine intervention?

"You're thinking about the week-eight assignment already?"

"Pastor said we should."

"That's what he wanted to talk to you about?"

"Yes." Smooth. No hesitation. "Since we're sort of the elders, he suggested we start brainstorming. I'm kind of busy with my new tutoring gig, but I was thinking Friday night. Mama Marian's downtown."

She blinked rapidly, as if I'd shined a bright light in her face. "Umm, okay."

I whipped my phone out, held it to her. "Let me get your number."

"If Pastor says so." Spooked, blindsided, and stunned, she still did exactly what I said, punching in the seven digits. I immediately hit the Call button, and she jumped, startled by her phone buzzing in her back pocket.

I said, "Now you've got my number, too. We'll be talking much more." I raised my hand for the customary Purity Pledge high five.

She slapped my palm sheepishly. "First Missionary Crew!"

Damn right.

Me and Kiera didn't speak much the rest of that night. Actually, I didn't speak much to anybody the rest of that night. Not Jameer. Not Mom and Dad. Not Qwan when he sent his texts asking me how it went. Despite that absolutely genius chess move I pulled from thin air to finally get a date with Kiera, Harvest Fest felt more like a fail than anything. It wasn't because of Mason—who was definitely a problem, but one that could be solved. Weirdly enough, the thoughts that made me toss and turn that night were about Healthy Living, and MJ.

I'd told the truth. That shouldn't be wrong, but the truth could be a weapon depending on who used it.

That wasn't Bible, but it was the kind of thought that would fit right in.

What was the worst Newsome could do with that info I gave him? In English class the next day, I got my answer.

We had a substitute. MJ never showed. I was too scared to ask anyone if they knew why.

In the gym, there was a sign posted on the classroom corridor: HEALTHY LIVING POSTPONED, DRESS OUT FOR YOUR REGULAR GYM CLASS.

It could be coincidence, right? Maybe MJ was sick.

Then why would the girls' Healthy Living class be postponed, too?

Get real, Del. How could anything you said during a conversation with Pastor Newsome last night have this much of an effect less than twenty-four hours later? You are not responsible for this.

But for someone who'd pulled off such a thrilling lie to get Kiera to dinner this Friday, I sucked at lying to myself.

CHAPTER 14

AS AGREED, SHIANNE MET ME by my car after the final bell for the first of our tutoring sessions. She climbed in with a crumpled Red Bull can and alarming wide eyes. None of the school vending machines sold energy drinks, but I knew who the caffeine plug was. "You copped from Kent Oster. You really are flaunting your wealth now."

"His one hundred and fifty percent markup only seems steep when you aren't desperate. I so needed this. Home, Jeeves!"

We did the slow crawl out of the school lot. While we inched along, I said, "You haven't heard anything about MJ today, have you?"

Her face crumpled. "Mister Jay? Why would I hear anything about him?" She jerked forward, snapping her seat belt tight across her body. "Oh, he isn't a Baby-Getter Dad, is he?"

"No! That's not what I meant. Never mind." Though that wouldn't have been too far off from escalating BabyGetterToo drama. Last I heard, a couple of the previously anonymous dads were getting sued for child support, or were going on the offensive by asking for DNA tests. Maury Povich shit I didn't care that much about, if I was being honest.

I hoped MJ was okay.

It was silly asking Shianne. Mom would've said this was my guilt talking. I turned up the music, focused on that.

There was virtually no traffic headed in the direction of Shianne's house. She lived in Green Creek's oldest-money neighborhood, Poplar Estates. These were houses built a long time ago, like over a century. Dad said my great-grandparents wouldn't have been allowed to live in this part of town, because back then you had two barriers to overcome: money and skin color.

Now it was mostly just money, which the Griffiths family had plenty of. Shianne's dad was some executive for the meat-packing company that ran a big plant in the neighboring town. Her mom helped start some software firm in college that she and her partners sold for big dough when Shianne was a kid. Now she worked on various apps and coding projects at her leisure. Their neighbors were the lawyers and doctors and bankers of our community. I knew all this from the times I used to bike to her place and eat Hot Pockets while doing homework in her family room.

I hadn't come to this side of town since I last visited her, way before Baby Zoey. It always struck me how the sky seemed wider and bluer over the rich part of town.

On her street, we passed Tanisha Thompson's house, location of our imaginary sexcapade. Tanisha and friends had gotten out of the school lot before us, and were in her driveway, exiting Tanisha's new Chevy SUV. At neighborhood speed limits, me, my car, and my passenger were easily recognized, and I saw the speech bubbles hovering over their scowling heads like a comic book panel: *Is that Shianne in Del's car?*

Shianne responded with a rock-steady middle finger that got Tanisha and crew popping their necks and angrily gesturing in my rearview as we cruised past.

I said, "Y'all are closer than ever, I see."

"I can't wait to get out of this town, Del."

We turned a corner and approached Shianne's distinct home, which reminded me of a mini version of the White House. It was pale, close to gray, with these columns bordering the front door. I parked in her driveway and she led me inside, triggering such a strong sense of déjà vu that the crying baby confused me a minute. Like, whose kid was that?

Missus Griffiths met us in the foyer, with a fussy little Zoey on her hip. "Shianne, this baby has been cranky all day and I couldn't get anything done." She'd been laser focused on Shi, and only seemed to recognize my presence after she spoke her piece. "Del, what are you doing here?"

"I'm going to help Shi get caught up on some schoolwork."

"Lovely. I hope you two can work with Zoey in the room," she passed the baby, who began shrieking like she saw evil spirits, "because I had to move all of my conference calls to late afternoon."

Shianne bounced her daughter lightly while flinching from

her screams. "Are any bottles ready?"

Missus Griffiths was already backing into her home office. "In the fridge." The last word was clipped by her slamming door.

Shianne said, "You remember where the family room is?"

"Of course."

She motioned in the general direction, and broke off to get Zoey's meal.

I delved deeper into the house, making familiar turns while cataloging changes. A thick hallway runner now covered what were once bare floors. The walls were a different color, pale green. It smelled different, some strong, cotton-y air freshener plugged into the wall.

The family room was pretty much the same, with the exception of a newer, wider television. I fell into my old preferred seat at the corner of a plush sectional sofa and turned on ESPN.

While random highlights played, my phone buzzed. I slipped it from my pocket, read.

Kiera: Del, I've been thinking of our final presentation. I have a couple of ideas, but maybe we should loop in Jameer? He's always got good input.

My head got airy, like the time me and Qwan spent way too long making our voices funny off the helium tank at the school carnival. I'd pulled a Qwan move, deliberately avoided texting Kiera first since we exchanged numbers. Risky, but important to sell the "Pastor wants this" part of the plan. I couldn't seem too eager. That she wanted to include Jameer didn't bother me much—I'd kind of expected it. He was on my team, so I could work that, too. I responded with giddy speed.

> **Me:** Cool. Should I pick y'all up
> on Friday?

> **Kiera:** I'll ask my dad to drive me and J.
> Less complicated that way, trust me. Six
> o'clock?

> **Me:** Yep

I knew this went against Qwan's mandate to not show too much interest, but I couldn't resist adding:

> **Me:** Can't wait

"Why you looking so goofy?" Shianne asked, suddenly beside me, her baby quiet now that a bottle was in hand. She leaned over my shoulder. "Who you texting?"

My phone went facedown on my thigh. "Nosy."

"Whatever." She went for the far end of the couch, began to sit, then stopped, scanning the area. "Crap. Left my books in the kitchen."

She lunged at me, thrusting the baby forward. "Hold her a sec."

I damn near somersaulted over the back of the chair. "Hell no. She's tiny."

"She's tougher than you think."

"I don't know how, Shi."

Huffing, she said, "You make a cradle with one arm, let your chest be like a backboard. Keep her head up, and hold her bottle with your other hand."

Running wasn't an option because, apparently, new mothers had cheetah speed. Before I could protest further, little Zoey was wedged into the crook of my elbow, only squirming in the moment her bottle left her lips while Shi made minor adjustments to my hold technique. Then the feeding resumed, with me tilting the bottle at an angle the child was happy with.

"Shi!" I pleaded.

"It'll be thirty seconds, Del." She was halfway around the corner. "If she doesn't make it we're both going to jail, so don't mess up."

Zoey's eyes pinned me, big brown marbles that expressed mild curiosity over her new food supplier, though no objections. When my initial adrenaline rush tapered, I realized my terror was unwarranted. Me and Zoey were doing fine.

Shi returned, slung her backpack onto the middle couch cushion, but did not reclaim her child. Instead she flopped, with her arms spread wide and head angled toward the ceiling, eyes closed, groaning. "Red Bulls do not last like they used to."

I said, "Do you want her back?"

"In a sec. Let her finish the bottle."

I did, observing what could only be described as ecstasy on

the girl's face as her belly filled. With her bottle nearly empty, I asked, "What are we studying?"

Shianne did not open her eyes when she said, "Del, so, real talk . . . I don't need you to tutor me. My grades were always better than yours."

What? "Why am I here, then?"

"My parents don't trust me to do things on my own anymore. 'You're still going to college! You're still getting a degree! In spite of your self-sabotage!' It's like they're mixing punishment with proactiveness. I don't know. They said get a tutor. You're the only person I can stand at that school right now, and they like you. So I got you. I'm sorry if that sounds shitty. Since Zoey was born, I don't have much of a filter."

That was unexpected. I tried to decide if I should be offended. "Am I still getting paid?"

"Yes."

I was not offended.

Though, I did wonder. "None of your other friends?"

"I don't have any other friends these days."

The baby drained the remnants of her bottle and squirmed. "What now?"

Shianne stretched toward me. "Hand her over. Gotta burp her."

That was definitely beyond my pay grade, so I walked Zoey to her mother, and let Shianne get about the business of baby gas. This did bring to mind all the subconscious warnings MJ's Healthy Living lessons were hammering into us.

My guilt-soaked questions about MJ's whereabouts tried to resurface, but I forced them back down. Focused on Shianne's problems, her worries.

She was always well liked in school. Now she had to pay me for company? No friends? "How is that possible? What about the other Baby-Get—" Shit.

She leaned toward me, patting Zoey's back lightly while her lip twitched. "Go on. Say it to my face. You wouldn't be the first."

I heavy-sighed. "The Baby-Getters."

"Right. To answer your question, why aren't I friends with them? I wasn't friends with them before, despite what News Channel 12 wants everyone to think. Besides, if the town's treating us like a coven of witches when we never really hung together, what would it be like if we all started mass playdates?"

"I didn't think about that."

She swiped a hand my way, slow, no energy. "Why should you? It's not your problem. I don't mean to take it out on you. Let's get to 'work.'" She made finger quotes with one hand.

It wasn't a total scam. Shianne didn't need my help with school stuff, but an extra set of arms for Zoey didn't hurt. I played with the little girl while Shi did pre-calc problems. When the room got suddenly fragrant in a way that made me think of despair, Shianne took Zoey for a diaper change while I texted Jameer about Friday's dinner with Kiera. Basically telling him we needed a good way for him to make an exit at some point in the evening. He didn't respond right away, but I'd be thinking on it for sure.

When Mister Griffiths arrived home, he greeted me warmly ("Del, long time!"), paid me my fifty bucks promptly, then quizzed Shianne on all the responsible things she'd done today. My cue to leave.

"See you in school tomorrow, Shi."

Glum: "We can only hope."

At home, there was no family dinner. Mom and Dad left a note about catching a movie, and I rummaged in the freezer for microwave sesame noodles. While my meal cooked, I caught sight of the ever-present car insurance bill sitting on the counter. I supposed I could've left the fifty bucks I'd earned being Shianne's study buddy on the envelope as a down payment, but, if I did that, I might come up short at dinner with Kiera on Friday. Unthinkable.

I slept rough again, my worries about Healthy Living and MJ attacking my defenseless subconscious. So I can't overstate the relief I felt the next day when I walked into English class and found MJ back behind his desk, prepping his teaching materials.

"MJ!" I said upon seeing him. As enthusiastic as a First Missionary Crew! high five.

His response crushed my delight like a hydraulic press. "Del, have a seat, please."

His voice was flat, emotionless. Very un-MJ-like. It was worse than if he'd yelled, "Del, you snitch."

I folded into my seat, as did my other classmates, and spent the rest of the lecture measuring MJ's every word, every movement. His energy was low, the lecture had a going-through-the-motions feel. At the end, I toyed with the idea of slipping out quietly. Probably would've been for the best. Instead, I lingered. When the class was empty, I said, "MJ?"

"Del, I have to tell you, if you have more questions like the kinds we've discussed over the past few weeks, I can no longer entertain them." It sounded rehearsed, and robotic.

"I—" I almost apologized, before recognizing that would be an admission of guilt. I didn't *know* this had anything to do with me. So, I said, "Is something wrong?"

He answered too fast. "No. There have been some directives passed along to me about what is and isn't appropriate subject matter on school grounds."

"Is that why Healthy Living was postponed?" It felt like a safe question to ask. Everyone saw that note.

"Healthy Living is canceled, Del."

That landed like a blindside slap. "For . . . good?"

He looked past me to the open classroom door, checking for spies. Waved me closer, and I moved to him reluctantly, halfway expecting a punch.

"Del, you haven't told anyone about me answering those questions for you outside of class, have you?"

"No. I didn't tell anyone about that."

"What about the Q and As at the end of Healthy Living?"

I swallowed hard. "Nope."

"Well, someone has."

"What do you mean?"

"Look, there are people in town who are dead set against any discussion of sex, biology, really anything even close to human reproduction—despite all of the real-world examples we've seen lately. I got called into a meeting yesterday morning about some of those parties being outraged over a strict curriculum being altered on the fly. Or something. I'm still not clear on what the exact issue is. It was enough for an already reluctant council to pull the plug on Healthy Living, so we can 'revisit the focus of the course.'"

There was a question I dreaded, but needed to ask. "Are you in trouble?"

"Naw. Not for real. A lot of people talked at me yesterday, but it's nothing that's going to cause me problems. I'm worried about you."

"Me?" Had he seen through my guilt? My lies?

"You students. The information from Healthy Living was super basic, I'll admit. But it was better than nothing. This whole community has seen what ignorance gets. Yet, year after year, the adults who are supposed to know better think that if we hide all the sex talk from you, you're not going to do it. It's something about getting old, particularly around here, that makes people forget they were teens once too."

It felt like he was talking to a wider audience than me. His usual lecture energy had returned.

Too bad the guy who betrayed him was the only one around to hear it. "I should get going, MJ."

"Yeah, of course. Sorry to unload on you like that. Enjoy your lunch."

He went back to the whiteboard, scrawling notes for his next class. I could tell he'd already moved on from the dismantling of Healthy Living. He'd washed his hands of it.

Somehow, I knew I'd have a much harder time.

In that Thursday Pledge session after my conversation with MJ, and before my night with Kiera, everything felt too fragile. I kept watching the door of the Pledge room, expecting Pastor Newsome to swoop in at any time and cast me out of the Lord's House for *my* impropriety. He got the scoop on Healthy Living from me. He didn't need me anymore.

We never saw Newsome that evening, though I kept looking over my shoulder even on my way out the door. When someone called my name, my brain turned that person into Newsome. I spun around, queasy.

It was Mya. "Hey, Del, wait a second."

"What's up?"

She fished something out of her bag, handed it over. "Here."

A comic book. *Shuri*, issue #1. Black Panther's sister in her own standalone book. This was unexpected.

"It's about a black woman by a black woman, so I bet you haven't read it."

That sounded harsh. I'd been meaning to pick it up. "This is what we're doing now? Trading passive-aggressive recommendations. If so, you should read—"

"Please don't say Batman. All you boys love Batman."

"Have you given *Tower of Babel* a try? Batman's plans take

down the whole Justice League!"

She groaned, pointed at her gift. "If you read that, I might consider a Batman book. Maybe. I want a book report on my desk by Monday." She kept on to her rust-bucket car.

"Mya! For real, why you give me this?"

"Good conversation the other night. Don't necessarily like what you said, but figured I might show you the light. See you in school."

Then she was gone, and I was driving Jameer home, that issue of *Shuri* resting on my backseat. For later.

Off church grounds, I started to relax a bit.

That wasn't the truth. I was getting excited.

"You know the plan?" I asked Jameer, wanting no confusion over the explicit instructions I'd given him.

"Mister Westing will bring me and Kiera to the restaurant, where you'll be waiting. We'll order an appetizer. I'll eat my portion quickly, then excuse myself to the bathroom, but really I'll step outside while you continue to chat her up. Eventually, she'll start to wonder where I am, at which point"—he snatched that clamshell phone of his from his pocket for review—"sorry, how's this part supposed to work?"

I kept it cool, didn't let any annoyance slip into my voice. "I'm going to send you a text when she gets antsy. That's when *you text her*, and say . . . ?"

"Right. My text will say I was feeling sick and I got my mother to pick me up."

"And?" This part was important.

"I'll mention that I didn't want to interrupt you two because it looked like you were having a good time."

I snapped my fingers. "Perfect."

It was plausible. Didn't put Kiera in a position where she felt she had to leave for Jameer's sake, and didn't get into a creepy setup vibe because we were still in a loud public place. We could talk about Purity Pledge, sure, but that wouldn't take all night. Who knew what direction things took after that?

"How are you getting home, by the way?" I asked.

Jameer said, "A friend."

I didn't know Jameer had other friends besides me and Kiera. But, okay. If he was good, I was good. Until . . .

We reached his house, and I thought about his doorless, mirrorless room.

I came close to asking more about it. Probing to make sure he was, indeed, good.

We were in such a solid place with the Kiera plan, though. Best not to spoil the vibe. I dropped him off, went home, and fell into my first good night of sleep that week.

In the morning, sunlight peeked around the edges of my closed blinds, waking me moments before my alarm would've went off. I didn't mind. Tonight was the night, me and Kiera. Wonder if I could convince her to take an after-dinner drive with me. I opened my blinds to look at this new day full of all the possibility in the world and found my driveway parking spot empty.

My car was gone.

"Mom!" I shot down the stairs barefoot, tugging a sweatshirt over my head, holding car keys that would do me absolutely no good. "Dad!"

Groggy at the top of the stairs, pulling the flaps of her robe closed, Mom said, "Del, what on earth?"

Dad, in a T-shirt and boxers, pressed up to Mom's back. "Junior?"

"Call the cops," I said, working my foot into my other shoe, "someone stole my car."

I reached for the knob, unsure what I planned to do when I got outside. Check the driveway for skid marks, fibers, and DNA?

Dad trotted down the stairs, grabbing my arm before I jetted into the cold morning. "Calm down, son. No one stole the car."

"What do you mean? I parked it last night and it's missing. Look."

Mom descended the stairs, groaning, massaging the small of her back. She removed her cell from her robe pocket, tapped the screen. "I'm texting Cressie now."

"Why are you texting Cressie? What's she got to do with—"

No. No. Nononononono.

Dad said, "She came home late last night. You were knocked out, so we didn't bother to wake you."

"But you let her take my car?"

Mom huffed. "That car's for both of you. Last time I checked, you weren't exactly honoring your part of our driving agreement."

"Where is she now?"

Mom's phone buzzed, and she read the incoming text. "'At Waffle House. Be home later.'"

"How am I supposed to get to school?"

Mom, ice cold, said, "The bus still stops at the corner. I'm having coffee. Anyone else want some?"

CHAPTER 15

QWAN CAUGHT UP TO ME in school, and risked his life by asking, "How was the bus?"

"Rolling purgatory. How the hell did you get here?" I'd been cranky when I texted him the bad news about my thieving sister this morning. Suspicious when he responded with a calm "ok, see you in class."

"Angie's van. It's all hers, D. Her uncle gave it to her because it's like half-a-deathtrap. But she watched YouTube videos and taught herself to fix it."

Jealousy gnawed. "You could've told her to come pick me up."

"Maybe, but then she might've been weird about us making out in the ride before homeroom. Bro, there's like a whole couch in that thing."

"Judas."

"I can't believe Cressie's back again. You think she missed me?"

"No."

"How she looking?"

"Bitch, that's my sister!"

"So . . . good?"

"I haven't seen her, Qwan." Perhaps the snap in my voice was as horrible as I imagined. He flinched. Backed off the totally irritating questions for the kind-of-irritating ones. "She gonna let you have the ride back for your thing with Kiera tonight?"

Who knew? Since Cressie's last update to Mom, she hadn't responded to any of my extremely detailed texts explaining my dire need.

Qwan, maybe sensing the land mine his foot hovered over, moved on. "You thought about how you gonna kick your game tonight?"

His assumption that I'd still make my date, and that I'd have the opportunity to work things in my favor, was comforting. The power of positive thinking, right? My best plan: "Go on the offensive. No more passive plans, or schemes, or whatever."

"That's what I'm talking about, D. Look, when you get seated at the restaurant, you gotta make it seem like you're used to this sort of thing, though. Take charge. Girls like that. Say something like hey, the hush puppies are great here. I'm going to order you some."

"Does that place have hush puppies?"

"Don't matter. The idea is you're in control. She don't even have to worry about trivial stuff like ordering her own food when you're around."

Even I knew enough to know how dumb that sounded. First

of all, Qwan might be a sexual dynamo, but the number of date-dates he'd been on . . . questionable. "Where did you get that from?"

"Saw it in a movie."

Wonderful. "Did it work with Angie?"

Qwan shrugged. "She don't like hush puppies."

When asked about the possibility of borrowing one of their cars, each of my parents took the time to remind me, in their own special way, about the difference between my automobile-related expenses and my recent income. Of course I tried Dad first, hoping for a little understanding. His rejection was gentle. "I'm sorry, but I really don't want your mom to kill me."

I found Mom in the kitchen, poring over a number of torn envelopes—power company, cable, mortgage—with her laptop humming, and her checkbook ready. Her frown was chiseled on, and I didn't immediately flee the room. Desperate times . . .

"Mom . . ."

"You are not getting my car keys. Boy, bye."

My recently retired Schwinn ten-speed sat canted between stacked boxes and old luggage in the garage. The tires were still plump and tight, something I might've considered good news if I wasn't riding a freaking bike to my dinner with Kiera freaking Westing.

The frigid breeze bit into my face and hands as I coasted through the Green Creek streets. It was a short ride, a couple of miles, but I did it fast so I could chain my bike to a lamppost a full block from the restaurant with time to spare.

Priority number one: a good dinner and alone time. If I nailed that, I could survive my carless weekend relatively unscathed.

Mama Marian's, with its African-themed red, black, and green walls, was a new restaurant in an old bank building from when Green Creek was founded in the 1800s. It still looked like a bank, vault and all. The big round porthole door was painted black, and permanently wedged open at the kitchen's entrance. A little weird, but since the only restaurant I'd spent time in lately was Monte FISHto's, I was fine with the decor. The earthy scent of seasoned greens, a whiff of sugar and cinnamon from fresh-baked sweet potato pies, the pop and sizzle of battered chicken hitting hot grease. My stomach contracted with anticipation, and I fired off a text to Kiera.

Me: I'm at the spot. You nearby?

Kiera: Close. Be there in like two minutes

Awesome.

"How many, sweetie?" The hostess shuffled menus and pre-wrapped cutlery behind her podium.

"Three."

"Let me know when they're here."

Right on time, Deacon Westing's car slipped into a spot at the curb, Kiera and Jameer piling out. On the fly, I made a decision. I exited Mama Marian's, walked right past Kiera and Jameer, squatted at the open passenger window of the car, and said, "Hope you're having a blessed night tonight, Deacon."

He was behind the wheel in a plaid shirt and khakis, the citrus notes of his cologne wafting toward me. "Same to you, Del. I'm happy to hear you all taking your pledge so seriously."

"I treat the Bible like an instruction book, sir. It's like Psalm 119:9 says, 'How can a young person stay on the path to purity? By living according to your word.'"

Deacon Westing smacked his thigh. "Well, ain't that the truth!" Suddenly, he was digging in his pocket, freeing a thick leather billfold. "Kiera has money, but here," he slipped a twenty to me, "in case you kids want to get some dessert. Gotta indulge sometime."

I played bashful while pressing the bill into my hip pocket. "That's true, sir. That's true."

When I backed away, he yelled past me to Kiera, "Sweetie, let me know if you think you're going to be late. Okay?"

"Yes, Daddy!" she said, eyes narrowed, scrutinizing me.

"You kids have a wonderful night of fellowship." His car motored away, and I faced my friends. "Shall we?"

Kiera still seemed perplexed, but Jameer, that look on his face was awe. He knew good work when he saw it. On our way into the restaurant, I said, "I'm going to order us some extra hush puppies. They're good here."

I requested the hostess give us a booth, and when Kiera sat, I slid in next to her. She seemed slightly surprised, but this was part of the choreography me and Jameer had discussed. It was better that I already be situated next to Kiera when he made his exit so we could remain close without me making things awkward.

The first basket of hush puppies arrived and Kiera got right to business. "Group work isn't always my favorite, but I think our Purity Pledge class is well equipped to pull off something special. I was thinking maybe a skit, or something. We can play out some of the good and bad scenarios we've learned about."

"A skit?" Jameer said, chomping a hush puppy in half. "We could do a purity rap, too?"

"Don't make me reach across this table and pluck you in your forehead, Jameer," Kiera snapped back in a way I hadn't seen before, sort of sassy.

Couldn't help but laugh a little, and Kiera turned on me, playful but direct. "You have a problem with my skit idea, too?"

"I'm not saying it's corny." I fiddled with the straw that came with my water.

"What are you saying?"

"I was hoping not to say anything, and the corniness could remain implied."

Kiera popped her neck, and made a show of flipping her hair over her shoulder. "The devil is a lie."

It was one of those phrases that got tossed around Purity Pledge, and I guess First Missionary, a lot. Something I'd logged into the corniness column at first, and had to get Jameer to decode. "The devil is a lie," not "a *liar*." It was like the black church version of "your initial hypothesis is incorrect" or "mf'er, you wildin'."

Kiera wasn't angry. She smiled. Was relaxed. Her hip brushed mine. While she looked away, I flicked a glance Jameer's way. *Now.*

Jameer made a show of rubbing his stomach. "I'm going to run to the restroom, guys. Be right back."

Of course he wouldn't. He slid from the booth, made his way toward the front of the restaurant as our waitress returned. "Y'all ready to order."

I started rattling off what I wanted, when Kiera interrupted me. "Shouldn't we wait until Jameer's back?"

Almost fumbled there. I still had to pretend I thought he was actually coming back. "Right, right. Can we have a minute?"

The waitress departed, while I slipped my phone out beneath the table, prepared to send the signal for Jameer to text back saying he was out for the evening. Kiera sipped on the lemonade she ordered, then coughed, and coughed some more. Loud, hacking explosions while she kneaded her fist into her sternum trying to stave off the choking fit. She stabbed a finger at her glass, and shook her head, signaling she'd swallowed wrong.

I smacked her back the way my mom did whenever it happened to me.

The coughs slowed. "Sorry . . . fine. I'm . . . fine. Sorry."

"You don't have to apologize."

". . . People . . . staring."

"Let them."

My hand remained on her back, massaging in small circles. Only noticed I was still touching her when she said, "Thank you. That feels nice."

The room brightened. Those three words flipped a switch, heightening my perception. Strawberry-scented body spray, boobs stretching her sweater, her thigh brushing against mine. All the stimuli hit me like a quick-handed boxer.

My jeans constricted suddenly, almost painfully. I snatched my hand away from her, reflex tugging the hem of my jacket, concealing the embarrassing insta-bulge.

Frowning, her eyebrows knitting closer together, she said, "Are you okay?"

My horror lasted a second, if that. Kiera looked past me. I twisted slightly, turning my unwelcome erection away from the object of my desire, and found a stricken Jameer, who looked as sick as he was supposed to be pretending to be. He shouldn't be here. This was not part of the plan.

"Hey," he said, "maybe we should go somewhere else."

"What? Why?" This was so far off script my knee-jerk reaction was rage, until I followed the panicked glances Jameer flicked toward the restaurant entrance.

Colossus Turner and three of his thick-necked wrestling teammates were coming our way.

My anger quickly became terror.

The wrestlers arrived and the scene unspooled with painful slowness before me.

Colossus kept examining all the players present. The social calculus didn't make any sense. Kiera wasn't on a date with two dudes. Nothing here seemed romantic. I kept tugging at my jacket, willing my unresponsive hard-on down.

Finally, cautiously, Colossus said, "Del. Jameer."

Jameer said nothing. I tipped my chin slightly.

Colossus said, "Kiera, can we talk outside?"

"No!" she snapped. "Go talk to your kid, or your baby mama!"

The smallest wrestler in the crew laughed lightly, and Colossus saved his most aggressive look of the night for that guy. He smoothed the annoyance off his face before addressing Kiera. Mostly. "Come on. I know you stuck believing all these lies about me, but I miss you, bae. I just want one minute."

"You don't stop, do you?" It sounded like another refusal, but the inch of space between us vanished. Kiera nudged me, pushing me from the booth. I'd have to stand up to let her out. My dick was . . . still . . . hard!

Not any erection, mind you. Harder than a missile. If I stood up, I'd look like the textbook definition of "perpendicular."

"Del," Kiera nudged harder, "let me out."

I nudged back. "Uh, are you sure?"

Colossus's head cocked, the neutral facade he'd maintained cracked. "Stay out of this, Del. Ain't none of your business."

"No," Kiera said, settling back into her seat, "he's right. You're not going to bully me into hearing your tired, trifling excuses. You should be at Taylor's changing diapers."

He wasn't even listening to her. All of his attention was on the attainable victory. "Del, dawg, I ain't never had no problem with you before, but I feel like I'm gonna have to check you now."

Eye contact maintained, I tried for the no-fear approach. Stay calm. Don't let him smell your fear.

"Leave him alone," Kiera insisted, and I finally felt my body soften, the humiliation of her standing up for me having the effect I'd been wishing. Not fast enough.

"Get up so I can talk to my girl!" Colossus snatched my jacket with one hand, effortlessly reeling me from my seat. Exposing me.

"Whoa!" one of the wrestlers said, eyes angled down. "He's like half-tent!"

Jameer saw it too, flinched.

Colossus's fist sprung loose like a reverse bear trap. He backed away, horrified. "Bro, what the hell?"

The other wrestlers laughed, and the embarrassment was the mental equivalent of cold water. I rapidly retracted, the cramped tightness in my crotch becoming cavernous. My only comfort being my back was to Kiera. No way she saw what had all the dudes around me acting like I'd pulled a gun.

"I'm done." Kiera slid from the booth, made for the door.

Colossus called for her. She walked backward while she spoke, her cell raised like a ward against evil. "I'm calling my dad. Would you like to speak to him, too?"

Colossus backed off.

People were staring now. The unwanted attention combined with my embarrassment ejected me from the restaurant. I wasn't chasing Kiera as much as fleeing her ex, but when I spotted her turning the corner in the same general direction of my parked bike, well, why not?

"Kiera, wait up!" She didn't slow down, but I caught her easily.

"You don't need to walk with me, Del. I'm fine."

"I want to walk with you." Blurted so honestly that I regretted it immediately. It didn't feel smooth, it wasn't game.

I went for a neutral follow-up, pushing for—needing—more conversation. "Did you really call your dad?"

"No. If I called Daddy for a ride, it'd cause all kinds of problems that I don't need right now. I'm trying to get an Uber home." She stared at her phone, then extended her arm like that would fix the problem. You couldn't get an Uber in Green Creek. Not fast. Most of the drivers were like an hour away.

"Crap!" she said, reality sinking in. "Where's your car?"

I cycled through dumb lies, but we were coming up on the bus bench I'd chained my bike to; lamplight glinted off pedal reflectors. To sell any of my fabricated stories, I'd have to abandon it for however long I was in Kiera's company tonight. Bikes left unattended too long lost tires, or sometimes got their locks busted and disappeared forever. I conceded and said, "My sister took it."

"How'd you get here?"

Like a magician making his assistant appear from thin air, I flicked my fingers toward my ten-speed with an exaggerated "Ta-DAAA!" gesture. "The preferred mode of transportation for eleven-year-olds across the globe."

She laughed. A sound like acid pumping through my ears, dissolving my insides from the heart down.

Kneeling, I spun the dial on my combination lock. With it unclasped, I freed my bike from the bench, then coiled the lock and chain around the seat post so they wouldn't impede my escape. Tonight's mission: total fail. Any hope for making this work in the future, likely gone too.

Angling the handlebars toward the street, away from Kiera, I said, "I guess I'll see you later."

"I thought you wanted to walk with me."

"I—?" That laugh from before left behind an easy smile. "Yeah."

"On one condition," she said. "I want to ride that bike."

As soon as Kiera mounted my Schwinn, we got a group text from Jameer.

Jameer: You two okay?

I hit him back with a simple Yep.

Kiera said, "I'll tell him where we are."

His next message came before she finished.

Jameer: I'll catch up later. A friend I
haven't seen in a while showed up.

Jameer: Kiera, don't go in the house until
I'm back. You know why.

She frowned, so confused. "What friend?"

I figured my dude was improvising. Still giving me and Kiera the alone time we'd planned for. Though that last text confused me, too. "Why can't you go in the house until he comes back?"

The Schwinn's gears tick-tick-ticked while she pedaled

slowly. "Have you met his parents? We left together, so we can't come back separate. That's trouble for everyone."

"Like how?" There was so little his parents seemed to allow him now, what else could they take away?

"Like getting Pastor involved." Kiera twisted the handlebars away from me, then back, making my bike coast in wide, swooping arcs. Close to me, then far, the wind soft-combing her hair with each turn.

"I don't know what that means."

"It means we're all very careful not to cross the line."

"What line? Who's 'we'?"

"Jameer hasn't told you about baring your soul."

A breeze had started pushing our way, strong enough to howl, so I thought I'd misheard her somehow. The words didn't make any sense.

She must've seen it in my face, so she clarified. "Confessing your sins."

"Oh." I'd seen that a lot on TV, and in movies. "Like in those booths where you talk to a priest behind a screen."

Kiera laughed. "You're thinking about Catholics. That's not how it's done at First Missionary."

"So, how's it done?"

She wasn't laughing anymore. "Publicly. In front of the whole congregation."

I considered that. It seemed kind of extreme, but, "I guess if someone wants to do that, it's their business, right?"

"*Want* has nothing to do with it."

"Wait. You don't mean—? That's a public shaming, Kiera. That's some *Game of Thrones* type sh—stuff."

"Like I said, we're careful. Confession's important, don't get me wrong, I talk to God every night about my offenses, and always ask for His forgiveness. But when Pastor makes you do it that way, it's— I just wouldn't want to."

"So don't. He doesn't actually make people do that, right? You can say no."

She started those wide loops with the bike again. Changed the subject, and I wasn't bothered at all. "Look, I apologize on behalf of my ex-boyfriend for making tonight a mess. Doesn't seem like we're going to get much planning done."

Not that I minded. "I take it there will be no Kee-Lossus reconciliation then."

"Ugh! I hated that stupid nickname."

"I couldn't tell."

She looped my bike around me. "You got jokes?"

"Alls I'm saying is, if you had a wedding gown on layaway, it wouldn't shock me."

Kiera smacked my shoulder hard enough to alter her balance. The bike wobbled and she had to plant a foot to keep from dumping it completely.

"Here." I seized the moment, and grabbed the handlebars. "Let me hop on."

She made as if to climb off. I said, "Naw, stay on. Give me some room."

"Wait, what?"

I got the bike upright with her still on the seat. "Grab my waist and hang on."

"This seems dangerous."

"Only if you don't know what you're doing." I didn't totally know what I was doing. I hadn't ridden a bike double like this since I was ten. "There are pegs on the back tire. Rest your feet on those, and let me do the work."

"Del, I don't know about this."

Hush puppies, I thought. Take control.

I pushed off, had a millisecond of panic where I thought I'd send both of us skidding across the pavement, erasing skin from arms, elbows, and knees. But it really was true what they said about never forgetting how to ride a bike—even double. After three healthy pedal pumps, we were cruising.

We came to a slight hill, went over, picked up speed. Kiera's arms squeezed my waist hard enough to hurt. I welcomed that pain. Had been waiting for it so long. She squealed in my ear.

"What's your favorite place in Green Creek?" I asked.

No hesitation whatsoever. "The library."

That was less than a mile away. An easy ride. A few minutes later, we came upon the glowing glass atrium of the GCPL. Squeezing the handbrake, I brought us to a smooth and safe stop by the bike rack. Once I got the bike mounted and locked, I checked the time on my phone. "We've only got a half hour before they close."

Kiera seemed giddy under the sodium lights' glare. "Then we better hurry up."

Door chimes announced our entrance, and a bored-looking librarian with copious tattoos informed us of what we already knew. "We're closing soon."

We kept it moving, me following her lead now. She walked directly to the modest teen section, where signs done in colorful graffiti font identified which chunk of the alphabet each shelf held. *A–G. H–P. Q–Z.*

Kiera took us to roughly the last section, of the last shelf, where she skimmed the *W*s. She perked up. "Oh! They got it."

When she pried a volume free, I saw the "it" was a novel by Jacqueline Woodson, glossy in its newness. Kiera flipped the cover open, skimming the writing on the jacket, then brought the open book to her face like she was going to lick it. She inhaled deeply; eyed me like she'd gotten hold of a strong drug. "New book smell is the best smell." She blinked. Put the book back. "You think I'm weird now."

"I don't. I promise."

"Colossus thought this was weird. We came here a couple of times. All he'd do is sit in the corner and read *Sports Illustrated*."

This . . . was an opening I couldn't have planned better if I wanted to. "Come here," I said. "Let me show you something."

I walked her to a wall display marked "Graphic Novels and Trades." Plucked some familiar covers from the rack. *The Walking Dead, Black Science, Miles Morales: Spider-Man*. "These are great, too. I really like *Black Science* because—" Her scowl stopped me. "What?"

"Zombies and stuff?"

"*The Walking Dead*'s about zombies. Not *Black Science*. That's more like interdimensional travel. You see this family . . ."

Her eyes were sort of glassy. "I'm sorry. It's not my thing. I never really got all that stuff. I like reading about real people and places."

"Oh. Right." I put the slim volumes back in the display rack.

Over the PA, the tattooed librarian's voice droned, "*Please make your final selections now. The library will be closing in twenty minutes.*"

My feet shuffled, and my brain scrambled. Why was there suddenly nothing to talk about? "Umm, you gonna check out that book you were looking at?"

"No way. My dad dropped me off at a restaurant. I can't come home with a library book."

"Hide it in your bag." She'd had a big-enough purse slung over her shoulder, and bouncing on her hip, since she left her dad's car. It would do. Also, I really wanted her to take home something she liked, a good reminder of our night.

But she was on her phone, texting. "Jameer's going to meet behind our houses. We better get going then. If me and him get in and convince our parents nothing dumb happened, then we can salvage this jacked-up night."

That stung more than her basically calling my taste in books silly. Up until then, I thought we'd both had a good time.

We walked the two miles from the library to her and Jameer's neighborhood, and had a really good conversation about college, and everything else after high school. Good enough that I thought the evening might end the way I wanted. With a kiss.

Both of us wanted to go to schools far away from Green Creek. She talked about Columbia University in New York City. I hadn't thought about going *that* far, sort of thought I might stay in state, but hearing her talk about the city made me want to look at New York schools now.

"I've got an aunt in New York so we go every summer," she said, during that last quarter mile, my bike gears clicking between us. "That energy. The smell. If there's a total opposite to Green Creek it's that, you know."

I didn't. I'd never actually been to New York. Still, I said, "Sure. I do."

"My mom thinks I'm crazy for wanting to be around all those people, crammed up together. Her words."

I grasped for something to say. "There is a lot of space here."

"I know. Maybe once I'm away from it, I'll appreciate it more. All I know is right now, I want something different."

"So do I." I stopped walking. We were still about a hundred yards from where we were supposed to meet up with Jameer, but I felt a now-or-never moment upon us.

Kiera stopped, too. We stood together. Only the bike between us. She said, "You okay?"

"When I saw you in that Dorothy costume at Harvest Fest, it reminded me of us in that play when we were little. My lion costume had been super itchy, but it was worth it. You know, to be up there in the light with you." My heart felt like those springy doorstoppers that you flick, and they twang back and forth real fast. "I've had a really good time getting to know you again since we started Purity Pledge. I've really seen a different side of you." I didn't know if that part was true. She seemed much like the same Kiera I'd always known. Or not known. But I also wanted her to say something like that back to me. That she saw me differently.

She nodded. "That's . . . cool."

Okay. "Tonight, despite the interruptions, I feel like we really connected. And . . . you know what, this." I leaned over my bike, one hand reaching for her hip, while my face—my lips—moved closer to hers. No doubts. No hesitation.

She pulled away. Two big steps back. "Del. No."

The now-or-never moment stalled. Screeching halt. Damn near left skid marks. "Oh, um. Sorry. I—"

"No. It's fine. I probably . . . maybe I made it seem." She took another step back.

"My bad. I felt we connected—"

She took a couple of deep breaths. "Del, with everything that happened with Colossus, I'm not really interested in something serious. Plus, the Pledge."

"I wasn't talking about doing anything that went against the Pledge."

She crossed her arms, hugging herself. "I know. I didn't mean to imply that. The timing."

The timing? Damn! She never needed this much time before.

She glanced away.

A car pulled up down the street, sat in shadow; its headlights prevented us from seeing anything but silhouette. We clearly heard a door slam. The car pulled off a three-point turn and drove away, leaving behind a waving figure in the wash of red taillights.

Kiera waved frantically. "Jameer."

"Jameer."

He closed the distance between us. While he walked, Kiera said the last words I'd ever wanted to hear from her. "I don't want things to be awkward between us. We can still be friends, right?"

"Of course." Spoken like the words were solid shards of broken glass crunching in my mouth.

An eternity passed before Jameer reached us, like he'd been walking from California. A goofy grin was plastered on his face when he joined us. "How was your night? What'd I miss?"

Can you hurt and be numb at the same time? Something like agony mixed with that shot the dentist gives you so you can't feel your mouth. That's close to what I felt in my bed, twisted covers around me, and my knees pulled to my chest. The red digits on my alarm clock showed 10:54. I hadn't been in bed that early on Friday since I was eleven. My phone shook beside me. I nearly ignored it.

Kiera: Hey, seriously, I don't want things to be weird between us. You're a really great guy. I hope you know I know that.

Kiera: We still have a Pledge project to
work out. Can we try again tomorrow?
At the library? We can actually check out
some books this time. LOL!

I sprang up, hunched over my phone, typed with superhuman speed.

Me: Yeah. Let's do it.

The light at the end of the tunnel was apparent. This was a second chance.

Our timing couldn't be bad forever. We were inevitable. It took her a while to see.

I could forgive her for that.

CHAPTER 16

IT TOOK ME TEN MINUTES on my bike, my laptop bouncing in my backpack. Ten minutes of imagining us squeezing in one of those tiny study cubicles in a dimly lit back corner. Two chairs wedged together, shoulders touching. Thighs, touching. While we discussed presentation options. She'd taken the lead by texting me, and inviting me here. She'd decide when things would go further. I was happy to be in her company.

Working my chain through my spokes and frame, I locked my bike down next to a rusted, tire-less ten-speed carcass someone abandoned a hundred years ago. While I did, a familiar minivan turned into the lot, releasing Bobby and Ralph Burton.

"Hey Del!" they said in unison, bounding past me into the library. Their mom gunned the minivan's engine, gone.

Panicky, I snatched my phone from my pocket, sending a quick message.

Me: Are you here yet?

Kiera: Yes. We are all inside.

We?

Wary, I followed Ralph and Bobby. They led me to a study room packed with my Purity Pledge classmates.

A round table was covered in books and papers. Extra mismatched chairs had been dragged in. When I pushed through the door, I recognized the space fit the bodies nicely, but may have been too small for the Burton Brothers' Axe body spray. I struggled to maintain normal breathing in a cloud of aerosol masculinity, and I wasn't the only one, judging by the way others not-so-discreetly pressed hands to nostrils. The jolly brothers didn't seem to notice, though.

Everyone greeted me, Kiera least enthusiastically, merely tossing a nod my way before refocusing on the open book in her lap. Jameer left his seat at the opposite end of the table from Kiera, pulled me into a bro-hug. "You're confused, right?"

"Little bit."

"Sit." He pointed to an empty chair next to his. On the opposite end of the table from Kiera. I sat.

Shanice chirped, "I say a fashion show."

Mya rocked back in her chair, her phone in a two-hand grip, only halfway with us. "What's a fashion show got to do with purity?"

"About as much as a dance number," Shanice fired back.

Helena and Ralph and Bobby laughed. I found none of this funny.

Kiera spoke without looking up. "I've been texting with Sister Vanessa and she suggested we be proactive. She's expecting us to impress. So, whatever we settle on, that's where the bar is set."

Jameer gave a wicked eye roll. "Total freedom to control our message. Y'all got ideas?"

Everybody spoke at once, and I only caught snippets of phrases. Purity comedy routine. Purity choir concert. The only thing anyone agreed on was purity.

With everyone trying to talk over everyone else, the competing voices grew into a loud dull roar, a library no-no. The tattooed librarian from last night was back, her eyes dark and bloodshot, giving us a dirty look through the study room window. Jameer clapped his hands together once, a thunder crack that made me jump in my seat.

"Stop." He squeezed the word through clenched teeth. The group complied. "We start on paper. We take a half hour, everyone makes a list of ideas they like, then we go through and pick the best ones. Narrow down from there."

Kiera tapped her phone. "Excellent plan. I'm setting a timer."

Mom and Dad had spoken. Everyone except me, Jameer, and Kiera tugged spiral notebooks or loose-leaf from the garden of school bags planted under the table and got to work.

Jameer retrieved a fancy-looking brown leather journal from his bag for his own brainstorming. Kiera, though, brought the book she'd been reading from her lap—the Jacqueline Wood-son novel she'd gravitated to—and splayed it on the table like she planned to keep her focus there and only participate in this activity at the supervisory level. Essentially, she was Tyrell counting the Cra-Burgers at FISHto's.

I signaled her with a hand wave. Her eyebrows arched high, waiting.

"Talk to you a minute?"

All the girls looked up, then quickly zeroed in on their papers when they noticed us noticing. Kiera gave me a tight nod, led the way, bringing the book with her, as if she didn't trust it to be there when she returned.

Outside of the study room, away from the windows and prying purity eyes, I said, "Hey."

"Hey."

Should I have told her I was hurt? Disappointed? Expecting something different than a purity class reunion? I motioned to the book in her hand. "You're checking it out today?"

"Sure. It won't blow my cover now."

"So it was all good when you and Jameer got in last night? No problems?"

"We told our parents it was a nice night so we decided to walk. They let us come out of the house today, so it seems like it worked."

"Cool." The awkwardness was thick between us. I said, "I'm sorry about—"

"It's fine. It is."

"Timing." I said it, hoping for, I don't know.

She shifted her weight foot to foot. Then her phone buzzed, and when she looked at the screen, her mouth turned up a bit.

"Hey, I'm going to—" She pointed at it, made some jerky gestures that I took to mean she wanted to address whatever text message had come through. Alone.

Inside the study room, it was all eyes on me. Mya asked, "Where's Kiera?"

I did a rough approximation of the gestures Kiera showed me a moment ago, and Mya was like, "Are you having an episode?"

I sat without answering and Jameer said, "We didn't get very far on the purity presentation. After you left *someone*"—he looked directly at Shanice—"wondered if you answered the last batch of questions I gave you."

"Dude." Maybe I should point out how I was the only one holding up my end of the bargain. *Fix my Kiera situation if you want your answers.* What I actually said: "That is the opposite of what we're here for."

Bobby spoke up. "Yeah, but we were all arguing about the presentation, nobody argued about this."

Jameer nudged my concession. "Do you have them with you?"

"No. I bet you do, though."

Jameer flipped his phone out.

I said, "Thought y'all wanted this anonymous."

"The *questions* are anonymous," Jameer confirmed. "No one here knows who asked what. It's like what Sister Vanessa says in class. A lot of times we're all thinking the same thing, so no one should be ashamed of what we discuss in our group. Every *topic* can help every*one*."

She did say that. Sounded, oddly, like MJ, too.

"Fine." From my seat, I dug out my laptop. "If this is what y'all really want?"

Kiera returned, beaming. "So, did we decide? Fashion show?"

Jameer broke the news. "Not exactly."

"No!" I spun my laptop toward the group, scrolled through a *MythBusters*-styled medical website in case someone needed proof. "It will not fall off, you won't go blind, or grow hair on your palms."

The girls laughed hysterically. The Burton Brothers blushed. The anonymity of these questions didn't hold up well to context clues.

We'd worked through half their list, body curiosity stuff mostly. Kiera, disappointed that the group wasn't more focused on Purity Pledge Squad Goals, zoned out fairly quickly. Earbuds in ears, eyes on phone.

Twenty minutes and we'd burned through the list Jameer provided. Eyes were lit with the madness of forbidden knowledge, and no one was interested in resumed purity presentation brainstorming. Jameer proposed we used Ralph's Lakers cap as a repository for everyone to toss in more anonymous questions on torn slips of paper. Ten minutes after that, a dense puddle of paper filled the hat.

I plucked the first one up. "Am I supposed to shave my hair off down there?"

"I think, only if you want to," I said. The thought of a razor anywhere near my junk freaked me out, but I knew from . . . other internet research, some people were into it. As was our habit, they didn't take my word for it. I entered the question in a search engine, and got several articles that echoed my answer, but also gave tips on how to accomplish the "landscaping" safely if it was your thing.

Next question: *I think my mom and dad do it a lot. They make noises. It doesn't sound like fun noises, though. Is that weird?*

Some quick typing and a moment of reviewing results. My response: "It might be weird. Not necessarily bad weird. I mean, your parents might be into unusual stuff. That's okay as long as they're both into it. At least that's what it says here."

Shanice asked a follow-up. "What kind of unusual stuff? Are there examples?"

I scanned my results again, tried not to let my shock show. "Some people dress up as fuzzy animal mascots."

Everybody in the room pushed back into their chairs a little.

I stirred the offerings, digging for a question at the bottom of the pile, really getting into my role as a sort of sexual raffle announcer. I touched a strip I liked, unfolded it, read the question a couple of times before I was brave enough to ask it.

My cousin has Down syndrome. Is God punishing his mom because she wasn't married when she had him?

Tinny music secreting from Kiera's earbuds was the only sound in the room. I couldn't even hear their breaths.

My gut answer was no. Hell no! I was still on the fence about

God as a thing at all, if I was being honest, but if that's how He worked, I didn't want any part of Him. Me and the Purity Pledgers had our ways, though. My answer alone wouldn't do.

I typed the question into Google, and immediately got links to several mental health and parenting sites. When I clicked on them, I didn't like them. Many were sketchy, badly in need of updates. Design aesthetics aside, there was no direct answer to the question—how could there be?—but the tone of the articles seemed really negative. Calling the syndrome a "death sentence" in some cases.

Naw. Not doing it. I adjusted the search, using only the term "Down syndrome," and got a great-looking site with simple stats and info. But, those didn't answer the question either.

They began to stir, shift, everyone uncomfortable. So much so, Kiera noticed and tugged the buds from her ears. "What's wrong?"

When I repeated the question, the flesh between her eyebrows pinched and her mouth became a flat line. She searched the faces of everyone in the room, read their concern. "Guys, no. Absolutely not. At least the God I believe in doesn't punish people—babies—because He doesn't like something their parents did. That's monstrous. Sometimes people are born . . . *unique.*" She leaned sideways so far, I wondered if she'd fallen from her chair, but popped back up with her personal Bible. Her flipping pages sounded like bird's wings beating the air, then she traced her finger down a particular page. "Here. Ezekiel 18:20 says, 'the one who sins is the one who will die. The child will not share the guilt of the parent, nor will the parent share the guilt of the child.'"

She gave a curt nod as if that cleared everything up. I got what the verse was supposed to mean. I'm sure it comforted some of the Purity Pledgers because it came from Kiera. But, I'd been thinking on the God thing more and more lately, and monstrous stuff happens on His watch all the time. Turn on the news.

Jameer wasn't sold either, obviously. With no Bible handy, or needed, he said, "Exodus 20:5 says the opposite. 'I, the Lord your God, am a jealous God, punishing the children for the sin of the parents to the third and fourth generation of those who hate me.'"

Kiera sucked her teeth loudly. "You're taking it out of context. The 'those who hate me' part is important."

"What's hate really mean? Let Pastor tell it, anyone who doesn't fall in line hates Him."

They bickered. Tossing out Bible chapters and verses back and forth like battle rappers. Then the Pledgers were in on it, the girls gravitating naturally to Kiera's point. The Burton Brothers drawn toward Jameer. Me remembering why I zoned into my happy place instead of absorbing all this confusing and contradictory info on Sundays.

The librarian shot us the stink eye again, on the move now, intending to shush us or kick us out, for sure.

"Hey," I hissed, "save the Bible Bowl for later and get studious fast. We got company."

The librarian popped in and I apologized profusely, assured her we weren't going to be a problem, and when we were left to our own devices again, I said, "Maybe we should talk about that fashion show, before we kill each other."

No one argued.

We spent all day getting absolutely nowhere on the presentation, and by three that afternoon our group began to disperse, happy to move on with the rest of our day. Missus Burton got Ralph and Bobby first. Then the girls piled into Mya's car for their ride home. Kiera remained preoccupied with her phone, breaking from her nonstop texting to say, "J, you okay getting home?"

Jameer said, "I'm fine. I'm going to hang with Del for a bit."

Awesome. We had much to discuss.

I gave my good friend Kiera a wave goodbye that she barely noticed. Mya's bucket puttered out of the lot, leaving me and Jameer to recalibrate our plans.

He shadowed me to the bike rack, where I undid my lock and asked, "Is she texting Mason?"

He twisted away, sighed. Delaying.

"Jameer."

"I think so."

I groaned at the sky. "How is this happening? Is he getting the same 'timing' excuses I am?"

"I don't know. Probably. She's said a bunch of times that she's not interested in a boyfriend right now."

"Because of Colossus." We walked my bike from the library lot in the general direction of my house. "That asshole. What happened after we left the restaurant?"

"Colossus and his friends got a booth. I guess they ate."

"You guess. Where did you go? Who dropped you off last night?" No quick answer that time. My overall frustration leaked. "It's bullshit that you're trying to keep secrets. I can be your perv question errand boy but you can't tell me what's got you so distracted that you don't seem to really care that our well-laid plans are falling apart."

My bike gears continued clicking as I walked, but I was suddenly alone. I turned, found a frozen Jameer a dozen or so feet behind me. Scowling. "They're not perv questions."

"What?"

He unfroze, stomped toward me. "Like you give a shit about anything in my life."

That "shit" made me flinch. I'd never heard Jameer curse before. "What are you talking about?"

"You're obsessed."

I dropped my bike. "I'm honoring the deal you proposed."

Jameer chewed his bottom lip.

"No comeback? I didn't recruit you, Jameer. You came to me"—I mocked his prim voice—"'Because Pastor won't like it.' What did that even *mean*?"

"It meant you were new, and interesting, and not brainwashed. That's all the stuff Pastor hates."

"Wrong. He thinks my collages are incredible."

Jameer blinked. Blinked some more. "That was pretty funny."

"I know, right." Some of the tension sloughed away. Not all.

Jameer said, "I like you, Del. I want to tell you something very personal. Can I trust you?"

"You have so far." He struggled with it. I felt it. "Go on."

"The person driving the car last night is . . . my . . . boy-friend." He turned his body sideways like boxers do when they want to become a smaller target, raised his hands halfheartedly, then went statue still. Waiting.

Was I surprised? Yes and no. I *hadn't* thought much about Jameer's life, let alone his *love* life. When did I have time? So any new information was surprising. Was I going to hurt him over this revelation? Hell no. For as long as I could remember, my parents have taught me and Cressie not to hate on people for who they liked or loved. Once there was something on the news about people in our state protesting same-sex marriage. Dad said, "Gay couples should be allowed the right to the same dumb arguments about which way the toilet paper roll should go as straight couples."

Mom said, "The correct way is under. Anyone who says over is a monster."

The point of all that: "Okay."

Jameer said, "Okay?"

"Okay."

"That's it?" His body sagged, abandoning the fighter's stance.

"I'm good if you are."

Relief came off him like a breeze; he wasn't used to that

reaction. Everything around us felt better. The tense energy from before . . . gone.

For a little bit.

Gathering my bike, I got us walking side by side again. "That's why your parents are so hard on you. No door, no mirrors. It's why you kind of hate Pastor Newsome. They don't like your boyfriend and they're punishing you for it."

His eyes got wide. "They don't *know* about my boyfriend. They *can't* know."

"I'm confused."

"They're fixing me, Del."

That phrase, the way he said it, made the day about ten degrees cooler. I wasn't going to pretend I knew much about being gay. I knew it wasn't something that you *fixed*.

His voice got fake deep, maybe mocking his dad. Or Newsome. "*You're confused. You have too much freedom. You've been corrrrupted!*"

"They told you that?"

"It's what they told me *to say*. To everyone in the congregation. Two years ago."

"Baring your soul."

His head jerked toward me, surprised, then not. "Kiera said something."

"The basics. It sounds horrible."

"It was horrible. The worst thing I'd ever had to do. My parents caught me looking at some shirtless muscular guys playing flag football in a YouTube video. It wasn't porn."

My cheeks and forehead flamed. I pushed Lindy Blue to the deepest part of my subconscious.

Jameer said, "Even then, it was a lie wrapped in a confession. Pastor Newsome was very clear that when I stood before the congregation, I was not to specify that my 'impropriety' was about someone of the same sex. Pastor told me, 'We want this to be something you can come back from in the eyes of the congregation.'"

"Dude, how do you keep stepping in that place every week?"

"God."

I thought it was a joke. I almost laughed. His clenched jaw and downcast eyes killed those giggles.

"My whole life First Missionary has been my church home. I love thinking about the good God does. The way there's comfort in His words when things get hard, like when my grandma died. I want to see her again, in heaven, Del. I believe that's something that can and will happen. I've seen how a little push from Him can help people be better, like when Jimmy Carmichael, the organ player at church, first came in saying he was addicted to drugs and thought he'd be dead within a year if we didn't help him change. The church welcomed him, and prayed, and he got the strength to go to rehab. Stuff like that happens more than the bad stuff. Because I do believe God's there with us."

"So why's there bad stuff at all?" I was louder than I'd intended.

"That's a big question."

"No. It's not. I'm not talking about why God lets bad stuff

happen in the world, though we could talk about that, too. I mean why, in a place where Newsome has the power, does he force you to tell your deepest secrets? That dude, Jimmy, *wanted* to tell y'all what was happening in his life. He wanted y'all to chime in with prayers, or advice, whatever. Totally in bounds, because it was his choice. But why does Newsome get a pass to stick his nose in other stuff? Why doesn't someone call him out on it?"

Jameer ticked off the words slowly. "Why doesn't someone at the church call out the pastor? You are, obviously, still very new at this, Del. Because you'd be considered an agent of Satan and nobody would listen. The faithful protect their pastor the way the really big guys in football protect that one slightly smaller guy who throws the ball."

"You're talking about the offensive line and the quarterback, which you obviously know nothing about."

"Sorry. I wanted to put it in terms you get. If you go after the pastor, a lot of big folks are in the way, and they'll hurt you. I don't want to get hurt anymore. I'm clockwatching, now. A year and a half until college. I'm going to the farthest one that will take me."

"Until then?"

"I continue to mount my tiny rebellions. I'm like the guy who puts itching powder in the quarterback's jockstrap before the game."

Does a guy like that exist? Were we still in sports analogy territory? "Do all of the Purity Pledgers know you're gay?"

"Maybe not Ralph and Bobby. I don't think they know much of anything beyond their video games and hormones. Kiera knows, so the other girls probably do, too. We don't talk about it."

"Why tell me all this now?"

"So you know I'm being honest when I say you really have helped all of us in the Pledge. My parents are extreme with the laser-focused holiness, but the rest of them have their own barriers. Thanks to Newsome. I hope you'll still want to help when I say this next, very honest thing."

He let that hang, like he needed me to agree before moving forward. "Okay."

"There's not much more we can do with your Kiera situation."

My stomach twisted like an old dishrag, but I couldn't say I was totally surprised.

"Don't be mad," said Jameer, "she's been really different since she broke up with Colossus. And, she needs—"

"Time. I got it. It's cool." I didn't want to talk about this anymore.

We'd reached an intersection, and though we still needed to go in the same direction a ways before we split for our separate neighborhoods, Jameer said, "I think I'm going to walk downtown and get a burger."

He didn't invite me to come along. I wouldn't have accepted if he had. I preferred him when he had more of a "can do" spirit.

"See you tomorrow," I said, and turned my bike toward

home before he could respond.

I stewed the whole way, recalling every little moment since the Sunday I joined the Pledge, looking for the missteps and missed opportunities that had me still trying to crack the code on Kiera. She needed time and space, but there had to be a way to, subtly, let her know a guy like me was worth giving some of that time and allowing into her space. More so than an ass dude like Mason.

The problem lingered, until I turned onto my street and spotted my car in our driveway. My carjacking sister had returned. I jogged my bike to our lawn, dropped it in the grass with no concerns about securing it, then stomped inside, up the stairs, and shouldered my way into Cressie's room without knocking. "What the hell, Cress?"

Harsh white light doused me, forcing a flinch. I threw my arm across my face like Dracula at high noon.

"Hey world," Cressie said from beyond the harsh glare, "meet my little brother, Del. Del, say hi to the viewers."

"What"—my eyes adjusted, I recognized the source of the light as some fluorescent halo fixed around her phone— "viewers?"

"We're live on IG."

Squinting, I saw the viewer count was at 157. Then 163. I gave her IG followers my coldest ice grill, no smile. "How long are you gonna be on?"

"I'm wrapping up." She turned the lens on herself, flashed a smile as bright as her portable studio lighting. "Thanks for tuning in, FemFam. Keep an eye out for more spontaneous content here, and definitely subscribe to FemFam Presents Channel on YouTube for new content every Monday, Wednesday, Friday. Until next time . . . Love. You. Too."

She ended the broadcast, then stared at me flatly. "Bro, we gotta work on your media training."

CHAPTER 17

"WHAT IS EVEN HAPPENING RIGHT now, Cressie?" Her room . . . cleaner than it had ever been. Her bookshelves had actual books on them instead of bras and old jeans. Her bed was made, like, neatly, not the comforter snatched to the top of the mattress as if covering a cadaver. I could see the floor!

She snapped the elaborate lighting rig off her phone. "Expanding the brand, little brother. What's up with you?"

"A lot of busing. A lot of biking."

She smirked. "Seniority has its privileges. It's my car, too."

"You could've given me some advance notice. I thought you weren't coming home again until Thanksgiving."

"Some things came up." She moved to the floor, pulling her stowed suitcase from beneath the bed, and I noticed her hair. Shaved into a buzz cut on one side, it was a little startling. When she was home, she treated her hair like her one true love. Stressed daily over how it was laying, if the ends looked broken, begging Mom for newer expensive products. Now, half of that obsession had been sheared away. Her left ear featured a new series of painful-looking sterling studs running along the edge. She looked tough. A little scary. I would not be deterred.

"Like what? What came up to make you mess up my whole weekend?"

"You know Taylor Burkin?" In her suitcase was more equipment. Another camera, a tripod, more lights. She placed the phone light among the gear, and removed some other stuff. "Originated that BabyGettersToo hashtag?"

"Of course. What's she got to do with this?"

Cressie placed more disassembled gear on her mattress. More stuff than I'd think anyone would need for recording YouTube videos in their dorm room. More stuff than my sister should be able to afford. "Why do you care about Taylor Burkin, Cress?"

"Because I'm doing my sociology semester project on Modern Feminism versus Societal Mores. My YouTube channel is part of it, but when I told my professor about the 'scandal' in my town she encouraged me to incorporate more points of view, and loaned me some sweet gear to make it happen. I reached out to Taylor and she wanted to talk, had a ton to say."

I didn't know how to respond. I also didn't know what a Societal More was, so I asked about that.

Cressie said, "Customs. Things that we may not talk about much, but are generally accepted as the way things are done. An obvious example that most societies agree with is you shouldn't murder people. An example that's less universal would be holding a door open for a person walking into a building behind you."

I sat next to her, repeated my earlier question. "What's that got to do with Taylor?"

"It's not obvious? Society expects people to reproduce. We don't have a species if there aren't new people. But, depending on the specific society, there are a lot of funky rules about who, when, how people have babies. I'm not arguing about which society has the best baby rules, but what's consistent in many parts of the world is when a birth happens outside of a society's rules, and people in power don't like it, blame is placed on the woman. She's fast, a whore, a slut. As if every birth that doesn't get the power player's stamp of approval is immaculate conception. No male participation at all. Sadly, nothing new there. What's interesting is Taylor's young, and calling out that behavior through the most powerful tool available to any oppressed class, social media." Cressie's beat-up, scuffed backpack was wedged against her nightstand. She hopped to it like a manic bunny, snatched the zipper open. "You should see these journal articles I found on . . ." She looked in my eyes and trailed off, her shoulders slumping. "You want to know if I'm done with the car, don't you?"

"No. I want to cuss you out. Then I want you to confirm that you are done with the car."

"Did you hear anything I said?"

"Taylor Burkin is helping you with your school project. Cool. I hope you get an A. You still messed me up last night, Cress."

She shook her head slowly, resealed her journal articles back in her bag. "I heard about your hot date. Kiera's nice, she wouldn't care that you rode a bike." Her gaze was shrewd. "Am I right?"

"That's not the point."

"If I was wrong, it wouldn't be a relationship worth pursuing. You boys always get it twisted." She resumed fiddling with her equipment, extended her tripod's legs. "You should watch my show. You could learn a lot. Or"—her head tilted, scrutinizing me—"if you let me do your makeup, you can guest on my next episode. A male perspective might help draw in some new subscribers."

"You're not putting makeup on me!"

"The light's going to show every pore on your face."

"There will be no light, Cressie. I'm not doing your dumb show."

"Rude!" She punched me in the chest, and I pretended it didn't hurt. There would probably be a bruise. She said, "If you're going to be typical Del, kindly close the door on the way out. I want to get one more video done before I leave tonight."

With her focused on her setup, I massaged my sore sternum. "You're not staying?"

"Naw, one of my friends is heading back to campus early. I'm bumming a ride."

"So you *are* done with the car."

A sneer, which I took as a yes.

I touched some of the equipment, to her dismay. A telepathic *be careful* shot into my brain, but I ignored her stern vibe. "Mom and Dad know you're leaving?"

"They're out shopping. I'll text if they're not back when I leave."

"Mom's not going to like that. She's been a bag of nerves since you went away."

Cressie sat her tripod upright, snapped her camera onto its mount. "Stop exaggerating."

"She misses you, is all."

"Nice to know someone does."

I nodded. "Fine, fine. Dad misses you, too."

She cocked her fist for another punch, and I grinned wide. Instead of hitting me, she said, "Cornball."

"So what's the other thing?"

"Huh?"

"You said you came home because some *things* came up."

"Oh!" She dropped to the floor, in her backpack again. Please God, no journal articles! A moment later, she handed me several sheets of paper and I thought the Lord had forsaken me. But, each page was the same. Flyers. The header read:

"JAYLAN KNOWS" LIVE!
PART OF THE AWARD-WINNING COMMONWEALTH UNIVERSITY LECTURE SERIES

"What is this?" I asked.

"Only my favorite YouTuber and the inspiration for *FemFam Presents* is coming to campus next week. I've been volunteering with the Student Government Association on planning this lecture series. It's the first time the school's brought in someone who's not like a civil rights activist, or famous writer, so it's important that we have a good turnout. I dropped in on some of my counterparts at NSU, and ODU, and HU, and . . . well, you're going to have to put some gas in the car, Del. Sorry."

"Seriously?" I reviewed the flyer more carefully. Jaylan had an angular face, short hair, shaved on one side—now Cressie's haircut made more sense—and a wide smile. It was a good-looking picture, confident. I guess you'd have to be if you're proclaiming to the world you KNOW.

Cressie went on, "Her videos are amazing. Timely and topical in a way that's so compelling."

Whatever. My car was back. "I'm sure you're going to have a great time. Tell me all about it over Thanksgiving turkey. Have a safe trip back to school, Cressie."

I gave her a limp, one-armed hug, and was down the stairs, still unclear on Jaylan's particular area of expertise.

Though, not for long.

At the nearest Exxon, I wedged the gas nozzle into my tank and let it autofill, leaned on my trunk, while shaping my evening via text.

> **Me:** I got the ride back. You trying to roll tonight?

> **Qwan:** My bad, bro. Made plans with Angie.

Me: You're whipped.

When he didn't respond, I took that as confirmation that he was indeed whipped.

The gas nozzle thunked off—THIRTY-FOUR DOLLARS was the tab, damn Cressie! Almost my entire take from tutoring Shianne.

Oh. Shianne.

> **Me:** Hey, you down for some "tutoring" tonight?

Shianne: Come by. I'll show you how to change a diaper.

> **Me:** On second thought . . .

Shianne: Come over PLEEEEZZZZEEE!

Why not? The weekend had been plenty crappy anyway. What was a diaper going to hurt?

CHAPTER 18

MISTER AND MISSUS GRIFFITHS GREETED me at the door, and Shi's dad slipped a fifty-dollar bill in my shirt pocket for my service.

"Come on." Missus Griffiths led me upstairs. "They're in Shi's room."

She nudged her door open, and I caught a bit of SZA playing low through wireless speakers. Shi's bedroom was huge. Big enough for a king bed, a desk like you'd see in the principal's office, her own beat-up couch, and, of course, a baby's crib. Shi, in baggy sweats, thick socks, and a Serena Williams Nike shirt, was tucked into the corner of her couch, bouncing Zoey lightly while scrolling through her phone.

Missus Griffiths said, "I'll take her so you two can focus."

"Thanks, Mom." Shi handed the child over.

"Thank me by working hard."

Missus Griffiths left us, and Shi said, "Hey, close the door."

I hesitated. "Your parents cool with that?"

"It's you, Del."

That stung in an unexpected way. I imagined her parents having discussed the possibility of me and their daughter getting into some lewd, X-rated behavior, then cracking up hysterically like naw, not him! As if it was so ridiculous to believe me and Shi capable of anything beyond this platonic and lucrative arrangement. I shook off the hurt and sealed us in, focusing on that crisp currency in my pocket. Flopping in her desk chair, I said, "What subject do you want to cover tonight?"

"I'm really interested in binging some Hulu." She switched from phone to the iPad on her nightstand, and fell back onto her bed, the tablet propped on her chest.

"Works for me." I'd brought along my laptop, and opened a browser. I tried some aimless surfing for a while, then checked IG and Snapchat on my phone, but nothing really interesting was popping. When my usual procrastination options were exhausted, I found myself thinking of Purity Pledger questions from that hat, ones we never got to, but I might've peeked at before we left the library.

At the Google search bar I typed: *What's the correct way to kiss?*

There were mad results! Almost information overload. Pictures. Step-by-step instructions. A disproportionate amount of the pages focused on a rainy scene from some old movie called *The Notebook*. I read through about a dozen articles, and found it really was a toss-up.

I mean, kissing was something I had limited experience with, but the correct way and the wrong way were subjective, right? "Shi," I said, "if I asked you to describe the correct way to kiss, what would you say?"

"Low spit."

I spun the chair. "That's it?"

Her tablet still blocked her face, and she flexed her socked feet like she was dancing. "Use lip balm. Flavored. I like strawberry."

"That seems very specific."

"You asked."

Jotting down some notes, I decided to revisit that question, and moved onto another wedged in my memory: *What's too young to fall in love, and is love the same as lust?*

That's kind of deep. "Shi, what do you think about this?" I read it to her.

She placed her tablet aside and came to me. "What are you doing?"

"It's this thing at my mom's church. Long story, really. I've been sort of finding answers to questions some of the kids aren't able to find on their own."

"All the questions are like this?"

I clicked over to a notepad file I'd started, let her see some of the prior questions and answers. She said, "I didn't know your family was religious."

"We weren't. Mom got into it this year. So I'm into it. Not voluntarily."

"She making you be the quizmaster for these kids?"

"Naw. That's a different thing."

She perched on the edge of her bed, considering. "That's why you been around Jameer Sesay more? I've heard his family is hard-core religious."

"You have? Like how?"

"We were in classes a couple of years during elementary and middle school, and he'd bring in notes that excused him from story time, or other stuff, because of his beliefs. We never really knew what those beliefs were—a lot of kids went to church, but didn't get excused the way he did."

"You ever hear anything else about him?"

"Nope. Give me all the tea!" She rolled onto her belly and propped her chin in her hands, anxious.

"I was just asking."

She pouted. "I don't understand why they're coming to you when the answers are right there." She pointed to the computer.

"It started kind of accidentally." That's when I gave her the high-level overview about Purity Pledge and Healthy Living. I didn't tell her everything, though. And she knew it.

"A Purity Pledge, Del? Don't take this the wrong way, but why are you doing all that stuff at 'your mom's church'? I know it's not charity. I'm your friend, and my dad's paying you to be here."

Sounded so harsh when she said it that way.

She pressed. "Seriously, why?"

"Kiera Westing."

Shi tipped her head back, groaning. "Still, Del?"

"Now I wish I hadn't said anything."

"Don't act like that. You've been Kiera-crazy forever. So, what's the deal? I know she hasn't been taking the Colossus and Taylor thing well. Are you and her talking now?"

"She's taking the Colossus and Taylor thing fine."

"You're such a boy. Dude, she's crushed. You know how I can tell? She's acting like she's not crushed. Everybody would be crushed by their ex fathering a secret baby while they were still together."

"Kiera's focused on other things."

Shianne's eyebrow hooked up. "You?"

"God."

She laughed. "Yeah, that's going to work out real well."

"We went on a date last night." I knew it wasn't a date, not with Jameer there, and Colossus crashing. Shianne's condescending tone irked, so I gave her something hard to dispute.

Her lips pursed. "Really?"

"Don't sound so surprised."

"Oh"—she stuck her bottom lip out, mocking me—"I wasn't trying to hurt your feelings, sweetie. Kiera seems a little uptight to me. I always thought you could do better."

Better, how? Kiera was fantastic. "You're a hater."

"Am not!"

"What Green Creek girl do you like? I'll wait."

"I've always gotten along with guys better."

"Like Zoey's dad?"

She flinched. "Low blow, Del."

I knew it. Didn't regret it. "Who is he anyway? No one at school seems to know."

"They're not going to know. Green Creek High can have that hashtag bullshit. You been talking about me?"

"No. You don't have to talk to hear the rumors. Some say he's a grown man, married and stuff."

"Well, *some* are lying. He's a football player in Richmond. Henrico High School. It's his senior year and he doesn't want anything to do with me or Zoey. Are you going to go throw that in the rumor mill now?"

No. I hated gossip for the most part. I did have questions. "He's not helping at all?"

"He stopped talking to me the minute I told him I was pregnant. Well, after calling me all kinds of names. Said it could've been anyone's baby even though I told him he was the only person I was ever with."

She told him the truth. Our lie/pact abandoned for a guy who later abandoned her. "Your parents, they didn't, like, I don't know, take him to court?" Some of the Baby-Getter situations had become contentious that way. Lawyers, child support.

"My mom and dad said we're not going to force someone to do the right thing. Money's not an issue for us, and he's not an influence we necessarily want in Zoey's life. So . . ." A shrug.

I struggled to fill in the blanks of what that meant. "What did you like about him? There was something, before he turned asshole, right?"

"His smile. His confidence. He was an athlete, so his body's amazing. Smelled good. Had a really deep voice. You should've seen him in those tight little boxer-briefs he wore, he looked like a superhero—"

"Okay, okay. Got it."

She exhaled, deflating right before me. "Funny part is that the way he acted with Zoey, all that stuff is gross to me now. His teeth are kind of gray; he's insecure and mean. If I ever smell his cologne again, I'll gag."

She was clearly uncomfortable, twisting and staring at the wall.

"Maybe we should really study something," I said, feeling guilty for taking us here.

"Don't try to be Mister Do-Right now." She repositioned herself, focused on her tablet. "I've got more TV to catch up on."

We resumed our previous activities. I clicked through open browser tabs and ended up on my YouTube home page where, because website algorithms are scary and know everything, a familiar face appeared in my recommended videos. Cressie's fourth episode of *FemFam Presents* was among the thumbnail offerings, and next to it, the YouTuber she'd been caping for in my car. *Jaylan Knows*, episode 202: "Sex Terminators."

Say . . . what?

Shi had screwed earbuds in, totally unconcerned with me. I clicked on the *Jaylan Knows* video and watched an engaging, humorous, informative breakdown about highly sophisticated sex dolls. It was the most bizarre thing I'd seen in a while. When it was done, I immediately clicked on episode 201: "Why Are (SEXIST) Dress Codes Still a Thing?"

Before long, I was on Jaylan's page, scrolling through various video titles, amazed at the topics from timely politics

("Bathroom Laws") to racy ("Orgasms 101") to hilarious ("The Five Worst Blind Dates Possible"). Didn't realize an hour had passed until a light snore caught my attention. Shianne had dozed off, her tablet slipping to the mattress. I, on the other hand, was surprisingly amped after falling down a YouTube hole. *Jaylan Knows* had given me an idea. One that might impress Kiera.

Gathering my things, I shook Shi's socked foot, rousing her.

"Huh?" She plucked her earbuds out.

"I'm gone. We can have another study session later this week."

Groggy-grunting, she mumbled, "Okay. Sorry about things getting tense earlier."

"Tense? What you talking about?" I tried to not hold grudges. Not with Shi.

"If you're into Kiera, be real with her. It shouldn't be so hard. Stop that faking church BS. Nothing's worth all that."

I didn't see how she was qualified to give relationship advice. All things considered. "Go back to sleep, Shi. I'll see you later."

I told the Griffiths family goodnight on my way out. From my car, I sent a text.

> **Me:** Hey, I got an idea. Wanna show you tomorrow. Can we meet like 20 minutes before service in the Pledge room?

Jameer: I'll be there.

Kiera: See you in the morning.

The next morning I drove myself to church, beating the earliest early birds. Jameer and Kiera arrived together and found me in the Purity Pledge classroom, where I already had my laptop on and ready. Jameer sat next to me, Kiera sat on his other side (even though there was an empty seat next to me, and closer to the computer, though I tried not to think about that too much). I cued up some of the shorter—milder—*Jaylan Knows* videos. One video was on sexually transmitted diseases and was way better than anything MJ showed us in Healthy Living.

Another video was called "First Date Tips," and was exactly that. Fun, humorous, with Jaylan and her friends role-playing dos (DO ask for that end-of-the-evening kiss, and be okay with it if the answer is no) and don'ts (DON'T expect anything more than pleasant company and conversation).

Jameer stopped the video midway, began scrolling through Jaylan's other offerings as I did. A full catalog of titles from "Mini-Rant: Stare in Her Eyes, Not at Her Boobs or Your Phone" to recorded multi-guest panels called "State of Your Virginity: Keep or Lose."

"These are great," he said, his voice airy with awe. "We gotta show the group."

"No," Kiera said. "Y'all know I'm not too comfortable with this Q and A situation you got going on. We definitely shouldn't be watching these videos *here*."

"I understand why you feel that way," I said, ready for this. "But I think this is where we get our purity presentation."

"How?"

Jameer seemed genuinely perplexed, too. "Yeah, Del, you lost me."

"We go to this Jaylan lady's event, see what it is she's talking about. Then we flip it. Do an opposite event. It's kind of like a skit, mixed with a panel. We know what we're going to talk about—purity—but we present it like we're experts schooling the congregation."

Kiera leaned back in her chair, considering. I was ready for that, too.

"See?" I raised my hands wide as if framing a huge neon sign that read, *"First Missionary Crew Knows Purity."*

The flyer was folded under my laptop. I pulled the slip free and passed it to Jameer, who skimmed it, then passed it to Kiera.

"It's at Commonwealth University? That's an hour and some change from here," Kiera said.

"Exactly." I grinned, finally reaching my closing point. "Road trip."

We had to get into the sanctuary for service before I could nail either of them down on a definitive answer. They both agreed to think about it, and I had a sense Jameer saw the beauty of my plan, even if he knew my ulterior motives. Regardless of why I was orchestrating this trip, it would get him away from his house, and Green Creek, for a few hours.

So, I felt good when I settled into the pew next to Mom, who beamed with all sorts of parental pride over the eager beaver routine that got me to church early that morning. I was even in a decent mood through all the announcements, and prayers, and overly long selections from the choir. My mood soured significantly when Newsome motioned toward the front pew while the choir *wooh-wooh-woo*ed through their last selection.

A familiar, but at the same time surprising, face rose above the heads of the congregation members between me and her.

Her name was Tavia Roberts. A Baby-Getter. One of the few who hadn't blown up a baby daddy with the BabyGettersToo hashtag. She hadn't come back to school yet, so seeing her here for the first time since before summer felt extra wrong, like she needed directions to where she was actually supposed to be.

She took a few steps toward the short staircase that would put her at Newsome's podium, hesitated, looked to a silver-haired woman I didn't know. Her grandma, maybe? The old lady rocked a sleeping infant, and prodded her along with a flicking hand motion, the way people shoo flies. Tavia continued her slow march, each time she lifted her leg to take the next step looking like her feet were five-hundred-pound lead blocks beneath her floor-length flower-print dress.

Newsome pulled his mic free of its holder, said, "We have a homecoming today, family. A hard homecoming, but a homecoming just the same."

Something in those words, they triggered an eerie premonition, and my gaze was drawn to Jameer like he had his own gravity. He didn't look at me though; he was locked on to what was happening at the font, like everyone else. My attention skirted back there too, but even before Newsome spoke again, I knew what this was.

Bare your soul.

"Young Sister Tavia has come back to the Lord's House. And we're so grateful for that. Not only has she come back, but she has chosen to take the Lord's word from Psalm 32:5 to heart. 'Then I acknowledged my sin to you and did not cover up my iniquity. I said, "I will confess my transgressions to the Lord." And you forgave the guilt of my sin.'"

"Amen!" Coach Scott shouted in his mousy voice, triggering a few more eager confirmations in the sanctuary.

"Sister Tavia." Newsome held the mic to her.

She didn't want to take it. I couldn't have been more sure if I was Professor X reading her screaming thoughts in an *X-Men* comic. Yet, she unfolded a sheet of paper she'd been clutching in her fist.

Tavia faced us, raised the paper so it nearly blocked her entire face, and only then did she take the mic and read her statement.

"First, I'd like to thank God for helping me see that me and my family should be here with you all, receiving the blessings of His word. Second I want to—" Her voice cracked, and never steadied. "I want to say I'm sorry for d-d-disrespecting God, Pastor, my grandmother, and all of you with my behavior. By . . . transgressing and giving in to temptations of the flesh, I have d-d-dishonored all the good God has brought into my life . . ."

There was more. More of the same. Tavia throwing herself before the people in this room, her classmates among them. Her sniffles were harsh echoes through the surround-sound speakers. I bounced around the sanctuary the way I did when Prayer Peeking, observed my Purity Pledge classmates. All stone-still, except Jameer. I swear I saw him flinch each time Tavia snorted snot to keep from sobbing, though at that point, what was really the difference?

I craned my neck to Mom, who was expressionless. Almost in a trance, horror or awe, I couldn't tell.

The final words of Tavia's confession were barely audible snivels. She pushed the mic back to Newsome and padded down the stairs back to her grandmother and baby's side. All to applause.

Newsome said, "It's hard to get right, y'all. It's hard to get right. But the children will lead us."

After service, I was glad me and Mom had driven separate cars. I didn't want to have a conversation about Tavia on the ride home. It's not that I didn't want to discuss it at all. I was afraid that if I discussed it with her, she'd say she approved.

Jameer caught me in the parking lot, tense and twitchy. "Pastor is hugging Tavia right now. Like they won something together. Nobody wants that prize, Del."

"Was it that bad for you?" Maybe it wasn't the right thing to say. What was?

"It was that bad. Like ripping off skin."

Him and his way with words.

"I'm down for the road trip," he said. "Anywhere but here."

That bit of good news brought me back to myself. "And Kiera?"

"She's still in there, too. Probably praise dancing with her parents and Pastor as we speak."

"No." I worked to ignore the disgust in his voice. "I meant can you get her to go?"

His head cocked, the slightest bit of annoyance wafted off him, and I got defensive. All he said was "I'll work on it."

Jameer walked toward his parents' car without a goodbye.

Later, at FISHto's, I had more to say about what happened in church, and Mya was my captive audience. "How often does that sort of thing happen?" I asked.

She passed a bulging, grease-spotted bag through the drive-thru window, gave the customary "Happy Sailing" goodbye, then called over her shoulder, "Couple of times a year. Depending."

"On?"

"How badly people want to be on good terms with the church."

"With Newsome, you mean."

She spun on her stool, faced me. "What do you really want to say, Del? It's just us here."

"I'm here!" Stu yelled from the grill.

Nobody cared about Stu. Tyrell was another story. I scanned the perimeter before I spoke. "I think it's bullshit. Don't you think it's bullshit?"

Mya got frowny. "You don't have to curse. I don't make the rules, Del."

"If you did, though, if you had a church, would you make people do that?"

"Tavia went up there because she wanted to."

"You couldn't have been looking at the same person I was if you believe that."

Mya fiddled with the bunches of drinking straws protruding from a cubby by her register. "Maybe she didn't *want* to be in front of everyone, but she wanted to get right with God."

"Newsome," I corrected.

Her eyes became slits. "I didn't like it, Del. Okay? It creeps me out every time someone does it. But I don't like that you keep trying to get me to talk bad about Pastor."

"I'm not."

She gave me a full-on Mom look. The "you know better" expression. Which I didn't understand because that wasn't what I wanted. At all. She made it sound so manipulative.

Stu chimed in. "That pastor dude does sound like a dick, though."

Mya threw her hands up. "I'm not doing this," she yelled toward the kitchen, "with either of you!"

Door chimes sounded, a family coming to my register to order. Then the drive-thru picked up with the Sunday-afternoon rush, and I didn't discuss church and the confessions of a Baby-Getter anymore. Not with Mya, my mom, or anyone else who'd witnessed that horror show. By Monday, the Green

Creek gossip mill was grinding with fresh Baby-Getter fodder and I'd all but forgotten about Tavia. Thanks to my sister.

Qwan rode to school with Angie, and I never saw him before homeroom, otherwise I might've gotten a warning since he kept tabs on Cressie so hard. It took till second period before I sensed something was off. Too many glance-aways when I caught someone kind of staring in the hall. Too many whispers.

As I was making a locker stop, a sophomore girl, Autumn Chan, approached me for the first time in life to say, "Del Rainey, is there any way you can mention me to your sister? I have so many things I'd like to talk about."

Her wide-eyed hopefulness was mad spooky. Her request seemed like nonsense. "*My* sister?"

"I want to go on her show. It's about time someone started listening to us." She pressed a folded slip of paper in my palm. "My IG, Snapchat, and cell number are there. Thanks for putting in a good word for me."

Autumn skittered into the hallway rush, leaving me so lost.

I whipped my phone out, opened YouTube. Cressie's latest episode, "Small-Town Scandal . . . But Is It, Really?" had posted. The thumbnail image was Taylor Burkin, frozen with a hand raised, and her neck tilted, and her mouth open as if she was giving someone—most likely Colossus—the business.

With no earbuds on me, I couldn't listen, and I didn't want to play it in the open. Had to get to class anyway, so I stayed in the semi-dark all the way until lunch when Jameer caught me by the cafeteria entrance. "I think something's going on with your sister, but I can't figure what it is."

"Same, Jameer. But we're about to find out."

Qwan was at our table, and I knew he had earbuds with him. Me and Jameer flanked him. "Have you watched it yet?" I asked, cueing it up on my phone.

"Yeah, man." No snark, no further explanation. Very un-Qwan-like, and it made me nervous. He passed me the buds. I took the right, Jameer took the left. Cressie filled the screen.

CRESSIE

Hey FemFam, Cressida here. I've been hearing from some of you new subscribers and I'm happy to see that we've crossed the pond. A few ladies from the UK have joined the family, I see the countries of Nigeria and Ethiopia representing, even have one subscriber all the way from New Zealand. Thank you for tuning in and dropping thoughtful comments. Means a lot.

The UK? Africa? New Zealand? I glanced below the video, checking Cressie's subscriber count. 2.4K. More than quadruple the number from when Qwan first showed me the channel.

CRESSIE

Got a special guest today. Y'all have heard me talk about where I'm from, and how it's not the most progressive place on earth. Well, over the last year there's been a situation of sorts. One that's gotten a lot of unfair attention in the local media. It has to do with a group of young women who have been ridiculed and ostracized for arguably the most natural thing on the planet: giving birth. I'd like to introduce you to one of those young ladies, Taylor.

The video cut to a wider angle so we could see Cressie and Taylor side by side on a love seat in, presumably, Taylor's house. Taylor wore a Green Creek varsity soccer shirt, triggering vague memories of her in a yearbook team photo. I think she was pretty good at the sport.

TAYLOR
Thanks for having me.

CRESSIE
Would you mind telling the FemFam about what happened?

TAYLOR
I sure don't.

She gave a recap of the Baby-Getters drama in a way none of us had ever heard before . . . because it came from an actual Baby-Getter. Not a news reporter. Not the Green Creek Rumor Mill. She dispelled the myth of a pact ("Nobody planned this, it was a time when everyone was stuck at home, bored. Sex happened, then the babies. Hasn't it always been that simple?"). She gave new information ("The vice principal kept saying stuff to my mom like do we think it's a good idea for me to return to a potentially toxic environment—it felt like he didn't really want me to come back to school"). And she said something that we probably all sensed on some level ("That stupid nickname they gave us hurts. A lot!").

Her voice cracked and Cressie took over, giving her time to collect herself.

CRESSIE

I hear you, sis. It's mad derogatory. The FemFam has heard me speak a lot on how we get labeled with the most demeaning things for simply existing in the same space as men, doing the same things men do. Which brings me to a movement you started when trying to reclaim that horrible nickname. Can you tell the fam about #BabyGettersToo?

Taylor. Went. In.

It's the stuff we'd all seen in her IG story, so not new to us. But Cressie made sure to edit in some of the original footage for the people in the UK, and Africa, and New Zealand. When Taylor finished, Cressie added her commentary.

CRESSIE

What I'm hearing: there's a double standard at play. The school administration would rather have you disappear than protect you. And the boys who should be held equally responsible, aren't. Not surprising. What are you hoping to accomplish with #BabyGettersToo?

TAYLOR

Everybody else was telling stories about me, and the other girls. I wanted to be heard. My words, my way.

CRESSIE

That, I can relate to. We already know we can count on a healthy number of critics to keep shunning you, blaming you, denigrating you. But know that the FemFam has your back. So, I'm sure there are people in my hometown watching this— I'm asking what can we do to protect these young women, and their children, from the continued scorn of the . . . well, I was going to say "community," but is it really? The comments are open. Until next time.

The video ended, and I tugged out my earbud. Unsure what to think, I focused on my friend, because other phones were out too, and I felt a lot of eyes on me.

"Is this bad, Qwan?"

"I think for some. I don't see Colossus being real happy someone in Ethiopia is probably calling him a deadbeat. But, that ain't on you."

"Could you inform the rest of the school?"

Jameer, the voice of reason, said, "Del, I believe you can keep your head down and this will blow over. It doesn't really have anything to do with *you*."

That was good advice. That's what I'd do. It didn't have anything to do with me.

School wrapped up, and I pulled a short shift at FISHto's,

pushing the Cressie/Taylor crossover episode from my mind. But that evening, before bed, I got some uncomfortable texts:

Cressie: Hey baby bro! My latest Fem-Fam episode has been BLOWING UP. You should watch it if you haven't already.

Cressie: Need to ask you something though.

Cressie: Got an anonymous comment from a girl saying that the faculty at Green Creek High canceled the sex ed class and I should do a show on it.

Cressie: Have you heard anything about that?

I didn't respond.
And I muted my sister's texts.

CHAPTER 19

AS JAMEER PREDICTED, in the days leading up to our road trip, the furor over my sister's video died down. Or was snuffed out, depending on how you looked at it.

Vice Principal Terrier couldn't do anything to Cressie—she wasn't a student—and though I caught him staring at me with murder in his eyes a couple of times, he couldn't do anything to me either. Through some tense PA announcements, he did make it clear that anyone caught with their phones out during the school day would lose them. Typically, that was a rule applied to the classroom only, but something was bubbling beneath the surface at Green Creek. So, things were changing fast and on the fly.

Fine by me. I could do without all the attention-by-association over Cressie's channel. Like, sis, you did your four years here. Don't make mine harder.

The week settled into the mostly normal routine.

Purity Pledge had its own difficulties as word about the CU trip spread to the group, and disappointment when I told them everyone couldn't come—I could only fit four in my car—spread faster than that. I was surprised by all the pouting over my denial, mostly from the Burton Brothers, who, for some reason I couldn't comprehend, thought I'd allocated two spaces for them.

In the church lot, our breath puffing in the autumn air, Jameer expressed some personal concerns about how his parents thought we'd all be studying together at the library on Saturday.

I said, "Look, we hit the road fifteen minutes after the library opens. We're at the university in time for the panel, then we're back here an hour before they pick you up. Who's going to tell them different?"

He motioned toward the sanctuary, to the chatty bunch that wouldn't be going with us.

"So what do you want to do about it?" I asked.

"What if I could find a way to get everyone there?"

"Whatever you need to do." I was going, and my passenger seat was reserved for Kiera. I wasn't concerned with the other logistics.

I should've been.

Wednesday night, I managed another Shianne "tutoring" session to get some pocket money before we made the drive to CU. Thursday, I pulled another (short) shift at FISHto's—I'd forgotten my belt, stupid, I know, and my pants were too loose, so I took orders one-handed and with the other hand kept them from falling and showing my customers what color boxers I had on. Tyrell sent me home, but with a warning. "No more messing up," he said. "It hurts everybody when you aren't doing what you're supposed to do."

It pissed me off. I had a lot on my mind, and the belt thing was an honest mistake. Maybe next week I'd see if McDonald's was hiring.

By Friday I had tunnel vision. All of the uncomfortable feelings from Tavia baring her soul, Cressie turning into Green Creek's Oprah Winfrey, and Taylor continuing to scorch the earth had subsided. Some. It wasn't on my mind, anyway.

I washed the ride, copped a crisp Hawaiian Breeze air freshener, and stayed up late putting together a perfect shuffle-ready playlist, nothing overtly romantic, but nothing super ignorant either. Sleep was a rough affair, the anticipation of Kiera time somewhere Mason, or Colossus, couldn't pop up felt, well, divine.

The next morning I showered, dressed, and was on my way to the library when I got a text from Mister Rules Tyrell.

Tyrell: Del, hey, you've been asking for more hours, and Stu called in with the flu. Could really use you on the day shift.

Me: That's a pass for me, Tyrell. Got plans.

All those times he sent me home and I'm supposed to be On-Demand Del now? Naw. Didn't give Tyrell or FISHto's a second thought. I arrived at the library five minutes after opening, thinking I was being early, but found the Purity Pledgers had beat me there. All of them.

Kiera sat on the library steps chatting with her girls. Ralph and Bobby hovered to the side, slapboxing childishly. Jameer greeted me as I approached. I said, "What's this?"

"I worked it out."

"Worked what out?" I'd forgotten his proposition of finding transportation for all. Still didn't get it until the van showed up.

The dull gold-and-maroon paint job, faded down to gray splotches in some spots, was unmistakable. As it coasted over a speed bump, the suspension squeaked and set the whole thing bouncing like a soap bubble on a breeze.

Qwan leaned from the passenger window, slapping the door like a set of bongos. "What up, peeps!"

The van came to a full stop. Angie clutched the wheel, smiling wide, and then not. Taylor and Colossus had been the hot drama in the Green Creek halls, but Taylor wasn't *the reason* Kiera's long-term relationship ended. That . . . was Angie.

Kiera stood among her girls, arms crossed. Jaw clenched.

I said, "Jameer. What did you do?"

"Made a way." He slid the van door open on a squeaky track.

The younger Pledgers looked to him, to me, and, for the final verdict, to Kiera, with the glossy, hopeful looks of kids asking if they can have ice cream.

"Go on," Kiera said, little enthusiasm in her voice.

The girls piled into the van, as did Jameer. Knowing no other option existed but to roll with this, I moved to my car.

Kiera . . . did not. She approached the van.

"Kiera?"

"I'm going where my girls go, Del."

"But . . ." *My Hawaiian Breeze air freshener!* Hey, it's what I thought! What I actually said, "Is that a good idea?"

She patted my chest, determined. "It'll be fine. It's only an hour drive. We'll see you there."

Kiera climbed into the van, closed the door behind her. Leaving me with the Burton Brothers, who vibrated with excitement as they rushed my car.

"Just the fellas!" Ralph said, clutching his backpack to his chest instead of utilizing the shoulder straps like a normal person.

Bobby said, "Yo, Del, we can play our mixtape for you. We got bars!"

"Your mixtape?"

Oh God.

I stopped counting time and began measuring the infinite trip in songs—nine so far—as the "R&B" (get it?) mixtape stretched on and on. It was everything I feared and more. Trash raps, off-key singing, amateur homemade beats. One song—a *love* song—was called "Blood Ain't Thicker Than Booty."

Yeah.

"This one's like a story," Ralph explained. "We're both in love with the same woman, and it's causing a rift between us."

"Got it." The van, visible in my rearview, fell behind a few car lengths, and my gut twisted with the possibility of Kiera and Angie at each other's throats. Colossus was trash, a fact that had been well established and documented. Was that enough to form a bridge between the girls, or an octagon around them?

"That line," Bobby said. "'She slayed me, but you betrayed me, I don't know which is worse . . .' I wrote that, Del."

"Okay." Both brothers watched me, eager. They wanted my approval. Flatly, I said, "It's fire."

With thirty minutes of driving left, upon the announcement that the next track was "Blood Ain't Thicker Than Booty, Part 2," I decreased the volume and asked, "I thought you two were church dudes, born and bred. These songs raunchy as hell. How and why?"

Bobby said, "We know what's up."

In that moment, I knew what Qwan meant when he said some half-ass, untrue boast about my sexual conquests sounded sad. "Try again. For real, where y'all getting this stuff from?"

Ralph, a little more honest than his brother, said, "We listen to other music. If we like it, we kind of imitate it."

"'Blood Ain't Thicker Than Booty,' though? Who are you imitating with that?"

"Everybody," they said together. Which was a glum assessment on the state of urban music.

Ralph said, "We're getting good enough to make songs that can sound like anybody."

"Why don't you make them sound like you?" I asked.

They sort of shrugged. Kind of their own answer. They were still figuring that part out.

"Our music's gonna be fire one day, Del. Everybody gonna be listening. Watch!" Bobby said, real slick.

Ralph smirked and nodded, still clutching his bag to his chest all weird.

I decided I did not want to know what *that* was about, and switched for the AUX input to radio.

"Hey! We still got seven more songs to—"

"Radio!" I said.

He pouted, and finally flung his backpack aside. I thought I heard it swish.

We got off the highway, and my phone navigation guided us into the heart of downtown Richmond. Plenty of traffic accompanied us into the city, which was already showing signs of seasonal cheer in the form of red "Happy Holidays" banners adorning lampposts and the "Come See Us on Black Friday" signs in stores.

We found a campus parking deck, and a couple of empty spaces. We all spilled out of our vehicles. Everyone who entered the van still appeared to be alive. There was no blood. Angie and Kiera, both smiling.

The entire group gathered at the van's rear bumper and moved in the direction of the parking deck elevators with only me and Qwan dragging. I sidled up next to him. "What happened?"

"What you mean?"

"Angie and Kiera. The Colossus thing. What happened in that van, Qwan?"

"They talked. I gave up shotgun to Kiera and rode in back so they could have their say."

"Talked? No screaming. No threats."

Qwan sneered. "Look, everybody ain't caught up in that silly shit the way you think. They were fine."

Whoa, whoa, whoa! "What's up with all that bass in your voice?"

He shook his head, then jogged to catch up with Angie, leaving me alone and confused.

I sped up, passed them all to take the lead. We came to the student union, the only building bustling with activity on a Saturday morning.

The whole walk over, the Pledgers chatted among themselves, Angie and Kiera most of all. It was benign stuff, admiring how pretty the campus was, and how tough certain teachers back at Green Creek were. How they got there from those icy stares this morning was a mystery for me, one nobody seemed eager to help me solve.

Inside the student union, where the marble floors were like mirrors under the streaming sunshine, and signs pointed us toward the auditorium where the event would be held, Angie said, "Is there a restroom nearby?"

Mya spotted the facilities, and all the girls drifted in that general direction. Bobby, Ralph, and Jameer announced a pit stop, too. Qwan's attention stayed on tall windows near the exit, the clear sky beyond. Though my bladder pulsed lightly, I took the opportunity to talk one-on-one, something we hadn't done since . . . when? "Hey, what's with you? I know something's wrong."

He blew air through his teeth, whistling slightly.

"Things not going good with Angie?"

"Yo, you think Tyrell might give me my job back? If I apologize?"

Now that was out of the blue. "Naw. You stole from the restaurant. It's like on tape. He probably told corporate and everything."

A grim nod. "I figured."

"Bro, you won that battle. A few Cra-Burgers to go with two girls and—"

"Those girls robbed me, D."

At first I thought it was some new slang I wasn't up on, not literal. Then, I thought back on that night. How Qwan had been working the front line by himself. I never saw how it all went down. "At gunpoint? They must've been starving."

"Naw. I gave them the food, and rolled out with them thinking it was about to go down. They were talking all slick like we were gonna get real freaky. Lindy Blue shit, you know. When we got to the edge of town, they pulled over, made me give up my shoes and any dough I had on me."

"The Jordan Elevens?" I always wondered why he didn't wear those anymore. "But you said—"

He threw his hands up, defeated. "I lied on my dick, D. Okay? You got me."

Qwan . . . lied on his dick? The cardinal sin? Him, too?

Some warm blossom of hope bloomed inside me. Maybe I could tell him the truth about Shianne finally. No more secrets. Except, why was he admitting this *now*? I said, "Have you always lied?"

"I wish."

Cryptic. Okay. "Why'd you lie that time?"

"Because I was embarrassed. It was stupid to mess up that gig over it. I been going around trying to get work, and ain't nobody hiring for real." His hands spoke his frustration, his fists balling and unballing with no target.

"Did your mom get laid off?" I asked, knowing how fast that could happen, how real it could get.

He shook his head. "Angie's late, bro."

"Late for—?" Oh. Shit. "She's pregnant?"

Qwan shrugged hard, exaggerated. His shoulders bouncing high like he was trying to crush his own head and put himself out of his misery. Then he walked to a different section of the floor-to-ceiling windows. To be alone.

Jameer appeared at my hip, squeezing a dab of hand sanitizer into his palm. "It's starting soon, guys. I think we better grab seats."

The crowded foyer thinned, people grazed into the designated space.

"Go get the girls," I said. "We'll see you in there." I never took my eyes off Qwan.

"But—"

"We'll see you in there."

The Burton Brothers bobbed closer; Jameer intercepted

them and angled them toward the ladies' room, where the girls had emerged. I couldn't help but examine Angie from a distance, smiling at something Kiera said, looking no different than every other time I'd seen her. You never knew what was happening underneath, not with anyone.

I went to Qwan. "How?" I said.

His eyes narrowed. "Bro, it hasn't been that long for you, has it?"

"I mean . . ." I recalled my lone condom. "Y'all ain't use nothing?"

"Not all the time."

Then it was MJ in my head, day one of Healthy Living. Birth control, and diaphragms, and a bunch of other stuff. I didn't bring that up because what good would it do? Instead, I asked, "What's Angie saying about it?"

"She scared."

So was he. It came off him like heavy cologne. I grasped for something, anything, to comfort him. "Are you sure? Because her period's late? I heard my mom and sister talking about monthly stuff before. Sometimes it can be off, right?"

"I—we—know that. But we're Green Creek, D. Babies are in the water." Qwan waved me off. "I didn't tell you so you can try to solve it. I had to say it, is all. You're the only one I could say it to. Let's go do what we came for."

He joined our crew, slid an arm over Angie's shoulders and pulled her into him, like shielding her from bad weather. She squeezed his hand like she was grateful.

Falling in beside Kiera, my vibe was all wrong, and she

sensed it. "What's the matter?"

Everything. This wasn't the plan. Every time I go for a moment with Kiera somebody else's shit gets in the way. Mason at Harvest Fest. Colossus at Mama Marian's. Now my own best friend was throwing salt in my game? I know he didn't mean it, but damn.

I told Kiera, "I hope this was all worth the trip."

Because I had my doubts.

Our line snaked through a set of double doors. We inched forward and inside; ushers directed us to seats arranged like rows in a theater. I watched the group closely, particularly the younger kids, in case they got noisy. Excited. They couldn't have sat more still if this was a church service and Newsome was on the stage.

Shortly after the room filled to capacity, the lights dimmed. I slid to the edge of my seat when a speaker emerged on the dais and gave the mic two thumping taps. Cressie.

My sister cleared her throat. "Good morning, everyone. My name is Cressida Rainey, and I have the tremendous honor of introducing today's lecture series guest. She's an internet sensation. A social media dynamo. A sharp-tongued, proud 'nasty' woman. Above all of those things, she is a lifesaver. If you don't believe me, listen to the excerpt from a letter our guest received yesterday.

"Aunna G from Clarksville, Tennessee, writes: 'I didn't think I belonged on this earth. I dressed different than people in my town dressed. I spoke different than people in my house spoke.

Inside, I felt different than what my body expressed to the world. I was so many things—Goth/liberal/Girl—different than what everything around me said I should be. It got hard to live that way, so I sought other solutions. When I put "painless suicide" in the search bar, I expected having to skip over the prevention hotline numbers, and the articles about how to deal with temporary depression. I was prepared for resistance. But, the second search result from the top was a bright colorful thumbnail for a YouTube video. The girl in the picture was gorgeous, beaming. Two things I wanted for myself so badly. The title of the video was "That Time I Almost Killed Myself, and Why I'm Glad I Didn't Succeed."

"'I don't know how long I sat there. It felt like hours. But the contrast of colors, beauty, and the casual way you spoke on a subject that was causing me immeasurable anguish made me click your next video, and your next, instead of deep-diving for ways to remove myself from this world. Without meeting me, and without knowing it, you saved my life . . .'"

Cressie's eyes glistened, reflecting twinkling stage lights. "There's more to the story, and much more to the woman who's about to take the stage, but I'll let you see that for yourself. Join me in welcoming the creator of *Jaylan Knows*, Jaylan Perry Monroe!"

We were a hive mind rising in unison, applauding, as two more people joined Cressie on the dais. A buttoned-up woman in a blue pantsuit like Mom wore, and the woman whose face I'd seen across dozens of videos over the last week. Jaylan was petite, shorter than my sister. Maybe one hundred pounds if you counted the sandalwood bracelets stacked up her forearms and the huge hoop earrings brushing her shoulders. Not a hair out of place; her brown skin glowed. Her smile warmed the coldest heart in the back row.

Jaylan hugged Cressie, who mopped starstruck tears from her cheeks with no shame, then took a seat in the nearest armchair as the professor type took the other, casually shuffling index cards in her palm.

Sixty minutes went by in a breath. The professor did not waste time getting into the topics Jaylan covered in her videos. Dating. Sex. Mental health. They touched everything, relating it back to Jaylan's own tough background—an inner-city kid whose parents worked so much she barely saw them. She always had questions, and spent nearly every afternoon and evening at her local YMCA in the teen computer nook, researching any topic that came to mind, filling stacks of single-subject notebooks with her findings.

"I had so many notebooks, they formed teetering towers along one wall of my room. My big brother said I kept manifestos like a serial killer"—big laughs from the audience there—"but what I had was an external brain. I couldn't keep all of my thoughts, and concerns, and worries up here." She tapped her temple. "They would've driven me insane."

The professor leaned into Jaylan, nodding. "Fascinating. You were very young when you started the habit of writing it all down."

"Yes, maybe ten or eleven."

"But"—the professor cocked her head, intrigued—"there came a point where your interests changed?"

Jaylan caught the pass handily. "Yes. When I began puberty, the topics I worried about changed. Before, I was concerned with music, and puppies, and science, and basketball. Almost overnight there was an urgent shift. I needed to know about the things my body was doing. Even though my mother made time to explain in the best way she knew how, it wasn't adequate."

"Why?"

"Because everything else I was hearing was wrong."

Down my aisle, each and every one of the Purity Pledgers tipped forward, drawn toward Jaylan as if she were a low-powered magnet.

"Nothing was consistent," Jaylan said. "The correct information was vague. The incorrect information was abundant. The confusion was maddening, and I spent all of my teen years in trial-and-error mode. Navigating a sexual awakening minefield in snowshoes, if you will. No one should have to go through that. When I got to college, on scholarship, I worked my butt off to get my first computer. When my parents saved up to give me a phone with a decent camera built in, I decided I'd trade in the notebooks for a video journal. My first entry was called 'Dorm Sex,' which was a facetious title because I was really talking about the pros and cons of coed versus same-sex dorms. A friend dared me to post it. Within a couple of days it had fifty thousand views with requests for more. Now, one point four million subscribers later, you all know the rest."

They talked more about the struggles of being *a brand*, how she dealt with critics, and trolls. Too quickly, the discussion was over, and a couple of polo-shirted techs dragged mic stands to either side of the room. The professor said, "We'll be opening the floor for Q and A."

People lined the outer aisles. Glancing down the row at the Purity Pledgers, I mouthed, *Well?*

Honestly, I didn't expect any of them to get up. Shanice proved me wrong. The bravest of us, she slid into the aisle. Shockingly, Mya, who'd sworn she was so not into my Answer Man role among the Pledgers, followed. As did Ralph Burton.

Further down the row, Qwan stood, letting Angie pass since his bony knees were butting against the seat in front of him. She joined the line right behind my people.

It was the first time I thought of the Purity Pledgers that way. My people.

The house lights came up. The mic line on the other side lengthened with folks anxious to ask Jaylan questions, too. I might not have noticed who else was in the building if not for the dress she wore. The same one from the day I started down this path and she quizzed me on my reasons for wanting to remain sexually pure.

Sister Vanessa had a question for Jaylan, too.

CHAPTER 20

SCRAMBLING FROM MY SEAT, shouldering past people who'd lined up behind Angie, I hissed, "Mya, Shanice, Ralph! We gotta go now."

Mya's mouth screwed up to argue like we were at FISHto's. I pointed and said, "Sister Vanessa."

Shanice spotted her. Like a lost toddler seeing their mother in a crowd, she took an instinctive step forward as if she intended to say hi, but then remembered all of us weren't supposed to be here.

Ralph and Mya caught on quickly and excused themselves from the line. The room was noisy with chatter and shuffling as people either moved to a mic line, or shifted to allow others passage. The professor's voice echoed through speakers as she asked people to settle down. Thankfully, they were slow complying, which allowed me time to wave the rest of my crew off the row and sneak from the room.

Everyone except Angie.

"We gotta go," I said, picturing a swift escape to the parking deck, cars, and back to Green Creek.

Angie refused to leave. "I don't know that woman."

Really? Was it too soon to call her a cranky pregnant lady?

Me and the rest of the Purity Pledgers couldn't stay; we'd figure a rendezvous later. Qwan joined Angie in the mic line, mouthing *Text me, bro.*

I led the Purity Pledgers to the auditorium's back exit, keeping them between the wall and the ever-growing mic line. Eager Jaylan fans provided ample cover until we were clear.

Once in the lobby, we gathered in a loose huddle.

"What is she doing here?" Kiera asked, brow creased, almost angry.

I had nothing. Maybe she was here to chastise Jaylan. Call her out for promoting filth on the internet. I didn't think anything I saw on her page was filthy, yet I could see 90 percent of her content being fodder in a Newsome sermon. Counterproductive to our purity mission.

"We gotta get outta here," Bobby said, afraid and decisive in a way that was more unnerving than spotting Sister Vanessa. He kept exchanging glances with his brother, who still clutched his backpack to his chest like he was protecting a baby. Strange.

Jameer leveled his gaze on me. "Where to now?"

"We should leave this building. Eventually people will start coming out and we don't want to run into Sister Vanessa th—"

"Del!"

I closed my eyes—shit!—cold fear icing every part of my body. Turning like a brave man facing a firing squad, I said, "Cressie?"

My sister approached, giving us a slow up and down. She

lingered on Kiera, smirking. Then, to me, "About time you got woke."

Cressie took us to an adjacent building, the campus gym. Sparse groups of students wandered in and out with towels, and basketballs, and weight-lifting belts while we settled in the near-empty foyer. I texted our location to Qwan, got the Pledgers settled in the bleachers, then prepared to deal with what I knew was coming.

"Why have you been dodging my texts?" she asked.

"I haven't. I've been busy."

She punched me in the arm. Playful and excited. "The Taylor Burkin episode of my show has been blowing up. I'm at like nine thousand subscribers now. It's wild! My viewers are Green Creek crazy."

"Why? It's Green Creek."

"Tell me about it. My professor says people are seeing us like an Everytown. We're the poster child for female oppression, and puritanical values."

"That's . . . something."

"Think about it. There are some teen pregnancies, the town treats it like a curse. Yet, the sex ed class that's teaching students about ways to be safe and avoid unwanted pregnancy gets canceled because of pressure from some religious zealots."

I glanced over my shoulder at the chatty Pledgers. "How do you know that's what happened?"

"My anonymous source. Since you won't help me, I've been leaning on her information. It's a gold mine. Whoever she is has documents, meeting minutes. Did you know the school lets clergy have a say in what goes into the sex ed curriculum? Whatever happened to separation of church and state?"

"You sound like Mom and Dad."

"I talked to them. They said you were taking that class, but they had no clue it had been canceled. Why didn't you say anything?"

"Because it was dumb." I felt defensive, needed to distance myself from ever caring about Healthy Living. "Stuff we already know."

"Apparently not." Cressie shook her head, not like she didn't believe me, but in apparent awe. "It's amazing we're this far into a new millennium and we're fighting battles that should've been won before we were born."

I said, "You working on a show about what happened with Green Creek's sex ed class?"

"Not just Green Creek, all across the state. The problem is systemic. Different standards, different texts from school district to school district. I'm shining a light on all of it."

"Awesome."

Cressie leaned and looked past me. "What's up with your ragtag group of rebels?"

Mya huffed. "Another *Star Wars* fan? It runs in the family, huh?"

Cressie, full attitude, said, "So?"

Mya backed down, none of the Harvest Fest sass I'd gotten. "Nothing. I don't want any problems."

Cressie said, "Y'all go to my mom's church, right?"

Like good criminals in the making, they kept their mouths shut. I answered, though. "Yes. We're all in Purity Pledge together. We dipped out because we saw our Purity Pledge teacher there."

"Purity Pledge? As in the sworn denial of any physical urges or pleasure to please a patriarchal oppressor?"

Mya, full attitude, said, "So?"

Cressie nodded, chuckled in a humorless way. "It's a choice, I guess. My bad. I don't want any problems."

"You can't tell Mom and Dad you saw us here," I said. "There could be trouble."

"I won't snitch. I'm glad you got a chance to come and expand your mind. I gotta get back; they're going to wrap up soon and I want some one-on-one time with Jaylan. You can hang here. No one's gonna bother you."

"Thanks, Cress."

She hugged me. No sneak pinch. No soft jab to the solar plexus. Just love. "It's good to see you here, baby bro."

Cressie began to step away when Shanice stopped her. "Ms. Rainey?"

"Oh no, sweetie. Let's not do that. Cressie's fine."

"Okay. Um, will Jaylan come back soon? I still want to ask my question."

Cressie frowned.

I said, "Shanice, probably not. She's pretty busy and—"

"Hold that thought, baby bro," said Cressie. "Don't hit the

road until you hear from me."

"I gotta have them back before their parents try to pick them up from the library."

"Boy, wait!" She stomped off, leaving us irritatingly perplexed and cautiously hopeful. My sister, a woman of contradictions.

Twenty minutes later Qwan and Angie entered the gym. His hands were stuffed deep in his pockets, like he was trying to scratch his knees from inside his jeans. Angie smiled when she saw us, a forced thing.

Kiera said, "Did you get to ask your question?"

Angie nodded. We waited, melting her with expectant stares. Maybe it was rude, but she'd asked the question in public. She could repeat it.

"Wow," she said, "you're like puppies waiting for kibble. I asked how she made difficult decisions. She seems to be killing the game, so I was curious about how someone like her thinks."

Mya piped in. "What'd she say?"

"I said"—Jaylan entered the gym with my sister on her heels—"Examine, evaluate, extrapolate."

The girls perked, with Shanice squealing a little.

Angie shrugged. "Well, there you go."

"Examine all of your current options." Jaylan paced before us like a drill sergeant. "Evaluate the pros and cons of each. Extrapolate each pro and con out one year, three years, and five years to determine the possible results. Thinking about it that hard, that clinically, will make things so much clearer. In case any of you were wondering."

The girls applauded. I had to admit, her swagger *was* crazy. It was like being in the presence of a future movie star, or president of the United States.

"Cressida tells me you all couldn't make it into the Q and A line. I wish I'd known. I don't get to speak to groups your age too often."

"Why?" asked Kiera.

"I'm considered a bit too risqué for school visits below the college circuit. Such a shame, because I remember being your age. What I talk about, I think you need the most." She sat on the bleachers, motioned for us to join. "So, let's do it."

"Do"—I felt slow on the uptake—"what?"

"Q and A. Just for you."

My sister beamed. "I asked as a personal favor."

"She's been an amazing guide," Jaylan said, arching her back in a cat stretch, obviously tired, but pushing through it for us, "and is doing some important work on her channel. This week in particular."

Cressie's smile almost split her head in two.

Jaylan said, "You're all from the same town? Green Creek?"

"Yes," I said. "We are."

The Pledgers swarmed. Settling into seats on the bleachers like bees settling onto sunflowers, ready to lap up all that could be taken. Kiera sat, and I nuzzled next to her. Qwan and Angie climbed higher into the bleachers, his legs sprawled, and her between them using his knees as armrests.

Shanice dived in, the need for anonymity abandoned. This whole trip was a pact: we'd all be keeping each other's secrets.

"Is it bad that I think about sex a lot? I don't want to do it, but I think about it all the time."

"Not bad," said Jaylan, "human. I thought about it a lot, too. Still do, if I'm being honest," she finished with a wink.

Ralph and Bobby asked various questions about approaching girls. Helena had her questions. Surprisingly, Mya jumped in. Even Qwan had an odd question about if girls liked dudes who could cook? This went on for about half an hour. When the group ran out of gas, Jaylan said, "Nothing I can help you with, Del?"

Everyone stared. Most had shared some secret yearning with Jaylan. Why not me?

"Um, sure. In relationships, how do you move forward from a situation that started kind of rocky?" I asked.

Jaylan popped an eyebrow high. "Move forward, or move on?"

"Forward," I said. My palms felt damp.

Jaylan said, "I ask because sometimes the available choices get confused. Particularly when there are rocky starts. Everything good doesn't have to be hard."

"How do you know all this stuff?" Jameer asked, tense, his voice gruffer than usual. "How do we know you know what you're talking about?"

"It's easy to give others good advice. The only time we're objective is when it's not about us. If I broadcast my mess-ups, I could have my own soap opera in addition to my channel. Is there something you want to ask me—?"

"Jameer," he said.

"Do you have something on your mind, Jameer?"

He shook his head and waved off the request.

"What about you, lady?" Jaylan focused on Kiera.

"What do you do if you've been hanging on to this old feeling, and you're guilty about it, but you want to move on to whatever's next?"

My pulse sped up. She was talking about Colossus, had to be. She wanted to move on. Wanted what was next. I squeezed her knee, and she jumped a little, surprised.

Jaylan scrutinized her. And me. "That's pretty vague."

"For now, it has to be. I hope that's okay."

Jaylan nodded. "Maybe you need to find the right person in your life to discuss that guilt you're feeling? Probably best not to do it in a large group. A single, good friend would do."

One corner of Kiera's mouth turned up slightly. "Thank you."

Kiera's question brought us near the end of things. Jaylan had a question for us, though. "Do you spend much time listening to each other?"

There was a stirring among us, no one stepping up. Maybe no one knew the answer. I tried anyway. "We talk a lot."

Jaylan said, "Not exactly the same thing. You all seem like really bright kids. You'll figure that part out."

She extended her hand, and I shook on behalf of my friends. "We appreciate you taking the time to speak to us like this."

She gave my arm a big pump. "It's not totally altruistic. This sister right here"—she motioned to Cressie—"is buying me the best Thai food in the state, right?"

Cressie said, "That is accurate."

"I'm determined to earn my keep. So thank her."

I hugged my sister. "Thanks, Cressie."

"You're welcome. Get those kids home safe."

That was always the plan.

The Pledgers filed past me in a line, like ducklings. When Ralph passed, I heard that strange swishing from his backpack again, and my Spider-Sense tingled.

We made our way back to the parking deck, divided into vehicles. This time, Kiera didn't angle toward the open van door. "Okay if I ride with you?"

I said, "You're not worried about your girls anymore?"

"Jameer's with them." She cut her eyes to the Burton boys. "I figured you could use a little relief on the ride home. They're very energetic."

My heart stuttered. This . . . was what I'd been waiting for, and wanting. Sure, I still had the Burton Brothers with me, but, whatever, I'd endured worse.

Bobby ran to the passenger door. "Shotgun!"

"Get your ass in the backseat," I snapped, and the entire crew froze for a beat before cracking up.

Bobby slid behind the passenger seat, mumbling, "What kind of world is it when 'shotgun' doesn't mean anything?"

Ralph joined his brother, sounded like a mobile wading pool, and I couldn't take it anymore. "What's in your backpack, Ralph?"

The twins exchanged villain grins. Ralph unzipped his bag and pulled out something I mistook for a lunchbox, until I didn't. "The hell?"

Kiera said, "Have y'all lost your minds?"

Ralph had a box of wine. Black with gold trim and lettering. "We stole this out our mom's pantry."

Bobby said, "It's a Malbec."

Like any of us knew what that meant.

"Is your mom going to know it's missing?" I was more worried than when I spotted Sister Vanessa.

"Naw," said Ralph. "Probably not. Mom's an extreme couponer and she's been stockpiling these for a while. There are like twenty in our basement."

"Take it back," Kiera ordered.

"But we thought it could be like communion. All of us."

Kiera's mom-like rage receded; she looked to me. I had nothing.

We followed Angie's van back to the highway, much later than planned. We'd get back close to the library's closing time, provided traffic was kind.

It wasn't.

Angie's brake lights flared as my phone GPS announced: "A collision is causing a half-hour delay."

The highway was apocalypse still.

The dread in the car became palpable. Boxed wine was the least of our worries.

Kiera fished her phone from her pocket and called Jameer on speaker. "Hey! We've got a problem."

"We know. Everyone's freaking. Helena especially."

What would happen to them—us—if we got caught? I couldn't imagine more than a Mom and Dad lecture on my end, maybe losing my car keys for a couple of weeks. But I'd seen the wrath brought down on Jameer. Humiliation, privacy stripped away. Never considered that his parents might not be the most extreme in the church.

Kiera went silent, thinking. "Jameer, tell everyone to text their parents. Say I suggested we all go for pizza and milkshakes to continue our fellowship. We're walking from the library, to Antonelli's Italian restaurant. We'll be done by eight."

"Yes," Ralph said, drafting the text.

"You're awesome, Kiera," said Bobby.

If it worked, that'd give us an extra three hours to get back to Green Creek. More than enough time. Impressive. More so because of who it was coming from. I was more turned on than ever.

Each parent approved the pizza date with no extra conditions, on the strength of Kiera's endorsement. Good thing, too. That half-hour delay became a full hour. The library was dark and abandoned when we pulled into the lot to regroup.

We piled out, crowded between our vehicles. Jameer said, "Now what?"

"We do what we told the parents we'd do." Irritation bled into Kiera's voice. "Go to Antonelli's, order pizza and milkshakes, then actually talk about our purity presentation. Enough fun for one day, guys. We're lucky this didn't go south."

Reluctant grumbles favored Kiera's thinking. Bobby Burton had a different idea. "We could get the pizza to go."

"And do what?" Kiera activated full mom-voice. An unspoken warning in the air.

Where Bobby faltered, Ralph excelled, finishing the proposal. "Communion."

He unzipped his bag and showed everyone his stolen wine. Sullen Qwan was the first responder here. "Whatever this is, I'm with it."

Angie cut him some wicked side-eye, but did not object.

Jameer said, "I would not be opposed to breaking bread and drinking drink with my brothers and sisters."

"Jameer!" Kiera scolded.

This particular demon was loose and hopping bodies. I was fascinated seeing the Pledgers so eager to break more rules.

"Unbelievable!" Kiera said. "We can't crack open a box of wine here in the parking lot, you know."

Jameer said, "I have a spot."

Qwan clapped his hands. "Then it's settled. What y'all like on your pizza? First person to say 'pineapple' getting slapped."

CHAPTER 21

WE POOLED MONEY, GRABBED THE pizzas—pepperoni, not pineapple—and a sleeve of red plastic cups. We let Jameer navigate to "his spot." Him in Angie's van, me following. The path took us to the edge of town, toward thick bands of forest. Turning off the main road onto a blink-and-you-missed-it passage, asphalt became a foliage tunnel. The ceiling was crisscrossed branches, the floor gravel tracks with lush grass between the treads. Angie's van bounced like a bad dancer ahead of us. My teeth rattled. "What is this place, Kiera?"

"I don't know."

Another minute and the ceiling lifted, exposing a darkening late-afternoon fall sky. I was so close to Angie's bumper that I couldn't see beyond. She veered left, opening up our view and, real talk, I was stunned.

We'd reached the creek our town was named for. A grassy bank ran right to the water's edge; to either side you could see it running from some unseen source, toward a train-track overpass and beyond.

I parked, and exited the car as the van's side door was flung open, Jameer the first one out. The Pledgers followed, then Qwan, then Angie. Kiera stood close to me, with the Burton Brothers circling, their boxed wine exposed. Ralph had it by the handgrip in the box's top, while Bobby punched out the perforated notch at the bottom, freeing the spigot.

"J." Qwan tore open the packet of cups. "This spot is *fire*. How'd you find it?"

"A friend showed me."

I knew what friend he spoke of. I clapped a hand on his shoulder. "Thanks, bro."

Qwan passed cups out to everyone, but hesitated when he got to Angie. She waved him off. A few eyebrows arched.

"We're driving." I stood tall next to Angie, and handed my cup back.

There was a question in her stare: Did I know? My answer, "I've got a case of water in the trunk. My dad's big on being prepared for emergencies."

Qwan bullied the Burtons away from the box, and filled his cup first. "Seniority, little ninjas."

When the brothers tried again for their portion, Jameer shoved past them, filled his cup like it was fruit punch. "Seniority."

Kiera said, "You don't need that much for communion, Jameer."

"My spirituality is deep."

When the Burtons leaned in, Kiera jumped forward, playful,

blocking them once again. "Seniority."

That got everyone laughing, even if she only took enough wine for a sip or two.

The rest of the Pledgers got in, finally. Most keeping their share of the wine closer to Kiera's portion than Qwan's and Jameer's. Except for Helena. I caught her trying to go all in. I reached over and flipped the spigot closed, then tipped her cup, spilling half of her overly indulgent haul onto the grass. "Chill, you little alkie."

"Boo!"

Angie poured water for me and her. Once we each had a cup, Qwan said, "How do we do this? A toast?"

"Grace," Kiera said. "Every head bowed, every eye closed."

Like church, they obeyed. Even Angie and Qwan. Like church, I Prayer Peeked.

"Oh Heavenly Father," Kiera began, "thank you for traveling mercies to and from the university today. Thank you for this time of fellowship. And may your awesome spirit remind us that we are not to lose control of our senses as we break bread and drink wine in your name. This is communion, not a drinking game."

Jameer coughed loudly. "Wrap it up."

Kiera huffed. "May we continue to love each other as You love us. And may You remind Jameer that I can still beat him up. Amen."

The laughter was thick as we brought those cups to our lips.

We cracked open the three pizzas we'd acquired, munching, chatting, drinking. Happy. Together.

The sun sank, throwing golden rays across green, mossy creek water. We told stories. Funny things from school. Funny things from church. Qwan slipped an arm around Angie's waist, pulling her close, and she let him. The two of them disappeared into the van, and I was concerned the situation might get a little . . . mature. But they kept the door open, and their ongoing mumbling conversation relaxed my fears.

Shanice asked the other girls, "Have y'all looked at any Purity Ball dresses yet? This is the one my mom bought me." She had her phone out, swiping through photos of the dress she planned to wear when our time in the Pledge was completed and we had our final celebration. The ladies gathered around her *oooohhh-hed* and *aaaahhhhed*.

Helena said, "I haven't looked at dresses yet. But I'm thinking I want something blue. That's my favorite color."

"I've been working extra hours," said Mya, "because I'm going to need a Purity Ball gown and a prom gown this year. My mom can't get them both on her own."

Jameer, who'd refilled his cup, maybe more than once, said, "You could wear the same one."

Even I knew better than that. While they sizzled him with heat vision, my eyes cut to Kiera. Mya brought up the prom, had me thinking about dresses, too. And tuxedos. Matching corsages and cummerbunds.

I nearly said something bold, feeling some magic in this secret place. Only Angie and Qwan's conversation got suddenly louder.

"Oh, *that's* what you're worried about?" Angie said, snatching everyone's attention.

"Chill. I was joking."

"Well, I ain't laughing, Qwan."

I jogged to the van's passenger window. "Everything okay?"

"I gotta go." Angie twisted the ignition and revved the van's engine. Party over.

"Dude?" I said to Qwan.

He had a dejected look, stared straight through the windows toward the dark forest. "She's right, let's go."

What. The Hell. Just Happened? We were doing so good. Me and a bunch of kids shooting for years of chastity, on purpose! Sitting by water that would probably kill us if we drank it, eating mediocre pizza, and sipping stolen wine.

It was awesome. Until it wasn't.

Kiera said, "Time to pack up, everybody."

Mostly everyone participated in the cleanup, stuffing used plates into a grocery bag and stacking emptied cups for later disposal. Jameer stood off to the side, though, thumbing something into his ancient phone. When the secret grotto was litter free, we piled into the vehicles, got back to the main road. The closer we got to the restaurant, the more it seemed like whatever spell we'd experienced was false magic. Kiera still rode shotgun, though. That was something. The glowing Antonelli's sign came into view.

Looking tense over whatever happened with Angie, Qwan remained on task, distributing Altoids to cover any lingering wine scent. Then, one by one, parents showed up to retrieve their particular Purity Pledger. Me, Kiera, and a slightly wobbly Jameer greeted each parent like the good chaperones that we were until only the Burton Brothers remained. They'd stashed the half-empty wine box in my trunk, and were buzzed enough to attempt some freestyle raps that were better than that mixtape. There was hope for them.

Their mom's minivan pulled to the curb, the automatic door sliding. They said their goodbyes and hopped in. Within seconds of them pulling off, a familiar car pulled to the curb in front of Antonelli's. Me and Kiera had seen it drop Jameer off the night we walked home from Mama Marian's. Jameer, suddenly overjoyed, ran to greet the driver.

He stepped from the vehicle, taller than all of us. Rail thin. His hair was all shiny curls. Sparse stubble covered his cheeks and chin like moss. He wore a plain gray hoodie and loose jeans, the opposite of Jameer's daily almost-formal wear. Wardrobe differences aside, the two embraced with warmth and longing that made me jealous considering the foot-long gap separating me and Kiera.

Jameer pried himself away from the boy, and said, "Kiera, Del, this is Ramsey. Ramsey, these are my friends."

Ramsey waved. "Hi!"

"What's good, Ramsey?" I dapped him up.

Kiera, reserved, said, "Nice to meet you, Ramsey."

Jameer patted Ramsey's chest, then came to us for a word. "I'm not going home yet."

Kiera went bug-eyed. "You can't be serious right now."

Jameer's demeanor darkened. "Is keeping this secret a problem for you, Kiera?"

"Yes. No. I mean not for the reasons you think. I can't go home without you."

"I know. So cover for me. Give me an hour. I've done it for you."

He had? When? For what?

She leaned in, her words pointed. "What am I supposed to do until then?"

The question stung. The answer seemed obvious to me. We—me and her—would talk. Get to know each other even better. But I stayed out of this. Jameer still seemed a little off-balance from all that wine. He smelled of sour grapes and desperation. "I need one night to be me, Kiera. Please."

She crossed her arms, stared at the sky. When she met his eyes again, she said, "Keep your phone on and don't be late."

Jameer threw his arms around her, kissed her cheek. "Thanks, K."

He ran to Ramsey's ride, hopped in the passenger seat, and the two of them disappeared to wherever. Leaving me and Kiera alone.

"Well?" she said.

"We don't have to walk this time." I motioned to my car, dangled my keys. "We could listen to music. Or talk."

She mulled it over. Each second feeling like a gut punch. Was it that hard to decide?

"Okay," she said finally. "We can discuss what our presentation will look like."

In the car, I turned to an old-school station. Smooth music my parents played when I was growing up, a quiet soundtrack. She didn't seem eager to talk about our presentation, or anything.

To break the awkwardness, I said, "I gotta ask, because I was super nervous when I saw her show up. What happened with you and Angie on the ride to CU?"

"We cleared some things up."

"Should I stop prying?"

"No. Everyone else heard us, and I knew some of the truth already. There were still enough lies in the mix to make me want to be between the girls and Angie. *She* brought up Colossus. Said she wanted me to know nothing really happened between them. Though he did try."

"You believe her?"

"Colossus tried stuff with other girls before. I didn't do anything because I didn't know how. I was taught to forgive."

I'd heard that lesson, too. On more than a few Sundays.

"Finally, got tired. Just in time, I guess."

I said, "He never deserved you."

She got quiet again. The need to make the conversation continue, to crack a joke or ask a question, felt urgent. I fought it. Jaylan's voice in my head. *Do you spend much time listening to each other?*

A couple of random turns, and an extra mile on my odometer later, she said, "Do you feel weird being in the pledge even though you're not a virgin?"

It stunned me enough that I couldn't respond quickly. She said, "I'm sorry. That's a little too personal, isn't it?"

"No," I said, recovering, amazed at how me and Shianne's lie still powered on. It was exhausting in ways, and I considered telling her the truth, right then and there, that we were both virgins.

Instead, "I feel like you can commit to purity at any time."

It was something I regurgitated from one of Sister Vanessa's lectures.

"You're right. Of course," Kiera said. "Do you ever feel tempted, though? Like maybe you can't be pure, even if you promise?"

The endless repetition from our classes became my crutch. "I remind myself there's something better waiting for me. With the right person."

I waited for her to catch on and say the timing was finally right, that *she* was the right person, that she felt all I felt for her.

She didn't.

Our small talk became stagnant. The drive aimless. She spent most of the ride staring at her phone, sending the occasional text. I got aggravated. It was kind of rude ignoring me like that.

When Jameer's requested hour was near its end, she was obviously irritated, so I had to ask, "Is this about time, or that he's with a guy?"

Maybe it sounded harsher than I meant. I wasn't in the best mood.

"I've known Jameer liked boys forever. He's one of my best friends."

"You're cool with it, then?"

"Yes." There was some bite in her voice. "I'm cool with it."

"Even though the church isn't?"

"My church means a lot to me, in many different ways, but I still think for myself. I won't be a bigot no matter what, and I believe my God is fine with that. Do *you* have a problem with Jameer and Ramsey?"

"Not in the slightest."

"So why's it feel like we're having an argument?"

I didn't answer fast enough. Couldn't.

"Can you start driving me toward my house? We can park on the back street and wait for him there."

Fine. As you wish.

The hour Jameer had asked for became an hour and fifteen minutes. Then an hour and a half. The tension in my car shifted by degrees, as Kiera kept checking the time on her phone.

"What is he doing?" She sent her dozenth text.

Her phone buzzed back. "It's my mom, asking where I am."

Understanding the stakes, I began my own text to Jameer, hoping the double harassment would get him in gear. Before I finished, headlights shone in my rearview.

Ramsey's car pulled within a few feet of my bumper, then cut the headlights so the glare wouldn't blind us. Kiera went slack with relief. Even though we were in the same vicinity, Jameer still wasn't in much of a hurry. I could see their silhouettes leaned into each other, gyrating with their sloppy kissing.

"Oh come on," she said, her phone vibrating with, most likely, another parental check-in.

Kiera reached over, triggered a short burst from my horn.

The silhouettes separated.

Jameer left Ramsey's car, shuffled over to mine, and pawed at the door handle until he was able to fall into my backseat, giddy.

Kiera killed his mood. "You better hope we're not in trouble."

Ramsey drove off, and I circled the block, parking between their houses. Kiera ran down their cover story.

"The three of us stayed late at Antonelli's discussing church stuff. We didn't text because our phones were dead, and we didn't think it was a big deal. At the worst, they're annoyed with us. Got it?"

Jameer gave a lackadaisical thumbs-up. "Whatever you say, boss."

Kiera sneered, said, "Thanks for the ride, Del. See you in church tomorrow."

Jameer clapped a hand on my shoulder. "Thanks for everything today, Del."

They parted, on the way to their respective porches, and I sat a moment.

Thanks for the ride, Del? That's it? I do everything it took to pull the day off and *Jameer* got more action than me?

This some bullshit.

Jerking my gearshift to drive, I made a hard turn out of Kiera's neighborhood. Pissssssed.

I couldn't shake the feeling the whole way home.

CHAPTER 22

Tyrell: Del, Stu's going to be out again. If
you could get here even a half hour earlier,
it would be super helpful. Let me know if
that's possible ASAP

Tyrell's text woke me up three minutes before my alarm was supposed to go off. That made me cranky enough to not hit him back. I'd see him later, during my regularly scheduled shift, thank you very much.

Honestly, though, I was cranky with or without his text. Last night kind of sucked.

I got dressed out of habit, rode with Mom to First Missionary with earbuds in, listening to ratchet-ass trap music; Mom could miss me with that gospel today. When we sat in our pew, I did a quick head count of the Purity Pledgers. All present, all in their usual spots. Those who'd had the most wine looked a little sluggish. Jameer's chin rested on his sternum like he could doze off at any second.

Kiera was settled in between her parents, greeted me with a cursory wave. I felt crankier than ever.

So I committed to zoning. No holy rolling for me that morning.

Service started. The choir sang. The announcements got read. Tried to keep it all in the background while I thought on more pleasant things. But every so often my gaze drifted to the front pew, where Tavia, her grandmother, and her kid sat. Flashbacks of last week's horrible forced confession made it difficult to think of better places.

Newsome took the pulpit, opened his Bible as if he meant to read, then gently closed it, staring at the cover. His silence went on for an extended moment, long enough to trigger concerned murmurs.

"Pastor?" someone asked, I didn't know who.

When he spoke, it was with the utmost sadness. "I have discovered we have a wolf in sheep's clothing among us."

Startled parishioners looked to each other for meaning. The wide-eyed faithful got rapturous, perhaps sensing a fire-and-brimstone sermon coming. Coach Scott squeak-shouted back, "A wolf in sheep's clothing. Amen!"

"I need to repent!" Newsome slapped the podium. "I made the mistake of thinking I could shirk my duties as the spiritual leader of this house, and let the Lord do all the work Himself. Now, we know He is able to do any and all things in heaven and on Earth, but he still requires discernment from us. I was not discerning when I let something other than a single-minded focus on God distract our young people. I looked the other way when I saw dangerous influences swaying them. I am not looking away anymore."

The dramatic pause was epic. Felt a month long. Long enough for suspicions to rise.

Newsome took a strange turn. "Television is Satan's tool, you know that. Shows everything except glory for the Lord. But, I recall many years ago, a public service announcement that used to air. 'It's ten p.m. Do you know where your children are?' Anybody else remember that?"

Some chuckles from the old heads. I had no clue what he was talking about.

"It was a good question. I know most everyone in here knows where their children are at that time of night. What about during the day? Do you always know?"

Some grumbling. Some cheers, probably from folks still thinking this was some abstract example.

"Did you all know where your children were yesterday afternoon?"

Oh. No.

"It has been brought to my attention that our bright, promising Purity Pledge class attended an event on the campus of Commonwealth University yesterday. It was hosted by a woman who makes sexually explicit internet videos, and I'm certain if you're the parents of these children, you were unaware until this very moment."

The ripple effect was wide and immediate. Parents twisting

in pews, asking stern questions of Helena and Shanice. Mya's mother pointed to her in the choir stand, making a silent promise for later discussion. Across the aisle, Jameer's parents remained composed. He shuddered. His punishment would not be public.

Ralph and Bobby Burton were by themselves, only contending with the flicked glances from adults who would undoubtedly fill their mom in later. The Westings craned their necks to Kiera, seated between them, flanking her with their disapproval.

On the front pew, Sister Vanessa hunched forward, head in hands, either in prayer or tears. Best I could figure, our escape from the CU auditorium wasn't as successful as I thought. She'd seen us. Had reported back. And now . . .

Newsome said, "We know here, at First Missionary, our children are not prone to bad behavior, or deception. At least they didn't learn it from us." He held his Bible high. "Or this. There has been an outside influence—a wolf—integrated among our sweet flock, and Lord help me, I let it happen."

Mom gripped my arm, like she used to when I was little and she needed me to stand still, or stop running through a store. Something like fear pulsing off her.

"The Purity Pledge was meant to be so, so holy," he said. "It has been sullied. It saddens me to say that I can't allow it to continue. Not in its current incarnation."

Sister Vanessa sprang up. "Pastor, no!"

His immediate response was ice. "See. Even my own niece rebels when under the shadow of the evil spirit that has taken hold of these children."

Evil spirit. Me. He was talking about me.

"The Purity Pledge is done. No final ceremony, no Purity Ball! Not until we cleanse this house! Can I get an amen?"

He got it. The amens rattled the foundation.

"Every head bowed! Every eye closed! We will chase Satan off this day!"

They obeyed, praying for the solution. To expel the evil spirit. Truth was, there might have been something to it. I never wanted to leave a place so badly.

If I wasn't evil, I was stubborn. I wouldn't give Newsome the satisfaction. Because this time he was Prayer Peeking, like me.

We locked eyes in a staring contest. I lost.

I bowed my head, closed my eyes. I stayed that way for the rest of service. It was easier than seeing all the disappointed faces surrounding me.

Service ended. A huddle formed at the front of the sanctuary. All of the Purity Pledger parents, converging on my mother.

What was said, I did not know. It seemed calm. At first. Like watching muted television without the subtitles. Then energy shifted abruptly.

Tense shoulders and jerky hand movements. Shanice's mother stomped away three paces, then spun back, speaking fast and wagging her finger. Helena's dad laughed a lot, but not in a funny joke way. It was the "I'm supposed to buy your bull?" laugh.

What was Mom saying? She didn't know anything about yesterday, none of them had until Newsome blew us up. It was only when he joined the huddle did things seem to calm.

Not among the Pledgers, though. We'd all stayed in our pews, flicking horrified looks at each other.

At Newsome's direction, the other parents relaxed their hungry lion poses, allowing Mom a small window to escape, summoning me with a finger snap. "Let's. Go."

I jerked to my feet and hopped into the aisle like she'd snapped an invisible leash. We climbed into the car silently, and were a half mile from First Missionary before the conversation I dreaded started.

"What did you do, Del?"

"Mom, all we did was go to Cressie's school to see—"

"You had those children lying to their parents and you took them out of the city without permission! Anything could've happened. Some of those kids are barely teenagers!"

"I know. I wasn't trying to take them at first. They sort of—"

"I don't care! *You* didn't have permission. You're not grown. You don't pay for that car. Are you rolling your damn eyes?"

"No." Maybe.

"Those parents are furious. At you. At me for not knowing what you were up to. They're right to be. Do you even get that? It's bad enough what I've been dealing with now that Cressie wants to be a NewsTuber or whatever."

"YouTuber."

"Boy, if you think this is the day for you to correct me, you are sorely mistaken."

I shut up. Though I had questions. Cressie's videos were

causing problems for Mom around town?

Mom said, "You better start explaining yourself, Delbert Lamond Rainey Junior!"

My whole-whole name. Damn. "Pastor Newsome is blowing the whole thing up because he doesn't like me, Mom."

"The pastor doesn't like you? So, it's his fault that you snuck behind my back, and did things you weren't supposed to. When are you going to grow up and take some responsibility?"

"I am, though!"

Mom said, "Oh sweet Jesus, I can't with you right now. Let's see what your daddy has to say about this."

In the garage, I ejected myself from the car as the door ratcheted down behind us. I entered the house first, thinking I might catch a breather while stripping out of my church clothes. Maybe sneak-text Kiera to make sure she was okay.

Nope. In the kitchen, I found Dad clutching the house phone, with his head bobbing, a fighter's posture. He said, "There you are. Sit your ass down right now."

The hell? Had Newsome called the house?

I did as told. When Mom stormed in and sensed trouble, she said, "What's wrong? Is it Cressie?"

"Naw. She fine." He aimed the phone at me like a gun. "Guess who I spoke to. Your boss at Monte FISHto's. Mister Tyrell."

My head dropped into my hands.

Dad told Mom, "He's been trying to get Junior some shifts. Moneybags over here has been turning him down with no explanation. When he does show up, he's goofing off and breaking rules so he has to get sent home early. Funny thing is I don't recall Junior coming home early any of those days he was supposed to be working. Do you?"

"I. Do. Not," Mom said.

With all the effort in the world, I lifted my chin, and looked my executioners in their eyes. "It's not what you think."

"It isn't?" Dad said. "Because I'm thinking you're in the streets doing dumb shit. Are you hustling?"

"No way, Dad. I know better."

"But you have money?" Mom countered, their double-teaming masterful. "How?"

"Tutoring. Shianne Griffiths. Her dad's been paying me to help her get caught up at school." It was the half-lie me and Shianne agreed to, so I felt justified in arguing like it was absolutely true.

That righteousness was not good currency today.

Mom said, "So something else you decided to keep from us."

Dad's head wrenched her way. "What you mean?"

"Let me give you a little recap of church service this morning."

Mom told him everything, with the added bonus of the huddled conversations after service. "The other parents tore me a new one. It's not about him being this ringleader taking their kids across the state like a human trafficker. The whole Pledge has been canceled because of our son's 'corrupting influence.'"

Dad's mouth twisted. "That's ridiculous. They're talking about him like he's the damn devil. Though I guess that kind of exaggeration can be expected from folks like that."

"Folks like who? Like me? Because I happen to think they're correct to be upset that a good thing their children committed to has been upended by our son?"

"You mean the thing that's a step above fitting those kids for chastity belts? I'm not saying Junior wasn't wrong, but I think the kids will be all right not having to publicly profess their virginity, or however it works."

"You'd know how it works if you stop turning your nose up at everything holy. Oh, wait. Only your opinion matters in this house, though. You know more right from wrong than Jesus Himself."

What was happening here? Did they forget about me?

I stood, thinking this a good time to slip away.

"Sit yo ass down!" they said at the same time. If God ever spoke to me aloud, I imagined it'd sound like that.

Dad said, "Mister Tyrell called here to say he couldn't maintain your employment if you weren't going to work. I convinced him to give you one more chance. You're going to your actual job this afternoon."

"Fine." Anything to get out of here. I tugged my keys from my pants pocket.

"Give me those." Dad extended his hand.

"You said I have to go to work."

"You are. I'm taking you. And picking you up. Same for school."

"For how long?"

"Until I can trust you again. Give me the keys."

I dropped them in his palm.

"And your phone."

"Dad!"

Mom backed him up. "Do what you're told. Any more back-talk is only going to make your situation worse."

I handed my cell over. "Can I go now? I need to change into my uniform if I'm going to FISHto's."

Dad nodded, releasing me. I got halfway up the stairs before he said, "Bring that laptop down here, too."

"What?"

"Until we say otherwise, it's only for homework, and you do that where we can see you."

Was this a Supermax now? Was I Jameer?

A slick voice in the back of my mind whispered: *You're not Jameer. You deserve this.*

There was no fighting this, just enduring it. They were old. They'd forget. Eventually.

It was the only way I knew to comfort myself as I was cut off from the outside world. From Kiera.

How was she? What sort of fallout was she experiencing?

Questions I had no way of answering anytime soon.

According to Dad, I had bigger fish to fry. Literally.

One cold comfort: this couldn't last long. This kind of tech lockdown, the car restriction, we'd been here before. They'd get tired of supervising, of being my chauffeur. This would go three, maybe four days if they were feeling hard core.

In my room, tugging on my FISHto's shirt, I thought, This is nothing. It won't last.

Seventeen days later, with Cressie home on break, Mom hauling in last-minute groceries, Dad prepping the Thanksgiving turkey, and me still as cut off from the world as my parents could manage, my conviction waned.

CHAPTER 23

NOT THAT THOSE DAYS BETWEEN Newsome's ultimate judgment and the holiday were uneventful; I simply had no effect on the twists and turns.

The only free contact I had with anyone outside my house was the cafeteria at school. That first day at lunch Qwan explained what happened between him and Angie at the grotto.

"Maybe I had too much of that wine, D," he began. "Things were going okay, I was trying to say the right stuff, but she kept talking about, you know, possibly being pregnant. It's all she wanted to talk about. It was freaking me out, but I kept it cool, until she asked me what kind of dad I thought I'd be. So I was like, 'Whatever kind you want so you don't blow me up on some #BabyGettersToo-type shit.'"

"Oh." We'd all heard how the rest of that conversation went. "Have you talked to her since?"

He nodded, slowly. I noticed the only thing on his tray was an orange, and Qwan generally didn't eat fruit unless you figured a way to fry it. My dude was off.

"She hit me up last night and said I didn't have to worry about getting blown up. Her period came." He picked the orange up, examined it like he didn't understand it either, dropped it back on his tray. "She also told me not to speak to her again. She said people here treat her bad all the time. She wasn't about to date one of them."

Whoa. "I'm sorry. You for real like her, don't you?"

"I love her, D." His voice was so low, I barely heard it. Louder, he said, "If you ever bring up that I said that, I'm kicking you in the chest."

"Noted."

Qwan, never one to let the shield down for long, turned us back to my messed-up life. "What's up with your situation? No car, no phone. How long's that going to last?"

Still under the impression my parents would cave after a few days, maybe a week at the most, I waved it off. Had no reason not to. So, my concern lay more with the Purity Pledgers and how they were feeling the fallout of the CU road trip. What I heard from pieced-together reports passed along from Jameer when I was at school and Mya when we shared shifts at FISHto's. Some punishments were more severe than others. The Burton Brothers got their game systems and music recording equipment taken away. Helena and Shanice were forced to sign up for extra chores at the church. Jameer couldn't be oppressed much more in his house, so nothing changed for him. Mya didn't get into any trouble at all.

"My mom yelled a little, but she's never come down on

me hard," she said while we unpacked the new shipment of Cra-Burgers in the FISHto's deep freezer. "She told me I do more right than wrong so she's a little relieved when I step out of bounds."

"Since you're still free, maybe you can bring me more comics to read."

"You checked out *Shuri*?" She sounded skeptical.

"I did." As of last night. With no connection to the outside world, I would've read the laundry tags on my shirts to keep from going stir crazy.

"And?"

"It was dope."

She sighed all dramatic. "Guess I gotta read some *Batman* now."

"That was the deal. You should have your Tuesdays and Thursdays free, so it shouldn't be too hard."

She stopped unloading patties. "That's not funny. Believe it or not, the Pledge meant something to most of us."

I believed her, but felt an accusation in her tone, so I let the conversation taper off and made no special effort to pick it back up that night. I didn't twist anyone's arm on the road trip—hell, I actually told most of them not to come. It wasn't my call to cancel the whole damn Pledge. All that, and she still wasn't mad at Newsome? Not my problem.

In any case, we were all accounted for with our individual sentences known, except for Kiera. I asked Jameer how the Westings were treating her. Because his parents were keeping such a tight leash on him, he had no clue.

"All the parents have been consistent on this," Jameer said, "the Pledgers aren't allowed to talk to each other. Everyone thinks everyone else is the bad influence."

I barely saw her in the halls at school, and when I did, Mason Miles was always near.

That made it hard to concentrate in English, and in gym where I spent the most time around Mason. An angry flip-flopping of two questions. How you, Mason? Why you, Mason?

In the midst of my stint in purgatory, Cressie dropped a whole damn series of videos calling out Green Creek High for allowing the harassment of the Baby-Getters, not providing a curriculum that educated the students in safe sex practices, and essentially calling our whole town a puritanical pothole. If anything, I could thank my sister for taking half the burden of Mom's wrath. I might've shamed her out of the church she'd grown accustomed to (sleeping in Sundays was the only bonus from all this), but Cressie made it so Mom had to answer questions about her daughter throwing dirt on the town's name.

Qwan told me Cressie's subscribers had jumped to like fifteen thousand, so I imagined Mom's irritation was a price she'd been more than willing to pay.

With no other time away from my parents' scowling and school, I found myself embracing FISHto's. Really throwing myself into the shifts. I used to wish for the clock to speed up so I could leave the oblong Flounder Fingers and Cod Crisps behind. Not anymore. With no other distractions, little stuff became obsession. The straw dispenser could never be more than half empty. The condiment cubbies beneath the counter could not be in disarray. When I found out the shrimp fryer oil was a week overdue for a changing, I lost my shit, to the shock of my wary coworkers, who remembered I'd once wished for a grease fire to take the whole building down.

Tyrell took notice of my newfound initiative.

The night before Thanksgiving, he caught me dragging two trash liners through the back entrance before dinner rush, the plastic bins bopping against each other while I worked the heavy latch with my free hand.

"Del," he said, lurking in the shadows like a serial killer. "What you doing?"

"Cleaning."

He leaned over the bins, scrutinizing. "You hosed these down?"

"Yes. We're expecting a crowd, right? Night before Thanksgiving, everyone's cooking for tomorrow. I do something wrong?"

"Not at all. Feel like taking drive-thru?"

That froze me. Drive-thru was, like, running point. The quarterback. The captain's chair. Qwan was still working here the last time I had a crack at it. During dinner rush, Tyrell often ran it himself because he was obsessed with wait times and didn't want any backups.

"You want me"—it was hard processing this handoff of responsibility—"to do it?"

"Grab a headset. If you're up for it."

I was.

• • •

When the dinner rush hit, it hit! For an hour straight, I was taking orders, and cash, and cards, while filling drink cups, and bagging up Cra-Burgers hot off the grill. Not only was I rocking the NFL coach–style headset, I'd donned the FISHto's parka, crimson like our swashbuckling mascot's waistcoat, because Virginia was acting appropriately seasonal for once, and opening the window for each order was like cracking the airlock on a ship in frigid space. Icy gusts slapped my cheeks and forehead, which I kind of liked. It kept me sharp. Focused on getting the orders right. So focused, I didn't recognize the voice in my ear ordering two Fun Flounder meals with extra cocktail sauce and Whale-Sized drinks.

I scooped ice, poured Cokes, dropped sandwiches and Clam Clusters in a bag, layered on some napkins, and placed the extra sauces on top. When I popped the window to pass them out, Mason Miles waited, a debit card extended while he chatted with his passenger.

Kiera.

I froze. Not from the wind. I couldn't feel the cold anymore. Couldn't feel anything.

Mason's neck twisted. "What up, Del?"

My attention was on her. Her eyes flicked down, though she managed a squeaky "Hey Del."

"Hey." That wasn't me speaking. Was it? I felt outside of myself, like my soul was leaving my body and watching all this from the outside. One final torment before moving on to a (hopefully) better place.

"Del?" Mason said. "You good?"

I still hadn't taken his card. Kiera wouldn't even look at me.

Muscle memory unstuck me, got me through. I swiped his card, returned it with his receipt, then passed him his order. All on autopilot. A robot performing a programmed task. Even mentioned, "Be careful with those drinks," as I pushed the cardboard cup holder to him.

"Thanks, man." He peeled away. No "the best man won" posturing. Nothing disrespectful. It was too cold for all that.

"Del!" Tyrell shouted, unmistakable disappointment in his voice. "We're backing up! Can you handle this or not?"

"Sure," I lied.

But he was talking about drive-thru, wasn't he?

"Hey, could you pass that cranberry sauce?" Cressie asked.

I'd barely tasted any of the food as my family chatted at the table Thanksgiving Day. Couldn't concentrate on the Cowboys game with Dad. Or Cressie and Mom's annual *The Wizard of Oz* viewing. My body was present, but my mind was still in that drive-thru window, catching a cold slap to the face.

The next morning, at 4 a.m., when Mom knocked on my bedroom door, asking if I was venturing out with her and my sister to watch the Black Friday retail brawls, I was awake but declined. What if Mason had Thanksgiving dinner with the Westings?

What kind of moping troll I looked like, I didn't know. The couple of times I glanced in a mirror, patches of my face alternated between oily and ashy. My shower game was not on point and Cressie wasn't shy about letting me know. On Saturday, when it was time for my evening shift at FISHto's, Dad lounged on the couch, enjoying some alone time since Mom and Cressie had taken a long drive to Richmond for hot yoga and lunch.

"Sorry to interrupt, Dad." I was fresh and clean simply because I didn't need Tyrell getting on me about BO. "But I need to get to work soon."

He didn't look away from the screen. "Talked to your mom about it. It's been long enough. You can have your keys back. You're on probation, though. Any slipups, and I might sell that car."

I noticed my confiscated possessions on the end table next to his sweaty cup of sweet tea. Keys. Phone. Laptop. Like the coveted power-ups in some video game that'd been kicking my ass. Snatching them, I ran from the house, fearing some trick or reversal. My drive to FISHto's was the most disciplined I'd done since testing for my license.

With twenty minutes before my shift, I powered up my phone and saw two weeks of missed texts pop and scroll. There weren't as many as I'd hoped for. Mostly everyone who would text knew I couldn't respond, so aside from a single "you still on lockdown?" message from Shianne, there was nothing.

So, I hit up Kiera.

> **Me:** Hey, I'm off punishment.
> What have you been up to?

The response bubble popped up. The ellipses danced as she typed her reply.

The bubble vanished.

I waited, stomach twisting. Fifteen minutes later she hadn't responded and I needed to clock in.

My entire shift, my phone bulged in my pocket. A few times it vibrated while I was ringing up a customer, and as soon as the order was complete I'd check it right there on the front line, even though that was against the rules. No return text from Kiera, only notifications from apps like ESPN and SoundCloud.

On my break I resisted the urge to text again, though I checked her IG. No new posts since before Newsome busted us. Old pics of her and her brother Wes, her and the Purity Pledger girls. The formerly prominent pics of her and Colossus had been scrubbed from her page. There was nothing new with Mason. That was motivation enough to get through the rest of my shift without having a total meltdown.

After my shift, I gave in and hit her up again.

> **Me:** You're really quiet. Hope you're okay.

An immediate response came through.

> **Kiera:** I'm fine. Thanks. Hope you're well, too.

Nothing more. No dancing ellipses, no questions about my well-being. I was salty the rest of the night. Feeling like, somehow, my punishment continued on.

No FISHto's shift, and no church, made for a Sunday that stretched like rubber. Mom drove Cressie back to school, Dad spent most of the day in his office doing work stuff. I escaped, hoping to see Qwan. He wasn't responding to texts, and when I went by his crib, Ms. Reid was like, "He at that girl's house."

Qwan was trying to fix things. Good for him, I guess.

I got away as fast as I could, and pulled over at the 7-Eleven to text Shianne.

> **Me:** I'm out on parole. Feel like some company?

> **Shianne:** Zoey had the worst night last night. So I had the worst night, too. Maybe later this week.

I toyed with the idea of texting Jameer. Naw. Knowing how his parents rolled, he was probably in a prayer closet at that very moment.

Already bored with my reclaimed freedom, I couldn't stand the idea of returning home. I drove, aimless at first, but quickly recognizing I'd picked a destination, if only subconsciously at first. The library.

There were authors whose names were drilled into me because of MJ. Gloria Naylor. James Baldwin. Walter Dean Myers. Tiffany D. Jackson. Kwame Alexander. Nic Stone. Meg Medina. Jason Reynolds. Gene Luen Yang. Lilliam Rivera. Cindy Pon. Before long, I was balancing a stack of books and duck-walking to an armchair, lowering the stack to the floor. Sampling a chapter or two, I worked through the pile, then revisited the volumes that struck me most.

When the PA announcement said the library would close in fifteen minutes, I checked out three books, and took them home to find Dad placing delivered pizzas on the counter. Mom joined us, and I told them about my reading. It was the first conversation I'd participated in that wasn't church related, job related, annoyance related in . . . I couldn't remember. Time passed quickly; by the time I got upstairs, and Kiera slammed back into my head with the force of a tossed kettlebell, dazing me, I recognized there was light beyond the all-consuming maneuvering to be in her world.

That light winked out.

Me: You home?

Kiera: Yep.

Me: I hope this doesn't sound weird, but, even though we don't have the Pledge anymore,

I thought we could still hang out.
Be friends.

Kiera: Friends sounds good.

Me: That's awesome. Glad to
hear.

Kiera: Yeah.

The texts went on like that for the better part of an hour. Her responses slow and erratically spaced. The drive-thru chill hit me again, and I couldn't take not knowing what to say, or do, or feel about it all. So, I went all in . . .

Me: I gotta ask you something
important. I hope it's all right.

Kiera: What is it?

Me: The night I saw you with
Mason at FISHto's . . . are you
two together now?

My worst fear was no response. The bubble appearing, then gone, with no more contact tonight. I'd probably die and decompose in my bed. But, her response was quick and direct.

Kiera: lol

Kiera: Me and Mason together? He's a friend. Nicer than I thought he could be, but, nope. No way.

I could've floated to the ceiling.

Me: Yo, let's hang out this week.

Kiera: Maybe. We'll see.

Mason wasn't her boyfriend and maybe wasn't no. That was something I could work with. Given the hours I'd been putting in at FISHto's, I had a nice check coming. Maybe we could get out of Green Creek. A road trip like the kind I'd originally planned. Without the burden of Purity Pledge, or Newsome, or Mason, or anything hanging over us.

We'd gotten through the worst of things.

It's what I thought then.

CHAPTER 24

SOUND CARRIED IN THE BOYS' locker room, so Qwan spoke low, filling me in on his Angie situation while we dressed for Monday's gym class. He tugged his extra-tight gym shirt over his head, talking through the thin fabric.

"A brother's been straight-up begging," he said. "I never thought I'd do it, but it's killing me that she's staying so distant."

I tugged on my faded sweats. "It's working?"

"I think she enjoys watching me grovel. She's grinning a lot as I do her various chores while her dad works his evening shifts. I've done the dishes, raked the leaves, cleaned the gutters."

"Her dad makes her clean gutters?"

"I don't think so. She be adding stuff to the list to see if I'll do it. But I get to be near her and she seems less mad at me every day. It's worth it."

Loud belly laughs erupted on the other side of the locker wall. Mason and his JROTC not caring about the amplified acoustics. I hadn't been paying attention to their conversation before. That changed quickly. One of Mason's extra-loud soldiers said,

"So what they say about them church girls is true!"

Thunderclaps from high fives. More laughs. My jaw clenched, and Qwan must've sensed the wrongness here. He said, "D?"

I was already moving. Slow, listening. I peeked around the corner, saw four guys leaning into Mason.

"Bro!" Mason said, volume lowering in a conspiratorial kind of way. "They. Ain't. Never. Lied."

More whoops and encouragement.

"In your car, though?"

"What you want me to say?" Mason wolf-grinned. "She's flexible."

Qwan grabbed my shoulder. Whispered, "Come on, let's get out on the floor."

I shook his hand off. "In a second."

Another of the JROTC guys said, "Don't let Colossus find out."

"Her and that dude are crazy done. She won't even mention his name. After last night," he paused, dramatic, "she probably don't even remember it. Feel me?"

"Bull. Shit." A new voice in the conversation. Mine. I rounded the corner fully.

"D, stop," Qwan said, tagging behind me like he was connected by an invisible tow chain.

All the bragging joy swirled from the room like dirty water down a drain.

Mason stood, smirking. "Huh?"

Volcanic rage unlike anything I'd ever felt bubbled in my

chest, over my tongue, into the world. "Everybody know you be lying on your dick. I'm not going to sit here and let you throw dirt on Kiera's name like that."

Mason looked perplexed, the way people in street magic videos do when they can't figure how the trick works. "Del, my dude, you need to stay in your lane. This don't have nothing to do with you."

"The hell it don't."

Mean laughs from the spectators, as crisp as cracking bones. Mason closed the gap between us. Meaner than I'd ever seen him. "I don't know what your problem is, but I ain't the one."

Qwan, from over my shoulder, said, "Back up, Mason."

"Get your boy, Qwan."

Qwan tried for my shoulder again. I shook him off again, jabbed a finger toward Mason's nose, a half inch from poking him. "Tell the truth. Tell them Kiera's not what you're saying."

Mason's shoulders slumped as if he'd grown suddenly exhausted. He stepped even closer to me, clamped a hand on my arm, almost comforting. "I can see this is bothering you, and I don't know what to say other than she was so, so good."

He stretched out the last word like a singer would, glancing back at his boys for clownish approval before facing me again.

I hit him.

It wasn't a great punch, or even a good one. As I clipped his chin, he rolled his neck in the same direction as my swing, so my knuckles only glanced off him.

He leapt backward, looking down his own body as if I'd

vomited on him instead of attempted to kick his ass. "The fuck, bro?"

He leapt forward, his punches quicker and harder than mine. Body blows, a left-right-left combination, had me folding at the hip, gasping. Mason caught me mid-collapse and flung me into the locker. My body generated a percussive blast like warped cymbals.

Qwan wedged himself between us, shoving Mason back so no more punches landed. His crew was gathered around, in case this became a group brawl—one where the odds weren't in me and Qwan's favor.

"Chill," Qwan told Mason.

"He's the one you need to be talking to." Mason glared at me.

"If Coach Scott even suspects y'all were fighting, we might all get suspended. Nobody says anything. Okay?"

Leaning, the lockers propping me up as I remembered how to breathe and various parts of my body throbbed, I watched Qwan show restraint, negotiating peace where he might've been throwing punches before, and had the strangest thought: Angie's really good for him.

Mason backed away, looking more frustrated at himself than mad at me. He pointed at the others. "Y'all ain't see nothing. I can't afford to get suspended over Del's punk ass." Then, to me, "Touch me again and you're getting worse."

They all poured from the locker room, snickering at my quick and effortless defeat.

Qwan said, "D, what was that?"

I didn't know. I only shook my head, pulled myself together, and left the locker room. Out there, Mason didn't acknowledge me. Coach Scott didn't drag me. Kiera spared me a single, concerned glance.

I went to her.

It'll be okay, I thought with force, hoping she'd sense my reassurance from across the gym. It will.

No way Mason wouldn't notice me and her talking, but we were all invested in no scenes on the open floor.

Kiera said, "What's going on?"

"Do me a favor. Let me drive you home after school? It's important."

"Important how?"

"Trust me. First Missionary Crew, right?"

A slow, skeptical nod. "Okay. I'll meet you at your car."

We got through gym without incident, though I could barely concentrate on any of the drills or the lackluster volleyball game Coach Scott insisted on. In the locker room, I got dressed fast, Qwan standing guard in case something jumped off, but Mason and his boys never even came back in. On my way to the exit, I spotted him and his crew in conversation with the sergeant that oversaw the JROTC. Though he flicked glances my way, he couldn't stop me without going AWOL or whatever.

Kiera met me at my car. My joy at finally getting time with her was tempered by the inevitable mood-killing conversation we were about to have. No way was she going to react well to Mason telling lies about her. I ran through likely scenarios—sadness, shame, rage—and wondered about the best way to comfort her, to remind her all dudes aren't trash like him.

She saw me coming, lifting her phone as if I could read the tiny texts from yards away. "People are saying you and Mason got in some kind of fight."

Of course they were, despite Qwan's warning.

"Get in," I said, "I'll tell you about it in the car."

With the school in my rearview, I worried about a kill-the-messenger situation. She needed to know, though. When Taylor Burkin dropped that first #BabyGettersToo video, Kiera had been happy I hadn't left her in the dark. Maybe she'd be happy again. We could figure a way to get in front of Mason's lies. "Look, what I'm about to say, nobody's going to believe it. Everyone knows Mason makes things up."

"Things like what?"

Do it, Del. Don't be a punk. "He was telling guys in the locker room that you two had sex in his car. They believed it because they don't know you like I do. So, I stepped in. We had an altercation."

She was quiet, processing it. I knew better than to expect a thank-you right away.

"He told people that?" she said.

I was outraged for her. At a stoplight, I turned to her, prepared for tears. Her face was slack. Unreadable. I asked, "You okay?"

"I don't know."

"He can't get away with making stuff up that way. That's,

what's it called? *Slander!* I know it might be embarrassing, but maybe you should tell your parents. Or your brother!" I thought better of that. "He'd probably rip Mason apart. Not that he wouldn't deserve it."

The car behind me honked; I'd missed the light changing. I put us in motion again.

Halfway to her house, she still hadn't said much. "What are you thinking, Kiera?"

She squirmed. I reached for her hand, trying to comfort her. When my fingers grazed hers, she pulled away. Her silence was suffocating.

"He was lying," I said, "right?"

She said, "I didn't think he was going to be talking about us like that."

My throat constricted. My hands felt shaky on the steering wheel. "Us? You told me he was a friend."

"He is. Was."

"So you didn't have sex with him? Because we were in a group that pledged not to do that, Kiera."

"I didn't plan to, it sort of happened."

My emotions shape-shifted. Sadness, rage, shame. "Did he—did he force you?"

"No! I'm saying we didn't plan it in advance. We were together and one thing led to another. I didn't expect for him to act this way about it."

"Well, you should've!" It was louder than it needed to be with only us in the car, not as loud as I felt like being. How could she?

"Excuse me?"

"You should've known better!" my voice echoed.

She twisted in her seat again, facing me now. "Who do you think you're yelling at right now, Del? You need to relax."

"Me? I'm the one you're worried about. Mason in there dogging you to his friends, but I'm the bad guy now."

"I'll deal with Mason. Okay? But you're a little too deep in my business right now. I don't know why, but I don't like it."

Deep breaths; I forced my voice softer. "Was the Purity Pledge a joke, Kiera? Because I seem to remember you questioning my motives and intentions from day one."

She shook her head. "No. I didn't."

"You pulled me aside, got all into my reputation, and if I was going to be a problem for the other kids, and—?"

"I wasn't questioning *you*, Del. I was questioning me."

"I don't understand anything you're saying right now."

"Are we friends, Del? For real? First Missionary Crew?"

I said yes because what else was I going to say.

Kiera wiped a hand down her face, like she could squeegee away the day's stress. "I wasn't a virgin when the pledge started. Me and Colossus, we'd been doing it. But when I found out he'd tried to cheat on me with Angie, I wanted a fresh start. When I saw you join, and I'd heard how you and Qwan be with all these different girls, it made me wonder if either of us had any business in that pledge. I came at you because I felt guilty."

My car felt unsteady. Maybe it was the road. Or the entire world. Everything was off. "You've been lying about your virginity?"

"I didn't lie. I never said I was a virgin."

You know this game, that slick, back-of-my-mind voice whispered. You know it well.

"But, Mason?! After you took the pledge. After you promised."

The first sob tore from her. "I know."

She was hurting; me rubbing her broken vow in her face was salt in a wound. Good! "Out here acting like a THOT." I was all rage then, none of the other emotions. It felt good being real about all this bullshit. For once.

"Like a what, Del?" She sniffed, cut off the tears, slapped me. Almost as hard as Mason punched. Then, she slapped me again. "I'm acting like a what?"

I swerved. We were in her neighborhood by then, and not going fast, thank God. "Stop! You're going to make me wreck the fucking car."

Her hand hovered, vibrating with the need to hit me again. Instead, she said, "Take. Me. Home." Like we couldn't see her house ahead.

I pulled into her driveway, and she was out the car before I was at a full stop, slamming my door with enough force to rock the suspension. She stomped up her porch steps, to the front door, then spun to deliver one last message.

Sweet church girl Kiera flashed her middle finger.

All my anger rushed back, and I drove home saying horrible things—more horrible than what I'd called her.

The anger lingered at home. I trudged through the kitchen, past Dad's office. On my way up the stairs he popped his head out and said, "What up, son. Good school day?"

I only grunted, barricading myself in my room. At dinnertime, I ate fast, aware of my parents watching warily, then communicating their concern in that silent way they'd mastered. They didn't ask, I didn't tell. I went to my room still chewing.

In bed, my thumbs hovered over my phone screen. I hesitated over the message. What good would it do?

Me: I haven't been acting like myself lately, and I want to see you. Can I come over tomorrow? Please?

Screw it. I hit Send.

The response was immediate.

Shianne: Cool. See you tomorrow.

CHAPTER 25

SCHOOL WAS HELL THE NEXT day.

Word of the locker room incident spread. Not so much to get me and Mason dragged into Terrier's office, but enough to get me joked on all damn day, dudes squaring up in the hall and shadowboxing close enough to my face that I felt the breeze off their knuckles. My newly swollen eye didn't help my cause. Too bad it wasn't swollen enough to hide the smug victorious looks Mason flicked my way as we crossed paths.

If the day was hell for me, Kiera's torment wasn't far behind. Mason's conquest tale made the rounds, too. I saw her once before our shared gym class, books held tight to her chest, head low, guys leering, inquiring loudly about how "gooood" she was.

Midday, while swapping books at my locker, I emerged and found an anxious, sad-faced Mya leaning on the locker next to mine. "What's going on with you and Kiera? I'm hearing all kinds of things."

"Maybe you shouldn't listen." I slammed my locker and kept it moving.

After school, I headed home for a quick shower, a few spritzes of Dad's best cologne, then straight to Shianne's, where she greeted me at the door with a screaming Zoey on her hip.

"What's wrong with her?" I scooted by, gave shrieking Zoey a wide berth. I sensed the emptiness of the house.

"Does it look like I know, Del? Mom passed her to me the minute I came in, warned me she's been cranky all day, then escaped. She's fed. Her diaper's fresh. I tried to put her down for a nap but she cried more. At this point, I'm leaning toward demonic possession. Do you have any holy water?"

"I do not."

Shianne groaned. Then sniffed deeply. "Are you wearing cologne?"

Proud, hopeful, I said, "You like?"

"It makes me want to sneeze. Come on."

She led me to the TV room. Zoey calmed slightly when Shianne laid her on the couch cushions. By calm, I meant her screaming became more of a persistent growl. Babies did that? "She sounds like a wolf cub."

Shianne scowled. "You've had a day, I hear."

"Everybody's heard. Something. Probably ain't the truth."

"You're alive, and Mason's not in jail. That disproves one of the stories. You two fighting over Kiera, though?"

"I guess. It was stupid."

"You're correct."

Zoey wasn't crying anymore. She made a gurgling sound that seemed suspiciously like agreeing with her mama's point.

I said, "Should've listened to you from the beginning."

Shianne jerked forward, a single eyebrow arched. "About what?"

"When you said Kiera wasn't worth it."

She ceased her baby wrangling, considering it. "I didn't say that. I never said that about her."

"I mean, you said she was uptight."

"I did. That doesn't have anything to do with her *worth*. I thought you'd like a different kind of girl. She all churchy, and you aren't."

"She ain't that churchy."

Shianne's eyes narrowed, but she was quiet.

I said, "You should've heard the way Mason and his dickbag army were talking about her. I can't figure why she put herself out there like that over that dude. I thought she was smarter than that."

"So you think she's stupid now?"

I shrugged. "What would you call it?"

"Del, you may not want to hear this, but Mason's ridiculous hot. Sometimes, that overrides common sense. I should know." Zoey cooed as if she agreed.

What the hell, Shi? I didn't come here to talk about Mason being hot. "Well obviously it wasn't worth it. And me, like a dummy, defending her when it was really true."

"Aren't you noble." It was tense, sharp. Zoey started crying again.

"What's that supposed to mean?"

"You tell me."

"I'm saying she's a liar. She played me." I grazed my puffy eye with my fingertips. "I got this because of her."

"Want me to get you a cookie?" She picked up the baby, rocking her. Shielding her, almost. "I should tell you how great you are. That's what you want me to do, isn't it? Give you a trophy. Because you've *never* said crazy disrespectful things about any girls the way Mason did. Right?"

Something had changed in the room. A different kind of pressure. Storm clouds. "What you acting mad at me for?"

"You don't even hear yourself."

"Yo, am I bothering you? Should I leave?"

"You should if you came here for me to cosign on your fake heroics."

"Fake—? I was trying to keep Kiera's name from being dragged through the mud."

"You just called her a liar and said she wasn't smart. You're dragging her fine on your own."

"Shianne, stop twisting everything I say. I know you're tired from the baby and all, but you acting like I did something to Kiera."

"Wowwww! I can't have an opinion about this nonsense you brought to my doorstep. I must be tired, and not thinking clearly. It can't be that you're wrong. Why exactly did you want to come here, Del? Why am I suddenly worthy of cologne?"

"I thought I was coming to see my friend."

"So, it won't bother you if my dad doesn't pay you."

You know what, screw this. I went for the door, but spun and faced her again, needing to get this off my chest. "I don't get y'all. For real. All of you say you want a nice guy, but you can't see one sitting right in front of you, then get mad at us when we tired of the bullshit."

She laughed. Laughed! The insanity of it enraged me. "What's so funny?"

"Del," Shianne said, not one bit of humor in her voice, "who told you you were nice?"

"I—" What?

"Since you have your gripes about us girls and what we don't see right in front of us, let me put you on to one of my pet peeves about boys. Warped perspective." She bounced Zoey, who squealed with delight, having fun now. "Her dad has given me many lessons over the last year. We're only right when we please you. When you're not pleased, we're crazy, or juvenile, or stupid, or not worth your time. Because you're so nice."

"You're—" I nearly said "crazy," but stopped short.

"You *think* you're nice, Del. You think you're nicer than Mason. You spent all that time in her church activities, doing pledges and praying, and whatever else you thought she liked. Things that ain't really you. But, because you were so nice when you were doing that fake shit, she owes you something, right? Mason's an asshole for talking about what him and her did in private, but he never pretended to be anything but what he is. Surprise, surprise, honesty worked. Who you really mad at here, Del?"

I chewed my bottom lip, tasted blood. Held back every horrible thing bubbling in my brain. I wasn't going to fall for this. She was . . . *baiting* me. Probably mad at her baby daddy and taking it out on me. "I guess I wasn't so horrible when you needed someone to run a game on your parents so you could watch videos on your iPad."

"Don't act like it wasn't mutually beneficial."

"I'm gone."

"Bye, Mister Nice Guy!"

"You're mean as shit, Shi."

"That's why we're friends, Del. You haven't figured that out yet? We're so much alike."

CHAPTER 26

AT HOME, I SLAMMED THE door and shook the house. Dad dropped his chopping knife and made a fist, startled by my entrance. "Junior, I know you know better than to come in here like that."

"Sorry." I tried to stomp past him, but he rounded the kitchen island, grabbed my arm.

"Hey, what happened to you today?"

Any thought of sulking alone in my room faded as I blurted, "Girls are insane, Dad!"

"In what way?"

"Every."

He tugged me toward the kitchen table. "Sit down. Explain."

So, I told him. All of it from the Sunday Newsome busted me and the Purity Pledgers to Shianne's meltdown. He took his chair at the head of the table, shifted positions a few times like he couldn't get comfortable. Crossed arms, slow nods, but he didn't interrupt.

". . . then Shianne goes off on me saying I was, like, using the church to fool Kiera and I got what I deserved." Or something. So much of it came from left field, and felt like a blur now. "That's totally not true."

Dad seemed to struggle with his words. "Son, when I asked you about that pledge thing a few weeks ago, you told me you were doing it because of Kiera."

"Yeah, but not *dishonestly*. Rainey Man!" I offered him my fist, so he'd understand.

When he extended his own hand, it wasn't to fist-bump. He wrapped his palm over my knuckles—paper beats rock—and nudged my arm down.

"Your mom's going to be home soon. We should all talk when she gets here."

"About what?"

"What you told me."

"I don't need another woman yelling at me today, Dad."

Anger flashed across his face like lightning in a cloud. Only for a second. "We're all going to talk. It's not going to be what you think. You do need to watch your tone. Believe that. You've had a bad day. I get it. Don't make it worse."

Fine. Everyone's lost their mind. "Can I go upstairs?"

"I'll call you when she gets here."

The garage door rattled open beneath my window, and Mom announced she was home and hungry. Then it got quiet, at least twenty minutes of what I assumed was conversation about I don't know what. There was a gentle knock on my door, and

Dad let himself in without an invitation.

He sat at the foot of my bed, clasping his hands together. "I get that you're pissed over a lot of stuff right now, but I'm going to ask you to come down and listen to your mother and sister. It's something I haven't been very good at. Me and you have work to do."

I sat up, confused. "Cressie's home?"

"FaceTime," Dad said, holding his phone like a talisman. "Our family meetings are high-tech now."

I swung my feet to the floor. "Fine."

Mom waited at the table, her fingers tap-tap-tapping. I sat, determined not to be bullied here. She got Cressie on the screen.

I said, "So what am I getting yelled at about now?"

Mom didn't answer—I thought this was her show—but looked to Dad.

He said, "The morning after you joined the Purity Pledge we talked. Remember?"

"Yeah, Dad, I remember. You reminded me like an hour ago."

"I was mad at your mom. We talked about you and that pledge, and she suspected you weren't doing it for the right reasons. I, basically, told her she was the one who dragged you to church with a bunch of crackpot Bible-thumpers and she shouldn't get mad at you for wanting to do something with the young people there. I—"

"Told me," Mom cut in, "I needed to stop overreacting. I was wrong. I didn't know what I was talking about because he knew his son so well. What harm could you possibly do?"

"Me? What about Newsome. He's the one—"

"Stop it, son," said Dad. "We're not debating Pastor Newsome. I mean, he sounds kind of like an asshole—"

"Del!" Mom snapped.

"Sorry, he does. That's a different conversation, though. We're talking about you. Your behavior."

My behavior. "Of course we are."

"That's what I mean, Del. It's scary sometimes," said Mom. I couldn't tell if she was talking to me, my dad, or both of us.

Cressie chimed in, her voice tinny through Mom's phone speaker. "Guys, maybe we should back off the intervention vibe here."

Mom said, "What would you call it then?"

Cressie said, "Enlightenment."

I said, "This feels like you're about to induct me into a cult."

"Show him, guys," Cressie said.

Mom produced her MacBook from the bag at her feet, woke it, then passed it to my dad. He glanced at whatever, shook his head, then passed it to me. It was a YouTube video. Cressie's show. The second episode she ever posted on her channel, an episode I never watched: "The Trouble with College Bruhs."

"Why do I need to look at Cressie's show?"

Dad said, "Press Play. You'll get it."

I tapped the icon and my sister was in motion.

CRESSIE

Hey, everyone, it's Cressida. The feedback for the first video has been awesome, and there have been a lot of great suggestions. I don't think I've seen a topic that I don't want to cover yet. However, something strange happened in the comments of my last video when "SarahThePatriarchy Slayer" mentioned telling scary stories. I thought she meant ghost stories, like at a sleepover. Until I read her example. Trigger warning, y'all. It said: "This guy asked for my phone number at a coffee shop. I politely told him no. He asked if I had a boyfriend, and I said no. He smiled, and placed an order for an extra-hot latte. When he got it, he took the lid off and tossed it directly on me. It hit me in the chest, so my shirt saved me from a first-degree burn. When I screamed, he said, 'It could've been your face,' and ran out of the shop. Now I give guys fake names and numbers. So it's not my face next time."

I paused the video, startled. "What is this?"

Dad said, "Keep going, son."

"But—"

"Do it."

CRESSIE

Y'all caught on faster than I did, because the replies were harrowing, but not surprising. Like "TaKeisha5219's" story about the strange guy who hopped into an Uber with her before she could close the door, because she was so beautiful. And when she told the Uber driver she didn't know the stranger, the driver said, "Well you ARE beautiful, learn to take a compliment." She had to endure a ride to her friend's house with two strange creeps, her only other option being to dive from the moving vehicle.

That thread is still there, and the stories range from frightening to grotesque, with more than a few heartbreaking tragedies among the tales. One reply that stood out to me came from a woman whom I consider a mentor now. Jaylan, of the Jaylan Knows channel. She wrote, "These are scary stories, but also entitlement stories. In every one of them a man felt entitled to a woman's time, attention, body because . . . reasons. And to appease their entitlement, we get left with scars. The wariness of animals who only want to forage but who always have to watch for the shadow of a predatory hawk, or slithering viper. No space is safe where toxic male energy is permitted, or simply invades. But, we all knew that, didn't we? It's the other gender that seems ignorant to their toxic colonization of a woman's right to breathe, and sunshine, and solace. Too bad they aren't reading these stories, too."

But—BUT!—that's not exactly true. At least one man read Jaylan's response. "CharlesSnarkly666" wrote, "Don't show ass if you don't want attention! #Yogapants"

My sister stared into her camera, blank-faced.

CRESSIE

Moving on. The replies to the one comment are well over three hundred. I've seen more than a few coming from some fellow CU students. It's very brave of you to share any of this. I know because I'm about to tell my own story, and it scares the shit out of me. But you've inspired me, sisters. Nothing changes if we stay quiet.

My first day on this campus, right after my parents dropped me off, I went to a dorm mixer and met a cute guy. I was very interested, as was he. We talked, exchanged numbers, then kept mingling. I met a second cute guy, and was very interested. What can I say? There are some fine men here on the CU campus. Well, guy #1 observed me flirting with guy #2. I didn't know this until I went to the restroom, and came out to find guy #1 waiting for me. I was startled but initially I thought little of it. Maybe he'd come from the men's room. That's how we rationalize, right. Then he says, "So, you're one of those."

I was confused. Remember, I didn't know he'd seen me flirting with guy #2, and that shouldn't have mattered anyway. I'd just met this dude.

Grinning like he'd cracked some kind of code, he says, "Should've told me you were a freak. I like that better than the nice-girl act anyway."

At that point I got nervous, and realized in this bathroom corridor there's only me and him. The party was back the other way, the way he's blocking with his body, and the music's

loud. No one's hearing anything happening in that moment.
I say, "Excuse me." And try to slip by him. He grabs my arm,
pulls me right up against him. "Hold up. We ain't friends no
more?"

I told him to get off me, but he clamped down tighter. I'm
talking pain; he was a big dude. Then he pushed me against
the wall, snaked his free hand under my skirt, rubbed my
thighs, said, "I saw how you were throwing it at that pretty
boy. If you want it that bad you don't have to shop around.
I'm willing."

I . . . was not.

I hit him in the chest, and I sucked in breath to scream,
when three more guys came around the corner. We saw them
at the same time, and Mister Assault let me go, trying to play
the whole thing off. He was smiling, and asking the guys what's
up. They had guilty looks on their faces; they'd seen enough
to know what they'd interrupted wasn't cool. But, eventually,
they smiled too. Comfortable with whatever they'd walked up
on being over.

Pushing my way between them, I made it back to the party,
then told my roommate I needed to leave, then spent the rest
of the night in my dorm room, under my comforter, shook
and confused. Questioning all the things I'd done wrong. I
went to the bathroom by myself. Stupid me. I socialized with
strangers. What was I thinking? I gave two boys my number.
I'm a monster. All this internal second-guessing leading to an
ever-growing checklist of things I'd never do again in an effort

to stay safe. A checklist I shouldn't need.

I know my near miss is relatively mild compared to the sto-
ries of uninterrupted assaults and rapes posted here. And I
now know I haven't lived up to my responsibilities by simply
running home and chastising myself. Not after all you've been
through, dear viewers. That guy could've done that same thing
to a dozen other girls by now, and maybe no one showed up
to give them a window of escape. My comfort in silence might
be helping him assault other women, so I'm not being silent
anymore.

I reported him to campus authorities this morning. Passed
on the name and phone number he gave me when he was pre-
tending to be nice and sweet. I'll keep you posted on what CU
does to protect women in this case. If you're a CU student and
want to know more about the reporting process, DM me. For
those of you not on campus, but still want help, DM me. And if
you're a man who isn't a piece of shit like "CharlesSnarkly666"
then check other men. Y'all don't listen to us, maybe you'll
listen to each other.

That's enough for one night. Until next episode . . .

I paused. Closed the MacBook. Stunned.

Mom said, "I've known that story since the day after it happened."

"Dad?" I said.

"Since last night, when your mom showed me that video."

"Why?" My voice cracked and I took Mom's phone so I could

talk directly to my sister. "Why didn't you say something when you were home?"

"I wasn't ready for Dad to know. I knew it would hurt him. I knew once you knew, he would, too."

"But it's online? It's got like"—I reopened the MacBook, checked—"like fifteen thousand views."

"You're not one of them. Or you weren't. So I was safe."

Something in that made me feel supremely shitty. More so than any conversation I'd had over the last two days. Which was saying something.

"It's hard to talk to you two about anything," Mom said. "You're never really concerned about what we think, or do, beyond half-assed criticism. All these months I've been going to church, neither of you asked me why the sudden change." To Dad, "You made it very clear that you thought it was silly." To me, "I was dragging you, I was a nag. You never considered there was a reason I sought a renewed faith in the Lord." She pointed at the MacBook. "It was that. My oldest child—my girl—would be leaving my home and encountering any number of things, and there was nothing I could do to protect her. It consumed me. Because I know what it's like for a woman. Doesn't matter age, looks, what we wear, where we go. There's always danger, because of, well, you."

You, meaning men. Hearing my mom say it made me bristle, even after what I saw.

Tears leaked from Dad's eyes. Mom didn't soften. "I know you're upset, Del. But it shouldn't have taken something like that happening to your daughter for you to get close to under-standing what I'm saying."

Isn't that what MJ told us during that last Healthy Living? Did it matter?

"Do what you need to do. Talk to him." She pointed at me, and my anger blazed.

"Mom. You don't think I'm like the guy who grabbed Cres-sie. That's crazy!"

"Is it? I see more than you think, son. I've seen you trying to force a situation with the Westing girl."

I stood so fast my chair almost tipped. "I didn't *force* any-thing!" I felt the need to be absolutely clear with my sister, who'd endured an attack in a loud hallway. "Cress, I didn't do anything like that."

"I believe you, baby bro. I don't think you're anything like my attacker. But there are degrees to this. Maybe he wasn't always like that. Maybe he got denied too often. Angry too often. I don't know. Maybe he built up to what he tried with me. But buildings have foundations. They start somewhere. Are you angry about anything Kiera's done recently?"

I didn't answer that.

Dad said, "Junior. It's not all your fault, because I've been encouraging you in a way that my father and my uncles and a bunch of other guys I looked up to encouraged me. It felt good-natured, like a rite of passage. 'Go get that girl.' But all I can think about now is that animal who put his hands on Cres-sie was probably getting good-natured encouragement from his dad, and his uncles, and all the guys around them. 'Go get that girl.'"

My hands shook. They were being so stupid about this, like I'd cornered Kiera in some dark alley.

Then Shianne's words came to me, ghosts in the room. *Del, who told you you were nice?*

Voice low, I said, "Can I be excused?"

Dad looked to Mom, and Mom looked disappointed. I didn't want to know what Cressie looked like on that tiny phone screen, so I turned away.

Mom said, "Go on."

Alone in my room, the anger got worse. Not in intensity, but in focus. Who was I mad at? Mom? Dad? Cressie? Kiera? Shianne?

Hours leapt by. I didn't eat dinner, or do homework. I tried texting Qwan, but felt petty when I thought about what he'd been through with Angie, so I deleted those texts. Then I tried locking my door, opening the private browser tab, and searching for new Lindy Blue videos. They were there, but they felt different now. Everything did. What was insatiable nymphomania before was now bad acting. What used to look like rough fun seemed painful. The hottest porn star on the planet looked way younger than I'd ever noticed. Take off the makeup, maybe she'd blend in at Green Creek High.

I had the hot and bright urge to snap my keyboard in half.

Who you really mad at here, Del?

My eyes burned.

Why Mason?

Why didn't Kiera pick me?

Why wasn't I good enough for her?

I cried, full on, in more pain than when that basketball smashed my face.

At least I could blame someone else for that.

CHAPTER 27

THE LAST WEEKS OF SCHOOL before Christmas break proved to be my most studious ever. After the Enlightened Intervention, I made sure not to have time for much else. When it wasn't algebra systems and inequalities, the Clinton impeachment from government class, or dissection prep for biology, I was snatching up every FISHto's shift I could get. I'd been a much better and focused employee, so Tyrell put me on the schedule way more. I didn't complain. By the time I got my mid-December paycheck, I had enough for my part of the car insurance bill and some left over for Christmas gifts.

Another Baby-Getter returned to school, even though it was late in the year—she apparently had kept up her studies at home—and she became the gossip that drowned the Me/Mason/Kiera drama. I saw Kiera, of course, even though I tried to look the other way. When she wasn't in the corner of my eye, she was in the back of my thoughts. So I worked harder, anything to stay occupied. Focused. Idle hands were the devil's playground.

The Wednesday before the holiday break, after the dinner rush at FISHto's, I crouched behind the front-line counter organizing condiments, when above me, I heard a cheery, "Good evening, Del."

Popping up, I was greeted by the eternally sunny face of Sister Vanessa. She was bundled up in a leather jacket with a bright blue Hampton University hoodie beneath it. She seemed to be waiting on something.

"Are you looking for Mya? She's off tonight."

"I know. Choir rehearsal. She has a beautiful voice, doesn't she?" Her gaze angled up and over my head, perusing the menu. "What's good here?"

"The platter is cool if you like a more traditional seafood meal. You get fish, fried or broiled, some shrimp, an ear of corn."

She stroked her chin. "Think I'm in the mood for something a little bolder. How's that Sriracha Crabcake Sandwich?"

"It's good. Spicy, obviously."

"Let's do that. The combo. For here."

I rung it up, took her money, and asked, "Do you like hush puppies?"

"Sure. Do those come with the combo?"

"Nope, just fries." I held up a finger, approached the food rack between me and the kitchen, signaled Stu. "Throw some hush puppies on, too."

"That is very generous of you, Del."

The freshly arranged condiments beneath the counter became super interesting. "It's the least I can do."

The order was up. I added a drink cup, plus the proper sauces, to her tray.

She said, "You wouldn't be able to take a break right now, would you? I'm not a fan of eating alone."

"Ummm . . ." My stomach churned with new nerves. I shouted, "Tyrell, can I take a break?"

"Go for it," he called from somewhere in back. Turns out he was a kinda cool boss when you actually showed up to do real work. We'd had no problems lately.

She filled her cup with sweet tea from the silver cylinder by the Coke machine, then joined me in a booth. Immediately, she bit into one of the hush puppies. "Ohhh, these are good."

"Thank you." Like I made them. This was awkward.

"Haven't seen you in the church lately. Your mother either."

"Didn't go so well the last time I was there."

"For either of us."

Then you shouldn't have snitched!

That . . . was not the proper response. I bit it back. She bit into her sandwich. Took her time chewing. The silence got to me. "How are they?" I asked.

Sister Vanessa dabbed crumbs from the corner of her mouth with her napkin. "Ralph and Bobby joined the Ushers' Board. They look very handsome in their dress clothes and those white gloves. Helena's found her way into the choir stand with Mya. Shanice has been talking about starting a praise dancing team. My uncle's not so enthusiastic about it, though."

That last bit was flat. Monotonous. Lacking any of the

inherent joy of most things out of Sister Vanessa's mouth.

"I don't mean to be rude, but I may not be able to sit here for long. I feel like you came here to say something to me."

"I couldn't just be curious about the cuisine?"

"Nobody, ever in the history of the world, was simply curious about the food here."

She rested the half-eaten sandwich on her tray, and wouldn't touch it again. "Kiera told me about things between you two."

"Y'all talk like that?" Despite my anger over the way things went down, despite the confusion and disappointment and embarrassment I felt when my family confronted me about it, despite the foolishness of everything I did and tried to do, hope sparked like an ember in my chest.

Did Kiera feel more for me than she'd ever let on?

Was Sister Vanessa here to tell me Kiera had been as miserable as me over these last few weeks? Had I crossed her mind every time her head touched the pillow, or her feet crossed the threshold into Green Creek High? I waited.

Sister Vanessa said, "I know it hurts when someone you like doesn't feel the same way, Del. I'm sorry your pain drove you to react badly."

That ember was snuffed with a knife's tip, the blade then twisted, scraping the soft things inside me.

"Despite that, I'd hoped you and your mother would return to First Missionary."

"Sounds like you'd be the only one."

"Not true. Believe it or not, you and your mother were good

for the church. We need new blood, with new ideas."

"I don't think your uncle would agree."

Sister Vanessa pushed back against her bench, taking her time, choosing her words. "Uncle Eldridge is an old man. He doesn't always understand that times change, as do the needs of the congregation. He hasn't adjusted well since my aunt passed. He really is a good person who does what he thinks is right. He's lost his North Star."

"I don't think all that matters much when he's forcing kids to shame themselves publicly."

"You're not wrong."

"Why doesn't anyone stand up to him, then? Why don't you?"

"Uncle Eldridge isn't the only one stuck in old ways. I was raised to not challenge the pastor. He's the leader. My role in the body of the church is to report to him."

The excuses and justifications grated on me, so I said more than I intended. Maybe too much. "Is that why you told him we went to Commonwealth University? Just doing your job? Maybe me and my mom wouldn't have had to leave if you could've overlooked that particular responsibility."

I don't know if I would've spoken to an adult like that in any other setting. She came here, though. She inserted herself into a night where I'd planned to do my job and go home and not bother anyone.

Sister Vanessa's eyes narrowed. I figured she was about to check me for my disrespect. She said, "I didn't tell on you and the Purity Pledge class, Del. I never even saw you at the event."

"You didn't?" Could I believe her? Should I? "Why were you even there?"

"New blood. New ideas. I'm seeking answers, same as all of you."

"Answers? Like us?"

"Yes, I know about the others coming to you with their curiosities. With no Pledge, and you gone, there was no reason to keep it secret anymore."

"And you still think me and Mom should come back?"

"I do."

The door chimes sounded and several burly road crew workers in reflective vests over heavy coats filed in for dinner. Break time was over. I slid from the booth. Said, "I'm sorry to disappoint you, Sister Vanessa. You're nice, and I like you, but can you honestly tell me if I did come back, your uncle wouldn't push me to 'bare my soul' before all was forgiven?"

She didn't answer. Didn't have to.

"That's what I thought. It was nice to see you again, and if you like dessert, you can't go wrong with the apple turnover here."

I left her to her meal; filled the road crew's order. It didn't take long, but when I glanced toward Sister Vanessa's booth, it was unoccupied and the table was spotless, like she'd never been there at all.

CHAPTER 28

SCHOOL COULDN'T END FAST ENOUGH.

Everything that had come at me in these last few weeks made my head feel crowded and mushy. Sister Vanessa's visit to FISHto's rattled me more than I liked. I didn't think I missed First Missionary, and I hadn't thought much about the Pledgers, but that was because I made myself not think about them. The task at hand became everything. At school I was like a bloodhound sniffing my way to class. Head down, eyes on my exact path, concentrating hard enough that I could almost ignore Mason's taunts over his superiority, Kiera's scowls over our last conversation, Jameer's attempts at any sort of conversation, and so on. Even when I shared FISHto's shifts with Mya I sought any and every task that kept me moving and quiet. She didn't try to force anything different, which I was grateful for.

We were two days away from a long holiday break; time away from everyone's drama might be enough to get me back to some kind of social equilibrium. I could become New Year's Del. Put all of my mess behind me.

So, one might imagine exiting school the Thursday before break, and finding Jameer sitting inside my car, being both unexpected and unwanted.

I considered an about-face. Hell, I turned all the way around, but spotted Shianne inside the school entrance. I'd successfully avoided her, too, and given the very real work I apparently needed to do processing my feelings toward all the women in my life, Jameer became the better option.

Climbing behind the wheel, I keyed the ignition, turned on the heat because winter had come, and said, "Did I leave the door unlocked, or did you break in? If you broke in, I'm going to have way more questions."

"The door was unlocked." He sniffed hard, like he might have a cold. But, his eyes were also red, puffy. He'd been crying. A lot.

"What's wrong, Jameer?"

"I messed up, Del. I'm sorry. I messed up."

"Messed up what?"

He cupped his face in his hands, folded himself almost in half. "If I tell you, promise you won't get mad."

"I promise I'll try."

"I told Pastor about our road trip, Del. It was me."

He didn't look at me. I was glad, because I'm sure my face would've betrayed my promise to try holding back my anger. "You? Why?"

"I overdid the wine that night. My parents knew I'd been drinking. They were so angry, they called Pastor—woke him up—to ask for prayer and guidance. They actually took me to his house, eleven o'clock at night, Del. And he drilled me. Who, what, when, where. I didn't say anything, though. Not at first. I swear. Then my parents said if I wouldn't confess to the three of them, maybe I'd do it for the whole church, and I couldn't go through that humiliation again. So, I told them about the trip. Not everything. Not that the wine came from Ralph and Bobby, because who knows what would've happened to them. I—"

"Told about my part in it."

He raised his face from his hands. Tears puddling in his palms. "You're not like the rest of us, Del. I knew Pastor couldn't crack you. I knew you could take it."

My anger siphoned off quickly because that wasn't true. Pastor did crack me, and Healthy Living went away. I'd been where Jameer was, and I'd broken, too. The difference, I never confessed my role to MJ. Let him think it was anyone else but me. Jameer was the bravest person in my car.

I placed a hand on his shoulder, squeezed gently. "It's cool. That's all behind us now and everyone's fine."

"No, Del. They're not." He choked up into fresh sobs, unable to speak through them. Gave me time to think and get worried.

I said, "Something else happened."

"My parents . . . found out . . . about Ramsey."

I twisted in my seat, paranoid, expecting his parents to swoop down like monsters and snatch us away. "How bad was that?"

"Not as bad as it could've been, because I was able to convince them of what they want to hear. They've chosen to believe my story that he's not my boyfriend."

"So what's the problem?"

"A couple of nights ago I was with him because I was covering for Kiera. Me and her went out together, then we split up. We were supposed to reconnect on the street behind our houses, you know, same old plan. But I got back first, in time for the most random evening jog my dad ever took. He ran right up on me and Ramsey in the car. We weren't making out, thank God, but there were questions. So many questions."

This was going in a direction I didn't like, for a lot of reasons. He'd been covering for Kiera. "How did you answer?"

"I couldn't go through it again, Del. Do you know how bad it would've been if I'd admitted I was with my boyfriend?"

Oh, Jameer. "You put it all on her."

He cried some more. I felt a familiar irritation, my mind going in different directions than what he probably intended. "Who was she with, Jameer?"

I thought he might not answer. Maybe he thought I'd gotten over it all—until that moment, I kind of thought I had. "Mason."

"Still! Even after—"

He flinched, pressed against the passenger door like he was trying to knock it off its hinges.

No, Del. No. It's not your business. "Why tell me?"

"Who else can I tell? It's eating me alive."

"You feel better now?"

"No."

"Good. Because I don't either, Jameer. What happened after you blamed everything on her?"

"You don't know?"

I had an idea. "They're going to make her confess in front of everyone, aren't they? You wouldn't be this upset if it wasn't that."

"It's my fault."

"Yes. It sounds that way."

He looked freshly wounded. Maybe I meant to hurt him. I still had work to do. Clearly.

I softened my tone, proposed the only thing that seemed logical. "If you feel this bad, then maybe you take it from her. Tell Newsome and your parents that you lied."

"My dad caught her when she pulled up with Mason. Can't take that back."

"She didn't snitch on you when she got caught?"

He shook his head.

"Then maybe you should both confess. Or maybe you both refuse to do it."

"You know it doesn't work like that."

It never would, not when First Missionary was stuck in the old ways, with that old blood pumping through its veins.

Most of our classmates exited the lot by bus or car. Jameer's heaving chest settled into normal breaths, and I didn't know what else to say on the topic he dropped on me other than "I know how it is to have Newsome press you. I'm not mad you cracked. I can't be. I can't say if I were you, I wouldn't have thrown Kiera under the bus. I don't have much to say beyond that. I'm not there anymore."

"I know. I still like talking to you, though. You're a good listener, Del."

Was I?

His hand rested on the door handle, tugged it, let in knifing cold air as he prepared to exit.

"I can take you home."

"No," he said, "it's best if I get home on my own. All things considered."

Jameer got out, but before he was gone, I said, "Are you and Kiera going to be cool again? You've been friends a long time." I didn't say they needed each other, but I always got the sense they did.

"I don't think so. I can't fix this. Even if I could, I don't think so. Do you?"

I couldn't comfort him with a satisfactory answer. That feeling was the worst in a while.

Home was filled with familiar smells, and sounds, and fullness. I felt the change as soon as I stepped in. The suitcase and bulging laundry sack confirmed my sister was home for the holidays.

Dad greeted me in the kitchen, tossing things for some meal into his new Instant Pot.

"Hey," I shot back, heading upstairs.

"You all right?" he asked. "You usually want to know what's cooking."

Getting into the complexities of what troubled me was not even an option, so I simply asked, "What is it?"

"Gumbo."

"Awesome, Dad." I got away before there were more questions. From him, anyway.

Cressie's bedroom door was cracked, and even with my best stealth moves, I didn't make it past unnoticed.

"Hey," she called, tugging the door wide. "You're not going to say hello?"

"Hello."

"Come in here."

"Are you live on IG?"

"Naw. Nothing like that. Come in."

I entered, found no bulky camera cases or other equipment this time. There was her MacBook, decorated with CU decals, and a yellow legal pad next to it filled with scribbled notes. She was perched in her desk chair, cross-legged and tiny. I said the most small-talkiest thing I could think of. "Your first semester go okay?"

"Straight As. The channel was a huge hit in my sociology class." She motioned for me to have a seat on her bed. I hopped onto the cotton candy comforter and waited for whatever this was. From that position, I caught a glimpse of her computer screen. It was her face, in a frozen video.

"New episode?"

"Yep, for tomorrow. I'm making some small edits and plan to post it right after midnight." Abruptly, she changed the subject. "You mad at me?"

"For what?"

"We haven't talked since the family meeting."

I scanned the posters on her wall. Migos. Cardi B. Luke James and Algee Smith. Traced my gaze over her bookshelf. The photos rimming her mirror frame. Anywhere but at her. "Naw. I'm good."

"You don't sound good, or look good, baby bro. Something on your mind?"

"What makes you ask?"

"Your face is like a children's book. Easily read."

"College went and made you corny."

"Better me than Mom. You let her see you looking like that and it's going to be a for-real conversation. What's up?"

"It ain't about the family meeting."

Her head bobbed. Waiting.

So, I told her, because I had to tell somebody. Not only the conversation with Jameer, or the FISHto's dinner with Sister Vanessa. I told her all of it, from the beginning. I don't know if I could've done this with Cressie even three months ago. Like I said, I'd been keeping up with her show. I'd watched her field tough questions and give thoughtful answers. My sister was more than the person who slept down the hall, and stole my Fruit Roll-Ups. Seeing her these days was like a fog lifting.

Midway through my story, around when Kiera and I walked

home from Mama Marian's and I didn't get my kiss, we heard Mom come in downstairs. Cressie closed her bedroom door fully, and motioned for me to go on, but quietly. It took almost an hour to get it all out, and when I did, I felt lighter than I had in a long time.

"Wow," Cressie said, "that's a lot. I picked up on some of it from what Mom told me, but it's way deeper."

"I agree. Imagine being in it."

She fidgeted. Chewed her lip. Looked more hesitant than I'd ever known her to be. I asked, "Why aren't you saying what you want to say?"

"I don't want it to sound harsh, is all."

"I'm beyond hurt feelings at this point."

"It seems to me like you understand this now, but I have to say it, because I love you, and it's better you hear it from someone close. Kiera . . . it's not going to happen."

Heavy sigh. "That became clear shortly after the dude she actually likes punched me in the eye."

"I'm sorry."

"You're a girl. Can I ask you a Girl Question?"

"I'm not sure I'm a fan of the phrasing, but go on."

"Why do you think she'd still be spending time with him— probably still boning him—after he ran his mouth and the whole school knows their business?"

"Honest answer? He appeals to something in her. Something good, or something flawed, or something in between. In time she might find that thing, whatever it is, isn't appealing anymore. Or, she might marry him and start a family. Whatever her reasons, we don't have to understand them. She gets to make her own decisions." She became suddenly timid. "Right?"

"Yeah, I get it."

Matter-of-fact, she said, "Also, the sex might be *really* good."

Spoken like she had way more experience in that area than what I was comfortable with. I said, "That's enough, Cressie."

"My bad."

Something in me felt freer. At the same time, something in me wasn't. I hadn't unloaded all of my burdens. "This isn't going to make a ton of sense, I don't think, because I didn't really like going to church with Mom every Sunday, but I miss parts of it. I miss my friends there."

"The ones I met at the university."

I nodded. "I messed up some stuff for them. I want to fix it, but not the way it's usually done. I think that way is as wrong— or worse—as anything I've done. But adults are funny, they don't seem to know when they're out of line."

"Preach!"

We laughed a bit.

"Hey kids," Dad called from downstairs, "dinner's ready."

Cressie popped from her chair. I rose, too. She said, "Maybe you'll think better on a full stomach."

"Maybe." When we left her room she flipped the light switch, so the only brightness was her face, on her MacBook, that video she needed to prep.

Something began to churn in the back of my head.

Food first, though.

● ● ●

After dinner, in my room, I tapped a text to Qwan, who was Angie-free for a night thanks to her visiting uncle taking her people to a movie. I was in socks, flimsy PJ pants, and a Green Creek sweatshirt, bundled beneath the covers because it was chilly. I chatted with my friend, my phone glowing like a lantern in a mineshaft.

> **Me:** What you told me, about those girls robbing you . . . you regret it?

Qwan: Hell yeah I regret it. Who doesn't regret getting robbed, D?

> **Me:** No! Do you regret telling me it was a lie? Technically, you lied on your dick. Cardinal sin.

Qwan: I'm not sorry I told you the truth. I actually feel better knowing you know. I never have to worry about getting found out later.

> **Me:** What if I'd clowned you for it?

Qwan: Might've mattered a year ago, back before I went through some real shit. But

thinking Angie was pregnant, and I might
be a dad . . . fronting about something
that didn't happen wasn't important anymore. Why you ask?

> **Me:** I'm thinking about doing
> something Qwan. It might be
> kind of big.

Qwan: Is it legal, though?

> **Me:** It's legal.

Qwan: And it's about getting some shit off
your chest?

> **Me:** Yep

Qwan: Then I got your back, D. Always

> **Me:** Unless Angie calls.

Qwan: Then you're on your own.

Qwan: lol

Swinging my feet to the floor, I didn't feel so cold anymore. I
checked the clock. 8:45 p.m. There was still time.

I left my room, went down the hall, and knocked on Cressie's door.

"Come in." She was in her bed clothes, still tinkering with her video.

I said, "I have a proposal for you."

"About?"

"A very special episode for your channel."

She perked. "I'm listening."

I closed and locked her door.

CHAPTER 29

NO NEW *FEMFAM* EPISODE WENT up after midnight. Or by eight a.m. Or even by the early afternoon. It was the Friday before the long holiday break, and I asked my sister to hold off on posting until I finished school. I wanted one last day of semi-normalcy if what we did went the wrong way.

I said "semi" because I broke my Extreme-Focus protocols for the first time in weeks. I had stops to make.

First, I tracked down Shianne between classes. She was at her locker, saw me coming, and went full attitude, expecting a fight. I walked up to her, locked eyes, then hugged her. She went limp, didn't fight it. Some passerby made a lewd comment and she told him to do crude things to himself.

I let her go, and said, "Thank you for being honest. I know it must've been hard to say such harsh things to me."

"It wasn't hard. I told you, post-baby, no filter." Her face softened. "But I'm glad we're still friends."

Next stop, midday, Jameer. I caught him by the school library, pulled him inside. He looked skittish, like I might beat him up. I said, "Relax. I want to tell you to do what you can to get to a computer tonight. I know you're not going to be able to watch at home, so maybe the library. I don't know."

"What am I going to be looking for?"

"Help. I hope. I'll text you later."

Finally, at the end of the day, after gym was done, while everyone filed into the cold, happy to be done with school for this calendar year, I caught up to Kiera as she exited the girls' locker room.

"Hey," I said. "I need to say something."

The hostility was immediate. "Is it like what you said last time? Because you can keep it to yourself."

"No. Not at all. I want to say I'm sorry."

"For?"

"All of it. I never came at you honestly."

She backed up, taking it wrong.

I waved the last statement off. "This isn't me trying to holler or anything. I know there's nothing between us. I'm not trying to change that."

She didn't relax. That was okay. I was almost done.

"You weren't wrong to be wary of me in the beginning, Kiera. I've earned whatever distasteful things you feel about me now. Whatever happens this weekend, please understand it's all part of my apology to you and the rest of the Pledgers. Okay?"

The corners of Kiera's mouth turned down. "I don't know what you mean."

"Yo, is there a problem here?" Mason sidled up next to her, close enough for their shoulders to touch.

"No. No problem at all. Enjoy your holidays."

In my car, my tasks complete, I gripped my steering wheel, ratcheting my hands around it. Deep breath. Deep breath.

Then, I sent my sister a single-word text.

Me: Now

We would see.

FemFam Presents Episode 15: Bare Your Soul w/ Special Guest My Baby Bro

CRESSIE

Hey, FemFam! It's me, Cressie, and I interrupt our regularly scheduled programming to present a special episode. As you can see, we're in my bedroom back home, it's late, so my hair's wrapped and I'm rocking my silk bonnet—black hair, don't care. Okay, that's a lie, I do care a little, but I didn't get all camera official because I'm not going to be doing the talking this time. This episode's going to be my brother's show. At his request. You see, he's recently turned the corner on some very Boy-ish Things. If you've been following the channel, you know Boy-ish Things refer to some of the sillier ideas boys get in their heads about what we like, and don't like. What they need to do to impress us. How they respond when they don't like what we say or do. He's got things to tell you. Thank you for listening. Del, it's all you.

The MacBook rotated so the built-in camera focused on me. The tiny green power light next to the lens felt like a laser boring into me.

DEL

Hey out there. I'm sorry if I'm not as polished as my sister, this is new to me. The camera and saying the stuff I'm about to say. I'm here of my own free will, though. No one is making me do this. It's important that you know that.

I don't know how to make this fancy, or do a good lead-in— like I said, not polished. So, I'm just going to say it. I've been lying about losing my virginity for two years. I'm a virgin. I've never even come close to having sex.

[quick cut—removing the footage of me hyperventilating— the video resumed]

I pretended I wasn't a virgin because not being one felt expected. So many of the guys and girls at my school talk like they're porn stars in training. Like they know all about sex because they watched some Lindy Blue videos. It was embarrassing to feel like the only person who didn't know what they were doing. And maybe—maybe—I could've found someone who was willing to help me lose my virginity for real, but this

thing happened in my town. If you've been watching my sis-
ter's channel, you know what I'm talking about. A lot of new
moms, and babies, and everyone around us freaking. Hon-
estly, sex got scary to me.

I kept pretending I wanted to do it. I'd go on double dates
with my best friend, and find something I didn't like about
the girl so I'd seem picky, not afraid. Then—this is the worst
part—I made up all these unfair expectations for a girl who
I thought was a virgin, too. I made her this ideal instead of a
human. We were meant to be together when the timing was
right. Then I tried to make the timing right by engineering all
these dumb schemes, and more lies, and really being the kind
of guy that—that's not good for anyone.

I hurt feelings, and caused problems, and I'm trying to tell
anyone out there who's feeling the sort of thing I felt, and you
know it's not right, then you can turn it around. Like I did.
With help.

See, I joined this group of people who also weren't inter-
ested in having sex yet. They became my really good friends.
Though I was still pretending, and scheming, and being an
overall asshole, I feel like I'm able to admit my wrongdoing
now, partially because of them.

This is me baring my soul. Confessing my sins. It's okay if
you're scared about anything in your life. It's not okay to lie and
manipulate to hide those fears. I know that now. I'm better for
it. I hope me telling my story helps you find ways to be better.

And—listen—I know this may not be for everyone, but I

couldn't wrap this up without giving you the opportunity to make the same sort of connections I did so I could be what I think is a 1,000 percent improved Del.

I was able to come to terms with the real me through the various programs happening at my mom's church.

That's First Missionary House of the Lord in Green Creek, Virginia. It's run by this great guy named Pastor Eldridge Newsome. And if you're nearby, and free on Sunday, I'm inviting you to join me there.

Service starts at eleven.

Of course there was more to the video than that. Cressie asked some follow-up questions about the perceptions of manhood, and how men create new generations of misogynists. We talked about the unrealistic sexual expectations on teens in general. The canceled Healthy Living class. How we needed to stop calling the Baby-Getters *that name*. But, there was really only one part I was interested in. Would that invitation work?

I didn't think I'd know until Sunday, despite the way that video racked up views among Cressie's subscribers. And it blew up, believe me.

Still, would people show? Would this final play actually work? I was worried. I wasn't the only one.

Saturday night, shortly after 8 p.m., I got a text.

UNKNOWN NUMBER: Del, this is Sister Vanessa at First Missionary. I'm reaching out to deliver a message.

UNKNOWN NUMBER: If you do indeed plan to attend service tomorrow, could you come a bit early?

UNKNOWN NUMBER: Pastor would like a word.

CHAPTER 30

SUNDAY MORNING, I DRESSED IN my suit, attached my clip-on tie, gathered my notes, my freshly purchased Bible, and went downstairs, expecting a silent escape.

My entire family was dressed in their Sunday best, waiting for me.

My confused glare bounced from face to face, landing on Cressie. She said, "Seems like straight As gives you clout around here."

I still didn't get it. Dad?

He said, "I thought she'd want money. Her asking me to go to church seems a small price to pay." He munched a spoonful of wet Frosted Flakes from a bowl in his hand.

Mom looked less comfortable. "I'm all for getting y'all churched up, but are you sure you don't want to try the AGAPE Church over in Simonsberg?"

"Nope," Cressie said, "First Missionary today. We can try whatever church you want after."

Jesus, Cressie. That didn't sound ominous at all.

But my parents didn't seem to catch on, and, honestly, as nervous as I was, this made me feel better. Like backup. We weren't the Justice League or anything, but the Raineys felt pretty unstoppable in the moment.

We showed up at First Missionary early, at my insistence. Good thing, too. The parking lot was almost full. Usually, there were spaces to spare in the gravel lot. Not that day, and I knew why.

Mom said, "Guess people are piling into the services close to the holiday. Good call on coming early, son. I want my usual pew."

"Don't mention it, Mom." Really, don't.

We spilled from our car, began the walk to the entrance, gaining an ample amount of side-eye from some of the regulars. Coach Scott left his truck, paced us to the door, radiating bitterness. I got the sense if he could order me to do a dozen suicides right there, he would've.

Inside the door were two girls I didn't recognize. One white, one Latinx. They were focused on their phones until I walked in.

"Oh, oh," said the white girl. "Are you Del?"

"Um, yeah."

The Latinx girl went bug-eyed. "Oh, oh. You're Cressida."

Cressie gave a slick grin, like she was used to this. "It is I."

"Your videos rock, especially the last one. Can we get a picture?"

Cressie eyed me for approval. I said, "Sure."

Me and my sister wedged between the girls, and the white

girl handed her phone to Dad. "Could you?"

Dad eagerly played cameraman, ignorant to everything. "This church is way friendlier than I expected."

Mom's narrowed eyes communicated something different.

I asked the girls, "Where are you from?"

"We drove from Hopewell. Had to see the place that inspired you to say all you said."

Hopewell was an hour away.

The girls thanked us and rushed into the crowded sanctuary for a seat. A lot of new faces—a lot of young faces—occupied the pew gaps that were usually empty at the start, middle, and end of service. If it was like this forty minutes before service started, I suspected it would be standing room only by the time things really got rolling.

Someone gripped my arm, spun me to them. I expected an angry Newsome.

It was Kiera, her face crinkled with fury. "Come. Here."

She dragged me from my family down the middle aisle until we were at the base of the pulpit, where we took our Purity Pledge a million years ago.

"I saw your video. I saw that you did"—she swept a hand over the growing crowd—"this. Do you know what I have to do today? Do you know you made it worse by bringing like a hundred strangers here to watch me do it?"

"It's not what you think." Though, it might be exactly what she thought. We wouldn't know until after I spoke to Newsome.

She huffed. "How much damage do you plan to do?"

She walked away without an answer, not that I had one to give.

Sister Vanessa emerged from the corridor adjacent to the pulpit, spotted me, and waved me over. I mouthed to Cressie, *Save me a seat*, then joined Sister Vanessa.

"He's back there, huh?" I said.

"He is."

"How bad should I expect?"

"I honestly don't know. But I want to tell you, I'm proud of you for being so open in your video. And my God, look at all those people in the pews. I don't care what my uncle may say, or do. This is a blessing."

I know I should've been more focused on the blessing part, but I was scared AF.

I shoved my hands into my pockets so he wouldn't see them shake. That familiar incense tickled my nose, and when I turned the corner into Newsome's office, I saw me on his computer monitor. He was watching my video.

"Del," he said, calmer than I expected. "Sit, please."

I did, and became instantly bitter, recalling the night he made me tell about Healthy Living.

He paused my video, and tugged his glasses off, folding them, then massaging the bridge of his nose. "What's this supposed to accomplish, son?"

"I was told for me to come back, I'd need to confess. I'm honestly not a fan of your way, so I did mine instead."

"You expect me to believe that's all this is? All those new

visitors out there aren't some sort of setup to disrupt our service? Because I'm going to be frank with you: if you think you're going to prevent our congregation from worshiping, I promise I'll have you escorted from the premises. I won't stand for any . . . *shenanigans* during this holy time."

My head shook the entire time he spoke. "It's nothing like that. Everyone out there, they want to be connected to a good place. I haven't planned anything beyond that. But I do have a request."

Pastor breathed deeply, looked to the sky. "Lord, this boy." To me, "What?"

"Let Kiera off the hook. Don't make her, or anyone else, get up there and tell their deepest secrets anymore. I got on the internet and told all of mine hoping you'd see that as a worthy enough sacrifice to save them."

Pastor leaned forward, nearly hissing, "Boy, you are skating dangerously close to blasphemy. You didn't sacrifice anything. You didn't save anybody. Only One has ever done that."

"Then let's follow His example. I was paying attention in those purity classes, Pastor. I know when you're forcing us into the pulpit to embarrass ourselves, that's not saving anybody either. I'm asking you to look at a better way.

"The way I figure it, you can say some stuff that inspires those people to want to come back. I'm certain there are a lot of options in the Bible that work for when you want people to feel encouraged, like they belong. Or, you can force young people to embarrass themselves for your own satisfaction and a few amens."

"If you think you can manipulate me—"

"No." I shook my head, meaning it. "Not manipulation. I know I don't control you. I'm not trying to. I'm stating the choices I'm sure you already recognize. You can do whatever you want, and that can be the same thing you've always done. This is your church. Or, you can do what your wife once said, and help protect the youth in our community. You might start by not scaring them away."

I stood, not waiting to be dismissed. There were fifteen minutes before service started. I bet Pastor had some things to think over. "I look forward to the sermon."

Emerging from the corridor, I gaped at a packed church, more people still cramming their way in. Among them, I spotted all of the Purity Pledgers. Ralph and Bobby ushering folks to the last few empty seats. Mya in the choir stand. Jameer sitting apart from his parents. All the rest.

Kiera was wedged between her mom and dad, staring daggers at me. That gaze was too intense, so I dropped my eyes and skittered to the seat Cressie had saved next to Mom and Dad. I sat, thought it over, then bowed my head and closed my eyes, praying that all would go well.

Service started on time, but the songs seemed longer. There had to be a record number of announcements, and so many cursory prayers that I feared the crowd would start to siphon off before Pastor took the lectern. One request always wrapped up announcements before the real sermon started. Missus Baines, in her creaky old-lady voice, said, "Would all visitors please stand so the First Missionary family might greet you properly?"

Every other Sunday the question was a formality. That day, dozens of people stood. Most were young. All were because of me.

Missus Baines, who wore thick bifocals and maybe couldn't see so well beyond the first pew, seemed startled by all this movement. She adjusted quickly, excited for so much company. "Well, praise the Lord! First Missionary, please greet our newcomers."

Another few minutes passed as every visitor got a handshake or hug from the regular attendee closest to them.

Newsome observed it all. No smile.

The greetings calmed, everyone sat. Newsome approached the lectern. "Every head bowed, every eye closed as we pray."

I didn't peek for once. Didn't want to see what was going on around me.

"Dear Lord," he began, "we are often faced with choices. Choices that lead to other choices. And more choices after that. We know choosing wrong can lead to a path of darkness, which is why it is best to seek your guidance in our decision making. Yours. Not earthly advice from a man, *or a boy*."

Uh oh.

"We know the domino effect can be devastating, as it was for Lot, whose decisions eventually led to his tragic fall in Sodom. . . ."

My stomach sank. I knew this story from Purity Pledge, and it was mad creepy. A city destroyed. A wife turned to salt. All sorts of implications that trash people have used for centuries to justify oppression, and racism, and homophobia, and misogyny.

Please, I thought—prayed, if there's anyone listening, steer him away from this. Don't let it be what it's always been.

". . . Lot's wife made the mistake of looking back," Newsome said, "and . . . and . . ."

Silence. A few light coughs rattled in the sanctuary. Murmurs as the quiet stretched a few seconds too long. I opened my eyes and watched a lone moth lurch up and down toward the pulpit.

Newsome seemed in deep thought, staring intently at his Bible's cover. Finally, he said, "As I gaze upon the faces of you all, the faithful I see every Sunday, and you newcomers, I'm reminded of what our church's First Lady used to say to me when we were home on quiet nights. She'd say, 'Everyone thinks of changing the world, but no one thinks of changing themselves.' Now, that's not Bible, y'all. And when she said it, she mostly meant my long-standing habit of watching *Wheel of Fortune* every evening. She despised that show."

The congregation laughed! Deep, genuine belly laughs. Had Newsome ever cracked a joke from the pulpit? Don't suppose I'd know, since I hardly ever listened. But I was listening then.

"There is some Bible that supports her thinking," he said. "Isaiah 43:19 tells us 'I am making a way in the wilderness and streams in the wasteland.' This is Green Creek. This is our stream, we can make a way, together. I'd like to lead you, but someone reminded me of my dear wife, who I miss so much. Reminded me that she had a lot of ideas for how we might change the world. I got too stuck in my ways to consider them. With that in mind, we're going to shift gears. For now."

He left the lectern, mic in hand, walked to the edge of the pulpit, eyes cast in the general direction of Kiera. "You First Missionary regulars, I'm going to change the plan a bit today. I will be the only one in the pulpit for the rest of service. No one else."

Kiera's shoulders sagged with relief. Her parents' heads cocked, quizzical, though they didn't object.

"We have so many new faces in the building, I think they should get a good, long look at the leader of the house, so maybe I can entice them to come back next Sunday, and the Sunday after." Then his gaze swung to me, pinned me. "I recognize an opportunity when I see it."

To the rest of the congregation: "Please open your Bibles, and turn to John 16:33, we're going to talk about hope."

We did. And it was good.

Exiting the church after service was an ordeal. Many of these visitors had spotted me and Cressie and wanted to say hello. We were almost as popular as Pastor Newsome.

He had an expanded crowd around him. The usual well-wishers, and some of the visitors who felt especially touched by his upbeat message.

Me and my sister shook hands, and gave hugs on the move,

as Mom and Dad were anxious to beat traffic. We cleared the foyer and were in daylight when I heard my name.

"Del!" Kiera called. "Del, wait!"

My entire family gave me the "what you wanna do here?" look. I said, "Go on. I'll catch up."

They left me to it.

Kiera, so beautiful, as hard to look at as the sun itself. I focused on the gravel at our feet. "Hey."

"Did you know Pastor was going to do that?"

"I asked him to. I wasn't sure."

"Why? I thought you were mad at me. And Mason. I thought—"

I knew what she thought. I didn't like it, but I also gave her reason to think I'd get some sort of pleasure from her shame. A few weeks ago, I probably would've. To answer her question, "First Missionary Crew!" I raised my hand for a high five.

She slapped my palm lightly. "Thank you."

Kiera turned away. She climbed the church steps, then faced me again. "It was nice getting to know you in the pledge."

"Same."

She disappeared into the church. Though we'd greet each other in the halls at school, and run into each other around town—Green Creek was so small—that was the last time we were First Missionary Crew.

Me and my family haven't been back since.

CHAPTER 31

NOT THAT WE GAVE UP on church completely.

After another family meeting—low-tech, face-to-face, immediately after that final First Missionary service—we decided we'd do a bit of a church hunt. Different towns, different denominations, all within a half hour or so of Green Creek. We've heard fire-and-brimstone sermons. Super-cool live-and-let-live sermons. Saw one preacher pull a gun in the pulpit (he said it wasn't loaded, but we still scratched that church off our list). It's been . . . educational.

Not going to lie, I was uncertain where I landed on religion, but the family agreed we'd do this, and I was a team player, if nothing else. Mom felt better when we sought divine guidance, Dad felt better being supportive of Mom, and Cressie, when she wasn't at school and running her increasingly popular YouTube channel, loved us doing the church tour thing together. She even did an episode on it.

My episode was still one of her Top Five most viewed, a surprising number of those coming from my Green Creek classmates. Post-holiday break, I'd expected jokes, and there were some, but not nearly as much as the support I got from many who expressed their own anxieties about sex. MJ asked me to stay back after English class, and when the room cleared, he said, "It was a brave thing you did."

"I'm not so brave," I said. "I'm the one who talked about you telling personal stories in Healthy Living. I got the class canceled."

Seemed I was addicted to this confession thing.

MJ wrote notes on the board, and didn't look at me when he said, "I kind of figured. Once I saw your video, and you mentioned First Missionary church, you were the only clear connection between the class and Pastor Newsome."

"Were you mad?"

He faced me, amused. "Not at all. By then, I'd already sent some anonymous emails to your sister about the whole thing. Local girl, big social media following, outrage. The curriculum committee is going to review the course again."

"That was you feeding Cressie info? I—" I recalled Cressie referring to her source as a "her." "I thought that was a girl."

"Your sister likes heroic women. Nothing wrong with that. Her assumption helped with the whole anonymity thing, so I let it ride."

"Will Pastor Newsome be a problem?"

"If he was still involved. I've been told a new religious liaison will be joining the curriculum committee. Vanessa Newsome. You know her?"

Sister Vanessa? New blood, new ideas! "I'm familiar."

"I expect good things."

So did I.

In March, Vice Principal Terrier instituted another new rule, and sentenced a bunch of people to detentions over it. For once, I didn't mind. The use of "Baby-Getters" and "BabyGettersToo" was pretty much banned at Green Creek. We had to opt for calling the participants what we should've been calling them the whole time. Students, and nothing else.

I quit my job at FISHto's despite Tyrell hounding me about the management program. Not that things weren't going well, but I'd been hanging in the public library on the day that tatted, cranky librarian tacked a "Help Wanted" sign to the bulletin board. I immediately took it down, handed it back to her, and said, "I'm it."

She didn't argue, and I've since become the fastest shelver they've got.

By late April, Jameer frequently dropped by during my evening shifts, and my librarian boss didn't give a damn if I was chatty during work, as long as it was a quiet kind of chatty. He tagged behind my book cart, and kept me up on how the Pledgers were doing. Ralph and Bobby were still making horrible—but improving—music, and apparently had girlfriends. More material for their songs, I guess. Helena and Shanice got that praise dance team off the ground. Apparently, they all missed me.

"They need their answer man, right?" I didn't intend for it to sound mean.

Jameer checked me immediately. "They miss their friend."

They were younger than me, so I rarely crossed paths with

them at school. I'd make a point to change that, even if it got me a few tardy slips.

"What about you?" I asked. "I know things have been changing at First Missionary, but I can't imagine it's changed that much."

"Actually, all those new people who came, a few were LGBTQ, Del. Openly. And they're still coming."

I was shelving books on theoretical mathematics, working the social calculations in my head. "What Newsome have to say about that?"

"He's . . . adjusting. Sister Vanessa is helping him navigate the new rainbow-colored sheep in his flock. No one's run away yet. So, progress."

"Your parents, too."

Sadness wafted off him. I rolled my cart to the next bank of shelves, still felt it as he followed. "Not so much. I honestly think if anyone leaves this new version of First Missionary, it's going to be them. But, their frustration has been more with Pastor than me. They don't have any new, great ways to punish me. No matter what they do, I'm not hiding myself anymore. So, it's acceptance or bust. I only know I'm not going to be the one who breaks. Not ever again."

"Damn. Ramsey ain't coming over for dinner, then."

Jameer scrutinized the spine of some rock-and-roll singer's memoir. "We broke up, so no."

"Why? Was it because of your people? They messed y'all up?"

"No, Del. He bored me. Everything isn't tragic."

"Oh." Moving on. I said, "Can you still help me after work?"

"You brought it?"

"In the car."

"Then I'm helping you. But you're going to have to practice a lot to get it right by Saturday."

"I know."

"You shouldn't have waited so late."

"I know."

"Don't say 'better late than never.' It's trite, and you can be more refined than that."

"I wasn't." I was. He still had a way with words.

I wrapped up my shift, walked Jameer out to my car, where warm, humid spring was in full effect. I passed him a small box from my passenger seat. He slid it open, revealing a simple black bow tie.

I said, "Now show me your ways."

Prom was right around the corner, and there would be no more clip-ons for me.

The limo driver took my twisting, inefficient route as instructed. We picked up Qwan first, rocking his black pants, purple paisley jacket, and black-on-black Jordan Elevens. Angie next, her purple sequined mermaid dress expertly coordinated with his ensemble. Her mom made them do the picture thing for like a hundred hours. Then we were off again because Shianne was losing her shit over us taking so long.

We did the picture thing, too. My classic black spy tuxedo ("Rainey, Del Rainey") contrasted with her flowy peach-colored gown. Zoey did wake up, but seemed hypnotized by the light sparkling off Angie's outfit, so she joined us in a few photos, snug on her mother's hip, grinning toothlessly as we got immortalized in our formal wear splendor.

Mister and Missus Griffiths were kind enough to distract Zoey with some applesauce while we escaped to the ride, and we completed the trip to the golf resort clubhouse where Green Creek High's prom cranked, classmates dancing even before they entered the building.

Inside, the juniors and seniors mingled, formed dance circles, mobbed the food and drink table, while chaperones tried to maintain control like survivors fending off zombies on *The Walking Dead*.

The ladies separated from us, greeting friends and friends-of-friends for selfies and IG stories, while me and Qwan made our rounds. We ran into Jameer almost immediately, looking dapper in a maroon tux with black lapels. He was playing wallflower, and I thought I'd encourage him to join us, but I backed off when a senior by the name of Carlos Lumbly brought Jameer a cup of punch with an easy smile that suggested more than casual buddies. I'd have some questions for Jameer later, but I knew better than to throw salt in his game.

Taylor Burkin was in attendance with some out-of-town dude. All the Baby-Getter drama had long tapered off but she was still a hot topic because of Colossus. In the wake of everything, girls started avoiding him like the plague. And with Taylor being so public with her complaints, his parents came down hard on him to own up to his responsibilities, if for no other reason than to save face. Seeing her here drew mad whispers because he wasn't in attendance.

Word on the street: he was home. Babysitting.

Center of the dance floor was Kiera, battling some college freshman she'd met while touring Old Dominion University. They were going hard, popping in and out of each other's faces, pulling cheers and "ooooohhhhs" from the onlookers and instigators. Really getting it in.

All the time I'd been around Kiera, I never knew she could dance. Never learned much about her at all, really. I hoped her college date was better about that sort of thing than most in her orbit were. She deserved that.

On the outskirts of the dance circle, covetously watching the show, were Mason Miles and his soldiers. Him and her hadn't lasted very long after New Year's, but she still drew his attention. Mine, too.

I'd learn to pull away.

After a circuit around the room, Angie materialized, grabbed Qwan by his jacket sleeve, and dragged him into the next dance battle. He loathed dancing, but didn't fight it. Angie had her way with him, and I thought it made my best friend better somehow. It put me on alert, though. Was Shianne going to swoop in and demand the same?

A quick search confirmed I didn't have to worry. She was with a couple of the other new mothers who'd made it out this evening, swapping phones—likely sharing photos of their little ones. Which left me looking lonely.

I gravitated to the preferred loner destination, the punch bowl, being watched by an eagle-eyed MJ. He saw me coming, popped the collar on a tuxedo jacket nearly identical to mine. "I see you've got good taste in attire, young man."

"Thanks, MJ. How long they got you on guard duty?"

"I'm doing this and the After Prom. My lady's going to bring little man so he can play some games. He's been excited all day."

He wasn't the only one. After Prom was back at the high school gym. Everyone knew it was the community's way of keeping us off the roads, or away from hotels, or from drinking. We all tried to play like it was goofy and childish. But, for real, the school went all out with games, and fire prizes. GoPros, iPhones, TVs, and game systems. The best stuff got raffled off closer to sunrise to make sure you stayed. A brother could use a new TV.

I dipped the ladle into the icy pink potion, and filled a cup. "How you been?"

MJ said, "Making it, Del. Everyone's tired by this point in the year. You know. I take it you've heard the good news."

"Healthy Living?"

"Well, it's going to be called 'Positive Prep,' but that's one of those 'ketchup' or 'catsup' things. The big difference is the committee agreed to make some adjustments, focusing on a wider variety of safe sex practices, consent, and self-care. In other words, things that were proven to actually be helpful in reducing unwanted pregnancy, disease, even sexual assaults. Plus, no questions will be off-limits. I'm sure you can appreciate that."

"Damn right."

A petite gloved hand extended over the punch bowl. "Question: Are you going to drink all this?"

I glanced sideways, almost didn't recognize her. "Mya?"

She looked, literally, like a princess. Not just any princess either. Her green-and-cream dress, those gloves, and the tiara fixed in her hair were familiar. "Your outfit? I've seen it somewhere."

"Princess Tiana, from *The Princess and the Frog*. First black Disney princess. If you're gonna go formal, go big."

"'I'm rooting for everybody black,' right?"

"Sure am."

I stroked my chin. Curious about something. "You're dressed like Tiana, but is she your *favorite* Disney princess?"

Mya shuffled uncomfortably.

"Tell the truth!" I said. "I've heard you humming at FISH-to's."

She was caught. "Fine. It's Elsa from *Frozen*. Okay?"

"I knew it. She's like the whitest one!"

"Shut. Up! That song is *bars*!"

We laughed, a little like the good times, but also a little different. A little better. "You look great, though!"

"Thank you."

"How are things at FISHto's?" I sipped punch.

"Fried."

I almost choked. "Good one. Who'd you come with?"

"Jameer." She cocked her head toward him in the corner with Carlos, cackling at something the upperclassman said. "I think he's ditching me, though. Guess our engagement is off."

Mya poured her punch, faced the dance floor. More people jumped into the dance circle, including my date. "You came with Shianne. That a thing?"

"Naw. Just friends. It works."

A pulsing beat couldn't totally erase the long, awkward pause. Mya resorted to one of the many conversations we'd engaged in during my last weeks at FISHto's. "Batman's an a-hole, Del."

"You finally read *Tower of Babel*?"

"I did not. I read *Kingdom Come*. Why do they name so many of the books after Bible stuff?"

"Gravitas."

"Eh."

"Batman is not an a-hole, though. He's stern."

"He took over a city with Batbots, or whatever you call them. Then sits back in his old-man smugness watching everyone, judging like some kind of—"

"God?"

She punched my shoulder. "Don't start!"

The DJ mixed in another song, and Mya swayed in her gown, eyes on the dance floor. "Del, I gotta get in there. Hold my drink?"

I rolled my eyes, but complied. She hiked up her dress and skittered to the floor, leaving me and MJ to our conversation.

He said, "You probably should've followed her."

"Why? For what?" My face felt suddenly hot.

"Uh-huh. She's going to the After Prom. I saw her name on the list."

I crossed my arms, swishing Mya's drink around. "Um, *thanks*."

MJ chuckled. "You know if you ever want to talk, get some advice, I'm here for you. Ask anything."

This was sliding into uncomfortable territory. Questions and answers hadn't worked out so well for me in the past. Though, now that he brought it up, one inquiry lingered. The story he never finished. "How'd you end up getting with your lady? After you'd said foul stuff to her in college."

"Oh, that. I didn't."

I wrenched toward him, sloshing Mya's drink. "You said her parents knew your roommate's parents."

MJ shook his head. "Naw, I said my roommate's parents knew the parents of the girl I immediately keyed on. The one who when I saw her, I instantly crafted this story in my head about how I'd get with her. She. Was. Sexy! I was convinced that us meeting in that moment was some kind of sign. I messed it up by coming at her sideways, but no one could tell me that. At first.

"She'd brought friends with her. Two other girls. One of those friends eventually told me how much of a dick I was by pressing up on someone who wasn't feeling me. Basically called me a harasser. I was pissed, too. Notice how you get most mad when the truth is something you don't like?"

My eyes flitted to Kiera, who'd taken a break from dancing to snuggle with her date, his arm looped over her shoulder.

"That girl did me a favor by checking me. She did me more favors by always telling me the truth. Got to a point where I couldn't imagine her not being there to tell me the truth. Fast-forward, you'll be meeting her and our kid later tonight."

"Wow, MJ. That story is kind of amazing."

"Yes and no. Yes, that I'm so lucky. No, in that it shouldn't have taken me so long to see what was right in front of me."

The crowd around the dance circle was going crazy. Clapping, cheering. Mya was in the middle, moving in ways that shouldn't be possible in that kind of gown, but the girl was killing it.

MJ said, "I'll hold her cup if you want to go. The question is, do you?"

The answer: Hell. Yes.

I passed MJ that drink, and worked my way onto the dance floor with my friends, and my enemies, and everyone in between. Mya saw me coming—there was a glint in her eye, as bright as the party lights sparkling off her tiara. And, I swear . . .

It was the purest thing I'd ever seen.

Can I get an amen?

ACKNOWLEDGMENTS

Here we go again. It's always nice to see you here, but I gotta admit . . . this gets harder every time. This is novel #6. You've probably seen this is a whole new direction for me. And when you're on your sixth novel, trying to do a bunch of different things, you require a lot of help. Let's see if I can do all my fabulous family, friends, and colleagues justice. I'll try to be brief. Special thanks to . . .

Dear Wife Adrienne, Mom, the siblings, nephews, niece, and the rest of the family . . . I love you all. Thanks for the support.

The team that makes sure I'm getting the best possible opportunities: Jamie Weiss Chilton, Eric Reid, Carmen Oliver, and Jennifer Justman. You're all godsends.

Team HarperCollins: Karen Chaplin, Bria Ragin, Rosemary Brosnan; Erin Fitzsimmons and Molly Fehr in Design; Mark Rifkin and Liz Byer in managing editorial; Andrea Pappenheimer and the entire sales team; and everyone in marketing and publicity.

The people who helped usher this thing from a seed of an idea to a fully realized novel: Olugbemisola Rhuday-Perkovich, Nic Stone, Sheri Reynolds, Janet Peery, and John McManus.

As always, the many, many, many, many friends I've made along the way.